Also by Richard Engling

Body Mortgage

Antigone and Macbeth: Adaptations for a War-Torn Time

Visions of Anna

Give My Regards to Nowhere

Romeo and Juliet Keep Their Eyes on the Prize

Praise for the Dwayne Finnegan Series

"Richard Engling knows Chicago's famously chaotic and glorious storefront theater scene like the back of his hand. It's the perfect setting for absurd comic hi-jinx."
– Chris Jones, *Chicago Tribune*

"As Carl Hiaasen does with his Florida-based satirical crime novels, Engling's gloriously silly narrative allows his readers to witness how the sausage gets made, which isn't always pretty but is often eye-opening... Engling's satire on storefront theatre is thoroughly entertaining from start to finish. His characters sparkle, his knowledge of the backstage issues of the medium is elucidated with keen insight and comic verve, and he is somehow able to make even the most seemingly unsympathetic characters...into people it's fun to get to know."
– Karen Topham, *ChicagoOnStage*

"Richard Engling is undoubtedly a writer's writer. It's hard not to read him without marveling at the skill of construction. But the technical virtuosity of *Give My Regards to Nowhere* is performed like prestidigitation: it's a magic trick performed in plain view. The novel is comic, wise, and riveting. It gives us the theatrical world, but also the world of anyone who has ever struggled against the odds. But Engling is also a reader's writer, those who read him without fretting about how these marvels are executed will turn each page with a thrill of discovery and immersion in this richly entertaining novel."
– Liam Heneghan, author of *Beasts at Bedtime*

"A scrappy, big-hearted backstage comedy layered with mordant wit and full of a deep, abiding love for its characters, which is wholly appropriate for a story set in the scrappy, big-hearted world of Chicago theater."
– Adam Langer, author of *Cyclorama*

"Without a doubt, the best examination of the theatre trade I've ever read. Insightful, satirical, painful, but joyous. Richard Engling brings a wonderful cast of characters together in a way theatre kids and non-theatre kids can thoroughly enjoy."
– Darren Callahan, dramatist for the BBC, SyFy, author of *City of Human Remains* and *The Audrey Green Chronicles*

"A meager bank account, a tiny Chicago storefront theater with metal seats flecked with rust, and an enormous dream of a Broadway hit that *no one will never forget*. That's the stuff of Richard Engling's engaging new novel. A longtime denizen of Chicago's famed storefront theater scene, Engling vividly captures the disparity between grand artistic ambition and what reality has to offer in this very funny, briskly written, and often touching book."
– Mark Larson, author of *Ensemble: An Oral History of Chicago Theater*

"The rollicking ride through the underbelly of the acting world and the determination of a man who sees his world fall apart and come back together in a new way as the show goes on will attract anyone interested in drama, theater, Chicago backdrops, or a drive to succeed against all odds."
– D. Donovan, *Midwest Book Review*

"Hilarious, witty, touching, intelligent, and spot-on. Engling's novel about the many joys and incessant headaches of running a storefront Chicago theater is truth that could only be told as believably as it is, as fiction. The characters pulse with life, conflict, tons of drama, and humanity. Entire chapters are laugh-out-loud funny, and issues of marriage, friendship, loyalty, and the nature of theater and art flow through every sentence. A one-sit read, I promise!"
– Nadeem Zaman, author of *The Inheritors* and *Up in the Main House and Other Stories*

The Very Last Production of King Lear

A Dwayne Finnegan Novel

Richard Engling

Polarity Ensemble Books

This novel is a work of human imagination. No AI tools were used in the creation or writing of this work.

The characters and events in this book are fictitious. Any similarity to real persons, living or dead, is coincidental and not intended by the author. Characters named after real people or characters who appear to share some history or even specific occupations with real people are also fictional. The details of those characters' personalities and lives in this book have been invented.

Polarity Ensemble Books
www.polarityensemblebooks.com
Cover design by Jonas Peres

Also available in audio and ebook editions.

ISBN 978-1-969110-00-9

Printed in the United States of America

Special thanks to Liam Heneghan, Martin Uthe, Bob Fiddler, Jeanne Fredricksen, Ann Keen, Jeff Jacobs, Zoë Engling, and Gail Wilcinski for suggestions and assistance concerning this book. Also special thanks to Robert Falls, Steve Scott, and Adam Belcuore for interviews and a wonderful inside tour of the Goodman Theatre backstage, offices, and working areas. And a very special thanks to Gail Wilcinski for being my partner in life.

Dramatis Personae
(in order of appearance)

Reginald Camper, MWM*, artistic director of the Goodman
Theatre

Dwayne Finnegan, MWM, artistic director of the Psychedelic
Dream Theatre

Ingrid Baardsen, SWF, set designer, executive director of the
Psychedelic Dream Theatre

Angela Monica Guiseppelli, MWF, fifth-grade teacher, wife of
Dwayne

Rockwell Nesbit III (Rocky), DBM, Coco's father, a wealthy
lawyer, and sometimes actor who suffers from Dissociative
Identity Disorder

A Young Lawyer (Cartwright), SWM, who works for Rocky

Coco Nesbit, SBF, gorgeous diva actor playing Goneril

Brianna, MBF, Rocky's office manager

Norman Plotz, MWM, Angela's new principal

Todd Bodkins, MWM, Angela's assistant principal

Ry Joodey, SWM, guitarist, music director

Tom Collins, SWM, Dwayne's long-time creative partner, fight
and dance choreographer playing Regan

Peaches Brown, SWF, bipolar costume designer

A Fireworks Store Owner

Sheila, MWF, and **Evan**, SBM, colleagues in telemarketing at
Rocky's office

Melinda Prentice, SWF, a pretty young ingénue playing Cordelia

Joan Dunam, SWF, stage manager, board member of the
Psychedelic Dream Theatre

Barry, MWM, the bartender at the John Barleycorn Memorial Pub

Wallace Proctor, SWM, veteran actor playing King Lear

Raymond Green (Green), MWM, manager of the Chicago
Repertory Arts Playhouse

Kate Bennison, WWF, an elderly widow Ingrid helps and befriends

Nick Sanchez, MWM, coordinating producer at the Goodman
Theatre

Bobby, SBM, charismatic actor who has a long history with
  Dwayne and Coco, playing Edmund

Chaz Ackersley, DWM, PR man, Dwayne's old friend

Orlando Gunn, SBM, handsome actor playing Edgar

Carol, MWF, one of Angela's teacher colleagues, who owns a nice
  house near the lake in Evanston

George Aleister (Aleister), WWM, Dwayne's oldest friend, a
  successful psychiatrist, and author of *The Soul in Grief*

Dr. Brenner, Angela's fertility doctor

Davy, a sound man for big rock shows

A Curandera, a Mexican healer with a storefront on Clark Street

Bonnie Ackersley, DWF, Chaz's ex-wife, lawyer, brilliant red hair

Peter Burden, SBM, a veteran Chicago actor playing Gloucester

Howie Grange, MWM, a union stage manager

A Homeless Man, with a shopping cart of aluminum cans

Doug Slivesky and **Haki**, rock show roadies

***First letter:** M=Married, S=Single, W=Widowed, D=Divorced
  Second letter: W=White, B=Black
  Third letter: M=Male, F=Female

Preface: The Story of King Lear

You can skip over this preface, if you like. You might find it helpful if you don't know (or don't remember) the plot of Shakespeare's *King Lear.*

KING LEAR decides to retire and divide his kingdom among his three daughters. He plans to be hosted at their castles, one after another, with his 100 knights for the rest of his days. He asks which daughter loves him most so she can receive the best share of land. GONERIL and REGAN, his older daughters, exaggerate wildly, flattering Lear. His youngest and best-loved daughter, CORDELIA, tells the simple truth, which drives Lear into a rage. He disowns her. He banishes his faithful knight, KENT, when Kent warns him he is acting rashly. The KING OF FRANCE takes the disgraced Cordelia home with him to be his queen.

Kent disguises himself and rejoins Lear as his faithful servant. Lear travels to Goneril's castle. She demands he reduce his entourage to 50 knights. Infuriated, he travels toward Regan, who he is sure will treat him better. He sends Kent ahead as his messenger. The DUKE OF CORNWALL, Regan's husband, puts Kent in the stocks. Lear is horrified at the treatment of his emissary. He begins to go mad. Regan insists Lear reduce his entourage to 25 knights if he wishes to stay with her. He says he will go back to Goneril, but she refuses to allow him to return with any knights at all. Enraged, he flies from them into the wilderness amid a torrential storm, accompanied only by his FOOL and Kent. His madness accelerates.

Meanwhile, the EARL OF GLOUCESTER has been tricked by his bastard son, EDMUND, into believing that his legitimate son, EDGAR, plans to kill him to inherit the earldom. Edgar flees from Gloucester's men, disguising himself as Poor Tom, a deranged beggar. Lear takes refuge from the storm with Poor Tom in a ruined hovel on the heath.

Gloucester attempts to aid Lear, but he is betrayed by Edmund. Cornwall and Regan gouge out Gloucester's eyes and cast him out of his castle. A servant wounds Cornwall while attempting to save Gloucester. Cornwall dies. Wandering blind, Gloucester comes upon his son, Edgar, disguised as Poor Tom, who leads him toward Dover, where Lear also has traveled.

The two older sisters both lust after Edmund. Goneril and Edmund conspire to kill her husband, the virtuous DUKE OF ALBANY, while Regan plans to marry Edmund after the recent death of her husband, the brutal Cornwall.

Cordelia leads the French army to Dover to rescue her father. The older sisters muster the British forces and defeat the French invaders. Edmund imprisons Lear and Cordelia. He sends an officer to hang Cordelia. Goneril poisons Regan out of jealousy for Edmund and then kills herself when Albany discovers her treachery. Edgar duels and defeats Edmund, who repents and reveals his plot against Cordelia as he dies. Edgar is too late to save Cordelia. Lear carries his dead daughter out of the prison and dies of a broken heart.

How's that for the centerpiece of a comedic novel?

1

Tuesday, January 17, 2005

"So there he is, Brian Dennehy, huge bear of an actor," Reg Camper said, leaning across his desk in the Goodman Theatre toward Dwayne and Ingrid, his voice rising, "and he rushes toward Patricia Clarkson, who is what? Five foot three? Beautiful, petite, wonderful actor that she is. Playing Mary Tyrone, the love of his life of whom he's so proud. She's off the needle. She's recovering—this is early in the play, before she goes back on the dope. It's our first time running the show at the venue." He grinned and shook his head, relishing this mad memory. "And he rushes forward and grabs her in his arms—but his momentum carries them right to the edge where his toe catches on the footlights channel, and suddenly they are in flight!" He extended his arm to demonstrate. "The two of them, Patricia in Brian's arms, over the lip of the stage toward the floor, eight feet below! I am screaming. Patricia is screaming. This gargantuan walrus of a Dennehy is about to land atop her in the center aisle of the theatre and crush the life out of her. Like a bug! But then a sort of monumental howl bellows out of Dennehy's mouth. Somehow in midair—and this is absolutely miraculous—he spins the two of them one hundred eighty degrees as they careen toward the floor, and Patricia lands *atop* Dennehy," Camper rose to his feet and clapped his hands together, his hair shaking around his face, "who lands flat on his back with an enormous thud in the center aisle of the theatre. This knocks all the wind out of him. She's fine. He's saved her life. It's like she landed on a huge, lumpy, ill-formed mattress. She climbs off him, shouting at him for this ridiculous display and endangering her life. But then she stops when she sees the horror of Dennehy's face. He cannot get oxygen back into his lungs! It's like he's drowning in the open air." Camper waved his arms in demonstration.

"I jump over to help him to his feet, and he bends over,

desperately attempting to pull air into his lungs, but all his internal segmental bronchi in his lungs are pressed flat closed. The horror on his face! He cannot breathe!" Camper himself gasped as he talked. "He pulls himself totally upright and then this distant whistling wheeze sounds from within, and he pulls in the first milliliters of air. He's bending back and forth, over and over, pulling in teaspoons of air at a time, so desperate to breathe." He bobbed his body in demonstration.

"The rest of the cast has gathered. The crew. The stage manager is down from the booth. His face ashen white. Everyone horrified! Are they watching one of the greatest actors of his generation die standing up in the aisle of a Broadway theatre? Patricia is waving a script at her own face, which has gone all red. But the whistling, wheezing slowly increases, Dennehy's face going from white to red, and he can gasp larger breaths and finally breathe again. He bellows out a cry of triumph! People are laughing. Hugging. The stage manager calls for everyone to take thirty minutes, but Dennehy raises his hand. *I just need fifteen*, he says. *Patricia?* he asks. *I'm okay*, she says doubtfully. She shrugs. *Let's just take fifteen*, Dennehy says. *Everyone wants to finish and go home*. The stage manager announces fifteen. Dennehy walks next door, has a shot of whiskey at the bar, and comes back ready to work!" Reg Camper laughed hugely, and Dwayne laughed along while Ingrid nodded without a grin on her face.

"My God!" Dwayne said. Could his heart swell any fuller? Here he was in the great man's office, hearing stories of bringing *Long Day's Journey into Night*, one of his favorite plays, onto Broadway with a stellar cast.

They were in Camper's office to discuss Dwayne directing at the Goodman Theatre. A huge step up for him. A step into a real paying career as a director of live theatre.

O, consummation devoutly to be wished!

"That's what makes Brian so great." Camper continued, shaking his head in admiration. His long, curly blond/grey locks shook with him. "He has such an appetite for the work. He goes through *that*, and he just wants fifteen minutes to recover and back to work. But how he managed to spin them in the air! Incredible."

Dwayne laughed with appreciative joy. Oh yes. This was *his* world. Was Dwayne's appetite for the work any less than the great Brian Dennehy? He loved this. Sitting here, chummy with the Tony-Award-winning artistic director of the storied Goodman Theatre. Absolute bliss!

"So yeah," Ingrid said, her face all business. "Great story. But I was wondering how *our* production is going to work. You said we'd get complete production support. But what does that mean? Is this going to be a Goodman Theatre production or our production?"

Reg Camper's smile faded.

Damn Ingrid! Did she have to spoil the fun?

"Well," Camper said. "There is no one size fits all. We just want to make sure that any production on our stages will be of the quality that people expect at the Goodman."

"Absolutely," Dwayne said.

"But what does that mean?" Ingrid said. She shook back her chin-length ice-blond hair and sat up higher in her chair. She looked like she was ready to dive over Camper's desk and wrestle him to the ground. "I mean, how much control do you intend to exert over our show? Design? Construction? Casting? What's it going to mean?"

Now Camper looked annoyed. "Honestly, most of that you'll work out with Nick Sanchez."

"Maybe Ingrid and Mr. Sanchez should get together," Dwayne suggested.

Reg Camper looked delighted with that idea. He picked up the phone and three minutes later Nick Sanchez whisked Ingrid away. Camper and Dwayne smiled at one another as though they'd scored a coup. "Let's take a little walk," Camper said.

They left the office, chatted with the receptionist who was stationed in the foyer between the artistic and the executive directors' offices, and stepped out a door onto a balcony above Randolph Street. It was a very short walk.

"This is what we call the *Via Maggio*. It's a little tribute to our dear old friend, Michael. I don't know if you knew Michael…"

"Not personally," Dwayne said. "But I certainly knew his work."

Had Dwayne ever, in fact, seen a play directed by Michael Maggio? He wasn't sure. But he'd quickly researched Michael Maggio after his first awkward meeting with Reginald Camper a few months back. Dwayne had come to the Goodman to propose that Camper create a program to encourage emerging directors in Chicago—with the hope that Dwayne himself would be one of those emerging directors—not realizing that Camper already had instituted the Michael Maggio Directing Fellowship for early career directors. Dwayne had embarrassed himself, but it led to Camper seeing his production of *Romeo and Juliet* twice. And now Camper was inviting him to direct at the Goodman.

"Come on out," he said, holding the glass door open. Frigid winter air blew in.

Dwayne stepped out into a glorious scene. Just to his right rose the Goodman marquee, spelling out GOODMAN in four foot high illuminated vertical letters, stretching up to thirty feet over the street. Randolph Street lay below them, bustling with traffic. A car circulated on the stacks of the parking garage straight across the street, right at their eye level. Off to the left rose the Leo Burnett Building and beyond that, on the other side of the Chicago River, the corn cob shape of one of the Marina Towers. So much city life!

Camper walked down the balcony and leaned over the parapet. "I love it up here," he said. "In the breaks between working, this is one of my favorite places." His breath swirled in clouds of fog.

Even though it was January, there was a table and chairs for anyone who wanted to lunch outdoors, and a series of chairs down the length of the balcony. Ah, to be working at the Goodman and come out here for a coffee and a conference about the work (when it was warmer, of course)! But then he had to pinch himself. Wasn't that exactly what he was doing right now? With the great man himself? What a dream!

Camper turned and leaned his buttocks against the parapet. "So tell me more about your vision for *King Lear*. You said you'd use music again, yes? Prince? Or something else, I think?"

"We did Prince for *Romeo and Juliet*. We used Jimi Hendrix for *Titus Andronicus*. I'm thinking about David Bowie for *King Lear*."

Camper nodded. He looked intrigued. Encouraged, Dwayne pushed on, feeling a bit giddy to be in this conversation.

This was where he needed to be! This was where he deserved to be! He was thirty-one years old. He'd studied at Northwestern. His mentor was Brad Cunningham, a Tony-nominated director. He'd studied with Frank Galati, a true genius. He'd acted and directed on Chicago stages through his twenties and paid his dues. His last two outings as a director had been critically acclaimed. His *Romeo and Juliet* had sold tickets like hotcakes.

He deserved to be here!

Didn't he?

Stop it, Dwayne. Be cool.

"We took the music further with *Romeo and Juliet*," Dwayne said. "Our music director, Ry, adapted lyrics from the text that moved the action. We replaced whole scenes with music and lyrics."

"I remember," Camper said. "I liked it."

"The challenge for Ry was writing music that had a Prince feel, but didn't violate the Prince copyright. There are a number of David Bowie songs I'd like to use, music and lyrics that'd work for us. The actual songs rather than our approximations. But we can't do that."

"Why not?" Camper said.

"The rights. That's why our music was *reminiscent* of Hendrix and Prince rather than *actual* Hendrix and Prince. We can't afford the performance rights."

"If you are doing *King Lear* here, we have a contract with ASCAP. You don't have to live in the storefront theatre poverty mindset."

"Wow," Dwayne said. This hit him like a thunderbolt. He could use *Fame* and *Cat People* and maybe *Changes* in the original? That would be so great. What was less great was that Camper had used the word "if" in that statement. *If* he were doing *King Lear* here? Dwayne wanted to hear *when* you do *King Lear* here.

Also not so great—it was fucking cold out here on the *Via Maggio*! He was beginning to shiver, but Camper showed no signs of being cold at all. In the past couple days the temperatures had dropped to the single digits. He longed for his coat, which was tossed over a chair in Camper's office.

But he would not allow verbal *ifs* or freezing temperatures to derail his conversation. "That really opens things up," Dwayne said, working hard to keep his teeth from chattering. "You know, I'd heard some rumor about the Rolling Stones coming to a show…"

Camper laughed. "Oh yeah. People said all sorts of things about that. But we had paid the rights."

"Mick Jagger…"

"No, Mick wasn't there," Camper said. "But it would've been the same if he had. Anyway, I met Mick in New York. Fascinating guy. Driven. Very business-minded. He and Keith Richards are like opposites. Mick is the Apollonian. Keith is the Dionysiac. Classic. But Mick wasn't at the show. Charley Watts was here. Dapper, lovely, understated gentleman. Beautifully dressed. Enjoyed the show. But there was no controversy. People love to chatter."

"So when we know what songs we'd like to use, do we submit a list to you?"

Camper stood up from leaning against the parapet and stuck his hands into his pockets. "Well, that's the thing," he said. "I'm still making up my mind. Should I go with an exciting but untried local company like yours or should I work with someone who is more of a known quantity? Our audiences were excited about seeing a La Mama production in Chicago—until that fell through. Otherwise, this slot wouldn't be available."

Dwayne felt something in his soul fall through. The slot was not his? He felt the cold penetrate him and his whole body began to shiver harder.

"Brad Cunningham has been lobbying me for the slot, too. That wouldn't be a visiting company. That would just be Brad directing a Goodman show. But I don't know. I'm tempted toward something new."

Fucking Brad Cunningham. Dwayne's relationship with Brad had suffered so many ups and downs over the years. Yes, he'd learned a tremendous amount from Brad, and Brad had opened opportunities for him, but he'd also laid his unwelcome drunken hands on Dwayne's crotch more than once. Plus, he'd somehow he'd led Camper to believe Dwayne was a funder who wanted to give money to the Goodman the first time they'd talked.

"Ah," Dwayne said. He was shivering so hard the word came out like he was bouncing down a set of stairs.

"You're cold," Camper said.

Dwayne's whole body was shaking uncontrollably.

"A bit," he said.

Camper shrugged as though Dwayne were making a questionable choice by being cold. "I suppose we can go in," he sighed. He led the way back into his office where Dwayne continued to shake.

"So this Agnes, your executive director, I take it she's your set designer, as well?"

"Ingrid. Yes. She's done set and lights for our past shows."

"Hmm…" Camper looked as though he felt that also was a questionable choice. "The Owen is our smaller stage, but people fail to realize it's still the third largest stage in the city of Chicago. A designer who's used to storefront stages may lack the monumental vision for a space like the Owen. You might want to consider that."

"I will," Dwayne promised, his muscles still clenched with the effort of bringing his body back to a reasonable internal temperature.

"I can give you the names of some excellent designers that I think you'd enjoy."

"That'd be great," Dwayne said. "But when do you think you'll decide whether we're in the Owen slot?"

Camper laughed. "Fair enough. Brad made me promise to let him pitch a show. I'm meeting with him this week." He flipped open a calendar on his desk. "Today is Tuesday. I meet with Brad on Thursday. Come back in on Monday, and I'll let you know." Camper stood up from his desk.

"Oh!" The meeting was over. "Yes, thank you." Dwayne got up and reached out a hand to shake. He walked out of the great man's office feeling profoundly deflated. What could he do about this? Would it be wrong to hire a hit man to kill Brad Cunningham?

2

That Evening

"I'm out there freezing, and I just don't know what to say." Talking about it now with his wife, Dwayne's throat tightened. The sorrow threatened to choke a sob out of him. "Even if I could've thought of something clever, I could barely speak. My muscles were so tight and shivering. I walked in there thinking we had the slot."

Angela tipped her head once to the side. She wasn't taking this as hard as he. Leaning her hip against the ancient, battered porcelain of their kitchen sink, she sipped from a bulbous glass of Chianti Classico. Dwayne flipped the pair of strip steaks in the oversized cast-iron skillet, sending up a wave of smoke and a roaring sizzle. The smoke detector on the ceiling began screaming. Angela sighed, set down her glass, picked up the broom and waved it at the device until it stopped. Dwayne opened the door to the back porch, then carried the salads and baked potatoes to the dining room table. Cold air came in, steak smoke flowed out. You couldn't get a good, crusty sear on a steak without a little smoke.

This was supposed to be a celebratory dinner after what he'd anticipated would be a triumphant meeting with Reginald Camper. Despite the lack of triumph, Angela encouraged him to cook it anyway. "Look," she'd said. "A year ago, did you think you could sit down with Reginald Camper to talk about directing at the Goodman? That alone is worth a celebration."

He couldn't argue with that. A year ago Camper didn't know who he was. Now they were on a first name basis. So out came the steaks. Dwayne served them up while Angela brought out the butter and sour cream. Dwayne topped off their wineglasses.

"So my mother called. She wants to know when I'm going to get pregnant." Angela imitated her mother's voice: "*Your father could sneeze on me, and I'd get knocked up.* That's what she says to me. So what's taking us so long?" She shook her head and took a sip of her Chianti. "I tell her: Ma, keep your nose out from the business between a woman and her husband."

"Good for you," Dwayne said. The past six months had been filled with drama regarding Angela's state of non-pregnancy and his insufficient contribution to said condition. It had made so much noise in his head that sometimes he couldn't get it up. So humiliating! There was no topic more likely to disturb his enjoyment of the seared beef on his plate. But he loved that she'd told her mother to keep her nose out. He forced himself to keep his focus on the positive. No thoughts of wilting penises. *Be here now,* as Ram Dass said. He sliced into his steak and saw the perfect gradations from brown sear to juicy pink to near red in the very center. Ah, beautiful! If one thing could be said about Dwayne Finnegan, it was that he knew how to cook a steak. He might not have advanced beyond adolescence in almost anything else in his life, but faced with a good slice of beef, he was a master.

Angela popped a slice into her mouth and chewed. "Nice steak," she said. "You go down to Paulina Market?"

"I found this at Dominick's. On sale." He popped a piece in his mouth. So very good. He would have paid twice per pound at Paulina. He may not have become a great bread-winner, but he was excellent at economizing.

"Really good," she said. "My grandfather never would've believed you could get a decent steak from a supermarket. For quality meat, you had to go to the butcher. For quality vegetables, you went to the greengrocer. You want quality pasta, you make it yourself."

"He was a giant among men," Dwayne agreed.

"At only five foot two! They made giants smaller back then."

"Yes, they did." Dwayne cut a larger slice of his steak and chewed it with pleasure.

"I was thinking it's time we visit the doctor. Ma has a point. You're going to need to go, too. I mean… Well…" She shrugged her shoulders as if she were hinting at something too delicate to discuss.

Dwayne set down his knife and fork. The piece of steak stopped cold somewhere along his esophagus. "This is supposed to be a celebratory meal." He swallowed hard to chase the piece of meat the rest of the way to his stomach.

Angela raised her eyebrows to the height of full innocence. "Hey, you were going to call it off. I said, no, it's worth celebrating your meeting. But, come on, you didn't get your production slot yet. So, hurrah, we celebrate, but we can talk about my thing, too. Because your meeting wasn't the *complete* big thing. Right?"

The steak on his plate looked suddenly pitiful. This wasn't a steak-level celebration.

She cocked her head at him. "Dwayne, don't get mopey on me. You're making good progress. I'm proud of you."

To Dwayne, she looked more like *impatient* than *proud*.

"Okay," he said. "So talk." He leaned back in his chair.

"It's time to find out if we need to do something. You know. They can do tests."

"Like poking us with needles?"

Angela snorted. "It's nothing for men. You jack off in a jar, and they look at your spermies, see if they swim okay. Maybe they're just doing a lazy backstroke, and they need a little boost or something. Who knows? I'm the one who has to take the hard tests."

"Yeah, okay." He took a forkful of his baked potato. It was already a little cold.

"Good. So stop looking sulky, Dwayne! Enjoy the beautiful steak. If you don't get the Goodman slot, you guys still have $150,000 in the bank. You can do a bang-up job of *King Lear* at the Playhouse. What did you spend on *Romeo and Juliet*? Like fifteen grand? And that was beautiful."

"Yeah," Dwayne agreed. "It got Camper willing to talk to me."

"Whatever he decides, you've got good options for where you lead your company next."

"True." This was a different way to look at it. Could he keep his mind in this positive direction? It wasn't about what Camper decided—it was about what *he* decided to do after Camper's decision. He was the artistic director of his company.

He thought about his father. Angus Finnegan had written and rewritten the same novel his entire adult life, sending it to agents and publishers, sometimes getting some interest, but never getting it across the finish line. He made a living writing for local periodicals like the *Evanston Review* and getting the occasional piece in the Tribune. But he always had an air of vague disappointment. Dwayne didn't want to be like that. And his mother—well, he didn't even want to think about his mother, the other member of the family who tried so hard and so long to make it on stage and screen. Her ups and downs were epic. He would like to be reasonably optimistic, but he struggled sometimes.

Angela stood up and lifted her wineglass. "So things are looking up for the Finnegan/Guiseppelli household. Right?"

He smiled and stood up to click glasses with her. "Yeah," he said. "Cheers."

Thank God for Angela.

She gave him a cockeyed smile. "So okay. Maybe doctor talk isn't the best thing for a celebration," she admitted.

"No, it's fine."

"It's not great timing," Angela insisted. "My steak is getting cold while I'm yakking on."

"I could give them another fast sear."

"Well," she said, sidling up to him. "If you can do that, maybe we should take a little break and reset this celebration." She put her arms around his neck and slowly leaned in to kiss him lingeringly on the lips. "If you know what I mean," she whispered into his ear.

"I think I'm getting the idea," he whispered back.

Now things were looking up. She took his hand and led him into the bedroom.

3

Wednesday, January 18, 2005

"Come on in here." Rockwell Nesbit III led Dwayne from the luxurious reception area into an equally luxurious conference room. Gorgeous Afro-centric art adorned the walls. A runner of kente cloth ran down the center of the conference table. Pretty much everyone Dwayne had seen so far in the office was Black. Dwayne wasn't exactly sure why Rocky had called him here, but he suspected it would mean money. Maybe Rocky wanted him to direct some of the commercials that made Rocky's law firm so lucrative. Dwayne had directed Rocky in *Romeo and Juliet*. Of course, that had been somewhat fraught, given Rocky's alternate personality as Uncle Bull, a loan shark given to breaking the bones of his clients. But it all worked out.

Floor-to-ceiling windows overlooked the south Loop from high above, all the way down to the museum campus. The offices were on the sixty-seventh floor. Rocky noticed Dwayne's look of awe and waved his arm toward the view. "Feast your eyes!" he exclaimed. Dwayne moved to the window and took it in. High above Michigan Avenue, the offices overlooked the south end of Grant Park. Beyond the park stood the Shedd Aquarium with its spurting fish fountain in front, the green copper dome of the Adler Planetarium, the neo-classic portico of the Field Museum, and the weird amalgamation of Soldier Field, which looked like a spaceship had landed atop the Roman Coliseum. Beyond it all lay the great freshwater sea of Lake Michigan.

"Awe-inspiring," Rocky said. "No other way to describe it."

"It is," Dwayne agreed.

"How'd you like to work here?"

"You mean directing your TV commercials?"

Rocky looked at him in amazement. "Directing my commercials?" He laughed loudly and derisively. "Damn boy! Ha! No, no, no, no, no!" He regained his composure. "No disrespect. You are an excellent director, but never fuck with the cash cow. My TV commercials are the hand on the tit that milks the almighty dollar that funds this whole gravy train. No, no, no, no. You know who shoots my commercials? *Spike Lee's cinematographer.* We do *not* mess with a winning formula. I'm asking if you want to work *here.*"

"Oh, yeah, this is a nice place," Dwayne said. His face felt extra hot. He must be blushing. He hated that. "What would I do?"

"Coco said you take office temp work."

Coco was Rocky's beautiful daughter. A terrific actor Dwayne had worked with many times, and a true diva.

"I've done a lot of office temping. And a lot of bartending."

"Well, I'll turn you over to my office manager, and she can put you where she needs help—and I'll pay you better than the usual temp job. Plus, you'll have a boss who understands the demands of the theatre."

"Wow. Yeah. That sounds great." It wasn't at all what Dwayne had been expecting. Working for someone so volatile worried him, but this looked like a really great office.

"Yeah," Rocky said. "I'd like to help you out. This place is just a money machine. Ninety-five percent paid for by insurance companies *settling out of court.*" Rocky laughed and raised his fists like a prizefighter. *"We put the insurance companies on the ropes, and get you the money you deserve!"* he said in the deep, resonant voice he'd used in countless late-night television commercials. The vast television-watching populace of Chicagoland knew Rocky's face and voice. Dwayne could practically hear the theme from *Rocky* that played in all his commercials.

"Help yourself to some coffee-and," Rocky said, gesturing to a spread of bagels and croissants, fruit, and coffee on an antique bureau against the wall. He poured himself a coffee, flopped a sweet roll onto a little plate, and sat down at the head of the heavy oak conference table. Dwayne followed suit.

"Coco said you struggle for work," Rocky said. They were interrupted by the conference room door opening.

"Say, Rocky," a young White man said, sticking just his head and upper torso into the room. "I've got a meeting here in five minutes."

Rocky looked at him with extreme displeasure.

"It's on the calendar," the young man said.

"Should we?" Dwayne started to get up from his chair.

Rocky held up his hand to Dwayne and swiveled his chair toward the young man in the doorway.

"Do I look like I give a good God damn what's on your calendar?" Rocky said. Dwayne felt immediately embarrassed for the guy.

"Um…" the guy said. "It's not *my* calendar, per se."

"Do I?" Rocky repeated.

The young lawyer took a deep breath. "We're looking to settle the Jones case. I've got the investigator and the insurance…"

"Do I provide you with an office in this building?" Rocky demanded.

"Um…yes, but it'd be…"

"Do you see *me* right now in this conference room? Am *I*, right now, not having a conference?" Rocky demanded.

"Um…yes, sir,"

"And did you notice *my name* on the door as you came into the offices this morning, and on the wall of the reception area, and on the wall down in the lobby of the building?" Rocky rose threateningly from his seat.

"Yes, yes, sir," the young man said, his face becoming more and more white.

"Well, then, since you have an office provided by me, why don't you take your meeting down there while you still have a job?"

"It's just…"

"It's just what?" Rocky said, stepping closer and closer to the young lawyer.

"It'll be crowded in my office. That doesn't look like we are coming from a position of strength, like you always say we should."

"We occupy this entire floor of the building and half the next floor up. Figure it out. Find a spot. And if you can't, then take them down to the Starbucks." Rocky's voice rose steadily with each sentence. "And if you don't like that, you can meet in the public library, or down in the dumpster in the alley, for all I care. But get the hell out of here!" he thundered.

The young man scurried away, his pale face turning a bright red. Rocky turned to Dwayne, his face transforming from furious to playful in an instant. He laughed heartily. "I like to give them a lesson in negotiating now and again. Especially the young *White* attorneys. Most of them been pampered their whole lives. Rich parents. Ivy League colleges. Never learned how to get tough. I show them how to intimidate the suits."

"That's how they learn?" Dwayne said uncertainly. He felt extra uncomfortable being White himself.

Rocky laughed again. "I guarantee you, that boy'll be a son-of-a-bitch now in that meeting. Insurance dude won't know what hit him." Rocky took a sip of his coffee, then lifted the cup toward Dwayne. "How do you like it? Hawaiian Kona. I have it flown in and roasted locally. I love it."

"It's really good," Dwayne agreed. Despite his momentary discomfort, he couldn't remember when he'd had a better cup of coffee. Fruity and floral and smooth. Delicious.

"I tried giving Coco a day job here," Rocky said. "She wasn't even good in the TV spots with me. Finally, I just put her on an allowance. Everybody's happy. But you ain't my kid. You'll have to work for your money." Rocky raised an eyebrow and laughed.

"Of course." Dwayne smiled uncertainly. "I've done a lot of office work. Spreadsheets at real estate offices, things like that, but I'm capable of much more. In the theatre, I hire and organize pretty much everyone, from designers to actors to backstage, and coordinate all their efforts. Procure space. Make sure ticketing works…"

"Right," Rocky cut him off abruptly. "I'm shopping for a new CEO, but you're not it. I hired one before, but he didn't understand that he was in charge as long as I liked what he was doing." Rocky laughed and slapped the tabletop, then looked serious again. "I just don't want to be bothered with the day-to-day."

"Okay," Dwayne said. "So, are you offering me a job now, or do I wait until the new CEO is in place?" He was feeling a little dizzy with Rocky's changes of mood and direction.

Rocky raised his eyebrows, stood, and pointed his finger at Dwayne. He laughed uproariously. Then he sat back down, shaking his head. He sighed. "Doing *Romeo and Juliet* with you all really whetted my appetite for the live stage. I'd like to do that on a regular basis. I was thinking you could put me in your ensemble."

"Oh," Dwayne said. Was this quid pro quo? Did he have to invite Rocky into the ensemble to get a job?

He didn't want Rocky in the ensemble. Once actors were in the ensemble, they wanted to decide what plays the company produced. They wanted to say how the shows were marketed. They wanted to decide all sorts of things for which they had absolutely no expertise.

Coco had brought Rocky into *Romeo and Juliet* as a replacement for an actor who dropped out. It turned out Rocky had a dissociative identity disorder and sometimes turned into a violent loan shark called Uncle Bull. On one of those occasions, Dwayne had to step in to perform Rocky's role in the show at the last minute. Dwayne still suffered PTSD from that episode.

Rocky grinned and pointed at him. "I see you have concerns. Never mind." He pulled out his phone, hit a button, and waited for someone to answer. "Dwayne's here," he said into the phone. "Tell him I'm staying on my meds."

He handed the phone to Dwayne.

"What's going on?" the phone said to him. It was Coco.

"I'm at your dad's office. He's talking about hiring me for a day job at the law firm and maybe becoming an ensemble member."

Coco laughed and laughed. "Oh, you fucked now," she said.

"What the hell?" Rocky said. "Is she laughing?" He grabbed the phone from Dwayne. "What're you laughing about? Tell him I'm staying on my meds." He handed the phone immediately back.

"Hello?" Dwayne said.

"Yeah, actually, he *is* staying on his meds," Coco said. "He moved back in with Mama, and that's her condition. She's going to kick him back out if he doesn't stay on the meds. And he doesn't want to be kicked out."

Well, that was something. He remembered Coco's mother. She was a formidable, exceptionally beautiful woman. Rocky was nuts about her in both of his personalities. Dwayne wanted to ask Coco what she thought of adding Rocky to the ensemble, but he couldn't do that with Rocky sitting across the table.

"Right," Dwayne said. "Thanks." He handed the phone back to Rocky, who promptly hung it up and stuffed it back into his pocket.

"So there you go," Rocky said. "No worries."

"Okay," Dwayne said. "Here's the thing. There can't be any connection between me working here and you being cast in our shows. If so, I'll look for a job elsewhere." He really wanted the job, but he couldn't have Rocky abusing him like one of his junior lawyers.

"Huh," Rocky said. "Fair enough. No connection." He said it sincerely enough, but then he winked at Dwayne. "But what do you think? What's the next show we're doing?"

How to handle this? He needed the job, but… He took a deep breath. "I'm not going to discuss theatre business here," he said. "If we talk about a show, that's going to be a conversation at a different location at a different time. No quid pro quo."

"No, no, no. No quid pro quo," Rocky said. "But you know what they say: One hand washes the other."

"Okay." This was not going to work. Dwayne stood up. "I'm going to look for a job elsewhere. I appreciate you taking the time with me."

Rocky laughed and waved his hand at Dwayne. "Sit down, sit down, sit down."

Dwayne hesitated, then did so.

Rocky leaned in and raised his eyebrows high. "You're a decent negotiator. I like that. You're a sharp guy." He glanced over as a smartly dressed woman walked past the fish-bowl windows of the conference room. He stood up and waved her in. "Brianna, this is Dwayne Finnegan. He's going to join the office staff. Find something for him to do."

Brianna looked at her watch. "Why isn't Cartwright in here? He's meeting with the investigator and insurance on the Jones case."

"He's not in here," Rocky said.

"He's *supposed* to be in here," Brianna repeated.

"He's not in here because *I'm* in here."

"And why are *you* in here, Rocky?" she said, much like Dwayne had seen Angela address one of her misbehaving fifth graders. "Are you here to disrupt business?"

For a moment, Rocky looked like he might explode at her, but then a sly smile crossed his face. He turned to Dwayne.

"Brianna is our office manager," Rocky said to Dwayne. "She makes everything work. Sometimes I think I should just make her the CEO!" He laughed. Brianna looked annoyed. He turned back to her. "So you can put Dwayne on the office staff."

"How are we using Mr. Finnegan?" Brianna's eyes cut toward him and back at Rocky.

"Entirely up to you. You can start him at an associate's salary."

Brianna looked confused. "Is he a lawyer?"

"No," Rocky said. "Office staff."

"Then why would he start at an associate's salary?"

"I want to be generous." Rocky raised his hands and laughed heartily.

She darted her eyes to Dwayne. Clearly she did not want to be having this conversation in front of him.

"Why would he instantly be the highest-paid person on the office staff? I don't even know what I'm going to do with him."

"You'll figure it out." Rocky looked at her, suddenly coldly.

"Office staff, starting salary," she said firmly. "I'm not having my people quit because they're pissed off."

"Office staff, one bump up," Rocky said.

"Starting," Brianna repeated. She darted a look that could kill at Dwayne.

What the hell was going on?

"One bump up," Rocky repeated. He turned to Dwayne. "You start Monday. Take your wife out to dinner tonight."

"I have a meeting with Reg Camper on Monday," Dwayne said apologetically.

Rocky's eyes lit up. "Reginald Camper? Artistic director of the Goodman Theatre? Oh, that's impressive." He turned back to Brianna. "One step up and a five-thousand-dollar signing bonus. Cut him a check today."

She narrowed her eyes. "Leadership, Rocky," she said.

He instantly held up a hand. "This is me. Leading." He turned back to Dwayne with a smile. "So what show do you think we'd do at the Goodman?"

"We don't have anything set up at this point."

"At this point!" Rocky exclaimed. "I understand. Never mind." He grinned and turned to Brianna again, his smile fading. "I'm done for the day. Cut him that check before he leaves!" He clapped Dwayne on the arm, walked out of the conference room, out through reception, down the elevator, and out of the building.

4

That Same Day

"One minute, Miss Guiseppelli." Angela's new principal strode up the hallway toward her, one finger lifted like he was testing the wind direction, his thick eyebrows raised high in his furrowed forehead. Angela stood in the doorway of her classroom, supervising her fifth graders returning from gym class full of high spirits, yakking, poking one another, laughing, complaining. What did this bonehead want? She needed to settle her kids down and transition back to classroom teaching.

"Mr. Plotz," she said in greeting.

"Plotz!" cackled the last of her boys to pass into the room. He poked a boy in the front row of the classroom as he passed. "Don't plotz on the floor!" he told him, and cackled some more. The word, plotz, plotz, plotz, popped up around the room.

Norman Plotz looked offended. "Do we need to talk about the discipline in your classroom, Miss Guiseppelli?" he asked tartly. He not only called her *Miss*, he pronounced her name as *Guys-eye-pally*.

"*Joe-Say-Pelli*," Angela said.

"What's that?" Plotz said.

"My name," Angela repeated. "*Miz Joe-Say-Pelli*. Not *Miss Guys-eye-pally*."

"Of course," Plotz said tightly. The light reflected off the lens of his thick black-framed glasses making his eyes momentarily invisible.

The noise level in her classroom spiraled up. A girl in the back squealed: "Hands off me, Jamar!"

"One moment," Angela said to Plotz. She gave Jamar the eyes-of-death, and he settled into his seat with his hands in his lap. Then she strode to the front of her classroom and clapped her hands twice. The kids quieted. "Okay," she said to them. "Mr. Plotz is your new principal." She gestured to the man in the black suit and black spectacles in the doorway. The kids looked at him curiously. He didn't look like their last principal. "I'm sure you all want to make a good impression. You don't want to be having a one-on-one in his office any time soon." She looked around at them meaningfully, holding the eyes of some of her usual suspects in particular. "Now, open your social studies to chapter fourteen and begin reading. I want it quiet in here. Your homework assignment tonight depends on it." A few groans rose from the desks. Angela raised her finger. Silence resumed. One hand went up. Angela nodded at the student. "What happened to Ms. Konacki?" the girl asked.

"Ms. Konacki and her husband moved to Wisconsin," Angela said. "She's the principal of a school in Madison now. Who knows a fact about Madison?"

A tall boy in the aisle along the window raised his hand with a studiously bored look on his face.

"D'Andre?" Angela said.

"Capitol of Wisconsin," D'Andre said while rolling his eyes.

"Very good, D'Andre. Madison is the capitol of Wisconsin. Now. Chapter fourteen. Social Studies. Reading quietly." She looked around meaningfully again and then stepped back to the doorway.

"If you could just close the door for a minute," Mr. Plotz said.

"They just got back from gym," Angela said. Any experienced teacher would know what that meant.

"This will only take a minute," Plotz said. He stepped forward and pushed the door closed. Angela could hear the whispers and giggles inside begin almost instantaneously.

"I'm sure Fran Konacki was a fine principal," Plotz said in a tone that made clear he thought the opposite. "However, I believe she neglected to review your weekly lesson plans. I don't intend to continue that lack of attention. I want to review detailed lesson plans for each coming week by the Wednesday of the previous week."

Angela tilted her head. "So you'd want lesson plans for next week by Wednesday of last week?"

"No, no," Plotz said. "Today's Wednesday. I'd want next week's lesson plans by today. You don't have them in a form you could give me, I suppose?"

"No," Angela said. The noise volume inside her classroom was rising. She wanted to get back in there, but she needed to straighten out this idiot. Plotz was adding a lot of work to her already difficult job. "Why do you want them?" she said. "You can't possibly have time to review the weekly lesson plans of every teacher in this building."

"The test scores at my last school, in Iowa, were twenty percent higher than at this school. I'll make the time. I intend to bring up the achievement level. A close eye on pedagogy was essential to my past success."

"Was it?" Angela said. She couldn't keep the doubtful cynicism out of her voice. Inside her room, the volume continued to rise.

Plotz looked toward the doorway and sighed. He shook his head disappointedly. "An article I wrote on classroom discipline appeared in *Teach Magazine* last year. I'll email you the link."

"I would certainly enjoy that," Angela said, controlling her tone as much as possible. She knew she just had to walk to the front of the room and give them the *eyes-of-death* look, as the kids liked to call it, and they'd quiet right down. "What grades did you teach before you went into administration?"

"I was never a classroom teacher," Plotz said.

Just as she suspected. He'd gone straight through to get his Ph.D. and then into administration. This guy didn't know shit.

"Once we get rolling, I'll be looking at how your lesson plans tie into the learning objectives I'll be adding to the district-wide objectives. We're going to pull this school out of the doldrums." He grinned grimly. "Now I think you'd best take care of *that* situation." He nodded toward the door as though full chaos had erupted rather than the totally predicable chattering of an unsupervised room of ten-year-olds. He nodded and headed off toward the next classroom to interrupt another teacher at work. Angela watched him go. He walked like he had a corncob stuck up his ass.

As soon as he was gone, Assistant Principal Todd Bodkins appeared around the corner and sidled up to Angela. "How did an administrator from Iowa get put in charge of a Chicago public school?" he whispered.

"What happened, Todd?" Angela asked. "You didn't kiss the right ass for the promotion? You going to be an assistant principal for the rest of your life?"

She didn't wait for an answer. She plunged back into her classroom and, with one clap of her hands, the room quieted.

5

Saturday, January 21, 2005

With Reg Camper on the fence about giving him a slot at the Goodman, Dwayne knew he needed to refine the concept for his *King Lear*. He had an appointment with Camper in two days and needed to wow him. He had talented people. Could he inspire them to greatness today?

He liked hosting production meetings in his apartment, but Angela wanted the apartment to herself today, so he scheduled the meeting at Ry's, which was also good. Ry's was a funky, creative space that he loved. Between one thing and another, Angela had been out of sorts lately. Dwayne wasn't sure what to do about that.

As he walked into Ry's studio, music blasted into his face like a gust of wind. Ry and Tom belted the words of Bowie and Lennon's *Fame* into the microphones with Ry on guitar and Tom on the drums. Who knew Tom could play drums? Of course, as an actor/dancer/choreographer, he totally understood rhythm, so why not? They sounded great. Dwayne bopped across the worn wood floor toward the stage at the back of Ry's studio.

The creative staff was already here. His costume designer, Peaches, danced in front of a Marshall speaker stack to the side of the stage with her eyes closed. No doubt she felt if she kept her eyes closed, no one could see her dancing. Or at least she couldn't see them seeing her dancing. She was painfully shy when she wasn't in one of her manic phases. But despite her shyness, she was wearing skin-tight purple velvet slacks with a pink tutu sort of thing over it and a pink blouse with a red satin jacket. It looked like she might have rearranged the array of pastel colors in her teased out hair, as well.

In their last show, the Indigenous Connection Church, the ayahuasca-taking cult that shared Dwayne's rehearsal space as their worship space, had set her costumes on fire. The actors had to perform in their street clothes. That had been devastating to Peaches. Dwayne wanted to make sure she had a better experience this time around.

Ingrid's big canvas bag stood on the bar that ran along the right side of the room. Ry's place had been a tavern back in the day when every neighborhood had its own little bar. Now the tavern was Ry's music studio. He lived in the apartment above. But where was Ingrid?

He heard a sudden yowl and saw Ingrid lying on one of the mattresses along the opposite wall. (Ry had mattresses to accommodate any of his musician friends who became temporarily homeless, or who were on a budget-level tour from out of town).

She sat up and raised a finger over her head. "I got it," she muttered. She began furiously sketching on her big design pad.

Ry clamped his hand over the guitar strings suddenly, and Tom stopped two beats later. "Our director has arrived," Ry announced.

"Hey, everybody." Dwayne pulled up a chair at a little café table in front of the stage. Peaches and Ingrid moved over to join him. Ry sat on a stool on stage, and Tom remained on the throne behind the drum kit.

"So we've talked about using Bowie for this show," Dwayne said. "The good news is that Reg Camper says the Goodman has an ASCAP account, and we can get the rights for the actual songs we'd want to use, music and lyrics."

Ingrid whooped, Peaches smiled, but Ry remained remarkably passive. "Yeah," he said. "That's cool, but I really liked how *our* lyrics replaced some of the transition scenes in *Romeo and Juliet*."

"Actually, if we are using Bowie," Tom said. "I'd been thinking Ry should play the Fool. The Fool is like a chorus character, commenting on the action throughout. That could really work."

"I like that idea. *Mark it, nuncle*," Dwayne said, half attempting to sing Fool lines: *"Have more than thou showest, Speak less than thou knowest, Lend less than thou owest."* Ry picked up his guitar and began playing a riff from Bowie's *Changes* beneath. Dwayne attempted to match the tune: *"Leave thy drink and thy whore, and keep in-a-door, and thou shalt have more than two tens to a score."* On the last phrase, Ry's guitar and Dwayne sounded together. Everyone applauded.

This was *fun*. He was already feeling happier about facing Camper again.

"So we can totally make that work," Ry said. "But I'm not so sure Bowie is best for this story."

"What do you mean?" Dwayne said.

"I was wondering, too," Peaches said. "Bowie's had a million costume styles. I have no idea how to design costumes from the idea of Bowie."

"Well," Dwayne said. "Everything, music included, does need to rise from the story."

"So, how do you define the story, Dwayne?" Ingrid said. "A poor old king is stupid, his daughters are mean, he goes mad, and everyone dies?"

Dwayne laughed, then raised a hand. "If I distill the play to one idea, I get *the inheritance of betrayal*. Lear starts the play giving out the inheritance. In his vanity, he betrays the daughter who loves him most and disinherits her."

"Cordelia," Tom said. He hit a rim shot on the drums.

"Yes," Dwayne continued. "Without Cordelia to protect him, his older daughters betray him and turn him out into the wilderness, where he goes mad. And the betrayals accelerate until most of the main characters are dead."

"That makes me think about the blues," Ry drawled. "Isn't that better for *King Lear* than Bowie?" He played a few bars of *Fame* again, and Tom joined in on the drums. Then they stopped. "I don't think Lear is tragic because of his *fame*."

"I'd agree," Dwayne said.

"Bowie doesn't write much about betrayal, but it's huge in the blues. The blues have got more of that tragic…whatever."

"Gravitas?" Tom suggested.

"Yeah," Ry said.

"Oh, come on!" Ingrid said. "We can't just drop Bowie just like that. *Putting out the gasoline…*"

"You mean *the fire*?" Peaches said.

"Yes, yes, yes," Ingrid said. "People love Bowie. Especially theatre people."

Ry took off his guitar and set it into a stand. "I want to use our own lyrics again, adapted from the script. That's what made the *Romeo and Juliet* music special." He sat down on the edge of the plywood stage. A splinter caught on the seat of his jeans, and he got up and moved over a bit.

"Any other arguments in favor of Bowie?" Dwayne said.

"For fights, and eye gouging, and movement, there's some good stuff," Tom said, still sitting on the drum throne.

"Eye gouging?" Peaches said, her eyebrows way up.

"Cornwall gouges out Gloucester's eyes. *Out, vile jelly!*" Tom quoted in diabolical tones.

"Oh, right." Peaches shivered.

"I love *Fame*. We've got to do something based on *Fame*," Ingrid insisted. "What's a word to replace *fame* that encapsulates something about Lear?"

"Lame? Came?" Peaches suggested. "Dame? Maim? Name?"

"It doesn't need to rhyme," Ry said. "Although lame and maim have possibilities."

"How about *reign?*" Dwayne suggested. "*Reign, your power's in the river,*" he sang. "*Reign, your kingdom's all asplintered.*"

Ry took a step back, nodding deeply. "Not bad, Dwayne. We're going to have to bring you in on the writing sessions."

"Ha!" Tom cackled with delight. "Yeah!"

Ingrid shook her head violently. "*Reign* doesn't have the punch of *fame*. So dump *reign*. Come on, we need something better!"

"You are definitely *not* invited to the writing sessions," Ry replied.

"Why? Can't Dwayne take a little constructive criticism?" She retreated behind the bar, put a glass under one of the ancient beer taps, and pulled the handle. Nothing came out.

"You get negative, it stops the ideas," Ry said. "That ain't how to collaborate."

Dwayne didn't remember Ry ever confronting Ingrid before, but he also couldn't remember Ingrid commenting on the music before. Usually, she was totally focused on set and lights and running the business side of things.

"I collaborate all the time. That's what we're doing right here." She waved her arms to include the whole space of the former tavern, with its walls covered with concert posters and its pressed tin ceiling with some of the tiles hanging down. A very dim light shone in through the storefront windows that hadn't been washed in decades.

"Critiquing during the flow is death," Ry drawled. "You keep adding until you got so much good stuff it's time to weed through it."

"*Yes and…* as the improv people say," Tom added.

"Well, spank my ass," Ingrid complained. "Everybody's got their own way."

"Okay…" Dwayne said, hoping to head off some rising tension.

"Right," Ry said. "And some people *don't.*"

"Are you trying to pick a fight?" Ingrid said, swinging herself out from behind the bar.

Ry looked at her, amazed, and then started laughing. "I was trying to be nice to you, working up the Bowie idea you wanted when obviously the blues are better suited to this script," he said.

"You don't know shit," Ingrid said.

"Why don't you step up here, pick up an instrument, and show me what you know about music," Ry suggested.

"Okay…" Dwayne said.

"You know what?" Ingrid said loudly. "Fuck you." She lunged to the bar, picked up her enormous canvas bag, and headed toward the door.

"Whoa, whoa, whoa, hold on!" Dwayne said. He shot to the door to cut off Ingrid's exit. "When I go back to Reg Camper, I need to wow the man. So let's hold up here and do what we came to do." He turned to Ry. "Right?"

Ry raised his eyes and shrugged. "Whatever. If you want *collaborate lite.*"

"Really, Ry?" Dwayne said disappointedly.

"You know what?" Ingrid said. "Fuck it. Here's my idea: Furniture. I'm thinking lots and lots of furniture. Like when the parents die and the kids argue who's going to get the antique armoire. Stacks of furniture. It's familial. That which is inherited. And yet uncanny. Epic. But betrayals erode it all the way through the show.

Termites are eating it, and sawdust falls. Crumbling. Diminishment."

"How is that going to work?" Ry said.

"*How is that going to work?* Seriously? You can't even do *collaborate lite*, fuckface. Maybe it doesn't crumble. Maybe it bursts into flames. *Putting out the gasoline.* Huge, monumental stacks of antique furniture. At the end, it bursts into flames. Lear's heart breaks as he carries in the dead Cordelia, and he dies, and everything burns." She pulled out a huge sketchbook from her bag and drew a high-speed rendering of the Owen stage surrounded behind by stacks of furniture going high over the actors. She tore the drawing out of her sketchpad and threw it on the dirty wood floor of the former tavern.

"There," she shouted. "Collaborate on that." She stormed out. They all looked at the door and then looked at each other.

"Okay, so she's having a great day," Dwayne said. Tom laughed and hit a rim shot on the drums.

"If I could say something?" Peaches suggested.

"Yes, please," Dwayne said.

"Your thing of the inheritance of betrayal and Ry's idea of the blues? That makes me think of post-Civil War south. You know? Like the betrayal of slavery and the inheritance of racism and poverty. The Confederate States attempting to split the country into North and South like Lear tries to give it to his two older daughters? Is that anything?"

"I love that," Tom said. "Lear is like the plantation owner whose time is gone."

"Or Robert E. Lee," Ry said.

"And then Gloucester is like the old house butler, still faithful to the master because he cannot see forward into any new way of life," Dwayne said, turning to Tom. "Maybe we cast the whole Gloucester family as Black."

Tom nodded. "We've been talking Wallace for Lear. Melinda is perfect for sweet Cordelia, and Coco would make an amazing Goneril. So we've got a mixed-race family there." He took a deep breath. "I'd like to take that farther. I want to play the third sister, Regan."

That stopped Dwayne. "Does that fit with the Civil War idea? How do you imagine this? Is she a gay man? So then is Regan's husband, Cornwall, gay? Are they a gay couple?"

"We don't have to be literal. This would be a nod to the practice in Shakespeare's time, men playing the women," Tom said simply, standing up from the drum throne and cocking a hip.

"But the other women would be played by women," Dwayne said. "I hadn't been thinking of you for Regan. I'd been considering you for the Fool."

"The Fool is a great role, too," Tom said, "but I want you to think about Regan."

"Okay," Dwayne said. "We don't have to decide now. You and I will discuss casting later."

"Right," Tom said, curtsying and looking pleased.

"Okay," Dwayne said. "I like Peaches' idea of *Lear* rising out of America's Civil War. Ry, go ahead with working up ideas using the blues and anything else of that period. Peaches, please pursue that with the costume design, as well. And I'll huddle with Ingrid." He picked up her drawing from the floor and looked at it for a long moment. He put it on the table, and the others gathered around. "You know, amazingly enough, this furniture stack set could work with that idea. Doesn't it kind of suggest a stately plantation home?"

"Yeah...." Ry's voice trailed off.

How was Dwayne going to get Ingrid integrated with the rest of the team again? She could show occasional real genius, but she could also be so damned difficult.

6

Monday, January 23, 2005

Dwayne spent all day Sunday attempting to reframe his *King Lear* pitch. He'd already told Camper they would use Bowie's music. They'd talked about the song, *Changes*, from *Hunky Dory*. You could say *King Lear* was all about changes. Unanticipated and horrifying changes. Would Camper be like Ingrid and think that dropping Bowie was a terrible mistake? Sweat broke out on his brow as he tried to adjust the presentation in his mind.

He had to stop second-guessing himself!

He was still trying to settle his mind as he walked into Camper's office Monday morning. Camper looked up from his laptop on the desk, and suddenly Dwayne had it! It was all about music! He would use *Bowie* to explain why he wasn't using Bowie! He would sing! Right now!

He broke into the chorus of *Changes*.

"*Ch....*" He did not get past the opening consonant, because instantly Angela's voice shouted a warning in his head: "*NO!*"

And he stopped.

As instantly as inspiration hit, he regretted the idea.

"What's that?" Camper said.

"Sorry," Dwayne said. He pulled out his handkerchief. "I thought I was going to sneeze." What was he thinking? He squinted his eyes and pretended to blow his nose. Camper looked at him strangely.

"It's certainly going to be interesting working with all of you," Camper said. Then Dwayne noticed his ensemble members' headshots spread out on Camper's desk.

"What's this?" Dwayne said.

"Astrid was here, first thing." Camper raised his eyebrows and shook his head slightly. "She brought in these headshots. Were you looking for my input on casting?"

"You mean Ingrid." Dwayne was not looking for Camper's input on casting. He always collaborated with Tom on casting. Suggestions from anyone else annoyed him. But if Camper wanted to collaborate on casting, that meant they would be doing the show at the Goodman, and Dwayne would put up with nearly anything to do a show at the Goodman. He sat down in the chair in front of Camper's desk.

"I'd love to get your input on casting!" Dwayne sounded ridiculously eager and borderline fake.

"Oh!" Camper leaned back away. "I hate having anyone other than my casting director kibitz on casting. But if that's what you want…"

"Does this mean we're in? In the Owen?" Dwayne said.

"Ingrid didn't tell you? Yes, you have the September/October slot. I hope she won't make me regret it."

"Oh, that's fantastic," Dwayne said. The Owen theatre was his! Oh, joy of beginning! The most beautiful theatre space in the city of Chicago. The best equipped. There was no other space in which he'd rather direct. He would direct there for free. He would pay to direct there! And he would be directing *King Lear*, the great Everest of the Shakespearean canon. There was no greater play in all of Christendom. Dwayne Finnegan directs *King Lear*. At the Goodman! Amazing! This was his first step toward a real, paying career as a director! Oh, consummation devoutly to be wished! And to think, he'd almost sung *Changes*. Camper might have *ch…ch…ch…*changed his mind right then.

"Ingrid told me you wanted to collaborate on casting," Camper said. "But I think she actually wanted to sound me out about using fire on the Owen stage."

"Really?" On Saturday, she'd talked about piles of furniture disintegrating, like termites were working away at them. Then she got mad and shouted about them bursting into flames. She was serious about that?

"Of course, we can't have a set burst into flames," Camper said.

"The fire marshal wouldn't allow Lady Macbeth to walk across the stage with a real candle. We are just around the corner from the site of the Iroquois Theatre fire. It's a hundred years ago, but the fire marshals seem to think it happened yesterday."

"Maybe she was just toying with the idea of flames," Dwayne said. But if that were the case, why did she visit Reg Camper this morning? She couldn't possibly have believed that Dwayne wanted Camper's input on casting.

"I understand she's your executive director, but are you sure you want her designing the set? Designing for the Owen is not like designing for a storefront."

"Right. Right." Working with a designer who'd worked at the Goodman before would be nice. Working with someone who wasn't a bulldozer like Ingrid would be even nicer. But Ingrid would never agree to step aside. He and Joan would have to vote her out of the job. Would Joan agree to that? And if they did that, what then? As crazy as she could be, Ingrid made things happen for the company. "I'll keep that in mind," he said.

"Good!" Camper leaned up and grabbed the first headshot off the stack and tossed it onto the space between him and Dwayne. "Wallace Proctor. He was fine as Capulet, but do you think he's got the chops for Lear?"

Okay, this was not a conversation he wanted to have.

"Yes," Dwayne said. "He showed me what I needed to see in the title role of *Titus Andronicus*."

"Titus is no Lear," Camper said.

"Maybe not, but it's a hell of an audition. And we are an ensemble company," Dwayne said.

"Right, right, right." He turned Wallace's headshot over and looked at his resume. "Still, there are more roles in *Lear* than you have ensemble members. Gloucester is a wonderful role for someone with Proctor's track record."

"Who would you cast as Lear?" Dwayne said.

Camper looked up from the resume. "Me personally? I'd call Brian Dennehy. Or Stacy Keach. But they aren't going to turn out for you."

"No," Dwayne agreed. Would the Brian Dennehys and Stacy Keaches of the world ever turn out for him?

"Peter Burden is a wonderful local actor with the chops and experience to take on Lear, if you wanted to consider a Black Lear." Camper noticed the next photo on the pile. "Ha! Speaking of Black actors." He picked up the headshot of Rockwell Nesbit III. "I was so surprised to see this fellow in your *Romeo and Juliet*. So many terrible late night commercials! And yet he was intriguing as Montague. Will you use him again?"

"Rocky is not actually an ensemble member." Why had Ingrid put his headshot in the stack? Had Rocky gotten to her? Cut some kind of deal?

"Montague was not a big role, but I found him mesmerizing. Maybe because we know his face so well from the TV commercials. He's like a mythic figure. You might consider him for something. Cornwall? Albany?"

"Coco Nesbit is playing Goneril…"

"Oh, excellent!" Camper said. "I look forward to her in that."

"Yes, so Albany is out. Coco is not going to play wife to her real-life father."

"He's Coco Nesbit's father? Ha! Well, it could be a nice acting challenge for them." Camper chuckled. "Maybe Cornwall is the better role for him, anyway. The cruel Cornwall, gouging out Gloucester's eyes…"

Dwayne felt immediately uncomfortable at the thought of Rocky playing Cornwall. Would Cornwall bring out Rocky's inner Uncle Bull? Sure, Rocky promised to stay on his medication, but he'd probably promised that before his misadventures last year as well, when he broke Chaz's finger with a pair of pliers.

"Okay," Camper said. "From the look on your face, I believe Ingrid lied. You have no more interest in my casting suggestions than the man in the moon."

"No! I'm just…"

"Listen, you want to direct your play your way. I'm beginning to realize Ingrid has her own agenda."

Dwayne laughed. "That's for sure."

"You want my advice on anything," Camper said. "You ask for it. I'll ignore Ingrid's entreaties on your behalf. Good?"

"Good," Dwayne said. "But, I mean, she *is* my set designer."

"Right. She should stay in her lane. But since you got me wound up, let me plug two ideas: Peter Burden for any gap your ensemble doesn't cover. He could do Lear, Gloucester, or either of the sons-in-law, Albany or Cornwall. And think about Rockwell Nesbit. There's something a little magical about him on stage."

After he left Camper's office, Dwayne stepped out onto the Via Maggio above Dearborn Street. Tiny snow flurries swirled around his head. The cold air felt bracing.

The Owen Theatre was his! He could hardly believe it. Reginald Camper just been giving him casting advice. It was going to happen! Dwayne Finnegan at the Goodman Theatre! Oh, joy of joys!

He looked at the huge vertical marquee spelling out GOODMAN in huge letters. It was not just the marquee of a great theatre. It was the marquee of *his* theatre! Yes! He couldn't stop himself. He let out a glorious whoop at the top of his lungs.

Oh yes! He was *here*. What fun if Angela were here with him right now on this glorious Via Maggio! They would hug and scream and dance. Whatever had been burdening her lately would wash away in the joy of this!

Cars flowed by beneath him. Tiny snowflakes swirled around him. Oh, glorious moment here in the heart of the world! This theatre where he had seen the very best shows he had ever seen.

Oh, love of life, oh glory!

He was *here*!

7

That Afternoon

Even though her meeting with Reg Camper that morning had not gone all that well, Ingrid was determined to move ahead. She turned up the music loud in her van and pressed harder on the accelerator. Sure, the Iroquois Theatre fire had been the greatest disaster in the history of entertainment, and yeah, it had been right around the corner from the Goodman, but that was a hundred years ago! Screw that. She could make fire on stage work. She *would* make it work, even if she had to do it entirely in secret. And once everyone saw it, the triumph would be hers. Hers alone. Her flames would be the crown on the head of this *King Lear* that would make it stand above all the rest. After this production, it would never need to be done again. This could be the very last production of *King Lear*, and everyone would be satisfied.

She turned off I-90 up the long curving ramp onto the Skyway toward Indiana. She'd already been to a magic shop and bought out their entire stock of flash paper. What she couldn't figure out was why everyone was being a pain in her ass. Dwayne. Ry. Reginald Camper. All those stupid actors. Tech people often shared an inside joke: *Theatre would be so much better if you didn't have actors.* But she did have to hand it to Ry. Once he pissed her off at the design meeting at his studio, she had her big idea. Flames! The foundational idea of her design was there already. Stacks and stacks of ancestral furniture, like the greatest estate sale in the history of man. Divvying up the wealth of the kingdom. That's what drove *King Lear.* But then greed destroys it all. The greedy sisters putting their old dad, the King, in his place. Pushing him down. Humiliating him. Leaving him to die in the storm. And the result? In the end, they are all destroyed. Nobody wins. Everybody's dead. *The Inheritance of Betrayal,* like Dwayne said.

Genius. Dwayne was a bright guy.

And what could communicate Dwayne's idea better than flames? Nothing!

She remembered the last time she'd left her family home in Portland. She'd used kerosene because it burned longer than gas. Not many people realized it, but jet fuel was kerosene. And she needed jet fuel to blow her out of that situation. She spilled kerosene all the way around the garage, lit it, and up it went. She would have liked to have burned down the house, too, but everyone was still asleep in there. She didn't want to kill them. Well, she did. But not really. Not like that.

Still, the burning of the garage was magnificent. It caught so beautifully. The kerosene first, the flame starting and then running all the way around the building until it was a full loop. And then the wood shingles of the siding catching, the flames climbing up the walls until the roof tiles began to curl at the edges. And the noise of it as it began to roar. Watching from the driver's seat of her car. And then her dad running out the back door in his dago tee and tighty whities, screaming. What a beautiful moment as she stepped on the gas and pulled away from that house for the very last time. She only wished she could've stayed long enough to hear the gas tank in his pickup inside the garage explode.

She'd figure out how to do the flames in spite of Reginald Camper, or Nick Sanchez, or Dwayne Finnegan, or Ry Joodey, or the Chicago Fire Marshall, or any other small-minded obstructionist. Rock shows used live flames on stage all the time. It could absolutely be done safely. And nothing communicated the disintegration of family like flames. She knew that from personal experience. So, why should she let anything stop her?

When she made up her mind, she'd do anything. She'd turn her whole life upside down if necessary. Change her identity. Who else had the balls to live through Chicago winters in a panel truck? Of course, Chicago winters were nothing compared to Minnesota. The polar vortex they'd had the winter of *Titus Andronicus* had been a taste of old home, for sure. But she'd survived that, too.

She took the exit for Hammond, and it wasn't long before she pulled into the parking lot for American Patriot Fireworks. It was a low, white, clapboard building with dozens of fireworks signs across the front wall, as well as illustrations of Uncle Sam with an exploding hat, flags flying, and a prominent, *Welcome Chicagoans to Yer Closest Fireworks!*

"This must be the place," she said to her van as she shut down the ignition.

The inside of the store took her breath away. So much inventory! Boxes and boxes of every imaginable type of fireworks in row after narrow row. What a catastrophe if this place were ever to catch on fire! The store seemed much bigger on the inside than it had appeared to be from the outside. "This should be called *Doctor Who's TARDIS Fireworks*," she muttered to a stack of huge skyrockets.

She wandered up and down the aisles for twenty minutes, carefully reading the few product labels that were actually printed in English, but found herself at a total loss. Finally, she made her way to the counter, where a rail-thin man in a camouflage jumpsuit sat reading *Guns and Ammo* magazine.

"Maybe you can help me," she said.

"Maybe," he agreed without looking up from the page.

"I'm looking for something that I think would be like a roman candle, but I want it to just shoot up a constant flame. I don't want any flaming balls or explosion. Just a controlled stream of flame going up about fifteen feet."

"Huh," he said, looking at her.

"You got something like that?"

"Maybe the flaming candles? They shoot up fairly steady sparkling flame that cycles through red, white, and blue twice before they burn out."

"I don't want any colors. Just flame. Steady, like yellow flame."

"Even a campfire has color to it. Blues and reds and yellows."

"That'd be fine," Ingrid said. "As long as it looks like natural fire. I don't want it to look like fireworks."

"You don't want it to look like fireworks?" The man leaned back away from her.

"Right."

"You do know this is a fireworks store?"

"Of course, I know it's a fireworks store. But there are fireworks that look like natural flames, right?"

"I suppose so," the man said. He slithered off his stool and tossed the *Guns and Ammo* on the counter. He led her down the third aisle and pulled out a long box with a half dozen spear-shaped fireworks labeled *Flaming Golden Candle #5*. He handed it to her. "This is about the closest thing to what you describe."

"Are these safe to use indoors?"

"The fuck?" He pulled the box back away from her. "You do know this is a *fireworks store?*" he repeated.

"Of course, I know this is a fireworks store. I mean, if I was in a big space, like on the stage of a big theatre with a big space overhead, would it be safe to light this? I mean, is the flame controlled, so you could aim it up into an empty space with twenty-five or more feet of clearance above it, and it'd be okay?"

"Are you out of your mind, girlie? There is nothing, not one God damned thing in this store, that would be safe to use inside a theatre."

"You know what? I'll just test these out myself. I'll take two boxes of these. No, three boxes. You're sure there's nothing else in here that fits my specifications."

"There's nothing at all, including these, in this building that fits your specifications. I'm not selling you anything you intend to use indoors. I don't need you coming back with a lawsuit to destroy my business."

Ingrid stood still for a moment. Now the man was standing in front of the rack, blocking her access to the *Flaming Golden Candle #5.* This would not do.

"Excellent, sir! Thank you so much. I'm from the *Chicago Tribune,* and we are doing a feature on safety for a variety of products. I'd like to come back next week with our photographer so we could feature your business and a number of others we've been researching for good safety procedures and good citizenship."

"So you're not going to light these indoors?"

Ingrid laughed. "Oh my God, who would do that?"

The man laughed with her. "You really had me going there. Fireworks in a theatre. But you'd be surprised what I hear people planning to do." He lowered his voice. "Last year, these two guys came in, tattoos all over their faces, never crack a smile, chains hanging on their leathers. Big guys. Muscles. They're talking quietly, but I hear them. They got some guy locked up, and they're going to stick a skyrocket up his ass and light it. Send a message, they say." He raised his eyebrows meaningfully.

"Wow," Ingrid said. "So I guess you didn't sell anything to those guys."

He rocked back on his heels. "Are you kidding me? You don't fuck with guys like that. Sell them what they want and hope they never come back."

Ingrid nodded sagely and bought three boxes of *Flaming Golden Candle #5*.

Back in Chicago, she pulled into an alley where she'd seen someone throwing out a tall, wood armoire. It was pretty beat up. She wrapped the armoire in flash paper and set a few *Flaming Candles* in place next to it and lit them up. Rather than flying straight up, as she'd hoped, the *Flaming Candles* spewed flames out in a fountain twelve feet wide, engulfing the armoire and blackening the closest garage door. The flash paper roared up in a super-white, unnatural, silent explosion. The armoire caught fire near the base, and Ingrid had to fetch a fire extinguisher from her van. She put out the armoire flames, then roared away in her van as an angry homeowner emerged from his backyard, shouting: *What the fuck do you think you're doing?*

8

Tuesday, January 24, 2005

Dwayne followed Brianna down the sumptuous hallway of the law offices of Rockwell Nesbit III. It was a beautiful place, but he was feeling ill at ease. When Brianna saw Dwayne, she gave him the same look of disgust as when she'd handed him the five thousand dollar signing bonus. Still, he needed this job. He might be doing a play at the Goodman, but his pitiful director's stipend came from the Psychedelic Dream Theatre.

Brianna took him to an office that contained four cubicles separated with sound-dampening materials. In one cubicle, a tall Black man looked at a spreadsheet and said into his phone: "Hello. Is this Mariah Richards?" He waited a moment and said, "Ms. Richards, I'm calling because we heard y'all sustained an injury." From the first sentence to the second, he'd shifted from middle-class White diction to that of an urban Black.

In another cubicle, a White woman sorted through spreadsheets.

"I got a new one for you," Brianna said to her.

The woman looked up. "Why?" she said. Her look of annoyance reinforced Dwayne's discomfort. "We aren't getting the referral lists like before. If you want to put us on salary instead of pay-per-signing, great, but we don't need a third person sharing the leads right now."

"Rocky hired him," Brianna said. "You don't like it, take it up with Rocky." She turned on her heel and clack, clack, clacked away down the hall.

"Take it up with Rocky," the woman muttered. She went back to looking through her stacks of spreadsheets.

Dwayne waited.

She didn't look up.

"She's kind of a tough cookie, huh?" Dwayne offered.

The woman looked up over the top of her glasses at him. "Brianna is the whole reason this place works at all. As long as she can keep Rocky out of the building, everything is fine."

"Keep him in the courtroom?"

"Oh my God, keep him out of the courtroom, especially," the woman said. "And don't let him hire the lawyers." She looked back at her spreadsheets. "Or anyone else, for that matter," she muttered.

Dwayne stood in silence for a while. "Ah, where would you like me?" he said finally.

She gave him an *Oh-you're-still-here?* look. "There's two unoccupied desks," she said. "Take your pick."

He selected the one from which he could lean back to catch the spectacular view out the window. He could see Soldier Field and the museums and Lake Michigan beyond. The air was exceptionally clear today. He could even see buildings far around the curve of the Indiana shore. He put his winter jacket, hat, and gloves into the other unoccupied cubicle.

"So what are we doing here?" he asked the woman.

"You mean in the existential sense?"

"Ah…" Dwayne began, but the woman rose from her chair with a spreadsheet in her hand just as the man finished his phone call.

"Wait a minute," the man demanded, back in his middle class diction. "What list are you giving him?"

"O'Connor."

"O'Connor," the man scoffed. "Yeah, give him O'Connor."

The woman circled around to Dwayne's cubicle and put a spreadsheet in front of him. Next to each name was a few-word description of an incident in which the person had been injured, the name of a hospital or other health care location, and in some cases the name of another party or business, and a phone number.

"These are your leads," the woman said. "I assume Rocky briefed you on what he wants you doing."

"Not at all, actually," Dwayne said.

She sighed. "I don't know what kind of telemarketing you've done in the past, but this is most likely different."

"I've never done *any* telemarketing," Dwayne said.

"Good God," the man said. "He's going to be a total waste of leads."

"I'm giving him O'Connor," the woman reminded.

"Right," he said. "Never mind." He rolled his chair back into his cubicle and started another call.

The woman brought another sheet from her cubicle and gave it to Dwayne. "This is a script outline. Memorize the gist of that, but when you're on the phone, make it personal. Each person has been hurt in some way. Traffic accident. Workplace accident. Exposed to toxins. Diagnosed with environmental cancer. Stuff like that. So, you need to be sympathetic and lead them around to their need for compensation. They pay nothing up front. No risk to them. Rockwell Law has a track record of the highest payouts in the Midwest. Blah, blah, blah. Got it?"

"Wow," Dwayne said. He held up the sheet. "How about I memorize this, and then listen in on a couple of calls you two make to see how you do it?"

"Yeah, I guess. You'll just hear our side of the conversation. It's not like we can put them on speaker."

"Say, my name is Dwayne." He reached out his hand to shake with her. "Dwayne Finnegan."

"Right." She shook hands with him. "I'm Sheila. That's Evan," she said, pointing to the man who was once again deeply engaged on the phone. She returned briskly to her cubicle.

Father Damien, patron saint of lepers, pray for me.

Dwayne spent a half hour memorizing the sample telemarketing script. He looked over his spreadsheet of prospects. Then he slid his chair over to Evan's cubicle, since Evan hadn't seemed quite as repulsed by his presence as Sheila. Evan was just finishing a phone call.

"Do you mind if I listen in on your next call?" he asked after Evan hung up.

"Knock yourself out."

"Are you an actor?" Dwayne asked.

"Actor!" Evan scoffed. "Yeah, I'm filming *Barbershop III* right after work."

"No, sorry. I just noticed how you change your diction

depending on who's on the other end of the line."

"That's not an actor thing," Evan said. "That's a Black thing."

"Really?"

"I guess you don't have a lot of Black friends."

"I have…some."

"Like Rockwell Nesbit the third?"

"Well, I'm not sure he and I are exactly *friends*," Dwayne said.

"Look. Just watch Black politicians. Look at Jesse Jackson. He has a whole other diction when he's talking to an all-Black audience than when he's talking to a White reporter or to Congress or something. He adapts. Code switching." He picked up his phone and called the next number.

Evan displayed impressive verbal finesse. He expressed sympathy for the prospect's injury. He inferred that he'd been requested to call her to make sure she didn't have trouble covering her medical bills when it might be difficult for her to work. He sounded her out on who ought to be held responsible—*if there were any justice in the world.* She apparently had someone in mind, because Evan sounded suddenly resolute. Money could be extracted from them. And there would be no money required from her up front or ever. She didn't need to worry. Rockwell Law's attorneys never failed. By the end of the conversation, he was telling her to expect a call from a Rockwell caseworker who would get her started with an attorney to handle her case. He hung up the phone and slammed his palm on the desktop.

"And *that's* how it's done!" he exclaimed.

Sheila stuck her head around the cubicle, holding the phone receiver to her ear with a cross look and a throat-cutting hand gesture.

"Oopsy," Evan whispered.

Dwayne, however, did not have similar good fortune on his first call.

"How did you get my number?" the man said after Dwayne's opening gambit.

"I, uh…" How should he answer that? He had no idea how the prospect's information was collected. "Well, we were informed you needed assistance because of your car accident? I understand you were back-ended?" Under the **Cause** column Dwayne's sheet said: *Car* *accident. Back-ended.* In the **Location** column, it said *Stroger Hospital.* That was all.

"How the hell did you find out? Who are you?"

"I represent a team of Chicago attorneys who have the highest track record of…"

"Ambulance-chaser! You're a goddamn ambulance-chaser! Who gave you my private information? You're violating my HIPAA rights. I'm going to find some lawyers, all right. I'm going to find some lawyers to go after *you.* What law firm are you with?"

Dwayne felt sweat break out over his whole body. The outraged man yelled, *Hello? Hello?* as Dwayne gently hung up the phone.

9

Thursday, February 2, 2005

Dwayne put the coffee carafe on the dining room table and lined up the cream and sugar next to it. This was something he knew how to do! He doubted Peaches would want coffee at this hour, but he found the aroma of fresh coffee in the air sharpened people's intellect. After the debacle of the last show with her costumes being set on fire by the cult lunatics, Dwayne wanted this show to go well for Peaches. Behind the coffee, he put a bottle of Rioja, half consumed, and an unopened bottle of sauvignon blanc. He'd already put out the crackers, cheese, pencils and notepads, mugs and wine glasses.

Dwayne believed in the art of preparing for a meeting. He'd selected his apartment and furnished it to create the perfect environment. He filled the horseshoe shape of the living room with well-worn furniture to offer plenty of seating and no fussiness. A battered steamer trunk and a wood cable reel offered coffee table substitutes that needed no coasters, offered surfaces on which to write, to draw, to set one's food and drinks, and to put up one's feet. It fostered collaboration and filled Dwayne with quiet pride. He was good at working with artists.

A director brought ideas to the table, but even more importantly, he called forth ideas from his team. He fostered creativity.

Was there a way to bring that to telemarketing?

Angela swept into the room and looked over the spread. "Who all is coming?" She grabbed a mug and poured herself a coffee.

"Just Peaches. Ry was supposed to come, but he got a last-minute gig at the Double Door, replacing a sick guitarist for some band or other."

"Fun for him." She added cream and sugar to her coffee.

"And I didn't want Ingrid. When Ingrid is there, Peaches hardly says a word."

"This is quite a spread for one designer."

"Peaches worked so hard on *Romeo and Juliet*. And then…"

"Oh, yeah." Angela made a miserable face. "Costumes in flames."

"I was afraid she'd never design for me again. So, a little extra TLC."

"Good idea." She took a deep sip from her mug. "I can't believe I'm drinking coffee this late. The dipshit new principal wants detailed lesson plans every week. He's started reading out the one he thinks is the worst in staff meetings. He thinks humiliation is leadership."

"Jesus."

"He should be like you, Dwayne. Cheese and crackers and wine for all the meetings."

"Talk to your union rep," he quipped.

"You think I don't do that, Dwayne?" A little coffee sloshed out of her mug, vibrated by the volume of her voice and the shaking of her arm. "Not about cheese and wine but all his…pedagogical interference bullshit."

"Yeah, sorry," he said.

The doorbell rang, and Dwayne went to the door and pressed the buzzer to let Peaches in.

"Maybe you could take out a contract." He raised his eyebrows.

"You know any assassins?"

"No. But I bet your Uncle Guido does."

"Ha!" she said.

"Hey, Dwayne." Peaches came in through the door, followed by Melinda. Peaches hair looked like it was done in yet another new arrangement of pastel colors. "Oh! It's Angela, too!" Peaches laughed nervously and looked at Dwayne. "Of course, Angela is here. This is your home. And you are married. To Angela. So this is Angela's home, too. Hi Angela!"

"Hi Peaches," Angela said.

Dwayne was pleased to see Peaches' awkwardness lighten Angela's mood.

"And you've got the beautiful Juliet with you," Angela said.

"Melinda," Melinda said, moving forward to shake hands with

Angela. "It's Melinda."

"Of course. I remember," Angela said. "I just called you Juliet because…"

"The play. Right," Melinda said. "Wow, I'm glad *you* didn't decide to become an actor. I'd hate to be up for a role, and you came in to audition."

"Oh?" Angela said.

"You're so beautiful. You'd get all the roles."

"Huh. What do you think, Dwayne? I'm about ready to quit teaching."

"Nothing pays the bills like live theatre," he said.

"Right. Oh, well. Have fun, girls." She turned down the hallway and disappeared into the second bedroom.

Peaches looked trapped in the doorway. She darted to the semicircle of well-used furniture in the living room. "We're in here?"

"Yep," Dwayne said. "I've got coffee, wine, and snacks on the dining room table. Whatever you like. All very relaxed."

An El train rolled by on the tracks outside the windows, filling the apartment with the sudden overwhelming rattle of train wheels. "Oh!" Peaches laughed, still standing in the middle of the room. "I'd forgotten you've got the El right there."

"Come here, baby," Melinda said. "Sit with me." She scooped up Peaches and located her on one of the couches with her arm around her. She planted a little kiss on the costumer's cheek.

Well, this is new, Dwayne thought. He poured himself a glass of the Rioja. "May I pour anything? Red? White? Coffee? Water?"

"Coffee! Oh God. No coffee," Peaches said. "I'm already so anxious. Like you couldn't tell."

"I'm here as Peaches' support animal," Melinda said. "And I'd gladly take a glass of white."

"Yes, yes, okay, me, too," Peaches said.

Dwayne took the corkscrew to the sauvignon blanc and brought them each a generous glass. He put the cheese and cracker tray on the wooden cable spool in front of them. He sat down with his wine.

"Why are you anxious, Peaches? Because we're at the Goodman?"

Her eyes flared open. "Oh, God, I hadn't even been thinking

about that!" She sat up abruptly and her knee connected with her wineglass, dumping it into the tray of cheese and crackers. "Oh, God!" she exclaimed. "You see?" She looked like she might burst into tears.

"No trouble. No big deal. No damage," Dwayne said.

The crackers were floating in sauvignon blanc, and the cheese looked like islands in the wine, but all the liquid was confined in the tray. He picked up the tray. "No problem at all," he said calmly. He carried it out to the kitchen. He grabbed the half-empty box of crackers and an open package of cheddar that looked a little dry on one edge. He put it on a saucer and cut off the dry part. When he brought the newish snacks back to the living room, Peaches was in Melinda's arms. Melinda kissed each cheek beneath her eyes.

So that's what a support animal does.

Peaches saw Dwayne entering and quickly broke away.

"Okay, don't mind me," Angela said, startling them all as she crossed the room from the other direction. "I'm just here to get a glass of wine. That coffee made me nervous."

"*Everything* makes me nervous," Peaches said.

Angela poured a glass of red and stopped on the way back toward the second bedroom. "You two are an item now?"

Melinda laughed. "An item?"

Angela frowned. "Wait. Weren't you dating Bobby when I first met you?"

Melinda looked embarrassed. "Bobby and I did have a thing for a while."

"No, no," Angela remembered. "It was Ry. Wasn't it? Weren't you and Ry a thing? Or was it you and Orlando?"

"Well…" Now she looked flustered. "Men have no…attention span."

"Oh," Angela said.

"Melinda's so beautiful," Peaches said, putting her hands between her knees. "I think she'll break my heart beyond belief, but I can't resist her."

Melinda looked shocked and embarrassed. "I'm not going to break your heart beyond belief."

"Okay," Angela said. "Good seeing you all." She scuttled back to the second bedroom.

"Oh my God." Peaches bent down until her face rested in her hands.

"Hey, we're all old friends here…" Dwayne thought he was heading somewhere with that thought, but he left it at that. He'd never seen Melinda with another woman, so that was different. Peaches, he knew, was ambidextrous in matters of gender and the heart.

He put the less formal arrangement of crackers and cheese on the table in front of them and brought Peaches a fresh glass of wine.

"Maybe I'm just bad luck." Peaches pushed herself back in the couch. "The first show I did with you, Dwayne, Coco had me crying so hard, I wet myself, and I had to leave."

Wet herself? Dwayne remembered the incident, Peaches crying and leaving the theatre. He'd had no idea she'd wet herself.

"And then *Titus Andronicus*, we had such a good show, but hardly anyone saw it because of the polar vortexes. And then *Romeo and Juliet*, those drug cultists set my whole costume collection on fire! I mean, I'm just bad luck."

"None of that was because of you," Dwayne protested. "Coco nearly brings *me* to tears sometimes. And the polar vortex? And those lunatics? None of that was your fault."

"What's the common denominator, Dwayne? I was costumer on all those shows."

"And I was the director. Maybe I'm the bad luck."

Peaches shook her head. Then she sat with it for a long moment. "You really think it's *you*, Dwayne?"

Melinda laughed.

"What?" Peaches said. "It's got to be somebody."

"It doesn't have to be *anybody*," Dwayne said. "Sometimes shit happens."

"With us, shit *always* happens."

"Hey, hey, hey," Melinda said. "What company went from zero dollars to one hundred fifty thousand dollars in the bank in the last show? What company is going from the Chicago Repertory Arts Playhouse to the Goodman Theatre for the next show? And finally, in what company did this actor meet this costume designer?" She took Peaches' face in her hands and planted a kiss on her lips.

Peaches looked shy and deeply pleased. "Well, when you put it like that…"

"Now, don't you two have costumes to discuss?" Melinda said. "Not to be rude, but I don't want to be here *all* night."

Dwayne had always liked Melinda, but tonight he had a new appreciation for her.

"Yes, yes," Peaches said. "Okay! So, David Bowie." She pulled out a stack of images and laid them out, side by side, across the furniture. "You see the problem." Each photo showed Bowie in another incarnation, from Major Tom to Ziggy Stardust to long-haired androgyne to the Thin White Duke to a Pagliaccio clown, and so on. "When we worked on *Romeo and Juliet*, it was easy to settle on a distinctive Prince look. With David Bowie, the looks are all over the place. It's visually incoherent. I suppose that could go with Lear's mental disintegration. Is that what you want?"

"Wait," Dwayne said. "We decided to move on from the Bowie idea. Right?"

"I thought so," Peaches said uncertainly. "But yesterday, Ingrid told me we needed Bowie for the fire in it, and she started singing that *gasoline* song again with the lyrics wrong."

Dwayne shook his head. "I'm not sure what's up with Ingrid. Ignore that."

"So nothing has changed since our last meeting? The music will be American blues?"

"Yes. Traditional blues. Electric blues. Ry played me a few ideas on the phone. I loved your idea of setting it in the Reconstruction period."

Peaches looked shocked. "Was that *my* idea?"

"Yes. I love it. Did you change your thoughts?"

"No, no! You're sure no Bowie? That would be a huge relief."

"No. Ignore Ingrid," Dwayne said. "I'm going to play you Ry's new music for inspiration. I want to go with your Reconstruction idea, if you feel secure with that."

"Am I ever secure with anything?" Peaches said.

"Oh my God!" Melinda exclaimed. She shook Peaches by the shoulders. "Dwayne loves your idea! Go with it!"

Peaches smiled shyly. "I do think it would be a fun look."

By the end of the night, Peaches was listening to recordings of Ry's music and fast-sketching ideas that Dwayne liked very much.

Now he needed to track down Ingrid, finalize her design, and keep her from pushing everyone else off the track.

10

Friday, February 3, 2005

Dwayne hunched over his desk, headset on his head, brilliant view out the window to his left, and the looming presence of Sheila, the team boss, behind him. It was so hard to concentrate with her listening in. In theory, this job at Rockwell Nesbit III Personal Injuries Law was ideal. With Rocky as the boss, he was assured of the flexibility his theatre career demanded, and they were paying him incredibly well. But he had yet to book a single new client....

"You don't have a broken leg?" he asked into the headset. He looked at the spreadsheet. The incident column said broken left leg from forklift accident.

"No, I don't have a broken leg," the woman on the other end said.

This was the last day of his third week here. Evan, who was very vocal about his successes, signed one or two clients *every day.* Wednesday last week, he'd signed five in one afternoon. Dwayne, zero.

"Any accident involving a forklift entails significant liability on the part of the, ah, business owner," Dwayne said. "We can help you win an, um, judgment, a sum of money, that will significantly aid you in recovery, medical expenses, you know, and the intangible costs of your, um, pain and suffering."

"Forklift? What the hell are you smoking? I dislocated my shoulder lifting a case of forks at the Amazon warehouse."

Lifting forks! Who was this O'Connor who gathered the data? It was always somehow wrong.

"Right. Right! Sorry. Amazon, however, is a deep-pocket employer. As an employee of Amazon..."

"I don't work for Amazon! I work for Lettuce Entertain You. I was picking up supplies for our restaurants!" She hung up the phone.

Blessed Gabriel, patron saint of communicators, pray for me!

"Seems like it's going pretty good for you, huh, Dwight?"

He turned his chair to face Sheila. She was standing so close. He scooted back a little and bumped into his cubicle divider.

"I think I'm getting the hang of it," he muttered. She put a hand behind her ear. He cleared his throat and spoke up louder. "It's just the O'Connor data is almost always wrong."

"I told you, never lead with information from the spreadsheet. Act like you know what their incident was, but get them to reveal it."

"Yeah, Dwayne!" Evan, who'd just finished another call, laughed derisively from his cubicle. "You need to *always be closing.*"

Dwayne couldn't believe it. "Are you making fun of me because I'm in theatre?"

"What's that?" Evan said.

"*Always be closing.* David Mamet. *Glengarry Glen Ross.*"

"What?" He looked so innocent. It had to be put on.

"Did you understand what I said?" Sheila asked impatiently.

"Of course," Dwayne said. "Right. I'm going to do that. I got it."

"I'm not sure you do." She sounded like she'd just made a decision.

Evan sang in a descending chorus of doom: "Dum, dum, dum, dum!"

"No, really," Dwayne said. "It's just a learning curve. I can absolutely do it." He smiled bravely and lifted a thumbs-up. Sheila sighed.

"This would be sad if it wasn't so pathetic, Dwight."

"Dwayne," Dwayne said. Why was it that when people got his name wrong it was always Dwight? Did he look like a Dwight?

"Whatever. Gather up your personal items and let's go talk to Brianna."

Oh, no. Not Brianna. Brianna hated that Rocky foisted him on her. How was he supposed to succeed here? Sheila and Evan both knew the O'Connor list was worthless.

Dwayne walked beside Sheila as her high heels clack clacked down the aisle. Were these floors marble? Heels made such a sharp echo as the fashionable women of this firm walked.

"Look," Sheila said quietly as they walked. "Here's a heads-up. If you are going to work at Rockwell Nesbit the Third Personal Injuries Law, you need to be useful to Brianna. She's the whole brains of this place. Rocky made the firm famous, and his ads draw in clients, but she finds the lawyer talent, the office talent. She drives the train. That's why she makes the big bucks."

Dwayne didn't know how to reply to that. He followed into Brianna's office. She had a corner suite with excellent views to the east and south. Rocky may not have made her the CEO, but she was set up in a CEO-style office.

Brianna looked up from a hyper-large screen on her desk. She looked from Sheila to Dwayne and back to Sheila. "Okay, what's this?" Brianna said.

"He keeps wasting leads," Sheila said. "He hasn't landed a single client. He's a drag on my team."

"Other than him, your team is just you and Evan."

"Right," Sheila said. "Add Dwight to my team of two, and we have the effectiveness of one and a half."

She was calling him Dwight deliberately.

"So, what do you want me to do?" Brianna said.

"Reassign him. Sell him to the gypsies. Throw him out the window. I don't care. I've had him for fourteen business days. I'm done." Sheila turned and walked out of the office.

Brianna sat and stared at him. "You can't be Rocky's love child," she said, finally. "Not as white as you are."

"They gave me a totally worthless list. Evan laughed about how worthless it was."

"You had fourteen days, Dwight."

"Dwayne."

She looked at him a few moments longer. "Go home. If you weren't Rocky's pet, I'd fire you. I don't need anyone else in the office right now. I'll see if I can think of something for you on Monday."

"It's only ten a.m."

"It's five o'clock somewhere, Dwight. Get out of here."

Dwayne felt a streak of shame running up the middle of his back all the way down on the elevator, all the way down the blocks to the

El, and all the way home on the train.

11

Saturday, February 4, 2005

It was only three p.m. on a Saturday, but Dwayne wanted a drink. He didn't really want to have a board meeting with Ingrid and Joan. However, the laws regulating Federal not-for-profit corporations like the Psychedelic Dream Theatre required them to meet on a regular basis. Dwayne requested a location change from the lobby of the Chicago Repertory Arts Playhouse to the John Barleycorn Memorial Pub, just up the street. The women did not object. He raised a finger as Barry circled the bar and ordered a pint of Guinness.

When he was half finished with his stout, the women arrived, and they approved preliminary budgets for *King Lear*. Since they now had $150,000 in the bank, no one was too worried about the figures. Plus, the Goodman would give them assistance. They were fifteen minutes into the meeting when Tom walked in.

Dwayne was mystified. "Why are you here?"

Tom looked equally surprised. "Ingrid said you wanted to work on *King Lear* casting."

Dwayne looked at Ingrid. "Okay. You are not going to sit here and kibitz."

"What?" Ingrid pretended innocence.

"Tom and I cast. You do not."

"The board should oversee the creative process in a production as important as this," Ingrid said.

Dwayne looked at Joan. "Are we finished? I move we adjourn."

"We aren't going to discuss casting? I had other things to do right now," Tom complained.

"I'm sorry, Tom. This was Ingrid's trick."

"No, no, wait," Ingrid said. "Just let me give a couple suggestions, and then you can make your decisions. Although I want the opportunity for a rebuttal if you don't like my suggestions."

"Forget it." Dwayne got up to leave.

"Okay! No rebuttal. But listen: You should think about Bobby for Kent."

"Bobby?" Dwayne said. "Bobby is in L.A. Bobby ran off with our cash before *Titus Andronicus*."

"Okay, maybe as Edmund would be better," she said. "The evil Edmund. Both Regan and Goneril want to get him into bed. Bobby would knock that out of the park."

"Bobby is in L.A.," Dwayne repeated.

"Bobby founded this company," Ingrid said. "Bobby has charisma out the wazoo. He's got Coco-level charisma. Bobby as Edmund and Coco as Goneril? Look out!" She laughed in awestruck amazement at the idea.

"Bobby founded Shakespeare and Friends," Dwayne said. "That ended when he split town with all the money. This company is a whole new thing."

"Well…" Ingrid shook her head this way and that. "We just continued with a new name and new funding."

"Bobby's not here!" Dwayne shouted in frustration. "He's making movies in L.A. with Buffy the Vampire Slayer!"

Ingrid shrugged with a secret little grin. "Maybe he's coming back."

"You'd be nuts to cast Bobby," Joan said. "I think you know that." She turned her eyes up to the ceiling.

"Do you need me for anything?" Tom asked.

Dwayne shook his head, but Ingrid pulled him back. "And what about Rocky? He's not in the ensemble, but you could use him, maybe as Albany?"

Could Rocky have possibly lobbied both Reg Camper and Ingrid? "I'm thinking Coco for Goneril," Dwayne said. "Cast Rocky as Albany, husband of Goneril? She'd kick my ass."

"Cornwall then! Even better. The brutal Cornwall, gouging out Gloucester's eyes for his faithfulness to Lear? Unbelievable!"

"Sure," Tom said. "Unless he turns into Uncle Bull and *actually* gouges his eyes out."

"Good point," Joan said in her oddly emotionless voice.

"Who are you thinking of for the Fool?" Ingrid asked eagerly.

"Oh yes! Who?" Wallace's rolling baritone sounded from behind Dwayne. When had he arrived?

"Did Ingrid invite you to this board meeting?" Dwayne asked. He flopped back onto his bar stool.

"I just came from a matinee down the street. *No Exit*. No intermission. Never was the title of a production more true."

Joan cleared her throat loudly. "The last item on the agenda is the question of a spring production."

"Let's not do one," Dwayne said. "The Goodman demands so many things prepared in advance. Let's skip spring and focus on *King Lear*."

"That would be just one production in 2005," Ingrid said. "We've got $150,000 in the bank. There's no reason to do just one show. I move we do both a spring and a fall production in 2005."

"Nay," Dwayne said.

"Aye," said both Ingrid and Joan.

Dwayne looked at Joan. "Are you kidding?"

"She made a good point," Joan said.

"So what do you want to direct in the spring?" Ingrid said. "We can approve a title right now."

"I'm not directing in the spring," Dwayne said.

"You are our artistic director," Ingrid said. "We've just voted in a production."

What bullshit. He was not going to be bulldozed into directing another show before *King Lear*.

He had a sudden inspiration: He'd suggest something they'd never approve. "Wallace here has been wanting to direct. Maybe we should give the spring slot to Wallace." Wallace looked suddenly electrified. Ingrid looked perplexed. There was no way they were going to turn over a spring slot to an actor who'd never directed before.

"Yes!" Wallace said. "Let's do *Oedipus Rex*! Ry could be the leader of the chorus. He could do all that music business with the chorus. See? I can be modern, too!" He looked around, proud as a kitty cat who's dropped a dead mouse on the kitchen floor.

"*Oedipus*," Dwayne said. "There you go." Now certainly they'd drop the idea of a spring show.

"Yes, *Oedipus*," Wallace said. "Say, I'm a natural to play the old soothsayer, Tiresias. Really, I'm the only one in the company who could do it convincingly," he mused. "No matter. I can play it and direct both!" He smiled broadly.

"If you are going to act and direct, you have to have a co-director," Joan said. "Otherwise, I'm voting no. I've done the actor/director thing with Bobby. Never again."

Wait a minute. Joan was going for this? She couldn't possibly believe this was a good idea.

"Hey, I could co-direct!" Ingrid piped up. "I could be co-director and choreographer of the chorus. I'm totally qualified. I was captain of the pom squad in high school!"

"Oh, for the love of God," Dwayne said. He looked at Joan. "No. Right?"

Wallace looked at her and started to laugh. "Pom squad!" he said. He laughed some more. "Sis boom bah!" He laughed so hard he bent over.

Ingrid looked like she had a dead frog in her mouth. Tom suppressed a smirk.

"Okay," Dwayne said. "I move we drop the idea of a spring show and focus on the Goodman." He looked at Joan. "Second the motion?" Now he felt better.

"No, no, no, no, no!" Wallace said. "Don't misunderstand me. I'm not laughing at Ingrid. I'm laughing because I LOVE it! Pompon choreography jibes exactly with the vibe I envision. It shocked me with delight. I love it. Yes!" He grabbed Ingrid's hand and shook it. "You're on, partner! I've always admired your take-no-prisoners attitude. We are doing this. Wallace and Ingrid. Watch out!"

"Okay then," Joan said.

"No, no, no, now," Dwayne said. "We need to keep our eyes on the prize. And the prize is *King Lear* at the Goodman. Not *Oedipus Rex* at the C.R.A.P."

"We can do both," Ingrid said. "You don't want to direct. That's fine. We've got a team." She grinned broadly at Wallace.

"*Oedipus* is a short script," Joan said. "It shouldn't take too much out of us. And Wallace directing was your idea."

Indeed. Why the hell had he tried that gambit? He'd led his company into exactly what he did not want.

12

Monday, February 6, 2005

"So you want one of the studios instead of a mainstage?" Green said. He rubbed his hand over the dry bulb of the top of his skull, releasing a little blizzard of dandruff to land on his shoulders and sift down the treads of the ladder on which he stood. He turned his head up to continue working on a lighting fixture over his head. He turned the wrench again and again. Dwayne suspected the bolt threads were stripped. "I don't get it," Green said, looking into the instrument. "You guys have been gangbusters. You opened up all the seats in here for *Romeo and Juliet*, and you were selling out. Three hundred seats. Now you want a sixty-seat studio?"

"He's right. We should take this room," Ingrid said to Dwayne. "To do an epic show, you need an epic space." She turned to Green. "How about you give us this room for a thousand a week?"

"We shouldn't be doing a spring show at all," Dwayne said.

"Trouble in paradise?" Green asked.

"Naw," Ingrid said. "Dwayne's just getting lazy. So, how about it? A grand a week?"

"Those days are gone." Raymond Green had given them this upstairs mainstage for *Titus Andronicus* for the price of a studio because he hadn't found anyone to rent it at full price. Even at that rental rate, the show had been a financial disaster. When *Romeo and Juliet* turned into a runaway hit, Ingrid volunteered to pay full rent and expanded the seating.

"You'll make a lot more money selling out a mainstage than selling out a little studio." Green yanked hard on the wrench, and it flew out of his hand. He reached quickly to try to catch it in the air, but his ladder wobbled in the opposite direction of his reach. He screamed as the ladder tumbled away, but he managed to grab the lighting pipe above him. Ingrid lunged to the ladder and grabbed it while Green's feet were still on it, his whole body stretched out nearly horizontally. She and Dwayne pushed the ladder back under him as he clung to the pipe overhead.

"Jesus, Green," Dwayne said. "If we weren't here, you'd've broken your neck."

"If you weren't here," Green grumbled, "I wouldn't have been distracted, and this wouldn't have happened at all." Ingrid handed him his fallen wrench, and he went back to working the bolt. "So why don't you want the mainstage at full price?"

"We've got a first-time director doing *Oedipus Rex*," Ingrid said.

"*Oedipus Rex*?" Green scoffed. "Who the hell wants to see *Oedipus Rex*?"

"Exactly," Dwayne said. Maybe that was the saving grace. If it was terrible but not too many people saw it, it wouldn't damage their reputation.

"Why don't you do something with some guts? *One Flew Over the Cuckoo's Nest* or *Balm in Gilead* or something?" He turned the bolt a few more times, but nothing was progressing. "Fuck!" He climbed down the ladder. "Goddamn people. There's no reason a bolt like that should get stripped. You got a saws-all with a metal blade in your truck?"

"I just might," Ingrid said. "Let's settle this, then I might get my saws-all and cut that bolt for you."

"Okay." Green flopped into a seat in the front row of the audience. "The knuckleheads scheduled for the upstairs studio for May canceled on me last week. I can put you in there. You'll be back on the mainstage for your fall show, right?"

"Actually, no," Dwayne said. "We're doing our fall show in the Owen theatre at the Goodman."

Green sat up abruptly. "Wait a minute. What the hell? You committed to being a resident company here. That's why I've given you all the perks." He hopped out of the seat. "Nobody else in this city would have given you the deals I've given you!"

"We can't pass up the chance to do a show at the Goodman," Dwayne said.

"We have a contract!" Green fumed.

Ingrid laughed. "You show me that contract, and we'll abide by it."

Green was famous for never getting around to drawing up contracts, although he was good about abiding by his promises. His promises, however, did not include light boards that would always work as needed.

"We have a verbal contract," Green said. "Fuck it." He picked up his wrench and started climbing the ladder toward the stuck lighting instrument again. "You know what? Find somewhere else to do your spring production. I'm done with you people."

"Come on, Green," Ingrid said. "You aren't going to let that studio sit empty."

"It won't be empty. I've got another little company that wants it. There's always more little companies popping up. I can always book the studios. It's the mainstages that give me trouble."

"We'll be back next spring," Ingrid said. "Or, who knows? Maybe we'll do three shows next season, and we'll see you in the winter."

"Maybe I'm tired of your high-handed bullshit anyway. What have you ever done for me?"

"I do things," Ingrid said. She walked out of the room.

Dwayne felt tempted to follow her. He didn't want to do a spring show. But there was certain magic to this ensemble. Maybe he should trust the board's decision. He'd directed two really beautiful shows in a row, despite the difficulties along the way. Sometimes leadership meant trusting your people. He turned back to Green.

"This show at the Goodman is going to raise our profile," Dwayne said. "That's going to be good for you, too."

"Instead of filling my mainstage, you're at the Goodman. How is that good for me?"

"Imagine our press releases: *Psychedelic Dream Theatre, a resident company of the Chicago Repertory Arts Playhouse, will present its fall production of* King Lear *at the Goodman Theatre under the invitation of Artistic Director Reginald Camper.*"

Green considered it.

"See? All the little companies will see the Playhouse as a path to the Goodman!" Dwayne said. "They'll be dying to work here."

"Huh," Green mused. "What made you guys want to work here? The shows you'd seen here?"

"Absolutely," Dwayne lied. They'd ended up at the Playhouse when Bobby left town with the company's money before *Titus Andronicus*. They'd lost their reservation at the Vox Populi Theater. Other venues were booked up a year in advance. The Playhouse was the only space in town available.

Ingrid came bounding back into the theatre with a toolbox, an extension cord, and a saws-all. She plugged it in, waved Green off the ladder, scampered up like a monkey, and cut the stripped bolt. She brought the lighting instrument down, used a tap hammer and a ratchet wrench to work the stripped bolt out, drilled out the hole, used a tap to cut new threads, and replaced the ruined bolt with one from her toolbox.

"There," she said. "I fixed your crappy instrument. I'll fix two more things of your choice, and we get the May studio slot. Done?"

Green looked from Ingrid to Dwayne and back to Ingrid. He sighed heavily. "Okay. Whatever," he said. He grabbed his wrench and walked out of the space.

13

Friday, February 17, 2005

Angela sat up in bed and gave a deep, happy sigh. "Yes." She leaned over and gave Dwayne a long kiss. She sat up and let out a little laugh of pleasure. "You are A-okay with me, Mr. Finnegan. And now I'm hungry." She hopped out of bed and put on a robe, shivering a little in the February air of their bedroom. She gave him a big smile and sauntered through the door. "That was definitely the way to slough off a week of teaching in the hellhole."

Dwayne had set up a happy hour spread on the dining room table and put some *Art Blakely and the Jazz Messengers* on the stereo for the moment she came home. She'd looked at the goodies, smiled, and dragged him into the bedroom.

He didn't complain.

He got up, pulled on his robe, and followed her, belting the robe tightly around himself. He'd have to talk to the landlord about turning up the heat.

Angela stood at the table, picking up a piece of *pan con tomate* and laying smoked salmon over it. She put it on a plate and tossed an olive into her mouth. "Nice spread, Dwayne."

"You, too."

She took a bite, stopped, and looked at him. "Are you making a naughty comment?"

He tilted his head coyly. "Maybe."

"Nice spread." She shook her head and filled her plate with sautéed mushrooms, celery and carrots, and cream cheese with anchovy on crackers. "It's a good thing you can cook."

"It is," he agreed, filling his own plate.

She plopped into a chair. "I hate to break the mood. I truly love practicing unprotected sex—and I admire how you got over your previous problems in that department—but Dwayne, we do all this fucking, and I'm still not pregnant. My ma had a bathtub full of kids by the time she was my age."

"I don't mind being patient," Dwayne said, stuffing a piece of *pan con tomate* into his mouth. *We do all this fucking, and I'm still not pregnant* was kind of a twenty-something dream come true. He sighed happily. "I enjoy the process."

"Right you do," she scoffed. "Everything is looking up for you. But my job has gotten a hundred times worse with this new principal. I'm ready for our next phase as a family, and I'm never getting knocked up." She waved her bread at him, the slice of salmon flapping. "I'm ready, Dwayne!"

"I hear you," he said. "I do. You want to go back in the bedroom?"

"Don't be rude. I'm hungry." She grabbed a couple slices of Manchego and poured herself a glass of Rioja. "I think we have to go beyond this random fucking and get scientific."

"You mean *more* scientific. You've already been tracking your periods and taking your vaginal temperature and whatever. Sometimes I feel like you've got a string tied around my pecker pulling me into the bedroom whenever the egg production seems most prodigious."

"Oh, right, like this is so tough on you."

"I'm not complaining." He waggled his eyebrows like Groucho Marx and flicked a carrot with his finger like it was a cigar.

"Don't do that," she said.

"Into the bedroom, my dear?" He waggled his eyebrows some more.

"Stop," she commanded. She took a deep breath. "Okay, Karen Kowalski, on the fourth grade team, told me about her fertility specialist. She's pregnant, so I think we should see him. And don't think you're not going."

"I didn't think…"

"You think you don't share the blame that I'm not knocked up yet?"

"I didn't…"

"You might be the whole problem!"

Dwayne opened his mouth, but Angela kept right on going.

"The Guiseppelli women have always been as fertile as rabbits. You have just one brother and one sister, and your family is Irish Catholic? That does not add up to normal fertility. The Finnegans are flagging."

Dwayne frowned. It was true; he had a million cousins on his mother's side. His maternal aunts and uncles all had big Irish Catholic families. But hardly anything on his father's side. Two cousins. Hardly worth mentioning. He'd never thought about it before.

"Okay," Dwayne said. "I'll be there."

"Damn right you'll be there. It's part of your marital duty. But there's another thing, too." Now she looked a little hesitant.

"What?" Dwayne couldn't help but be alarmed at her sudden change of mood.

"You know that nice signing bonus you got from Rocky?"

"Yeah?"

"You have to kiss that goodbye."

"Why?" Dwayne said. "I wanted to take you to Italy again. Maybe we could even bounce over to Ireland. I have all sorts of ideas. It's free money! It should be enjoyed."

"I know," she said regretfully. "But this fertility doctor is expensive. Our medical insurance doesn't cover much. You'd think the school district would provide health insurance that was excellent for women. Most of the staff are women, but the administration's mostly men. The cocksuckers. Do they get us what we need? Absolute shitheads."

"The whole signing bonus?" Dwayne said sadly.

"That's just the beginning. Your entire salary may end up at the doctors."

Dwayne leaned back into the chair. Since the day Sheila escorted him to Brianna's office, he'd been assigned to two other departments. He felt like he'd done better in the second, but none of his colleagues at Rockwell Nesbit III Personal Injuries Law were pleasant. He was a nice guy. Smart. Friendly. But when anyone heard Rocky hired him, that was the end of any welcome.

"Everything going okay over there?" Angela said.

"Yeah, um…" He didn't want to worry her. She was stressed enough. "Maybe just a little period of adjustment."

He couldn't lose that job. Would he have to cast Rocky in *King Lear?*

14

Saturday, February 18, 2005

Ingrid helped the old lady open the garage door. She remembered her father's garage: the smell of burning kerosene, the whole edifice going up in flames, her father bursting from the house, screaming in outrage.

Revenge. It was glorious.

And wasn't that really like Lear? He wronged his daughters. They had their revenge. They all ended up dead, of course. But wouldn't flames be the perfect cap to all that *King Lear* disaster? She knew it would.

Fireworks and flash paper had been entirely wrong for bringing flames to the stage of the Owen—no doubt about that—but every failed idea was one idea closer to the winner, they say. After all, how many hundreds of types of filaments had Alexander Graham Bell tried before he found the right material to invent the light bulb?

Wait. Was that Alexander Graham Bell? Did he invent the light bulb as well as the telephone? Or was it George Westinghouse? No! Thomas Edison! Of course. Thomas Edison invented the light bulb.

Anyway, it didn't matter. The point was: every failure brought you closer to success.

The old lady looked up at the heavy wooden garage door, now open. "I always wanted to install a garage door opener, but Bernie thought that was a waste of money."

"They are expensive," Ingrid agreed. "But it's not a waste of money if you can't open the darn door without it."

"That's so right!" She led Ingrid to the back of the garage. "I don't even keep a car in here anymore. After Bernie died in the Ford, I didn't want it anymore. He did most of the driving, anyway." She pointed to an old refrigerator with a large dent in the door. "There it is. I'm glad you're going to take it away. You know it doesn't work, right?"

"Right," Ingrid said.

"When Bernie ran into it, one of the tubes in back got punctured and all the gas leaked out."

Ingrid grabbed the side of the refrigerator and pulled hard to shift it around so she could see the back. Perfect! It was old enough that they still used copper tubes for the refrigerant instead of some cheaper metal. She could see where one of the tubes was crushed and punctured, but the rest was in good shape. If she couldn't build a fire trick with this, her name was not Ingrid Baardsen!

"So your husband just ran into this by accident?"

"No, no, no," the old lady said. "He was backing the car into the garage, and he had a massive stroke. The car kept right on going into the refrigerator. That was the moment he died. He liked to buy stuff on sale and keep it in the refrigerator. There was a turkey in the freezer that stunk to high heaven by the time I got it out of there." She waved her hand and shook her head as though smelling it once again. "Well, you can imagine. My husband dying, cleaning out that refrigerator was not the first thing on my mind. I didn't even realize it wasn't working at first."

"How horrible."

"It was. I was sitting next to him in the car. You should have seen his face. I still have nightmares about that face."

"Oh, I'm so sorry." The old lady looked like she was about to cry, and Ingrid moved to her and gave her an awkward hug. Despite her awkwardness, the old lady seemed to appreciate it and smiled weakly at Ingrid.

"Anyway, I'm glad to get this refrigerator out of here," she said. "I don't need those reminders."

"No."

"Not that I even come into the garage very often. But I was thinking I should get an opener installed, and maybe I could rent out the garage. You know, make a few dollars. Social security doesn't go very far."

"People always need parking."

"Not that it's necessarily my business, but what do you want with a broken refrigerator?"

"I just want these copper tubes," Ingrid said, putting her hand on them. "I'll take them out and sell the rest for scrap."

"You're going to take the copper tubes out yourself?"

"Sure."

"You must be handy." The old lady took a deep breath and blew it out. "Bernie was handy. He kept up the house. Now that he's gone, one thing after the other breaks down, and I can't afford a repairman. I can barely afford groceries. When my legs are bad, I have to get them delivered. That adds so much cost."

Light bulbs went off in Ingrid's head. This old lady reminded her so much of Ingrid, her "namesake," the old lady she'd assisted in Minneapolis. It started as a part-time job with *Rent-an-Angel*, doing tasks for the elderly. She'd loved helping Ingrid, who was also a struggling widow. She'd helped her for years, even after she'd been fired from *Rent-an-Angel*. In the end, the elderly Ingrid returned every favor without even knowing it.

"Say, what's your name?" she said to the old lady.

"I'm Kate Bennison. And you?"

"Ingrid. Ingrid Baardsen. Actually, I need a place to do some work with the copper tubes and all. If you'd let me work in your garage here for a while, I'll do repair jobs on your house."

"But it's so cold in here."

"I've got an electric space heater I can plug in. I'll fix things up for you, and I'll pick up your groceries when I pick up mine."

"Really? I've got a wall switch that doesn't work anymore, and a bathroom faucet that won't stop dripping, and that little curvy drain pipe under the laundry tub in the basement rusted through. I've been washing my clothes by hand in the kitchen sink because I can't run the washing machine. The laundry water empties into the laundry tub and goes all over the basement floor. When that happened, I just sat down and cried."

"Oh, Kate, that'll be the first thing I'll fix."

Kate's eyes opened wide, and she put a hand on Ingrid's shoulder. "You know how to do all those things?"

"I either know, or I can figure it out. Nothing mechanical,

electrical, or physical defeats me."

"Well, aren't you something! Would you like to come in for some coffee and corn bread? I've got butter and honey. You can use my garage as long as you like."

"Kate," Ingrid said. "I think this is the beginning of a beautiful friendship."

15

Monday, February 20, 2005

While Dwayne was once again trying to make good at Rockwell Nesbit III Personal Injuries Law on Monday morning, Ingrid was following Nick Sanchez up the stairs to the light grid over the Owen Theatre at the Goodman. She stopped at the top of the stairs and sucked in her breath. "Oh, Nick, this is so beautiful, I might just faint." She took three steps toward the catwalks and grabbed the railing, her eyes raking the scene. "Oh my God in heaven," she breathed. "Nirvana."

Catwalk after catwalk crossed the open space over the audience. In front of each catwalk were multitudes of lighting instruments focused on the stage far below. So many lighting instruments! So many lighting instruments in wonderful, like-new condition. She practically swooned.

"I guess you like it," Nick Sanchez said. He breathed heavily, having climbed all those stairs, not being in slender and robust shape like Ingrid.

"I might just have a spontaneous orgasm." She crept across the center catwalk, crouching down occasionally to look past the lighting instrument in front of her to the stage below. Then she got to the end of the catwalk and circled up to the next catwalk and crossed it as well. The catwalks were metal with safety railings. Everything was metal and industrial, with cables slung neatly to connectors. So perfectly wonderful.

"To focus lights without having to stand atop a rickety ladder and hope the lamp won't be flashing from a worn-out connector. Or trying to revive Dwayne after he gets yet another life-threatening electrical shock! Oh my God, I am going to dream about this place tonight. An absolutely *wet* dream."

"Thank you for sharing that," Nick said dryly, his lips turned down.

"You betcha." Ingrid circled off the last catwalk and toured the light booth at the back. Such beautiful light boards and sound boards and everything for which one could hope! Nick followed her in.

"Joan is going to love this."

"Joan?"

"Our stage manager."

"Is she Equity?" Nick asked.

"None of our people are union."

"Since you're an outside company, your cast and designers can be nonunion, but the stage manager has to be Equity to work in this booth."

"You're kidding."

"I seldom kid." He stood with hands on his wide hips, practically a giant of a man. His curly gray hair softened his look, shifting his appearance from that of a grizzly to more of a teddy bear. His gaze, however, remained stern.

"I believe that about you. You said this stage had a trap system? Could I see that?"

Nick nodded and led the way down the stairs to the stage. Halfway across, Ingrid stopped and faced the audience. The stage jutted out in a thrust, like the stage they'd been using at the Playhouse, but this thrust was elevated and had two balconies wrapped around the ground floor seating.

"Wow," she said. "That's a lot of seats. You can change things around, right?"

"Most productions use this configuration," Nick told her. "But it's flexible to your needs." He pointed up. "There isn't a fly system, per se, and not much room in the wings, so the usual thing is a unit set. The focus in this space is the acting."

"Yeah, that's good," Ingrid said. "I'm planning on surrounding the acting space with monumental stacks of antique furniture. I'm thinking they'll be on trucks, so they can be shifted to represent the different castles and the cliffs. The biggest challenge is the flames in front of the furniture."

"Flames?" He said it like someone might have said *live elephants?*

"I've been working on how to channel it safely. Very doable."

"Not in here, it's not doable," Nick insisted. "We couldn't get clearance for Lady Macbeth to carry a real candle."

"I need it to look like all that antique furniture is absolutely in flames," Ingrid said. "The lighting effects that simulate fire always look ridiculous. I'll figure out how to do the real thing safely."

"I don't think so," Nick sniffed. "No way in hell you are using live flames on a Goodman stage. Did you never hear of the Iroquois Theatre fire? It was right around the corner from here."

"Sure, sure, sure. Reg Camper said the same thing. But that was what? A hundred years ago? I know you and I can come up with a solution." She gave him her best ingratiating smile.

"No, you and I absolutely can not. No flames leaping up antique furniture. No bonfire in a garbage can. No tiny campfires in the center of the stage. No actor striking a match. No flame whatsoever."

"Huh," Ingrid said. "How about giving me some good news?"

"If Reg already said you couldn't do it, then this is not *news*, good or bad. If you want lighting effects that simulate fire, I know some excellent resources. Maybe you haven't seen the latest stuff."

"Yeah, okay." But inside, Ingrid was thinking: *No way, buddy.* In her head, she could hear her father screaming as he emerged from the back door to see his garage on fire, his pickup truck inside. That was the perfect expression of Dwayne's *the inheritance of betrayal.*

Nick led her down to the basement below the stage so she could see the trap doors from below.

"Yeah, this is nice," she said. "And you've got equipment for raising people and materials onto the stage?"

"Of course," Nick said.

"I like it. Maybe I can replace the flames idea. Do you mind if I look around down here a bit?"

"Knock yourself out." Nick headed back to his office, glad to be done with her for the moment.

Crates and set pieces atop rolling trucks created something of a maze in the space. Lots of little hidden nooks and alcoves. Ingrid could hide whatever she needed down here. There were plenty of electrical outlets. Space to hide gas canisters. Then she could snake gas lines up through one of the trap doors to the stage. Yes, there were many, many possibilities here. Nothing would stop the excellent designs of Ingrid Baardsen!

She was well pleased.

16

Friday, February 24, 2005

Dwayne leaned against the bar at the John Barleycorn Memorial Pub, sipping at a Jameson neat, when Bobby burst through the doors, stood there, and raised his arms.

"Ah, Chicago," Bobby cried to the drinkers milling about the tavern. His voice and his grin radiated across the room as he took in the familiar scenery. All eyes turned to the handsome, charismatic actor at the door, beaming back at them. He wore an enormous fur coat, a silk scarf around his neck, and perfectly trim black leather gloves on his hands. The dark flesh of his bald skull gleamed. He was magnetic.

How many shows had Bobby performed in this particular neighborhood? He'd been a favorite with the directors at Victory Gardens, playing several roles that traditionally featured White actors. His Hamlet was particularly admired.

"Dwayne! Dwayne! Dwayne!" he said, striding to him and embracing his old friend at the bar. With Bobby in the huge fur coat, Dwayne felt like he were being crushed by an impressively muscled teddy bear. "Coming back to John Barleycorn is like old home week."

"Bobby. Good to see you." He tugged at one of the furry sleeves. "What is this thing? Is it real?"

Bobby chuckled in his deep baritone and raised an eyebrow. "What do you think?" He grinned. "Barry!" he shouted as the bartender came near. He leaned far over the bar and shook the publican's hand. "Still holding together the soul of Chicago, I see. Good to see you!"

"Hey Bobby," Barry said. "You been out of town?"

Bobby laughed long and hard. Then he pointed at Dwayne. "Whatever he's been drinking and will be drinking, put it on my tab.

And bring me a White Russian, if you'd be so kind."

"Sure thing," Barry said.

Bobby grasped Dwayne's shoulders in his hands. "Thanks so much for meeting me. You were the first person I needed to see. Let's get a table." They moved to one of the high tops along the wall, Bobby commanding the seat that faced the door. High above them, model sailing ships decorated the space near the ceiling. Classical music filled the air. The aroma of stale beer filled their noses.

"This place never changes," Bobby said. "Thank God!"

"Nor do you," Dwayne said.

"Oh, no, so many changes!" Bobby said. "So many changes and yet so much the same! Congratulations on wooing Reg Camper, my friend! The Owen! So magnificent. I did a developmental production in the Owen. A little thug role, of course." He shook his head. "But you are doing *King Lear*! Congratulations."

Barry waved from the bar as he set up Bobby's White Russian. Bobby bounded over, retrieved it, and clicked glasses with Dwayne. "Do you know," he said in a low and secretive voice, "I started drinking these instead of beer because I thought they would be less fattening?" He laughed uproariously at his own ignorance. "These are so much more fattening than beer! All that heavy cream! Ha! But I developed a taste for them. I add a half hour of aerobics to my routine for every White Russian I drink!"

"I tried to warn you."

"You did?" Bobby looked amazed. "I should listen to you more often." He lowered his voice again. "And I *never* should have left Chicago. The things you've been doing! I should never have abandoned our partnership!"

Partnership would not have described the former relationship between Bobby and Dwayne. When Bobby ran the company, it was Bobby's company from top to bottom. Whatever Bobby said was the law. Somehow Bobby got the money to produce a series of shows under the Shakespeare and Friends name. He asked Dwayne to direct *Titus Andronicus*, but then ran out with what remained of the cash while the show was in pre-production. The Psychedelic Dream Theatre was founded on what remained of Shakespeare and Friends, but it was a new company.

"Let me guess." Dwayne leaned back on his stool and took a sip of his whiskey. "You heard about *King Lear* from Ingrid, and you want in."

"I have not been in touch with Ingrid," Bobby said, looking unjustly accused.

Dwayne noticed the aroma of expensive perfume, then felt the gentle fall of a well-shaped hand on his shoulder from behind. "Hello boys," Coco said.

Bobby laughed with delight and got up to embrace his beautiful friend. "Coco, my deepest, dearest love," he said. He gave her a long kiss on the lips.

"Oh là là," Coco said. "You should go away more often."

He pulled a chair up to their high top and took Coco's long black leather coat and draped it over a fourth chair atop his fur. "Now we're all here," Bobby said. "The talent trust of Shakespeare and Friends. We three are the pillars from which all the great art descends."

"Well, now." Coco cocked her head back. "We been doing just fine with you gone." She leaned toward Dwayne. "Don't you think Orlando is actually better looking than Bobby?"

Bobby scoffed. "Didn't you tell me that boy is gay?"

"That don't stop him from being extra fine," Coco said.

"Extra fine. Ha!" He threw his hands up in the air. "Ain't even in the race."

"Oh, he in the race," Coco said. "He's a beautiful, dark, Black man, and he is *extra fine*." She was enjoying this.

"So you found out about *King Lear* from *Coco*, not Ingrid, and now you want in," Dwayne said, correcting his earlier statement.

"Well…" Bobby said.

"Yep, you got it," Coco said. She leaned in toward Bobby. "If you don't want to spend the rest of your life in claptrap like *Dark Don't Wait*, you need to get in on this."

"*Dark Doesn't Wait* is doing great business," Bobby objected, correcting the title. *Dark Doesn't Wait* was the action horror flick Bobby had been hired into when he decamped for L.A. It had already earned out its budget and was making money for the investors. Bobby wished he had a percentage of the take, but as a first-time movie actor, he'd been paid scale, and that was that. The good money was going to the star, the former Buffy the Vampire Slayer.

"By the way," Bobby said to Dwayne, "did you know that Sarah Michelle Geller is married to Freddie Prinze Jr.? I thought I had a shot there."

Coco snorted. "And I suppose if you'd known she was married, that would've kept you from taking your shot?"

Bobby looked at her as though wrongly accused, then started to chuckle. "You know me too well."

Coco turned back to Dwayne. "So where you going to put him? Edmund? Kent?"

"Kent!" Bobby said. "Put me in as the faithful Kent. The virtuous Kent. I'm tired of playing the thug."

"I don't know that I'm putting you anywhere," Dwayne said. Bobby had run things by whim when it was his company, and there was no way Dwayne was going to let him waltz in and take over. *King Lear* was *Dwayne's* shot.

"Oh, come on," Bobby said. "You know how good I am. I started this company."

"You started Shakespeare and Friends, and you ended Shakespeare and Friends," Dwayne said. "This is a whole new day."

"Well, okay, so I did leave town with the cash," Bobby admitted. "But maybe that was the best thing. Look how you blossomed! Come on, Dwayne! Let me show my face at the Goodman. You know we do magic together."

Dwayne did know. Having Bobby on stage was like having Coco on stage. They performed with intense focus, always fascinating to watch. For all the potential difficulties of working with a diva like Coco, he would always cast her if he could. Bobby was at that same level, but Dwayne still felt the sting of his betrayal. "How can I trust you?"

"Trust me? We're old friends."

"That didn't stop you running out on me when I had my shot with the Public Theatre," Dwayne said. "You have no idea how hard it was to pull *Titus Andronicus* out of the fire."

"But you did it! And two shows later, you're headed to the Goodman! That's incredible."

"Sure," Dwayne agreed. "But what if someone offers you another movie as we're about to open?"

"He's not going to run out on this, Dwayne," Coco said.

"You see that? Coco trusts me. And doesn't Coco have casting privileges? Didn't she put her pops in *Romeo and Juliet*?"

"Don't push it," Coco warned him. She turned to Dwayne. "Listen. You don't have to rely on his friendship, or good will, or sense of honor. We both know none of that exists."

Bobby snorted in outrage, but Coco kept going.

"This is simply in his own best self-interest. That's always top for Bobby."

"You totally misjudge me." He gave his best wounded expression.

Coco waved him off. "The number of times I let you back in my bed when I very well *knew better*…"

"But if Wes Anderson sees *Dark Doesn't Wait*," Dwayne said, "and he calls Bobby to join Owen Wilson, Angelica Huston, and Willem Defoe in his latest film, is Bobby going to stick around here?"

"Have you seen *Dark Don't Wait*?" Coco said. Dwayne had not. "Wes Anderson ain't going to call."

Bobby turned and pouted toward the bar.

"Go ahead. Tell him," Coco said. Bobby gave her a look that could kill. She shrugged. "He called me in tears," she said to Dwayne. "The reviewers hated him. His big chance was blown. Hollywood doors closed. He begged me to tell him something good happening here." She turned back to Bobby. "Go on. Tell him. Tell him the rest."

"Yeah," Bobby said at last, looking uncharacteristically humble. "I told Coco maybe karma was biting me in the ass for letting you down. I'd like to make it up to you."

17

Saturday, February 25, 2005

Ingrid had spent some time nearly every day that week doing handyman projects at Kate's house. She addressed all the most egregious problems first. Kate was beside herself at being able to run her washing machine again. As an added bonus, the two of them truly enjoyed one another's company. Ingrid was not only getting space to work, she was getting a warmer place to sleep. She pulled her van into Kate's garage at night and plugged in her electric heater to Kate's outlet to keep the van warm. That was a luxury on these cold February nights.

"Bernie was a pretty good husband," Kate told her one night when she'd made dinner for them both. She was so grateful to Ingrid for picking up groceries, as well as all the work. "He drove a cab, and that was good until Ronny died and he started drinking. Then the income dropped, and he wasn't so fun to be around."

"That's so sad."

"Yeah. Before he died, Bernie would get furious with Ronny. I wanted to send Ronny to rehab, but Bernie believed in tough love. He'd read it in the newspaper. He kicked Ronny out. He was just eighteen. A month after that, Ronny had an overdose and died."

"That's horrible."

"Bernie blamed himself. He never admitted it, but I could see. He started drinking more and more."

"Your husband didn't have any siblings or anyone who could set him straight?" Inside, Ingrid felt a little embarrassed. She wasn't asking for conversation. She wanted to know if Kate was as isolated as old Ingrid in Minneapolis had been.

"No siblings. We fell out of touch with everyone back in Ohio. We made new friends here, but we lost a lot of them after Ronny died and Bernie's drinking went haywire. He got surly. We weren't so welcome anymore. And then when you get to a certain age, a lot of people you've known start dying off, too."

Ingrid felt even more embarrassed at her relief at this news. She really did feel fond of Kate. When Kate found out Ingrid took showers in skuzzy theatre backstages, she insisted Ingrid use her bathroom. More luxury.

Once Ingrid had removed the copper tubing from the refrigerator and carted the remains to a metal dealer for a few dollars, she began manipulating the metal into what she thought would work for a fire trick. By the end of the week, Ingrid had constructed a prototype. She'd taken a Christmas tree stand and soldered three curved copper tubes to the bolts that usually held a tree in place. The copper tubes were connected to flexible gas lines and then joined by a three-way connector to a single connector of the type that kitchen stoves used. Each of the open copper tube ends were fitted with electric igniters she'd salvaged from a junked stove. She waited until Kate's afternoon nap, pulled out Kate's kitchen stove, disconnected it from the line and hooked up her fire trick. She plugged in the controller that remotely controlled the igniters to spark.

This was the moment! She flipped open the gas line and pressed the button for the igniters. They spark, spark, sparked as the gas roared toward the copper tube ends and burst into a rocket of flame upwards, all the way up and spread immediately across the full surface of the ceiling and then puffed out with a loud pop. Gas poured into the kitchen. Ingrid dove for the line to shut it off as gas filled the air. She held her breath and opened all the windows that would open, feeling grateful that Kate's bedroom was upstairs and the old woman was hard of hearing.

She opened the back door to let more air flow in and put the fire trick equipment into the backyard. She reconnected Kate's stove and turned on the oven to combat the cold from the open windows. Then she put the fire trick into the garage.

She'd discovered another thing that did not work. Didn't that make her one more step toward success?

It didn't feel like it.

"Say, does it feel a little cold in here?" Kate said later when she came down to the kitchen. She went into the dining room to adjust the thermostat. As she came into the room, Ingrid noticed for the first time that the paint all across the ceiling had blistered.

"I noticed your paint is peeling in this room," she said.

Kate looked up. "Oh my goodness," she said. "I never noticed that before. Am I going blind?"

"I'm sure you're not," Ingrid said. "And don't worry. I get free leftover paint from set constructions. I'll repaint it for you."

"You are too good to me," Kate said.

Again, Ingrid felt a little embarrassed.

18

Monday, February 27, 2005

Dwayne looked up from his desk in the billing department of Rockwell Nesbit III Personal Injuries Law to see Rockwell Nesbit III and Chaz Ackersley walking toward him. Rocky had a huge grin on his face, while Chaz had a slightly reserved smile. Rocky's presence struck Dwayne once again. He moved like a man in charge of his universe: A handsome, powerful Black man accustomed to getting his way.

"We have a change of venue for you," Rocky said, hands on his hips before Dwayne's desk. "You don't mind giving him up, do you, Chantel?"

"Not at all," Chantel said, a little too enthusiastically for Dwayne to enjoy, despite the fact that he wouldn't mind getting out of the billing department.

"Come with us," Rocky said, as boisterously as if he were leading him to a surprise birthday party.

"Okay." Dwayne followed Rocky and Chaz down the corridor to another office. The office was small, but it was private and empty, with a nice desk and credenza and a beautiful view of the museum campus and the lake to the south.

"It's all yours!" Rocky said magnanimously. "Tell him," he commanded Chaz.

"Rocky and I discussed his PR needs, and we're moving to the next logical step. Chaz Ackersley Public Relations will continue to oversee his needs, but now he'll have an in-house PR person who can interface with the attorneys and collect the best information to write up the stories we place. That'll be you."

Dwayne was stricken dumb. Chaz knew how miserable Dwayne had been at Rocky's offices. Nobody but Rocky wanted him there.

Now he wouldn't have to report to any of those resentful people. He wanted to cry and hug them both and give them kisses on the cheeks. "I'd be delighted," he said. "This is my office?" He loved it already.

"It's all yours!" Rocky said. "You'll work on our payroll at the same salary, but you'll take your direction from Chaz. What the hell do I know about PR?" He laughed heartily. "But I do know it's improved our business. So, I'll leave you boys to it." And with that, he swept out of the office.

But then popped his head back in.

"Oh, and let me know when you decide on *King Lear* casting." He laughed and made a zipper movement across his lips with his fingers. "I know, I know! We don't talk about that in the office!" And again, he swept away and down to the elevator and out of the building. He'd spent less and less time in it over the years, allowing his people to make the piles of money that financed his extravagant lifestyle.

Dwayne got up and closed the door. "Oh my God, you have no idea. You saved me! Thank you."

Chaz sat on the edge of Dwayne's new desk and gave him a cockeyed grin. "Frankly, I saved us both. You might hate it here, but I hate coming here more. I cannot look at Rocky without seeing Uncle Buck. Every time I walk into this building, I can feel him breaking my finger with a pair of pliers. Now I don't have to come back."

"Good. Everyone wins. I can't afford to give up this job. Now Angela is launching into…" He stopped himself. She didn't want anyone to know about their fertility business.

"Launching into?" Chaz said.

"An…initiative at her school," he invented. "And she wants us to donate to it."

"Can't the CPS fund its own initiatives?"

"It's extracurricular. Never mind. Tell me how this PR job works."

"I've got an appointment to interview one of the attorneys here about a case she just closed. You come with me, and we'll do the interview together. Feel free to pop in any questions that occur to you. Then you'll write it up, and I'll do a revision. Next time, you do it on your own."

"Sounds good," Dwayne said.

Chaz slinked over to the door and peered out to make sure the boss was gone. "Are you really going to cast Rocky in your show?"

"I might," Dwayne said. "I'd definitely have a good understudy for him. Well, understudies for everyone, really. But maybe two for Rocky."

Chaz laughed. "And what about Bobby? He's good on stage. But *Dark Doesn't Wait?*"

They looked at each other and shook their heads. "I couldn't believe that," Dwayne said.

Chaz and Dwayne and Angela had gone to see *Dark Doesn't Wait* together Saturday night. Sarah Michelle Geller was terrific. Bobby, however, seemed to be in an entirely different movie—some kind of over-the-top thing with super-exaggerated emotions.

"It's like he was playing for the back row in a big theatre," Dwayne said.

"I don't think you have to worry about him being yanked away by Hollywood."

"This morning, he emailed me a copy of the sublease agreement for his apartment in L.A. to prove he's here for the duration. It's sublet until a month after *King Lear* closes. He's got no home there to go back to," Dwayne said.

"Sounds like he's yours if you want him." Chaz got up and surprised Dwayne with a strained smile. "So, if you don't screw the pooch on this PR job for Rocky, everything will be rosy."

19

Wednesday, March 1, 2005

"I'm really torn," Tom said. He squirmed in his seat and glanced out at the traffic passing by Cunneen's Bar on Devon Avenue. They were sitting at Dwayne's favorite table, up on the platform in the storefront window. Tom turned his gaze abruptly back on Dwayne, and the hanging spider plant babies hit him in the face. They would have been above anyone else's head, but Tom was so tall. He brushed them away and shifted down the repurposed church pew that provided seating at the window table. "Maybe we should hold auditions before we cast ensemble members," he said. "We might find more dynamic actors, and that could propel the company as a whole. This is the Goodman. We have to take our best shot."

"I hear what you're saying, but you know every veteran actor in the city will want a crack at Lear. We'd be seeing people who've done more Shakespeare than Wallace. And more than Coco. And more than you and I, for that matter."

"I know, I know, I know," Tom whined. "But I have to ask myself, am I being selfish wanting to play Regan? Should I be satisfied just doing the choreography? I mean, are we doing the best thing for the company?"

"That depends on what we're calling *the company*," Dwayne said. "Is *the company* our ensemble, or is it whoever you and I cast? The Chicago talent pool is incredible. If we replace all our actors, is this still a company show?"

"Right, right, right," Tom said. "But I have to say it: Aren't you worried about Wallace?"

Dwayne took a deep breath, got up and walked to the bar without a word. He remembered Wallace freezing on stage in the last show, lost in his demons. He'd really had to work to get him past that.

He waited a moment as though he were about to order another round of drinks, then came back to the table.

"What the hell was that?" Tom asked.

"I needed a moment."

"So you *are* worried about Wallace!"

"Of course I'm worried about Wallace. I do believe he could do an amazing Lear. He looks like a weathered warrior king. He's got that great penetrating baritone voice. He was terrific as Titus. But he also has his weird baggage."

"So, what are you going to do?" Tom said.

"A wise man once said: *People appear normal in an inverse proportion to how well you know them.*"

"What does that mean?"

"*Everybody* has baggage. We might cast actors who look like they'd be better, but then be in for an unpleasant surprise."

"Better the devil you know?"

"More than that." Dwayne thought about it for a moment. "This ensemble continues to build on its relationships."

"Right. I was already imagining how the sibling rivalry between Melinda and Coco could play out as the sisters," Tom said. "Then there's the love affairs that've come and gone. It's kind of like when Fleetwood Mac had their huge hit with *Rumours.*"

Dwayne cocked his head. "I guess it's sort of like that."

"I see it," Tom said, suddenly more enthusiastic. "Yeah, let's cast this puppy with our people and fill in the gaps after that."

"And hope that I can keep you all from killing one another."

"Pish posh." Tom pulled out a notebook and a pen with lavender ink.

"Let's start with the obvious," Dwayne said. "Wallace as Lear. Coco as Goneril. Melinda as Cordelia."

Tom wrote them down and then looked up at Dwayne with puppy dog eyes. "And me as Regan?"

At that moment, Dwayne saw Coco stepping out of a cab in front of the bar. She stood up and smoothed down her long leather coat and arranged her purse on her shoulder. She handed some money to the driver.

"What the hell?"

"What?" Tom said. He turned to see Coco turn smartly on her spike heel and smile brilliantly when she saw Dwayne and Tom on the other side of the glass. She entered Cunneen's and gave them a thrilling: "Hello!"

"Hello?" Tom said uncertainly.

"Hello, indeed," Dwayne agreed.

Coco held a hand to the side of her mouth as though shouting over a long distance. "A dirty martini back here with these boys, dear heart," she called to the barmaid. She settled herself on the pew next to Dwayne.

"It's lovely to see you, but what are you doing here?" Dwayne said.

"I had to make sure you two weren't committing us to any mistakes," she said.

"What kind of mistakes?" Tom sat very much upright and puffed out his cheeks.

"In casting, of course."

"How did you even know where we were?" Dwayne said.

"And how did you know we were casting right now?" Tom demanded.

"Oh, you boys," Coco chuckled. "Ingrid told me. You know how she is."

"I didn't tell Ingrid. Did you?" he asked Tom, who shook his head.

"Whatever," Coco said. "I didn't like how we left it about Bobby last week. You don't think you can trust him. I get that. But we hadn't actually started *Titus* when he pulled out. He would never run out on a show in production. And you know, on stage, he's almost as charismatic as me."

"Bobby's in town?" Tom said.

"He's in town, and he wants in. He wants to play Kent."

"Kent," Tom scoffed. "He's no Kent. You know who should play Kent? Dwayne should play Kent."

"Have you forgotten?" Dwayne said. "I'm directing."

"Bobby directed and played Hamlet. That was a great show."

"And the rest of us figured out our parts on our own," Dwayne said. "That's not what I want for *King Lear*."

"Right, right, right," Tom said. "Oh! Bobby should play Edmund!" he squealed. "The deviousness. The ruthlessness. The sexual magnetism. I've seen productions where you wonder why Goneril and Regan are fighting over this guy. No one would wonder why Coco and I have the lust for Bobby!"

Coco laughed low in her throat. "Can't argue with that." She cocked her head to the side. "Wait a minute. You're playing Regan?"

"What the hell?" Dwayne said. At that moment, tall, handsome Orlando came bursting through the door. He swung around to their table, nearly knocking over the barmaid as she delivered Coco's dirty martini.

"Thank God you're still here," he said.

"Ingrid told you, too?" Dwayne said.

"Yes." He pointed at Coco's martini. "Could I have one of those?" he said to the barmaid. She nodded and left. Tom slid down the church pew to let him in.

"I don't want you to think of casting Edmund with anyone but me," he said.

Coco gave a long trill of laughter. "I think you might be three minutes too late, darling," she said.

"No!" He looked horribly shocked. "No, no, no, no, no!"

"Oh yes," she said. "That little boat appears to have left the harbor."

At that moment, Wallace appeared at the door. He grinned hugely when he saw them all at the table. He knocked on the window and waved as he came in.

"This is ridiculous," Dwayne said to him. "Did you think I was going to cast someone else as Lear?"

"Not at all, old man," Wallace said, pushing back his great leonine hair with both hands. "But since you're talking casting, I was hoping we could kibitz a bit about *Oedipus Rex*."

"Sure," Dwayne told him. "But not today."

"What do you mean that boat left the harbor?" Orlando demanded of Coco.

"Bobby's back in town. Bobby would knock Edmund out of the park. It's probably Edgar or Kent for you."

"Bobby!" Orlando said. "Isn't he the guy who stole the company money?"

"He's the guy who came up with that money in the first place," Coco said to Orlando. "Suck it up, buttercup. It's not like you'd have to play the Nurse."

Suddenly, there was a rap at the window. Ry stood like a sudden apparition, an acoustic guitar slung over his shoulder. He entered the building and stood at the head of their table.

"Why are you here?" Dwayne said.

"I got an idea for a song to end Act One," Ry said. "I wanted to try it out on you."

"And Ingrid told you we'd be here."

"Well," he drawled. "She didn't tell me *everybody* would be here, but she did say you and Tom would be here. She wanted me to remind you that the best casting would be members of the ensemble."

"*Saint Christina the Astonishing.* Can that woman never stop interfering?" Dwayne turned to Tom. "Okay. Let's listen to Ry's song, then you and I will finish the casting at my apartment. *Alone!* I'll double-lock the door."

20

Friday, March 3, 2005

Angela stopped in the parkway in front of Carol's house. Carol liked to throw happy hours for their colleagues, which Angela always enjoyed, but today she had a mission. She needed to know how Carol, who was a fifth-grade teacher like herself, had afforded a gorgeous old house near the lake in Evanston.

Carol and her husband had raised two girls to adulthood in this house. One of them had children of her own now. Carol's big, dumb, friendly golden retriever stood up on the front porch and began wagging his tail when he saw Angela. Steam rolled out of his mouth in the chilly air, but his thick fur kept him warm. The dog could be left on the big front porch, and he'd remain there watching the action of the neighborhood without running away or chasing a squirrel. The dog stayed where Carol put him. What kind of magic did she possess? A wave of envy washed over Angela. What enchantment did Carol and her husband employ that they had such an ideal life? And how could Angela get it?

Back in her apartment with its periodic cockroach invasions, Dwayne was reading academic criticism on *King Lear*. Their second bedroom was now stacked with books on *King Lear*. He haunted secondhand bookshops collecting research on the play. Books that he couldn't find used, he borrowed from the library, but he much preferred to own them. He liked making notes in the margins. Sometimes he'd even cut a page out of a book, highlight a section, and tack it to the wall, which struck her as a violent abuse of a book. He always did this when he prepared to direct, especially Shakespeare. So much research. He'd get all absent-minded and start talking randomly about what George Bernard Shaw had said about *Lear*, or how Kurosawa adapted the story into his film, *Ran*, or the shortcomings of

Laurence Olivier's performance in the role.

She loved Dwayne. Sometimes she found all this charming. But sometimes she wished he were the kind of guy who could help her afford to live in a place like Carol's and raise two girls in a nice house with a yard and a big, friendly dog. She'd grown up in a big family, and she adored that. Could she not at least have a little family? A home to call their own?

Was that too much to ask?

She patted the doggie's head on the way into the house and found the living room already full of her colleagues talking in excessive volume, mainly about how much they hated Norman Plotz and his ridiculous demands which made it harder to do a good job teaching, and why the hell would anyone think a principal from Iowa would know his ass from a hole in the ground when it came to running a school in the city of Chicago? Former principal Fran Konacki, who had once been the subject of a multitude of complaints in this very room, was now being held up as the epitome of good sense.

Angela was greeted with a level of enthusiasm that indicated Carol was mixing her famously potent margaritas. As she dumped her coat on the coat-buried love seat under the front windows, she heard Carol's blender jump into life in the kitchen. She followed the sound back to its source.

"Angela!" Carol greeted. She stepped back away from her blender to give the younger woman a hug. Angela and Carol had been on the same fifth-grade teaching team for five years. Carol's husband was a visual artist. His paintings were all over the house. An easel with a work in progress stood in the sun porch off the kitchen. A large, eye-catching nude hung on the wall above the kitchen table.

"Is this new?" Angela pointed to it.

"Yup." Carol nodded. "Ted is quite *enthusiastic* about the new model. I'm sure a pretty young thing like that is not going to give the time of day to an old fart like Ted. So, he can have his fantasies."

Angela laughed. "Did he paint her here?"

"Oh, no. He's in a group of five artists who pool resources to hire the models and paint together."

"He must do really well."

"You mean selling his work?" Her eyebrows raised high, then she laughed uproariously. "Apparently, you haven't noticed every wall of this house is covered in his paintings!"

"Well, yes," Angela said uncertainly. "But at some point he must have…"

"At no point was Ted a big seller. Why would you think that?" She poured Angela a large margarita from the blender and handed it to her.

"Well, his work is…" She looked around the big old-fashioned kitchen. Her eyes lingered on the built-in arts-and-crafts cabinets, the high ceilings and dark stained crown moldings, and the well-worn wood floor.

"Oh!" Carol said. "You want to know how a schoolteacher and an artist afforded a big old Evanston house like this. Right?"

"Well," Angela felt her face flush. "Yes…"

"No. Absolutely. Fair enough, Ms. Schoolteacher with a theatre director husband. First, Ted made his *living* doing illustrations and layout for advertising. He was on staff at Leo Burnett for years. He spent a lot of time cutting up images with an X-acto knife and pasting them in place. But now computers do all that work, so they laid him off. He still does illustrations freelance. He doesn't make the money he used to, but the girls are grown. The mortgage is paid. It's just the real estate tax that's a killer."

"So it was the ad business…"

"Even at his old salary, we would never be able to afford this house now. Real estate around here has gone through the roof. If you two wanted to buy a house in this neighborhood, your boy would need to direct a Hollywood blockbuster. Or maybe a lot of TV commercials."

"He tried to get a job in commercials last year."

"Oh." Carol made a face and took a sip of her margarita. "Well, I know exactly how the starving artist thing goes. Ted didn't want to work for Leo Burnett. Fair enough. I didn't want to teach fifth grade every day to eternity, either. But that's just reality. It's not like I was going to let him have a free ride on my back my whole life. I kicked his butt until he found a decent job. As an illustrator who could also do layout, he made a good buck. And *Voila*!" She did a little turn with her arms out to her domestic surroundings.

Kick his butt? Is that what Angela needed to do with Dwayne?

21

Saturday, March 4, 2005

"Why are we doing this again?" Angela said. She tossed the spoon with a clatter into the sink, spattering red sauce up the sides of the ancient porcelain and the wall.

"Doing what?" Dwayne said, coming back from setting the dining room table.

"This dinner. Why are we hosting this dinner?"

Dwayne stopped. "You said to me on Wednesday, *Let's have a few friends for dinner.* I said, *Great.* So now they're about to arrive."

"Why does it always have to be your friends?" she said, hands on hips. Her face glowed rosy red from the steam of the pasta pot.

"It *isn't* always. The last party we had was a Friday happy hour with your teacher friends. You went to another one at Carol's place last night."

"Oh, sure. My drunken colleagues. Like that isn't just like extending the teaching day into my weekend!"

"This was your idea," Dwayne complained. "Wednesday, I said, *Who should we have?* And you said, *I don't care. A small dinner with the usual suspects. And invite Bobby since he's back in town.* That's what *you* said."

"But is that what I *wanted*, Dwayne? Is that what I actually wanted?"

"How the hell would I know what you *actually* wanted if you don't tell me?"

"Come on, Dwayne! What is the point of being married all these years if you can't even tell what I want?"

The doorbell rang.

"*I'll* get it," she said. "And *you* finish the cooking." She pushed past him to get to the door.

Dwayne looked over the kitchen. He'd been reading research on *King Lear* in the office bedroom until she shouted for him to set the table. What had she been cooking?

He lifted a lid off the Dutch oven. Red sauce with small meatballs, mushrooms, and peppers. Water boiled in the pasta pot. A bowl of fresh, uncooked pasta waited on the counter. Since it was fresh pasta, it'd just need a few minutes in the water. Lettuce, carrots, and celery sat next to it. He started washing those for a salad. That solved the mystery of the menu. But what about the mystery of his wife?

Meanwhile, Angela answered the door. She opened it to discover Bobby waiting with a sly smile. "Angela Guiseppelli, you sexy, sexy thing," he said. He took her in his arms, gave her a robust hug and a kiss on each cheek.

"You big, ridiculous flirt," she said back to him. She looked pleased. "Come on. Dwayne is finishing the dinner. Let's you and I get the drinking started."

"You got yourself a deal." He followed her into the dining room. "Hello, chef!" he shouted to Dwayne.

"Hello, Bobby," Dwayne called back, not sounding as welcoming as he'd usually be.

"Don't mind him," Angela said. "He's easily confused by cooking." She looked at the bottles on their little wine rack. They had two medium-level Chianti Classicos, a Rioja, a California cabernet, and one high-priced Barolo that Dwayne was saving for a big occasion. *Fuck it*, she thought. She pulled out the Barolo and handed it to Bobby with a corkscrew. "Make yourself useful."

"Charmed if I do," he said. He uncorked the wine and poured them each a healthy glass. He clicked glasses with her. "Cheers." He took a sip.

"*Cin cin,*" she said.

Bobby wiped his chin. "Did I dribble?"

"Don't be an idiot." She drained her glass, grabbed the bottle, and gave herself another healthy pour.

"Ah," Bobby said. "So we're *drinking* drinking."

"Well, *I* am," she said.

The doorbell rang again, and she let in Aleister and Chaz, who'd managed to arrive at the same time and joined Angela and Bobby in the drinking until Dwayne finished cooking.

As Dwayne served the dinner, Bobby raised a glass. "To old friends," he said.

"Old friends," they repeated.

Dwayne was impressed with the wine. "What is this?" he said. Bobby held up the bottle. The Barolo he'd been saving. The bottle was empty. He'd only got a half glass. What the living fuck? Was she deliberately trying to make him angry?

"Are you acting with the company again, Bobby?" Chaz asked.

"I wanted to play the faithful Kent," Bobby said. "But maybe Dwayne will want me as Edmund. He's the romantic lead, after all."

"Ha!" Dwayne said. "Now that's an interesting way to describe Edmund."

Bobby leaned back and grinned. "Edmund is an evil man that the two evil sisters want to fuck. So if *King Lear* has a romantic lead, Edmund is it."

"I guess I can't argue with that," Dwayne said.

"Are you using Rocky again?" Chaz asked. He looked a little worried.

"You see the face on Chaz?" Angela said, her voice beginning to verge on reckless amusement. "You'll see that face on him whenever anyone mentions Rocky." She lowered her voice to a conspiratorial whisper. "That's because Rocky broke Chaz's finger with a pair of pliers."

"No!" Bobby began to laugh at the dark absurdity of it.

"Oh, yes!" Angela said. "And I know because I had to set his finger bone for him."

"You are a woman of unfathomed qualities," Bobby said.

"I certainly am. I learned from my grandmother." Angela shrugged and took another sip of her wine. "She was always doctoring up Uncle Guido or Uncle Paolo. But Dwayne there is a starving artist."

What the hell?

The conversation lagged for an uncomfortable moment as Angela stared into her wineglass and everyone else attempted to process the non-sequitur. Then Bobby twisted his body in Dwayne's direction. "Cornwall! You've got to have Rocky play Cornwall. A man who deliberately breaks bones with a pair of pliers has got to be the man to gouge out Gloucester's eyes!"

"Unless he goes *too* method on you," Aleister said.

"Aleister is a man of many talents, too," Angela said. "He once hypnotized Rocky to get him out of his alternate personality. Dwayney boy told me all about it."

"Ha! Did he, Dwayney boy?" Bobby said. "Rocky has an alternate personality?"

"He did indeed," Dwayne said, trying his best to take it in humor.

"Rocky really wants to be in Dwayne's play," she said. "He gave Dwayne a five-thousand-dollar signing bonus that might have been an encouragement to cast him. But I'm spending it all, so that takes care of that."

"Aha!" Bobby was enjoying this all inordinately. "Well, that's the way it should be, right? After all the years *you've* been paying the bills."

"That's right!" Angela said, slamming her hand on the tabletop as though it had just occurred to her, even though that's what she'd been thinking about all evening.

"And Wallace is going to be King Lear?" Bobby said.

Angela pointed at her husband. "Reg Camper told Dwayne that if it were up to him, he'd cast Stacy Keach or Brian Dennehy, but neither of them will work for Dwayne."

"Did you contact Stacy Keach and Brian Dennehy?" Chaz asked.

"No," Dwayne said.

"What about Peter Burden?" Bobby said. "He's a powerful local actor."

"Reg Camper mentioned Peter Burden," Dwayne admitted.

"Burden is a monster," Bobby said. "If I were casting Lear in Chicago, he'd be the top of my list. And why not cast a Black Lear? It's about time. Let my people act!" he cried.

Angela pointed at him. "I remember what the *Sun-Times* said about you as a Black Hamlet." She snorted a laugh. No one knew what to say for a moment.

"Have you seen Wallace on stage?" Aleister asked Bobby.

"A number of years back. Nothing the size of Lear," Bobby said.

"Wallace is just another starving artist," Angela said. "Middle-aged man living in a tiny studio. Does that strike anyone else as kind of pathetic?" She poured herself a large glass of the Chianti Classico that Dwayne opened after the demise of the Barolo.

"Well, he's dedicated despite all the odds," Bobby said. "What matters is what Wallace can do *now*. I haven't seen any of his recent work."

"So Chaz," Angela said. "Are you still living in the crappy efficiency you moved into after Bonnie gave you the boot?"

Again, nobody said anything for a moment.

"Well, yeah, actually," he said.

"Even though you own your own PR agency, you're living like a starving artist?" She cocked an eyebrow at him.

"Bonnie cleaned me out. I'm mostly at the office, anyway."

"No healthy work-life balance nonsense for you!" she exclaimed.

"No," he agreed uncertainly.

"But Aleister, you still have the house you and Alison bought."

"I do," Aleister said.

"The only homeowner among us! A table full of college-educated men in their early thirties, the prime of fucking life, and only one homeowner." She was beginning to slur her words. She refreshed her glass of Chianti.

"Angela?" Dwayne said.

"Look, Dwayne." She gestured around the room. "No houses. No wives. No Bonnie or Alison at my table. I loved those women. But now, it's just you four. And all you can talk about is who is going to pretend to be this person or that in fucking *King Lear*."

"Geez, Angela," Dwayne said.

"Maybe we should go." Aleister started to get up.

"No, no, no, no, no." Angela got up clumsily and sat him back down. "I'm just in a mood."

"Are you sure?" Chaz said.

"I'm Italian!" she shouted. "I'm a woman! I have moods!" She looked around the table. "You should see your faces." She began laughing. "You're all too much."

They were all quiet. Angela picked up the Chianti bottle and discovered it empty. She shook it over her glass to collect the last drops.

"So," Bobby asked uncertainly, after a moment. "Who's going to play Edgar?"

Angela laughed abruptly and loudly, then quieted herself. "I'm sorry. Yes, Dwayne, who is going to play Edgar?"

There was another awkward pause.

"If Bobby is going to be Edmund, Orlando should be Edgar." Chaz suggested, attempting to make his voice sound normal. "The two of you could pass as brothers."

"Because Black people all look alike to you?" Bobby said sternly. Chaz looked guilty, then Bobby laughed. "Just shitting you," he said.

"Family resemblance! Very big," Angela said, slurring again. "And then you've got Coco, a Black woman playing one sister, Tom, *a White man*, playing the next, and Melinda, a White woman, playing the third. A lot of family resemblance there!"

"Tom and I are not announcing the roles yet. We're pretty well decided where to use the ensemble members, but we still have to audition to fill in the rest of the cast. That might change things."

"*You* should play the virtuous Edgar!" Bobby said to Dwayne. "Edgar is all about pathos. Betrayed by his bastard half-brother, so his father's men are hunting him. Pretending to be Poor Tom, the wandering half-wit. The pathos! No one is more pathetic than you, Dwayne!" Bobby roared with laughter. He stopped abruptly when he saw the gimlet stare Angela was giving him.

"Don't be a prick," she said. "Dwayne is not pathetic."

The party didn't last much longer after that. On the way out, Aleister asked Dwayne if he'd meet him for a drink soon. He'd hardly said a word the whole evening.

22

Saturday, March 18, 2005

How to present the question? *Should* he present the question? "Ingrid told me you've directed almost as many productions as our friend, Dwayne," Wallace said. That was as good an opening gambit as any. He raised his bushy eyebrows high and leaned back in his chair, pushing his great bushels of salt and pepper hair back with both hands.

"I'm not sure that's quite true," Bobby said. "But Dwayne is a *director* who sometimes acts. I am an *actor* who sometimes directs. I directed shows in which I played the title role. I just moved everyone else around to suit my performance. *Hamlet. Henry Five. Macbeth.*" He also leaned back and winked at Wallace. "I directed those shows, but Dwayne, he *directs* a show. You feel me?"

"I believe I do," Wallace said. He took a large inhale that could be heard halfway across the bar, his barrel chest expanding so that his next words boomed as though he stood central to an amphitheatre. "And I must wonder, too," he resounded, "what type of director I am destined to be."

"It's your first time, this *Oedipus Rex*?" Bobby asked.

"It is. What are you, mid-thirties?"

Bobby gave him a sideways nod in approximate agreement.

"I have a good twenty years on you. So it nags at me, what impact have I had on the culture? In live performance, our work exists, and then it's gone. All that remains are memories. To create a lasting effect, the experience must be intense! I've had a lifetime of attending performance. How many shows do I really remember? A blessed few."

Bobby leaned in as though he were about to share a secret. "That's why we must do film, as well. Film lasts."

"Does it, though?" Wallace squinted his eyes. "I saw your inaugural outing, *Dark Never Waits*. Will that endure the sands of time?"

"*Dark Doesn't Wait,*" Bobby corrected. He shrugged. "You've got to start somewhere."

"How was Sarah Michelle Geller?" Wallace said eagerly. "I loved her as *Buffy the Vampire Slayer.*"

"You and the rest of the world. When we had our first rehearsal…" Bobby barked a laugh. "Actually, our *only* rehearsal. We had a read-through the day before shooting started. After that, it was all piecemeal shoots, shot all out of order, according to whatever was convenient for locations and lighting. Nothing about what made sense for the actors."

"Ha!" Wallace said.

"So I invite Sarah out for a drink after one of the first days of shooting. We're in this little bistro, sitting in this dark little booth. I'm thinking, wow! She's getting us some privacy! But no. She's just getting a table where she's not constantly being told: *Oh, I loved you as Buffy, blah, blah, blah.* So I start making a move, and she clears her throat and holds a hand in my face. She says: *You know, I'm married to Freddie Prinze Jr.* Well, fuck me if I knew that. But maybe she'd like a little extramarital activity? One minute more, and that was clearly not on the menu."

Wallace chuckled deeply. "And yet, you had the experience of putting the moves on Buffy the Vampire Slayer. Even if you were shut down, it's a memory to be savored."

"I hadn't thought of it that way." Bobby looked pleased. "I believe you are right."

Wallace lowered his brows and lowered his voice. This was the moment. "I've been thinking about *Oedipus.* I believe the secret of good directing is making sure you've got the strongest cast."

"When I was directing, I would cast an actor I could trust over a flashier actor, every time."

This was a new thought. "You mean someone easy to work with over someone with chops?"

"Doing theatre is a marathon. If you pick people who wear you down, you'll never finish the race."

"Huh." Wallace nodded his head. "I've certainly been in shows where one volatile actor makes everyone else's life difficult."

"But then I always made sure I had a genius actor in the title role." Bobby laughed deeply and long, and Wallace joined in with him.

"I did see your *Henry Five*," Wallace admitted. "You were electrifying. I thought the rest of the production was a little uneven."

Bobby waved him off. "So did the critics!"

Wallace leaned toward Bobby and looked in both directions. "What do you think of Orlando Gunn?" he breathed in a low rumble.

"Dwayne certainly likes him. And Dwayne has good taste."

"He's not done a title role yet. I've promised him Oedipus, but I wonder, is the boy ready?"

"Wait a minute," Bobby said. "Didn't he just play Romeo? If Romeo isn't a title role, I don't know what is."

"Yes, yes, yes, of course. But Romeo is a confused, love-sick teenager. You know what I mean. He's never played a title role like Titus Andronicus, or Hamlet, or Henry Five, or Prospero. Something epic. Something tragic. Something to prepare one for Oedipus."

"Okay, I hear you," Bobby said, still with doubt in his voice. "Who's playing Jocasta?"

"Well…" Wallace shrugged. "I was thinking Coco."

"Oh, my God. Don't wait another minute. Make sure you've got Coco."

"Really?"

"How can you say *really*? Haven't you done two shows with Coco?"

"Yes," Wallace admitted hesitantly.

"If you can get Coco, you always cast Coco." He leaned in toward Wallace. "Coco is almost as magnetic on stage as myself. You put Coco in the cast, your worries are over."

"But isn't Coco something of a…diva?"

"Of course she is!" Bobby waved his hand around. "How else could she be so brilliant? You've shared scenes with the woman, no?"

"Yes."

"To be on stage with her! Have you ever felt more alive?"

"It is bracing," Wallace allowed.

"Her diva shit is nothing. Enjoy it! It's the price of admission to a beautiful experience."

"I wish I'd seen the two of you together." Wallace considered it for a moment. "And what about you, Bobby? What's it like working with you?"

Bobby laughed and shook his head. "Wallace, Wallace, Wallace. What is the point of asking *me* that question? Ask Dwayne. Ask Coco. I never work with me. I *am* me."

23

Saturday, March 24, 2005

"This is so nice of you!" Kate said. The thanks made Ingrid feel a little guilty. All of Kate's financial papers from the year were spread out on the dining room table. Ingrid would never do anything to harm Kate, but the old woman would not be happy if she knew what Ingrid had done. "I never thought my tax return was all that complicated," Kate said. "The year Bernie died, I thought it might be. But since then, frankly, it doesn't seem like there's much to it. And then this year he tells me how much his fee had gone up. I couldn't believe it! For my simple little return!"

Ingrid had finished repainting Kate's kitchen after blackening the ceiling with her experimental fire trick. She'd gone on to do several other home repair tasks, as well. Ingrid was living in her van in the woman's garage, using Kate's electricity to run its heater, and taking showers in her house. She didn't have to worry about a cop tapping on her windshield with his billy club or anyone attempting to break in while she was asleep. She handled it when those things happened, but it always left her feeling wired up—and her baseline state was wired up enough already. Having the sanctuary of Kate's garage was absolute bliss. She enjoyed talking with Kate over coffee, as well, which they did fairly often. The two had become fond of one another.

"Anyway, thanks so much for doing my taxes. I just didn't see how I could afford my accountant anymore."

"I'm happy to do it. I always do my own taxes," Ingrid said, which was not true. "I also did the taxes for the lady I helped out in Minneapolis." That was true. Doing the other old lady's taxes and having access to her financials and personal information had, in fact, been a lifesaver for Ingrid. She'd never used any of that information in any way that harmed her—she made very sure of that.

"You've got no dependents listed," Ingrid said. "Did you and Bernie have any children other than the one who died of an overdose?"

"We had two sons, Josh and Ronny. They'd be much too old to be claimed as dependents now. Josh died when he was seventeen. Hit by a car on Ashland Avenue. The impact of the car didn't kill him, but he smacked his skull on the pavement and his brain swelled. That cut off the blood." She waved her hand by her head. "And then he died."

"I'm so sorry," Ingrid said.

"Yes. I told you about Ronny. He saw Josh get hit. He never got over it. Bernie kicked him out when he got into drugs."

"Right," Ingrid said. "And then Bernie started drinking after the overdose."

"Yes." Kate sighed. "Yes. So no living children. No grandchildren. Both my sisters have passed. Bernie had a brother back in Ohio, but we aren't in touch. Frankly, I don't know if he's living or dead. You'd think someone would contact me if he died, but you never know."

"You were never close?"

"Bernie's brother was nine years older. They never got along."

"Well, that's too bad." Ingrid felt a little guilty again. Kate's isolation could make things easier for her.

"What about you?" Kate said. "You have family in Chicago?"

"I grew up in Washington state," Ingrid said. "I still have family back there, but I haven't talked to any of them in years."

"Oh, how come?"

Ingrid took a deep breath and let it out. "None of them ever liked me."

"Oh now," Kate demurred. "At least your mother…"

"Especially not my mother. I was a different species. They were all cows or sheep. Slow moving, chewing the grass. I was like a ram or a wolf. High energy. Banging into things. And my father was kind of a pig. I made them nervous. They were glad to see the back of me."

"How often do you get back to see them?"

"I never get back."

"Don't they call you? Ask if you're coming home for Christmas?"

"They don't have my phone number anymore."

"They could mail you a note," Kate suggested.

"My van doesn't have a mailbox." She felt a slight regret. She didn't really believe they'd want to contact her, not after burning down the garage and all. But it'd be nice to know if they did.

24

Tuesday, April 11, 2005

"All right, everyone! Good fellows, well-met!" Wallace exclaimed, standing in front of them in the third-floor rehearsal room at the Chicago Repertory Arts Playhouse. He stretched out his arms to the room. "This is the space in which Dwayne," here he nodded deeply to the company artistic director seated among the actors, "led us into the wonderful production of *Romeo and Juliet*. And now I will be leading us into this wonderful production of *Oedipus Rex*!" The ensemble members politely applauded.

"Before we begin our first read-through of the script," Wallace continued. "I want to welcome the cast. Coco as Jocasta!" Everyone clapped. "Rocky as Creon. Melinda as Antigone!" He continued on through most of the casting, getting applause for every role. Then he stopped and scanned the actors with his eyes. "I do have a few changes." He held up a finger to stave off any objections. "No changes to the script for those of you who have fully memorized your lines, as I requested. Like professional companies, we are only rehearsing three weeks rather than the longer five or even six weeks storefront productions demand."

"Yeah, about that?" Coco said. "Professional companies rehearse eight hours a day, not three hours a night, like storefront companies."

"Yes, yes, yes, that's true," Wallace said. "But *Oedipus* is a short script. And with this ensemble of seasoned actors, accustomed to working with one another, we shall have no problem. Am I right, Dwayne?"

Dwayne smiled and shrugged. *No problem* was not part of his experience, no matter how many weeks of rehearsal he scheduled.

"All right then," Wallace continued. "As I said, I do have a few changes because of some intriguing new possibilities. First and foremost, in casting." The actors looked at one another with the first intimations of alarm. "One of the original ensemble members has returned to Chicago. It seemed impossible for me to contemplate, after having met and gotten to know him, that I would not use him in *Oedipus Rex*. In fact, it seemed patently necessary that I use him *as* Oedipus Rex. Stand up, Bobby."

Bobby stood up and waved to the rest of the cast.

"What the everlasting fuck?" Orlando said incredibly loudly.

"I know this must come as a disappointment…" Wallace began.

"A disappointment?" Orlando shouted. "You asked me to memorize the role. I walked in here today off-book. All that for nothing? You've got to be kidding me!"

"You won't be without a role," Wallace said. "I'd like you to play the Shepherd."

"The Shepherd? I memorized Oedipus. I told everyone I was playing Oedipus!"

"You told me to prepare the Shepherd," Tom piped in. "I'm fired?"

"No, no, Tom," Wallace said. "You're promoted. I want you to play the Leader of the Chorus."

"All right now," Ry drawled. "You asked me to play the Leader of the Chorus. You asked me to prepare a folk music scheme to support the action."

"I'm sorry, Ry. I talked to you about the music before I talked with Ingrid about the choreography. We won't use a folk music theme, after all. The music will be percussion only: the pounding of the staffs by the chorus."

"Stupid motherfucker," Ry said, barely loud enough to be heard. He gathered up his things and headed toward the door.

"Wait, wait, wait," Wallace called. "That doesn't mean you're out. I still want you as a chorus member."

Ry kept moving out the door.

"Actually," Coco said. "I think that *do* mean he's out."

"Well, that was unfortunate," Wallace said. "I don't want him to go away mad."

"That ship has sailed," Coco said.

"You know what?" Orlando said. "I'm with Ry." He gathered up his things and headed out the door.

"Oh dear," Wallace said. "I think I miscalculated how this might go."

"Dwayne?" Ingrid said. All the actors looked to him.

This was a novel situation. It was the first time Dwayne was not the director of a show but was still the leader of the company. How would he navigate this? He'd unintentionally put Wallace in the director's chair.

King Lear tried to give away his leadership duties. We know how that turned out. So even though the company was not on a course Dwayne chose, he still had to lead. He sighed and stood up, but before he could speak, Rocky stood up. "This is the way it is, people," he said. "Sometimes heads will roll. The director is the director. Suck it up."

"Rocky?" Dwayne said. "Not helpful."

Rocky looked around at the other cast members, who mostly looked deeply disturbed. He shrugged and sat down.

"Okay," Dwayne said. "I'm going to say a few words. This is Wallace's first time out as a director. We can all agree he's made some big mistakes right off the bat."

Coco and Bobby laughed. Others shouted various epithets. Wallace stood back behind Dwayne, looking painfully stoic.

"So Ry and Orlando have left the room," Dwayne said.

"Say, Dwayne," Wallace piped in. "I know you intended to sit this one out, but how would you feel about playing the Shepherd?"

Dwayne held up a hand to him and turned back to the other actors.

"Most of you are ensemble members," Dwayne said. "A few of you, Wallace cast for your first show with us." The few strangers in the crowd nodded at Dwayne. "There is no production without a willing cast." He turned to Wallace. "Any more changes? Does everyone now know the roles you want them to play?" Wallace gave him a regretful nod.

"Okay then. Wallace has made disturbing changes at the last minute. We are three weeks away from tech. Are you willing to forgive a first-time director and get behind *Oedipus Rex,* or do we cancel this show?"

"Ut…up," Ingrid stuttered. "We can't cancel the show!" she said. "We have to pay the rent on the rehearsal room and the performance space, whether we do the show or not. What if *you* direct, Dwayne?"

"Now, now, now," Wallace rumbled.

"The board gave Wallace this slot," Dwayne said evenly. "The question remains: does he have a cast? I'd suggest we forgive him. One of the joys of being in an ensemble is getting to do things we might not otherwise have a chance to do. We get roles we might not get in competition with every other actor in the city. We get to develop deep onstage partnerships by doing role after role together. We've all seen Wallace as a fine actor. What might he do as a director? It's up to you. Do we cancel this show today? Or do you want to continue on with Wallace?"

"And Ingrid," Ingrid said.

"Yes, and Ingrid as choreographer," Dwayne added, thinking maybe that wasn't the best thing to add at this moment.

"May I?" Joan said, her voice typically without emotion.

Dwayne had no idea what she wanted to say. "Yes," he said anyway.

"Take fifteen," Joan announced. "Come back prepared to answer Dwayne's question."

"Thank you, fifteen," all the actors responded. A moment of stunned silence was followed by a cacophony of debate.

25

Thursday, April 13, 2005

"We've got an afternoon of tests ahead of us." Doctor Brenner looked up from his screen and gave Angela a reassuring smile. It might have been a side effect of being married to a director, but the doctor looked to Angela like someone who could have been cast for this role. Graying at the temples. Strong jaw. Intelligent and sympathetic eyes. And that reassuring smile. Did they teach that smile in medical school?

"You'll start with a blood test and ultrasound with my nurse, and then I'll be back for the scope."

"Okay, doctor."

Angela had taken one of her precious personal days for this. Neither her health insurance nor her schedule allowed for easy access to this treatment.

"From our interview, I can't help but think your stress levels have something to do with your difficulty conceiving," Doctor Brenner said. "It might be that no matter what we do, you won't conceive until you are off for the summer. You don't teach summer school, do you?"

"Actually, I've taught summer school every year," she admitted. "Dwayne and I carry a lot of debt."

"Sometimes the body resists bringing new life to an overstressed situation. I don't know if you have any options for reducing the stress, but if you do, it could be the key."

So, was this doctor giving her the real goods, or was he providing an advance excuse in case he couldn't help her get pregnant?

"You know what's also stressful, doctor?" She leaned in toward him with what her students called her intense, *beady-eyed look*. "I'm a career teacher. Making my job the problem is an extremely stressful proposition."

"I can see how that would be the case," the doctor said, leaning back. He slid his chair away from her a little. "I can only make suggestions. It's up to you to see what's useful."

"Yes, of course." Angela felt only slightly regretful for her outburst. "I'd like to take a year off, but we can't afford that."

"Don't schools offer a sabbatical year? Maybe this is the time to take that."

Right, Angela thought. *Like the CPS is going to offer me a year off with pay to get knocked up.* "I'm sure that's worth looking into," she said dourly.

"Good," Doctor Brenner said, intentionally missing her tone and patting the back of her hand. "The nurse will be in to give you instructions for today's tests. Then we'll see what's what. After the scope, we can have another conversation and see where we are. And, of course, we need to have your husband come in to take a look at his sperm."

He exited quickly.

Teaching had always been stressful. Last week, the janitor stopped a fifth grader bringing a handgun into the school. You had neighborhood violence. You had active shooter drills. Thinking that some madman with an assault rifle could come into the school and start shooting kids and teachers at any minute upped the stress for everyone. Plus, there was the constant stress of keeping order. You always had some disruptive kids. Even though Angela was really good at it, it demanded a constant level of alertness that wore on you. Then you had the shifting demands from the school district, constantly updating their standards, changing what they thought would improve learning results. And now her new principal demanded more and more documentation, as though that would accomplish anything other than pulling their focus from teaching the kids. Plotz was ridiculous. He should just let the teachers do their jobs!

She realized her hands were trembling, just thinking about it. That couldn't be good for her health. It wasn't good for her happiness. Apparently, it wasn't good for getting knocked up, either.

Dwayne finally had a good-paying job with Rocky Nesbit. Maybe between his new job and his rising reputation as a director, she could afford to take a leave of absence. Imagine taking a few years off to take care of their new baby! She could go back to work once the kid was a toddler and ready for preschool. Or even kindergarten. To spend the first five years at home with the baby until kindergarten! What a luxury that would be! By the time she came back, Norman Plotz would be long gone. That Iowa hayseed couldn't possibly last.

Maybe everything would work out beautifully.

Two hours later, after enduring a series of tests culminating in one that was painful enough she wished they'd given her drugs, she was sitting across from Dr. Brenner once again. His smile was not so reassuring now.

"Well, it's not just stress," he said. He went into a longish technical explanation that Angela could not follow. Angela was a college-educated woman, and the nomenclature of fertility was not totally foreign. But the expression on the doctor's face and her own disappointment interfered with truly following what he said.

"So," he said at last, "here's what I think we should do. Let's start with medication. Let's have a look at your husband. Let's watch what the medication does. Also see if there's some way you can reduce stress. I still think that's a factor. Maybe look for assistance from a therapist. If we don't get anywhere with medication, we can talk about in vitro fertilization. One way or the other, we'll get you started on that family you want." He gave her a wan smile and got up. "The nurse will be in with your prescription. She can answer any questions you have about the drug regimen."

And he was gone.

Questions? Yes, she had questions. Like what the hell had he just told her?

26

Saturday, April 15, 2005

"They're taking his direction, but you can still see the suspicion in their eyes," Dwayne said. He raised a finger, and Barry came down the bar. "A pint of Guinness for me."

"Hennessey neat," Aleister added. The bartender nodded and went away to get their drinks. Aleister swiveled his barstool to face Dwayne. "Rookie mistakes?"

"Re-casting the first day of rehearsal goes beyond rookie mistakes. They decided to forgive Wallace and do the show. Actors can be amazingly generous. Plus, they'd already memorized their roles."

"Makes sense," Aleister said.

Barry brought their drinks. They clicked glasses and drank.

"Since Ry and Orlando quit, I'm playing the Shepherd. I'm not called for many rehearsals, but it's enough to keep a little eye on him. But how are you? Last time I saw you, you were looking pretty down."

Aleister took a long, deep breath. "I think I might have made a mistake writing *The Soul in Grief.*"

"Why? You're getting great reviews. You're going on *Oprah*. It all looks fantastic."

"My latest new client lost his wife to gun violence. He came to me because of the book. Listening to him reminds me so much of Alison that I can't hear him properly. After the sessions, I'm so depressed, I feel like I should give up my practice. Writing the book backfired."

"You can't give up your practice." Dwayne set down his glass. Becoming a psychiatrist had been Aleister's dream since high school. Going through medical school, his residency, all that work, had been monumental. Alison had supported the two of them through that long, expensive slog until he could begin his practice. And he was unique. Unlike most psychiatrists, he relied on talk therapy as much as drugs. He'd become amazingly successful. First as a popular therapist and now as a self-help author.

Aleister lowered his voice. "I'm not doing right by my clients." He swiveled on his barstool to see if anyone was listening. Two stools down, two young women chatted excitedly. They weren't hearing Aleister.

"You're probably doing better than you realize," Dwayne said. "But if some clients are difficult for you, you could refer them to someone else."

"That's just it. *All* my new clients are coming in with intractable grief of some kind. It's hard with all of them. I wrote the book because that was *my* problem. It's rebounding on me with a vengeance."

"You should approach your client sessions like an actor," Dwayne suggested.

"What do you mean?"

"Sometimes you get a role that's loaded with baggage," Dwayne said. "Rage or grief or you're playing a rapist or something. If you're Anthony Hopkins, you don't want to take Hannibal Lecter home every night. It's destructive to your life. You have to create boundaries around it so you can live it fully onstage, but walk away from it at the end of the night."

"How do you do that?"

"The question is: how would *you* do that?" Dwayne put some money on the bar and got up from his stool. "You've always done so much for me. Finally, I get to do something for you. Come with me."

"We're abandoning our drinks?"

"Yes." He led Aleister out of the John Barleycorn Memorial Pub down the street to the Chicago Repertory Arts Playhouse and up to the rehearsal room on the third floor, which he knew was empty. The *Oedipus* rehearsal this afternoon had been the only thing scheduled. Actors were bustling around the backstage areas, getting ready for the Saturday evening performances. Dwayne used his key to get into the rehearsal room and closed it behind them.

"When I play a really loaded role, I perform a ritual of meditation techniques before the show and then another set after to let all those emotions go." Dwayne pulled two chairs into the center of the rehearsal space. He signaled Aleister to sit in one. "For you, the role you are playing is Dr. George Aleister, M.D."

"A role? I'm pretending to be myself?" he said, taking the seat.

"Right."

"What is the point of pretending I'm myself instead of simply *being* myself?"

"The point is creating a container for doing your job that doesn't bleed into the rest of your life. You want to do this magnificent service that you've trained to do and love to do, and not feel like quitting afterwards."

"Well, if it works, it'll be an amazing thing."

"Oh, it works," Dwayne said. "It's something I've taught to other actors. There's no reason it shouldn't work for you."

Aleister began laughing.

"What?" Dwayne said.

"In your *Oedipus* rehearsal today, you had to watch someone else directing, so then you make us abandon our drinks so you can direct me instead."

"And what do you call this? Bouncing the attention away from yourself. What's that called? Deflection?"

"Yeah, well, not exactly, but never mind. You win." Aleister spread his arms in a gesture of submission. "Teach me, oh Master."

27

Sunday, April 16, 2005

"Okay, and then both arms up to the side." Ingrid demonstrated the move for the chorus members. They all had dance experience and were able to follow her direction. Tom, playing the Leader of the Chorus, had a doubtful look on his face, but he replicated the movements perfectly. "Good! Okay, now let's take the whole thing with the lines."

Wallace stood up from behind the director's table. "Hang on a minute, Ingrid." He spoke in a quiet baritone meant just for her ear, but it put everyone in the room on the alert. She looked annoyed, but walked over to him. "Do you think they're beginning to look a little *too* much like…cheerleaders?" he suggested.

"This is the style we agreed to, Wallace," she said pointedly. "We can discuss after rehearsal, but don't interrupt while I'm working with the cast."

"Um…hmm…" he rumbled. He turned away from her to face Tom. "How does this seem to you, Tom? You're the real choreographer."

"Wallace," Ingrid said, loud enough to set everyone's nerves on edge. "Sit down or go away until I'm finished."

"Now that I'm seeing this, I'm not sure we are on the right track," Wallace said. "What if we had Tom take over?"

"Oh, dear God!" Tom exclaimed. "First, I was the Shepherd, then you moved me to Chorus Leader, and now I'm supposed to choreograph this thing? What the living, technicolor hell?"

After Tom's outburst, there was silence as everyone noticed the dangerous look on Ingrid's face.

"Is there any reason," she said, evenly and quietly, but loud enough in the overwhelming silence that no one could hear anything but her, "any reason in the world that I should not fire you right now?"

"Fire me?" Wallace said. "I'm the director. You're the choreographer. I outrank you."

"I am executive director of this company. I *outrank* everyone."

Wallace looked deeply shocked. He turned to Joan. "Can she do that?"

Joan got up. "Take ten, everyone," she said.

"Thank you, ten," all the actors said. Every one of them, other than Ingrid, Joan, and Wallace, left the rehearsal room. Dwayne was not called today.

Joan looked at a point ten inches above Wallace's head. "Listen to me," she said. "You will make no more personnel changes or alterations of responsibility in the course of these rehearsals, tech, or performance." Wallace made a sound of objection, but she held up a hand to his face. "You will not interrupt any personnel in carrying out their duties in the course of these rehearsals, tech, or performance. Do you understand?" He made one more sound of objection, but she continued again. "Ingrid and I are two-thirds of the board of directors of this company, and if we decide you are out, you are out."

Wallace opened his mouth and then closed it, opened it again, and again closed it.

"Do you understand?" Joan said.

"I believe I do," he said at last.

When the actors returned, Ingrid went back to directing the movement without interruption. The cast was unusually quiet, and everyone left afterwards with a minimum of the usual hubbub.

After they were gone, and Joan had put the room back to rights, she called Dwayne. "What is the responsibility of the artistic director vis-à-vis a production he is not personally directing?"

Dwayne looked up from the tome he'd been reading, deep in *King Lear* theatrical theory. "An artistic director's responsibility is to select the best work for his company and put the most appropriate people in positions of authority and let them do their work," he said.

"Oh," Joan said. "Okay." She hung up.

Now, why was she asking that? he wondered. But he was soon lost back in the world of *King Lear.*

28

Sunday, April 23, 2005

Dwayne was in for the Sunday afternoon rehearsal the following week. He arrived just before the work was to begin, so he didn't get to talk to the other cast members, but he noticed some of them looking at him quizzically. Everyone seemed unusually quiet. Joan called everyone to order, and Wallace blocked the Shepherd's scene, Dwayne's only scene in the show, and they ran it twice before moving on to the next scene. As soon as Dwayne sat down in the chairs, Ingrid was at his side.

"Come with me," she whispered in his ear as Wallace began work on the next scene. "You're not going to believe this!"

"Am I done for the day?" he whispered to Joan.

"As an actor, yes," she replied. "You're leaving?"

"Ingrid wants to show me something."

She shook her head. "Whatever."

Ingrid pulled his arm, and he followed her down the stairs, through the lobby, and out onto the sidewalk in front.

"Feast your eyes!" she shouted. She swept her arm in the direction of an old car parked by the curb.

Dwayne looked up the street. "What am I looking at?"

"The magnificent Pinto, silly." She waved her arm at it again.

"This thing?" Dwayne stepped closer to a rusty old Ford Pinto in a hideous shade of orange. The passenger side fender was crunched and rust-marked from a minor traffic scuffle. The tires looked bald. It hadn't been washed since the twentieth century. "Why am I looking at this?"

"It's yours!" she shouted. "Well, ours, actually. But you'll be the main driver. It's our first company car. Because we're in production at the Goodman, we've got two free designated parking spots. That's too good to pass up. So I found this beast." She patted the hood of the car affectionately. "A guy I knew was getting rid of it. He just wanted a hundred dollars. Can you imagine? A hundred bucks."

Dwayne walked around the pathetic-looking vehicle. "Well, actually, yeah," he said. "I can easily imagine."

"Sure, maybe back in the eighties you could get a beater for a hundred bucks, but not anymore. This was a steal."

"Was it though?"

"How many storefront companies have a company car? This is huge!" She gave him an enormous grin.

"Huh," Dwayne said.

"You've got a vehicle to drive to rehearsals and performances, and park in one of our free Goodman-provided parking spots. And now we have a second vehicle for picking stuff up and whatever, so it's not just me in my van anymore. It makes sense! You're going to love it." She tossed him a set of keys. "Let's take it for a spin!"

Ingrid meant this car to play a part in her long-term plans. She really needed to nail down parking spots in the Loop. Her next step would be to figure out how to keep the spots permanently. She couldn't rely on Kate's garage forever. She needed a base of operations downtown.

"Okay," Dwayne said. He walked out into the street to the driver's side door and unlocked it. Ingrid hopped in the passenger side. He pulled on the door; it opened three inches, made a hideous metallic squeal, and stopped. He pulled harder. He couldn't pull it out more than a few inches, and then the door would pop back closed like a spring.

"The hell?"

"Pull harder," Ingrid yelled. "It has a little rust problem."

Dwayne pulled and pulled and pulled again, but the door would not release past the five-inch open spot.

"Hang on!" Ingrid shouted. She carefully hoisted her legs and buttocks over the hand brake and stick shift in the space between the front bucket seats and put the flat of her feet against the door. "Now!" she shouted.

Dwayne pulled, and Ingrid pushed with both feet. The door gave a teeth-grindingly horrifying, soul-panicking scream of rust-complaining metal, and sprang open past the stuck point.

"See?" Ingrid said. "It's fine." She pulled her legs back over the stick shift so that Dwayne could get into the driver's seat.

"Have you driven this thing?" Dwayne said.

"Of course I've driven it," she said. "How do you think it got here? Divine intervention?"

"Wouldn't surprise me," he muttered.

"Start it up!" she commanded.

Dwayne slid the key into the ignition and turned. *Rum! Rum! Rum! Rum! Rum!* the starter motor said. Dwayne let up on the key.

"Don't stop!" Ingrid said. "Give it some gas. Johnny had the thing sitting around, so it's a little sluggish. Once we blow the carbon out of the cylinders, it'll hum like a top."

"Like a top, huh?" Dwayne turned the key again. *Rum! Rum! Rum! Rum! Rum!* the starter motor said. *Rum! Rum! Rum! Rum! Rum!* Dwayne let up on the key and turned it again, all the while pumping the gas. *Rum! Rum! Rum! Rum! Rum!*

"Okay, okay!" Ingrid said. "Don't flood the engine." Ingrid hopped out with her tool bag, opened the hood, and began working at something under there. Dwayne was going to get out, but he couldn't get the door open again.

"Okay," she shouted. "Turn it over now."

Dwayne turned the key, applied the gas, and the engine roared into life. It was surprisingly loud for a little car.

"Okay," she shouted enthusiastically as she hopped back in the car and tossed her tool bag into the back seat. "Purrs like a cat, huh?"

The car had a scary, deep-throated rumble. "Like a jungle cat, maybe, while devouring the natives. How about a new muffler?"

"Mufflers…" Ingrid blew a raspberry. "This vehicle had a rust hole in the exhaust pipe. I wrapped a V-8 juice can around the exhaust pipe and tightened it on with a pair of clamps. Quieted it right down."

"It was louder than this?"

Ingrid blew a raspberry again. "Come on. Let's take it for a spin."

Dwayne pulled the Pinto into traffic and accelerated up Lincoln Avenue. He noticed clouds of black smoke behind them. "This thing is an ecological disaster."

"I'll put something in the oil," Ingrid said. "Take it out to Lake Shore Drive so we can blow some carbon out of this thing."

Dwayne turned right on Fullerton and drove down to the lake and turned onto the entrance ramp going north up Lake Shore Drive. The engine sounded like an amped up Harley-Davidson motorcycle. Out the rear-view mirror it looked like he was driving a mosquito fogger.

"Hit it!" Ingrid said. "Blow that carbon out!"

He pressed harder on the accelerator, and the roar of the engine deepened, and the fog behind them swirled like the beginnings of a tornado. "Yeah! That's it!" Ingrid yelled.

Dwayne glanced over at the passenger in the car next to them, who was looking back at him with a quizzical, annoyed expression. Dwayne felt grateful it was no one he knew.

"Now, isn't this better than sitting in a stupid *Oedipus* rehearsal?" Ingrid shouted.

He wasn't sure it was.

29

Friday, May 5, 2005

Oedipus had just two run-throughs before it went into tech, and Dwayne felt nervous. He'd only attended the rehearsals for his scene as the Shepherd. He hadn't realized how much the show was struggling. The actors were unnaturally loud, and the movement and the percussive pounding of the chorus members' staffs looked disturbingly like a pompon squad. This was much worse than he'd anticipated.

"Listen, Wallace," Dwayne said, taking him aside. "This show is awfully heavy on the bombast."

"Isn't it, though?" Wallace said enthusiastically. "This cast is just terrific!"

Dwayne stopped for a moment. Did Wallace think he was praising?

"No, what I mean to say is, I'd like you to get more variety out of their performances. It's like they're all angry all the time. We need more subtlety. More variety. More quiet moments."

"Oh, sure, Dwayne," Wallace agreed. "And I won't lose the epic approach they've mastered. I'm really proud of these guys."

"You do understand what I'm saying, right?" Dwayne said. "The show is too loud and overpowering right now."

"Oh, absolutely. Power-house. I'll urge them to get some more variety in that. Don't you worry."

Two days later, on Friday, May fifth, it was opening night. Wallace came through the dressing room before the show. "Okay, everyone," he said. "Remember, *Oedipus* is epic tragedy. Play it like you're playing in a Greek amphitheatre. Don't hold back." He winked at Dwayne, gave him a thumbs-up, and then swept away.

"Play it like in a Greek amphitheatre?" Dwayne said to Coco.

"If I hear him say that one more time…" She shook her head and went to the costume rack.

Like in a Greek amphitheatre. How had Dwayne missed that? Had Wallace paid any attention to Dwayne's notes?

As the show started, it was clear the cast had taken Wallace's direction to heart. They boomed out their lines. They crashed down the pounding of staffs. They stamped their feet with all their might. The sound overwhelmed all the way through the wall into the dressing room. In the sixty-seat upstairs studio, the audience's ears were ringing.

When Dwayne got out on stage for his scene, he was amazed at how loudly the other actors delivered their lines. Stage actors were typically proud of how well they could project. Especially those who'd performed Shakespeare in the park as many of these actors had done. But in this space, the audience members looked uncomfortable. Some of them held their hands over their ears.

Dwayne lowered his voice as he began his lines, but in responding to him, Bobby, playing the role of Oedipus, only got louder. When Wallace came out to play old Tiresias, he practically blew the roof off the place.

After the actors took their bows, the audience scurried out of the place, looking annoyed.

Dwayne felt depressed. He climbed to the light booth. "What did you think of that?" he asked Joan. He felt in utter shock.

"Ridiculous," she replied.

"Jesus," Dwayne said.

"You should have been coming to the rehearsals," she said.

"Why didn't you tell me?"

"I asked you what are the responsibilities of the artistic director," she said evenly. "You said to put the right people in charge and let them do their jobs."

Dwayne did remember having that exchange. "But all that shouting. There's no space for subtlety."

"Subtlety," Joan repeated. She did something that was very much like chuckling and walked off to finish her post-show duties.

Dwayne felt horrible about the whole thing. He didn't want to go to the opening night party. He felt embarrassed. *His company* had done this. He sat in the dressing room for the longest time after everyone else was gone.

What *was* his responsibility as artistic director? He'd told Joan it was to select the best works and the best people and let them do their jobs.

Right.

But he'd had no reason to think Wallace was ready to direct. Instead of supervising him, Dwayne had stayed focused on his *King Lear* research. Now he started to wonder: was Wallace ready to play King Lear? Had he misjudged that, as well?

He thought about Rocky. His law firm was highly successful, but he didn't appear to be supervising anyone, at least not in a positive way. Rocky attracted clients to the firm, and Brianna kept the place running. Between the two of them, it was a cash machine. But you couldn't say people loved working there.

Rocky achieved what King Lear did not when Lear divided his kingdom between his daughters. Rocky left all the *affairs of the state* to Brianna, but he refused to name her as CEO. He could still sweep in like a tyrant whenever he felt the urge. Otherwise, he left the operations to her and the lawyers.

Dwayne should not have left *Oedipus* so completely in Wallace's hands. Wallace, obviously, was no Brianna. And the Psychedelic Dream Theatre was no law firm.

How should Dwayne focus his leadership? On bringing out the best in his ensemble? On providing the best experience for the audience? Or should he be making sure the company was financially successful?

Whatever, he'd blown it on this one.

30

Monday, May 15, 2005

"The boss wants a word." Brianna stood at the door of his office, looking beautiful and fashionable. Her sleek, black sheath dress seemed more like cocktail attire rather than office wear. Most of the attorneys and even the office staff dressed like models in *Ebony Magazine*. However, her face looked disgusted. She hated it when Rocky came to the office.

"Okay," Dwayne said. He saved the notes he'd been making about a case from an attorney he'd just interviewed. Things had been going well here since he'd started working as the in-house public relations person. He'd written and placed four articles in the press, and he'd proposed a newsletter to be sent out to past clients. His idea was to keep past clients aware of the company's latest cases, so they'd be more likely to recommend the firm to others.

When Brianna and he arrived at Rocky's spacious corner office (twice as spacious as any other corner office in the building), Dwayne was surprised to see Chaz there.

"Come in, come in, come in," Rocky said. Rocky sat at the head of the walnut conference table with Chaz to his left. Dwayne sat where Rocky was gesturing him, to Rocky's right. Brianna remained standing at the far end of the conference table.

"This is a little progress report meeting," Rocky said. He had the periodicals in which the articles Dwayne had written were printed. "You delivered on what you promised. These case history articles make our lawyers look like heroes. You get into the backstory of the clients' injuries—really heart-tugging stuff! And then you expose the brilliant moves the lawyers make on the insurance companies or whoever might be at fault. Gripping! It makes anyone with a claim want to come to Rockwell Nesbit the Third Law. Really fantastic!"

Dwayne felt good about his accomplishments. But the good feeling passed as he noticed the look on Chaz's face.

"See…" Rocky said, elongating the eeee vowel excessively, "there is a downside here. Sorry to say. When we discussed all this public relations business, I did not realize it would entail putting our business secrets and strategy into print so that any other law firm out there could read them and say: *Well, well, well, well, look at how Rocky Nesbit is managing to make so God damned much money. Hum. Hum. Hum. We aren't making as much money as Rocky Nesbit. I think we could do those very same things that Rocky Nesbit's lawyers are doing and take away a nice chunk of all that delicious money Rocky Nesbit and his band of merry litigators are making. Why don't we do that?"*

"Well, that's not really the point…" Chaz began.

Rocky raised a finger abruptly. Chaz closed his mouth and put a hand over his finger that had been broken with a pair of pliers wielded by Rocky's hands.

"I have decided," Rocky said. "No more PR. We were doing perfectly well without it. My late-night TV commercials continue to pull in the business. My lawyers don't need to look like heroes. Rocky Nesbit is the hero! Let the clients flock to me! We tried the PR. Now we are done with it."

No one spoke for a while.

What else was there to say?

"What about him?" Brianna nodded her head in Dwayne's direction.

"What was he good at before the PR?" Rocky asked.

"Absolutely nothing," Brianna said, totally deadpan.

"Hum. Well, he was good at the PR," Rocky said. "No question. Too good. Where else can you put him that might be like that?"

"Nowhere," Brianna said.

"Nowhere?" Rocky said.

"Not a single solitary thing."

"What about you?" Rocky said to Chaz. "You won't be getting any more business from me, but he was pretty good with the PR here. You got other business you can put him on?"

Chaz looked uncomfortable. Was he being commanded to hire

Dwayne?

Dwayne felt equally uncomfortable. He didn't want to be employed by Chaz. What would that do to their friendship?

"Well, we have been moving into a new market," Chaz said. "We've got our first business-to-business clients, which is not something we've done in the past. I guess I could try Dwayne in that."

"Excellent!" Rocky clapped his hands. He walked over and shook Dwayne's hand. "Now I don't have to worry about talking theatre with you at business, because you're not working for me anymore!"

"He hasn't been here long," Brianna said. "Shouldn't he return the signing bonus?"

Rocky waved her off. "Water over the bridge. Glad to help him out. In fact, give him an equal amount as a severance package." Brianna made a choking sound, and Rocky turned his face up to the ceiling. "No! Not equal. Half the amount. That's plenty. Excellent. I'm off." And Rocky walked out of the office, down the hall, into the elevator, and out of the building.

Dwayne felt that queasy sensation of uncertainty once again. He'd been doing well here, finally! It was fun interviewing the lawyers and clients and crafting their stories into compelling case histories. He had a knack for telling human interest stories. He'd found a perfect niche, and now he was out.

He certainly wouldn't want to go back to being supervised by Brianna. That had been miserable. If he could do PR so well here, why not at Chaz's office? Still…

Brianna shook her head. "I don't get it," she said. "Even the halfway decent work you did turned out to be something he didn't want. And he gives you a severance package? What the hell? Were you sucking his dick?"

31

Friday, May 19, 2005

"Hey, Miss Guys-eye-pally." Assistant Principal Todd Bodkins approached the table where Carol, Angela, and three other teachers were sharing happy hour drinks. He smirked at his mimicry of Principal Norman Plotz's horrible mispronunciation of Angela's name. In his advanced state of inebriation, he found himself hysterical.

"Go away, Todd," Angela said.

"Hey, hey, hey!" He rocked back on his heels. "You're going to hurt my feelings. And just when I have a fantastic offer for you."

"This is a teacher table," Angela said. "It's Friday happy hour. No administrators invited." A few of the other teachers laughed at her boldness.

"That's…that's…" Todd searched for a concept. "That's…discrimination. And discrimination is illegal in the Chicago Public Schools."

"Is that right?" Angela said. "Tell me this, Mr. Racial Justice: How come the only two White men in our school are you and Plotz? Just three male teachers, all Black. The rest of the teachers are women, mixed Black and White. The maintenance staff is all Black and Latino, as is the cafeteria staff. Why is that? Why are the two top jobs White men and all the rest of us women and people of color? Does that reinforce your notion that discrimination is illegal in the Chicago Public Schools?"

"Well…" Todd looked truly confounded, then inspiration struck. He pointed a finger at Angela. "You are not even correct, Miss Guys-eye-pally! What about the school psychologist? Huh?"

"Mei is Asian American," one of the other teachers said, a mystified look on her face.

"Exactly!" Todd exclaimed. "Not Black. Not White. I rest my

case."

"Thank God for you, Todd," Angela said. "You really are the brain trust."

Todd leaned in to her ear and whispered. "I looked up the specialty of the doctor you saw on your personal day. If your husband is having a hard time giving you a baby, I've got four kids already, and we weren't even trying. I'm happy to step in."

Angela felt the pressure of rage rush into her head. She hadn't liked including her doctor's name on her personal day request. And this sleaze-bag had read it and looked him up?

She stood up so abruptly that her chair clattered to the floor behind her and her rising shoulder caught Todd on the underside of the chin, making his teeth clack together like a pair of castanets. Already off-balance and staggering backward, she gave him a good shove with both hands to help him along. He tumbled backward, his head rocking back with a thump against the wood floor of the bar.

He sat up, rubbing the back of his head. "Fuck! That hurts."

"Get your ass out of here before I call your wife to come collect you," Angela said.

"My God, what did he say to you?" Carol asked. All the teachers were chattering in a mixture of astonishment and horror.

"That's assault," Todd said. "I could have you up on charges."

"Yeah, let's call a cop right now," Angela said. She pulled out her phone and extended it toward him. "And then I can file a grievance with the union. Let's see how that turns out."

"Hey," Todd said, now looking embarrassed. "Come on, Angela. A little joke between friends. A little joke! Let's not get all…litigious about it."

"Get out, Todd. Maybe if I have another margarita, I'll forget what you said."

"What did he say?" Carol asked again.

"Never mind." The last thing Angela wanted was everyone discussing her fertility. The medication Dr. Brenner put her on sometimes made her feel queasy, and Dwayne's seed had not yet been tested. Why was everything taking so long? The whole business annoyed her.

Todd got uncertainly to his feet. He stood for a moment, thinking things over, and then pulled out his wallet. He put three twenties on the table. "I was out of line. Next round is on me." He turned and left without another word. Five seconds after he was out the door, the women all cheered. Even Angela smiled a little.

32

Sunday, June 3, 2005

"What do we do about this?" Joan asked Dwayne. "Look at them." There wasn't the usual camaraderie as the cast carried the pieces of the *Oedipus* set down to Ingrid's van. As soon as they were done, they were gone. A few of them headed down to John Barleycorn for a closing night drink, but there was no big celebration. The show sold poorly through the run, and the small audiences who had shown up always looked overwhelmed by the Greek-amphitheatre-level performances. Some nights had no audience. After the second week, they dropped Thursday nights from the schedule altogether.

It did not feel like a good way to head toward their debut at the Goodman.

"Every company has a dud or two," Ingrid said cheerfully, tying down the platforms in the trailer behind her van. "Even Steppenwolf had shows that sucked. No big deal. We still have money in the bank."

"*Oedipus* lost thirteen thousand dollars," Joan said. "That's more than the entire budget of *Titus Andronicus*. And what did we spend it on? You just had these platforms and a few fake pillars for a set."

"We had more money. We spent more money," Ingrid said simply. She went back to stuffing cardboard boxes of folded costumes into the back of the company Pinto. Peaches had folded them, labeled the boxes, left them on the sidewalk, and disappeared with the rest of the cast. "So *Oedipus* wasn't optimal. But wait until you see our new digs!" she said excitedly. "We've got space to store things. We've got space to rehearse, rent-free. We could even think about performing there!"

"Getting licensed for a performance space is no easy task," Joan said.

"Don't forget," Ingrid said. "I *know* people."

Dwayne got behind the wheel of the Pinto and turned the key. *Rum! Rum! Rum!* the starter motor said, but the engine did not start. "Oh shit," Ingrid said. She got under the hood of the Pinto with her screwdriver to the carburetor, and Dwayne was able to start the car.

Ingrid and Joan got into Ingrid's van, since the entire back of the Pinto and the passenger seat were filled with costumes and props. Dwayne followed the van with its bouncy trailer stacked with wooden platforms to an industrial district some miles west of the Loop. They pulled up in front of an old factory.

In the block to the east of them, *The Onion*, a satirical newspaper, had some kind of studio on one side of the street with a metal plating factory on the other. On this block, all the buildings looked vacant. Large parking lots lay between them with weeds growing up out of the cracks in the pavement. A rusting, graffiti-covered school bus sat on flat tires in one of them.

They heard the rattle of the CTA on the elevated tracks two blocks south of them, heading into the west side and toward Oak Park.

"This is charming," Joan said dourly.

"Wait till you see!" Ingrid unlocked the heavy wooden front door and tugged it hard to open. She led them into a foyer. A waist-high wood partition with a glass window above separated it from a receptionist's desk on the other side. She opened a second door to a wide-open factory floor. "Feast your eyes. All rent-free!"

They could see where machines had once stood. The concrete of the floor was a brighter color where the machines had protected it from the daily assaults of oils, dirt, and wear from years of activity. The ceiling made a high arc overhead, with beams stretching across the space and beams radiating up from the center like spokes to support the arching roof. Chain hoists hung from some of the beams. Along the east side of the space, a wall sectioned off a row of offices with a series of doors.

"Wow, huge," Dwayne said. "You could put quite a theatre in here."

"This is more square footage than the Theatre Building on Belmont. And the height of that roof! You could have three or four good-sized theatre spaces in here with plenty of room for sound isolation between them. And room to build sets! And room for rehearsal space! And room to host benefits! I mean, it's endless. After the Goodman, to move into our own theatre? This is the next logical step!"

"That'd take a lot of money," Joan said.

"Oh, yeah," Ingrid agreed. "To do it right? Our money would be a drop in the bucket. But to set up something with the storefront aesthetic, on the cheap? We could absolutely do something wild in here. I could put a bed in one of these offices and stop living in my truck!"

"How is this rent-free?" Dwayne said.

"That's the fantastic thing." Ingrid spread out her hands to set the scene. "I know this guy. He has a load of money. He financed a local indie film. I did the sets for it. Anyway, we did some locations in this area, and he looked around. He said to me, *You know, you can buy these buildings for song. In ten years, they'll be worth ten times as much. Everything is moving west toward this.* I offered to help him find a likely building at a good price. I found this one, and he bought it, but he decided he wanted to live in San Francisco. He told me if I kept this place looking lived in, I could use it for the cost of the utilities. I just have to keep up the building so it doesn't look abandoned, because then the windows get broken and all that. But if I wanted to put a theatre in here, all the better, because that would make property values go up faster."

"That's crazy," Dwayne said.

"Let me see that lease," Joan said.

Ingrid led Joan into the reception area. The lease was in a manila envelope on the desk. Joan sat down to read it while Ingrid continued to give Dwayne a tour.

"You know what sold him on this building?" Ingrid said. "*The Onion* on the next block, and two blocks away, a pair of sculptors bought a space. He says once the artists discover a cheap area, they move in, spruce it up, and it's just a matter of time before it gentrifies and prices go through the roof. There's no bars or restaurants near here yet, so it'll take time. He figures a decade. So we should have this space for ourselves for some time."

"But that also means audiences won't want to come here," Dwayne said.

"The adventurous ones will."

Joan came out of the reception area, carrying the lease. "This says we could be evicted with one week's notice."

"Well, yeah, that's true," Ingrid admitted. "But in the meantime, we can do what we want."

"Can you get a little more leeway put in this?" Dwayne said. "What if we're in the middle of doing something? A week is no time at all."

"The agreement was that I keep this place up, and I don't bother him," Ingrid said. "He wants to be able to come back in ten years or whatever, and make a bundle selling this place. He wants the maximum convenience for himself, and in return, we don't have to pay rent. It seems like a pretty good deal to me."

"I noticed this lease is not with you, it's with the Psychedelic Dream Theatre," Joan said.

"Well, yeah," Ingrid said. "He wouldn't sign with me. I have no money. The theatre company has over a hundred grand. So that was a no-brainer to him."

"All right, I'm going to have to read this way more carefully now," Joan said. "And you need to stop spending money and signing leases without consulting us." She thought for a moment. "I'm calling a board meeting to order right now. Who seconds?"

"I'll second," Dwayne said.

"The meeting is called to order. I nominate myself to replace Ingrid as treasurer. Who seconds?"

"I'll second," Dwayne said.

"Let's take a vote." Dwayne and Joan voted her in as treasurer. Ingrid looked on like she couldn't believe what was happening.

"You two don't like me as executive director and treasurer? I'm always finding us golden opportunities!" she said.

"Checks and balances," Joan replied. "We three are liable for this company's debts. I don't intend to let that bite me in the ass."

33

Wednesday, June 6, 2005

Ingrid was excited. Finally, she'd have a solution! She pulled into an alley in the North Central neighborhood. It was just a few blocks from the Breadline Theatre on Berenice where she'd designed a few sets. ATC was around the block on Lincoln Avenue. She hadn't worked there yet, but hoped she would. It was a block of modest brick bungalows and two flats and bigger apartment buildings on the corners.

When she got to the fifth garage down the alley, the old man and Davy were already there, talking. The garage door and the back of Davy's van were both open. Ingrid pulled over her van and hopped out. This would be great!

Davy was the key. He'd designed lights and sound for some of the first shows Ingrid had done in Chicago. Then he'd moved on to doing sound and lights for rock shows at small clubs, then bigger clubs, and then he graduated into really big shows. He'd done Kid Rock, and My Chemical Romance, and Kiss, and Billy Idol, and the Dropkick Murphys. He'd even been one of the stagehands for The Rolling Stones at the United Center and Comiskey Park. He was a good guy. But best of all, he'd learned a lot about onstage pyrotechnics.

She joined Davy and the old man in the alley. "See, I got the designs from Popular Mechanics," the old man was telling Davy. They walked into the garage, which was crowded around on all sides with piles of junk. He gestured to pair of huge speakers stacked in the corner. "You base the inner cabinet volume on the low frequency response of the woofer, but you also have to account for the volume needed for the midrange, the volume of the port and the space occupied by the physical drivers in the system. I'm talking about volume in cubic centimeters, not volume in decibels."

"I hear you," Davy said. "Hey, Ingrid!" Davy smacked her hand in greeting.

"Davy," she said. "Wow. These must be the speakers."

They were monumental. She was glad. Connecting Davy with speakers like these would totally make him happy. Trading favors was how you got things done.

The bottom speaker was triangular shaped to fit in the corner of a room. It stood nearly five feet tall and four feet wide, made of unfinished plywood stained by decades of age. A huge woofer filled the bottom, partially baffled over with plywood. A large horn with a body of cast iron occupied the space all the way across the top. A big rectangular-shaped speaker cabinet sat atop it, just as large. The plywood cabinet of the second one had a surface layer of something like linoleum.

"You must be the girl that called about the speakers," the old man said.

"I am," Ingrid said. "So nice to meet you." Ingrid always kept her eyes on the classifieds for useful stuff being given away or sold cheap. When she read about these speakers, she saw an opportunity. She'd connect Davy with the speakers. Davy would teach her how to put fire on the Goodman stage.

"Yeah, these babies put out an amazing sound," the old man said. "Building the cabinets with the right baffle shapes is one thing, but then designing the crossover is a whole other issue. You have to measure each driver for frequency response and electrical impedance. It's a lot. A friend of mine did a similar setup. He had everything right, and then he ruined it with sloppy soldiering." The old man laughed. "Can you imagine? All that work and then sloppy soldering?" He shook his head. "What a moron."

"So, why are you giving them up?" Davy asked.

"I didn't make them pretty. The wife got tired of looking at them." He sighed. "So I brought them out here to the garage, and I thought I'd figure something out. I finally realized I'm never going to figure anything out. I don't want them to go to waste."

"They won't go to waste with this guy," Ingrid said. "He's a sound guy for big concerts and clubs."

"Yeah," Davy said. "A buddy of mine and I plan to open a music club. We could build these into the house sound system. Whole loads of people will enjoy them."

"That'd be nice," the old man said. He laid a hand on one of the speakers. "I put a lot of labor into these. We had some nice parties. The sound was amazing."

Ingrid noticed a tear forming in his eye.

"It's nice your work will live on." She patted the old man on the back, and he nodded. "Davy will send you an invite to hear them when the club opens, right, Davy?"

"Absolutely," Davy said. "Free admission for life. My honor."

"You kids go ahead and take them." He sounded choked up. "Just close the garage door when you're done." He shuffled back into the house.

"Poor guy," Davy said. "It's like he's giving up his pets."

"Better they get used than sit here until he dies and his kids junk them," Ingrid said.

They muscled the big rectangular cabinet off the top into the back of Davy's van and pushed it as far forward as possible. But when they lifted the larger, triangular cabinet from the garage floor into the van, a rat jumped out of the bottom of the cabinet and disappeared under the front seats.

"Motherfucker!" Davy shouted. "A fucking rat! And now it's in my van. I can't drive around with a rat in my van. It'll come out and bite me in the back of the leg." He opened the front doors of the van. "You stand behind and watch. I have to know he gets out." He began banging on the walls of his van, yelling at the rat to get out. He pounded on the van until he had to stop and shake the pain out of his hands.

"God damn it, Ingrid. I wish I'd never come here."

"Hey, hey, be cool, Davy. The rat is just scared. He's hiding."

"I don't care about the rat's fucking psychological condition!"

"Right," Ingrid said. She had to think. If she didn't get the rat out of there, she'd be lucky if Davy ever talked to her again, and she didn't know anyone else who knew anything about stage pyrotechnics.

She couldn't hire someone with company money now that Joan was keeping an eye on the dollars. She needed fire, and it had to be safe.

Ha! That gave her an idea. She ran to her van and grabbed her CO_2 fire extinguisher. It's not like she didn't believe in fire safety. She had a propane stove built in to the back of her van. She kept the fire extinguisher in case a fire broke out from cooking.

"Okay, Davy, you watch on the driver's side." Ingrid pointed the fire extinguisher under the passenger seat and blasted the CO_2. She could hear little claws scrambling and the panicked squeals of a terrified rodent. The rat scrambled out from under the passenger seat to under the driver's seat, but Ingrid pursued him relentlessly, fogging the truck with billows of CO_2. Then she heard Davy whoop and holler.

"Yes, ma'am! All right. The little bastard jumped out!"

"Okay," Ingrid said. "But now stick your head in the van and keep watch."

Davy looked confused, but he stuck his head in the driver's side door and watched as Ingrid circled around to the back of the van. She stuck the extinguisher nozzle into the bottom of the triangular speaker cabinet and blasted it with CO_2. More squeals erupted from within the cabinet and two more rats scrambled out, but these two headed right out the back of the van and into the alley and away.

Ingrid gave it several more safety blasts. Hearing nothing further, she blasted the rectangular cabinet, as well, though since it had been up atop the other cabinet, there was little chance rats had made their way into it. And indeed, they heard no rodent squeals from with that one.

Then Ingrid blasted the heck out of the entirety of Davy's van, just to make sure it had no more uninvited guests.

"I think you're good, pal," she said at last.

"That was genius," Davy said. "Okay, let me show you something." He pulled a twenty-pound propane tank from the back of his van and connected a hose to a length of black pipe with a cap on the end. The pipe was drilled with angled holes all along the sides.

"This pipe was a prototype from Barry Johnson of Apex Stage Pyrotechnics to test a concept." Davy turned on the gas and held a lighter to the side of the pipe. Flames roared from the holes in the sides of the pipe and created a spiral of fire rising up from the pipe. It was impressive.

"Wow," Ingrid said.

"Yeah," Davy said. "You can have this one. The nozzle. Not the propane tank. This is the spiral design. It's simple to make. A length of black pipe with a cap, and then drill the holes." He turned off the gas and disconnected the hose from the tank. "You can have the hose, too." He grabbed a manila envelope from this glove compartment. "There's designs in here for making about a dozen different types of nozzles. You have to make your own. It's not the kind of thing you can order on Amazon." He laughed.

Ingrid pulled the sheets from the envelope and looked them over. She *could* absolutely make these herself. This was great!

"The nozzles are not the big thing," Davy warned. "You've got to mount them safely, and then the bigger thing than that is the propane feed. You have to have absolute control over that. You also have to have people monitoring the stage at all times with effective kill switches, so if someone wanders too close to a nozzle they can cut the flames instantly. You set Mick Jagger on fire; you're in a lot of trouble."

34

Friday, June 15, 2005

Angela was free. She smiled and patted the shoulders and heads of her fifth graders as they exited her classroom for the last time. They were a nice group of kids. None of them had killed anyone. All of them had learned something. Many of them made excellent strides. For the first summer in her career, she would not be teaching summer school. They could've used the money to pay down some debt, but she and Dwayne had decided: No teaching this summer. They'd use his signing bonus and severance pay toward fertility. Probably his earnings from Chaz, as well. Finally, she was going to conceive a baby. She felt happy—until she saw Norman Plotz hurrying toward her.

"Miss Guys-eye-pally," he called to her.

She looked at him like someone had taken a shit in the hallway. "My name is Angela Guiseppelli. *Miz Joe-Say-Pelli.* Not *Miss Guys-eye-pally.*"

"Absolutely," he said, raising his super thick black eyebrows above the tops of his thick, black, plastic-rimmed glasses. "Before you take off, I'd like to have a word about the lesson plans for the coming year."

This absolute cretin.

"I came in mid-year, and perhaps we didn't get off on the right foot. But now we have the summer to regroup. Given the need to review lesson plans in time to revise and rethink, I'd like to have your first quarter's plans by July first. Then we could meet on the fifteenth to review, so I could get your revisions by August first."

"You want to see my lesson plans this summer?" Angela said.

"Right," Plotz replied. "And if it wouldn't be inconvenient, I'd like to see the second quarter lesson plans on August 10th. Those we could review after the fall semester starts."

"Where did you get your Ph.D., Mr. Plotz?"

"*Doctor* Plotz. The University of Iowa."

"I was thinking I might go back to school. Get my Ph.D. Maybe I'll become a principal. It can't be that hard, right?"

Plotz looked as though he wasn't sure if he should be insulted or not. "Actually, it's an arduous path to becoming a principal," he said. "I'll be sending out a memo about the lesson plans by the end of the day. I just wanted to give everyone a heads-up."

"Thanks," Angela said. "I'll be sure to forward it to my union rep."

"I don't think I see the point of that."

"The point is that your request violates the terms of my contract with the Chicago Public Schools. That's something of interest to my union rep."

"This isn't a contract issue, Miss Guys-eye-pally. This is in the interests of student achievement."

"Is it?" Angela said.

"If we work together, we can pull up the achievement levels. That's the whole reason I came to this school."

"Well, good for you, Mr. *Plaatz*. My responsibilities for this school year are finished. You have a terrific summer." She turned away from him, grabbed her purse and her shoulder bag, and walked on past. Even though she didn't look in his direction, she couldn't help noticing in her peripheral vision that Plotz's face was redder than normal.

Out in the parking lot, assistant principal Todd Bodkins was waiting by her car. "Did Plotz tell you his summer plans?" he whispered.

"Take it up with my union rep, Todd," Angela said, unlocking her car.

"No, no, no," Todd said. "I'm on your side. Totally. You need a principal that understands Chicago kids and parents…"

"One that doesn't try to get his hands down the lady teachers' pants would be nice, too." She slammed her car door and drove away for the summer.

35

Saturday, June 16, 2005

Dwayne took the Red Line down to the Loop and then changed to the Green Line west to the stop near the vacant factory Ingrid had found. He felt so annoyed. Once again, Ingrid had jumped ahead of everything. She purchased what she referred to as *a shitload of antiques* for the set before Dwayne had seen and approved her final sketches.

Ingrid was out in the parking lot next to the factory, wiping her hands on a rag and taking deep breaths as Dwayne walked up the cracked and crazily tilted sidewalk. In the distance to the east, the skyline of Chicago looked like the magical Land of Oz.

"Thank God you're here," Ingrid called. "I need so much help." The rusty Pinto, the van she lived in, and the rental trailer were the only three vehicles in the weedy parking lot. She slapped the trunk of the Pinto. "I fixed your car, by the way. You know how to use a manual choke?"

"I don't even know what that is."

"Ha! You're too much!" Ingrid said. "When an engine is cold, it needs more gas and less air, so you choke off the air until it starts and gets warm. Then you open up the choke so it gets a full mix of air and gas. That's what a carburetor does. It mixes gas and air. But you knew that."

"Did I?"

"Ha! Dwayne, you're a riot. Let's try it out."

Ingrid attempted to open the driver's side door, but it was rusted shut. The passenger side door was stuck, too. "Well, no matter." She opened the trunk, leaned in, and grabbed the springs that went across the back of the back seat. She lifted hard, and the back seat slid up and fell forward.

"See?" Ingrid maneuvered herself in so she was lying on her back in the trunk, then shimmied herself forward. She wriggled in and climbed over into the front seat.

"Come on in," she shouted back through the open trunk.

"Can't you kick open the passenger side door from the inside?" Dwayne shouted.

"Wimp," she muttered. She put a foot against the door while releasing the handle and gave a push from her thigh. The door gave a screaming complaint of rusted metal and opened. Dwayne got in beside her.

"See here?" She indicated a white knob below the dashboard. "That's the choke fully open, which is the opposite of all other manual chokes in the world." She pushed it in. "Now it's fully choked." She turned the key, and the Pinto started up. "Now listen!" Ingrid shouted. As it ran, the engine started to struggle. "See? The gas mixture gets too rich." She slowly pulled back on the white knob until the engine ran more smoothly. She shut it off.

"Voila!" She rolled down the driver's side window and climbed out. Dwayne exited in a more conventional manner. She tossed him a set of keys. "All yours."

"Thanks," he said. The car being such a pile of junk, he didn't feel entirely grateful, though it would be nice to drive to the Goodman and park in the garage.

He followed her into the building.

"*Holy Odo of Canterbury*," Dwayne said. Ingrid had filled half the room with ancient dressers, armoires, hutches, vanities, nightstands, chests, bookcases, desks, stools, and other objects of design he could not identify.

"Who is Holy Odo?" she asked.

"Patron of dealers in antiques and old clothes. How did you find all this?"

"How do I find things?" Ingrid laughed. "You kill me, Dwayne. After all this time: *How do I find things?* Come here." She led him over to a table against the wall. On it was a two-dimensional set rendering and a three-dimensional model. He could immediately see how it would fit on the stage of the Owen Theatre. As she had mentioned, huge stacks of antique furniture going high over the heads of the actors surrounded the background of the playing area. She'd arranged the stacks so that they gave an impression of an antebellum plantation home.

"Now watch this." She turned each of two furniture stacks one hundred eighty degrees. From the other side, the stacks gave an impression of a plantation in ruins. "See, the stacks are on trucks that we can revolve."

Dwayne turned the stacks back and forth, seeing how the impression of the space changed.

"And here's the rendering of the second position." She lifted the first drawing to show a second drawing underneath.

"I have to say, Ingrid, I love it," Dwayne said quietly. "I wasn't sure when you described it, but now that I see it, wow."

"Yeah?" she said.

"This really feeds the story."

"God, I'm so relieved," she said. "I tried to think of other ideas, but this one always crowded everything else out of my head. I think it fits your civil war idea as well as the inheritance of betrayal. When I was driving all over Illinois and Indiana and even into Kentucky and Tennessee collecting, all the time I was thinking: *If he doesn't like this, what'll I do with all this stuff?* But once I had the actual pieces, I could really see it. Look at the model. Those aren't just any pieces of antique furniture. Those are *these* pieces." She waved to the furniture around the room.

And Dwayne saw it. She'd fashioned tiny replicas of the furniture in this room from balsa wood and stained them to put in her model. "That is amazing," he said. Then he started laughing.

"What?"

"You suck as a collaborating artist," he said, "but you are something of a genius."

"No, no, no, Dwayne." She rushed toward him. "I absolutely was collaborating. I listened to what you wanted. I heard what Peaches said, and that fuck-face, Ry. I based this on the show you said you want to direct. I just didn't get you to sign off on the minutia before plunging ahead." Dwayne opened his mouth to say something about that, but she plunged on again. "But listen. Half of this stuff needs to look like prime, expensive, perfectly maintained antiques. We need to strip and re-stain a whole lot of furniture. Will you help me?"

"Wait a minute," Dwayne said. "What about the end of the show? You're not still thinking this needs to look like it's going up in flames, are you?"

Ingrid laughed abruptly. "Oh, God, no. Reg Camper and Nick Sanchez went on and on about the Iroquois Theatre fire and how we can't even light a match on stage." She laughed some more, sounding nearly hysterical. "No, no, no, no, don't worry your pretty little head about that. I'm working around that. Totally. No worries." She kept chuckling.

Something about her hilarity left Dwayne feeling deeply unsettled.

36

Monday, June 18, 2005

Dwayne looked at his watch again. He needed to get out of here. He had to drive to Itasca to visit a beverage closing machine manufacturer for Chaz. He was meeting with engineers who'd designed a new piece of equipment. He needed to leave now, but he didn't want to take the untrustworthy Pinto. At last, he heard Angela's key in the lock.

"What's up with you?" she said. "You're all dressed up."

"I was waiting for the car. I have to drive to Itasca. I told you that." He grabbed the little briefcase Chaz had given him.

"Right," Angela said, still standing square in the doorway. "I forgot about that." She looked stunned.

Dwayne wanted to plunge past her, but what was wrong with Angela? "Did your appointment with Dr. Brenner go okay?"

"I can't even say." She still did not move out of the doorway.

"What do you mean?"

"What they told me. It's too much. It's too much to say."

Dwayne felt a trickle of sweat roll down his side. He didn't want to be late to this meeting. He'd done really well with the PR at Rocky's, but this technical stuff was entirely different. He was afraid he was blowing it. But he didn't want to leave her like this.

"Come on, tell me," he said.

"All the tests are bad, Dwayne. My tests. Your tests. All the tests are bad."

"Like, how?"

"Your sperms are deformed. Some of them are swimming sideways. Some are swimming in pathetic little circles. A few of them are good. One or two are Olympic-level swimmers."

"Olympic-level. That's good."

"Sure, but you need hundreds of Olympic-level to be normal.

Not just a few."

"Okay." He looked at his watch. This seemed like a really big conversation. He had engineers to interview. "Did the doctor say what we do?"

"That's not even the whole story." She walked past and sat on one of the love seats in the living room and looked down at the floor.

"What's the rest of the story?"

"I can't look at you."

"Okay," he said. "Don't look. But what's the rest of the story?" She sighed deeply.

"This seems like a big conversation," Dwayne said. "Should we wait until I get back from Itasca? I don't want to be late. This is a brand new client for Chaz. He wants a good first impression."

"I just want to go to bed."

"Okay. You aren't teaching this summer. Take a nap."

"Take a nap?" She threw her purse at the sofa on the other side of the room. "Like that's going to solve anything? Is that what you think, Dwayne?"

"It's just a suggestion!" Dwayne said. "We can talk later. I'm really sorry about what you learned today, but if we're going to keep up with the doctor bills, I can't lose my job."

She sat up abruptly. "Lose your job? Jesus, Dwayne! Am I supposed to take on your anxiety, too? I'm supposed to relax so I can get knocked up. We fuck by the calendar, by the temperature, by the viscosity. We take tests and talk to the doctors, but guess what? No relaxing! No babies! And you want to know why?"

He felt afraid to ask. "Because you can't relax?"

"No! Because I have an *inhospitable fucking womb*. That's what Doctor Fucking Brenner, M.D., told me at my appointment today. I have an in-fucking-hospitable fucking womb. How do you like that?"

"Well." He took a deep breath. "I can't say that I like it at all."

"*You can't say that you like it at all.* You know, that's a really dumb thing to say, Dwayne. *You can't say that you like it at all.*"

"I'm sorry. You are just catching me…" He was about to say *at a bad time*. That would be a bad idea. "I'm really sorry. Did Dr. Brenner have any suggestions?"

"Dr. Brenner had a whole flock of suggestions. One of them was adoption. You go to this expensive fucking fertility doctor, and he suggests *adoption*? Speaking of expensive, I'd appreciate you *not* losing your job. A lot of his suggestions were unbelievably expensive. Like hugely, hugely, hugely fuckingly expensive." She sighed deeply. She looked at him and frowned. "You know what? Let's talk later. You just want to get the hell out of here."

"Don't be mad. I'm sorry. I'd like to sit with you and talk this over right now."

"No. No, you wouldn't, Dwayne."

"I would."

"No. *I* don't even want to talk it over right now. I'm too…upset. Inhospitable fucking womb. My mother was a champion baby-dropper. What the fuck? What the hell happened to me?"

"I don't know."

"You don't know." She huffed. "Maybe it was you. Maybe your terrible swimmers are actually toxic, and they turned my womb inhospitable. Maybe that's what happened. My mother told me I shouldn't trust you."

"She did?" Dwayne always thought Angela's mother liked him.

"She said you were too pretty. She likes good-looking men, but she doesn't trust pretty men. She thinks you are too pretty."

Dwayne had no idea what to say about that.

"Go," Angela said. "Just go. Get out of here. If I'm sleeping when you get home, for the love of God, don't wake me up."

37

Tuesday, June 19, 2005

Dwayne had been working at Chaz's PR firm for four weeks. He was beginning to feel like a burden there, which was exactly what he'd feared. At Rocky's, he'd written affectingly about the injuries the clients received and the heroic efforts the lawyers had made. Now Chaz had him writing about technical products that he didn't really understand. Yesterday, he'd gone to Itasca for a meeting with Hamilton Bottling Equipment and then come back to his miserable wife, who was sullenly quiet the rest of the night. Dwayne had finished typing up his notes from the interview this morning, but now he was sitting at his desk, feeling stressed. Instead of focusing on his work, he kept puzzling over the words: *inhospitable womb.*

Chaz stuck his head into Dwayne's cubicle. "How did it go yesterday?"

Dwayne froze for a moment. Of course, Chaz meant at Hamilton, not with Angela. "They gave me a nice tour of the place," he said. "I got to see the machine running. I had no idea you could fill a beverage can and close the lid so fast."

"Close it?" Chaz said.

"The machine puts a lid on the can and then crimps the edge all the way around to seal it. That's called closing."

"Excellent. Write it up. Let's make some money." Chaz started to move away.

"Wait!" Dwayne called.

Chaz stuck his head back in the door.

"They want me to put the customer benefit of the machine in the headline."

"So?"

"I don't know what the customer benefit is. *They* don't know what the customer benefit is," Dwayne said.

"It's fast, right? The fastest machine ever?"

"They already had the fastest possible machine. This new machine runs faster than physics will allow. If you run it at its full speed, the pop or the beer or whatever will fly out of the can before the lid goes on."

Chaz came in and sat on the edge of the desk. "So they already had the fastest machine?"

"Right. And this one's faster than that. So I asked them: *Why would anyone want to buy this?* And the head guy goes: *That's for you to figure out. We're just engineers. You're the creative guy.* And they all laughed. The guy claps me on the shoulder and says: *Good meeting!* And they all file out laughing."

"Well, that's why they come to us, I guess," Chaz said uncertainly.

"Yeah, but if they don't know why their customers would buy this, how would we?"

Chaz stood up. Certainty returned to his face. "Come on, Dwayne. I think it's kind of obvious."

"It is?"

"Sure. When a rich guy buys a 200-mile-per-hour Maserati, he's never going to drive it at top speed. Same here. Hamilton's customers are Anheuser-Busch and Coca-Cola, the biggest beverage companies in the world. They're like those rich guys who want a Maserati. You tell them: *No matter how fast you run it, for this machine, it's an easy cruising speed.*"

"*An easy cruising speed.*" Dwayne was impressed. That *would* be a reason to buy.

"Yeah. So come on, Dwayne. Why don't you come up with stuff like this?"

38

Wednesday, June 20, 2005

Angela pushed open the door of the *Curandera Botanica Espiritual* on Clark Street, a few blocks north of Pratt. It was a narrow storefront. Fanciful drawings of herbs and potions, a neon hand illustrating the major lines of the palm, and a mandala of the zodiac decorated its single window. It sat between a taqueria on one side and a discount furniture store on the other. Ximena Martinez, one of Angela's fellow teachers, had taken her aside when she'd learned Angela was seeing a fertility specialist. Angela had kept it secret, but assistant principal Todd Bodkins had been loose with her private information the next time he was drunk before the end of the school year.

"Don't tell anyone about this," Ximena had whispered to her in the hallway as the kids streamed noisily to lunch. "The other teachers would make fun of me forever. But when the doctor fails you, the curandera delivers. It's always been that way for my family."

"Did you go to a fertility doctor?" Angela asked.

"I went. He offered options, but so much money! I could *buy* a baby for less than what he wanted!" Ximena sighed. "So I went to the curandera. She'd already cured my uncle's cancer! We never would have got little Alejandro without her."

And so Angela, desperate after the revelation of her inhospitable womb, pushed open the heavy door of the curandera's storefront and went inside. Bells jingled at the top of the door. It took a moment for her eyes to adjust to the dim light. Some kind of incense scented the air. Low mysterious music played. On one side of the room, three padded chairs surrounded a little table. Floor-to-ceiling shelves covered the wall beyond that, filled with jars of herbs and liquids and other things Angela could not identify, as well as a variety of very old books bound in well-worn leather. A couch stretched along the other wall.

A black-haired woman with a tranquil smile came through a set of dark curtains from the back. "Welcome," she said.

She was maybe five feet tall. Her irises were as black as her pupils, giving her eyes an otherworldly look. She gestured to the table, and the two sat across from each other on the padded chairs.

"What brings you to me?" she said.

The woman surprised Angela with her aura of vast intelligence. Why so surprised? Maybe deep down, she'd been expecting a charlatan?

"Ximena Martinez recommended you. I want to have a baby."

"And?"

"My doctor says I have an inhospitable womb."

The curandera's eyebrows raised as high as they could go, then she broke into musical laughter. "Now I have heard everything! *You* have an inhospitable womb? You who spend your life with children?"

Angela sat up straight. "How did you know that?"

The curandera laughed harder. She shook her head. "I'm not a psychic. You don't look like you're Ximena's sister, so I'm guessing you teach with her?"

Now Angela laughed as well. "Yes. I do."

"Okay, let's figure out this *inhospitable* womb." She smiled at Angela and winked. "Lie down on my couch, please, on your back."

"Okay." Angela felt a little uneasy as she crossed the room and lay back on the couch. What was she getting herself into?

She was a little tall for the length of the couch, so she put her feet up on the armrest. "That's fine," the curandera said. She fetched a couple of pillows from behind the dark curtains and put them under the backs of Angela's calves to make her comfortable. Then she pulled a chair next to her and sat.

"First, I listen to the problem from your body. I put my hand on you so I can hear. Is that okay?"

"Yes," Angela said, though it made her nervous.

"Good," the curandera said. "While I do that, I want you to think that you have a baby in your womb right now. Imagine it as fully as you can. Do this, and I will be able to hear what is important."

"Okay," Angela said. "But you know, I've never been pregnant."

She patted Angela's wrist. "I know, *querida*. Close your eyes. Just imagine." She laid her hand flat on Angela's abdomen, just below her navel. Angela nodded and closed her eyes. After a few moments, the curandera's hand felt less like a hand and more like a warm presence. The curandera hummed along with the hypnotic music in the background. Angela relaxed into the humming and followed it to a place deep inside herself. She imagined a little fetus in her womb, a curled baby lizard of a fetus, which began to unfurl and develop tiny fingers and open big eyes in its overlarge head.

"Let it grow," the curandera whispered. It was like a voice in her own head in harmony with the hypnotic music. Her fetus enlarged, developing more and more into the dimensions of a human baby. Angela's belly expanded to allow it space. It turned and rolled and grew, attached to Angela's blood supply, growing healthy inside her. Oh, how she loved it! Tears rolled out of her eyes, feeling cool down the sides of her cheeks.

One part of her felt astounded. How could this be happening? How could she be imagining this in such perfect detail? But that doubting voice was low, in the background. In the foreground of her mind was the utter reality of this experience. Oh, how she loved it!

"Yes, yes, it is beautiful," the curandera whispered. "Yes, this is very good." The presence of the hand moved over her stomach, around the full rotundity of her pregnancy. It felt like a solemn blessing. "Yes, beautiful. You are doing very well." She sat with her hand on the very top of Angela's rounded stomach and hummed a comforting tune. Angela felt utter bliss. "Enjoy that feeling, and then let it go. Absorb it all into your body to make way for the real thing."

"No…" Angela moaned. She didn't want to let go of this feeling. It felt so beautiful. She never wanted it to end.

"You must," the curandera said gently. "This is preparation. Absorb it joyfully. Make way for the real thing."

More tears leaked from the sides of Angela's eyes, tears now of mourning rather than unexpected joy. Yes, of course, she would do what the curandera said. This was a part of her cure. She must embrace it.

The curandera waited until Angela acquiesced and had absorbed it all. Angela breathed gently and accepted this feeling of loss until she was back to her original state.

"Very good," the curandera said. "Now, I want you to imagine *becoming* pregnant. The moment of change. The moment you and your husband contribute, and it all begins."

This was a daunting thought. How was she supposed to imagine that? Did a woman ever actually feel that change at the molecular level? She was tempted to open her eyes and ask questions, but that seemed like a bad idea. She sank deeper into her imaginings as the curandera's hand slid lower on her abdomen.

Angela felt suddenly embarrassed. She was becoming aroused. This wasn't the moment the curandera requested. This was the moment *before* the moment. But maybe that's what you had to imagine to get *to* the moment. Because without that moment, there was no moment of molecular transformation.

"You are doing well," the curandera said. "Let yourself go. Don't be embarrassed."

And so Angela let herself go. She felt herself pleasurably opening. She felt her nipples hardening. And then her consciousness zoomed in and in and in down to the molecular level in which the swimmer came swimming and the egg greeted it with joy as her body orgasmed in bliss.

How in dickens?

"Excellent. Excellent," the curandera breathed. "I have what I need. I'll wait for you at the table." She lifted her hand from Angela's abdomen, and suddenly Angela felt profoundly alone. She opened her eyes and felt further surprised when she broke into tears. She sat up on the couch and wept openly. The curandera had left a box of tissues on the chair where she'd been sitting, so apparently she'd been expecting Angela to have tears. She wept and wept and then wiped her eyes and blew her nose.

Over at the table, the curandera wrote down notes.

Once Angela felt more normal, she went over and sat at the table.

The curandera smiled at her reassuringly. "The news is good," she said. "We can do something. But you and your husband must follow all my directions."

"Okay," Angela said. "Is it the same thing you had Ximena do?"

The curandera looked shocked. "Did Ximena tell you what she did?" The fierceness of her expression frightened Angela.

"No. She didn't tell me anything. She said she came to you, and you made little Alejandro possible."

"Okay." The curandera calmed. "This is a sacred ceremony. It is for you and your husband only. You must never discuss it with others. That would be an insult to the spirits on whom we call."

"You call on spirits?"

"Of course. Already. I am a human woman. I cannot transform your womb. For that I call on the spirits. Some of them live in herbs. Some of them…" She looked up at the ceiling for a moment, then she closed her eyes. When she opened them again, she spoke more quietly, but with a deeper toughness. "I call on them in a variety of ways. That is not your business. I am here to help you have a baby. Is that enough for you to know?"

Again, Angela felt a little afraid. "Yes, that's all I want," she said.

"Okay. Take notes."

"Okay." Angela fetched her purse and pulled out a pen. The curandera had had such an easy smile at the beginning. She seemed so loving when she had her hand on Angela. What had happened to that? Now she seemed so stern.

Angela looked through her belongings, but she didn't have a notebook. "I don't think I have any paper."

"Look again. It is important you write on something of your own."

She searched, but the only thing of paper was her checkbook. She held it up.

"Yes," the curandera said. "Write on the backs of those. You can't use them to pay me, anyway."

Angela wondered why not, but decided not to ask. She poised her pen above the back of the first of the checks.

"First, you must prepare a nursery for the coming of the baby. Everything the baby will need. Crib. Diapers. Blankets. Toys. As you add these items to your home, love them as though they were your baby. In a place of honor, add pictures of the women of your line.

Your mother. Your grandmothers. Great-grandmothers going back as far as you can. If you don't have photos of these ancestors, find something to take their place. Little figurines to stand in for them. Jewels. Vintage drawings. Call on them to bless your womb and assist in the continuation of your maternal line. The ancestors carry power. They've been waiting for you to give them something to do. Pray to them three times a day."

"Okay." Angela made notes as small as she could on the back of the check and continued the notes on a second check.

"You must pray to the spirits. I can call them, but if you don't win them over, nothing will happen. Meanwhile, I will gather all the useful ones I know. To receive their blessings, you and your husband will burn and breathe the aroma of herbs I will supply you. I will give you other herbs and instructions to brew two teas. One for you and another for your husband. You must drink these teas every day. I will prepare a medicine pouch to keep on your person at all times. Also, a medicine to spread on your belly at the new moon. It may give you a furious rash. That is normal. Let it run its course."

"You're going to give me all those things now?"

"No. You must pay seven hundred dollars for the herbs. I have them collected by another curandera in Mexico and shipped to me. They don't grow here. This is not cheap. If they are not collected properly, they can have the opposite of the desired effect. Plus, you must pay one thousand dollars for the ceremony. You must take the cash out of your bank account at the bank in person, in bills no larger than twenties. You must spend at least an hour handling all the bills. Carry them with you for a day. Imbue them with your energy. Seven hundred dollars is for me. Three hundred I will burn. This is because one of you is too concerned about money. You or your husband. This must stop. This concern for money warps something physical in the two of you. So I will burn the money, and you both must let go this concern. After all, people with no money at all have children all the time."

"Will we watch you burning the money?"

"No. You must accept it in faith. Faith is the power that drives the healing."

That made sense to Angela. She realized it also sounded like what a con artist might say, but she believed the curandera.

39

Saturday, June 23, 2005

On Friday, Angela went to the bank and took out one thousand seven hundred dollars in twenty-dollar bills. She gave a little prayer of thanksgiving to the weirdness of Rocky and his severance package for Dwayne. The teller gave Angela an odd look as she counted out the bills. Somehow, the weird look penetrated Angela's heart, as though the teller had observed everything. Angela wondered if she was participating in a scam on herself and Dwayne. But Ximena had had little Alejandro. Her uncle had been cured of cancer. Didn't this seem like a better chance than she had with the fertility doctor? She battled against feeling foolish as she made her way back to the storefront on Clark Street.

Angela delivered the seven hundred in twenties to the curandera and collected bundles of herbs and directions on how to burn and brew them. The curandera also gave her the lucky clay pot Ximena had used to brew her herbs and told her to bring the pot back once she had her baby. She stood in the storefront with the clay pot sitting in the palms of both hands, and suddenly all her doubts flowed away. Ximena had used this lucky clay pot! It had sat on Ximena's stove and brewed the strange herbs the curandera had selected for her. And Alejandro was a beautiful, healthy boy. A handsome, smart boy. How could this be wrong?

So Saturday morning, Angela began brewing the herbs. First, she brewed the herbs for herself and poured the tea into two mugs: one for the morning and one to be drunk before bed. Then she started brewing the tea for Dwayne. She measured the water and herbs and brought them to a simmer. She set the timer for twenty minutes of simmering and went to the bedroom to wake her husband and tell him what was happening. This would be the first he was hearing of it.

His head kept cocking farther and farther to the side as she explained it.

"We're doing all that?" he said, looking sleepy in the bed, sitting up, his hair in a mess hanging down on his forehead.

"This is our best chance, Dwayne. You have to have faith."

"But isn't that exactly what a charlatan would tell you? You have to have faith? They come to you promising the world and take your money?"

"She didn't come to me. I went to her. Ximena was in the same shape as me, and this curandera had already cured cancer in her family. And then this." She held up her phone showing a photo of a smiling three-year-old. "See? Isn't he beautiful? That's Alejandro, Ximena's boy. She never could have had him without the curandera."

Dwayne sat up more erect on the bed. "What's that smell?"

"Your tea is brewing. You have to drink one this morning and another cup before bed, every day."

"That's something I have to drink?" Dwayne made a horrible face and got out of bed. Angela followed him into the kitchen. Now that Dwayne was looking at it, the old clay pot on the range looked horribly rustic, like it had been fired without glaze in a wood fire in the forest, brown and black and weird.

"That smells horrendous," he said. "That's safe to drink?"

"Well…" Her tea had smelled rather nice, if a little grassy. Dwayne's tea smelled like someone had grabbed a handful from a compost bin that geese had shat on and worms were crawling through and threw that into the pot. "I wish you had met her. She inspired so much trust in me. I felt a baby growing in my womb! I've never felt anything like that in my life. It was totally magic, Dwayne. Please don't pour doubts on my hope!"

"I don't want to pour doubts on your hope," Dwayne said. "But I'm not sure I want to pour that stuff down my throat, either."

Suddenly, Angela felt that baby in her womb again, but now it was shrinking. Its growth was reversing, shrinking back down toward that tiny lizard-shaped fetus. Would it shrink and shrink and shrink until it disappeared and was gone forever?

She burst into tears and collapsed to the floor.

"Hey, hey, hey," Dwayne said. He sat down beside her on the floor and took her into his arms. "Come on. Don't cry. Give me a chance. I didn't even know you were going to a curandera. I didn't even know what a curandera was. I thought we were putting our trust in Dr. Brenner. This is a whole different…idea. Give me a chance."

"I felt my baby shrinking," she cried, putting her hand on her abdomen. "It was shrinking away to nothing because of your doubts."

"I'm sorry." Was he supposed to just jump into her fantasy? They were supposed to handle money and let it go? The curandera would burn three hundred dollars, but they weren't allowed to watch? Was there any chance in heaven that the curandera would do anything other than put that three hundred dollars in her pocket?

On the other hand, why bother to include that detail? She could've just said the fee was one thousand dollars instead of seven hundred. Was the burning of three hundred somehow more acceptable than handing over a thousand? It was all weird, magical thinking.

The kitchen timer rang, and Angela got up off the floor. She dried her tears and strained Dwayne's tea into two large mugs. He got up and stood next to her.

"This is the same brewing pot that Ximena used," she said quietly. "It brought her all the luck. Alejandro is such a beautiful little boy."

"It does look like a magical pot," Dwayne admitted.

"I believe it is," Angela said. She spooned a large spoonful of honey into each of Dwayne's mugs, as the curandera had told her to do, and stirred it vigorously.

"You don't think I'll die if I drink that?" Dwayne said.

Angela grinned through her tears and laughed a little. "That would be counter-productive. I'd have to go out and find a whole new sperm-donor."

"That's what I am? The sperm-donor?"

Angela hugged him abruptly. "You know you're not. The curandera stressed how we needed to do these things as a couple. As I bring in things for the baby, we both have to love those things as though they *are* the baby. While I call on the ancestors of my maternal line, you have to call on the ancestors of your paternal line. Drinking the teas and burning the herbs is not like taking medicine; it's a form of prayer. The prayer effects a change in our bodies that welcomes the baby. Can you do this with me, Dwayne?"

The look in her eyes was so pleading, it broke his heart. Could he bring himself to believe in all this mumbo jumbo?

He knew about the transformational properties of ritual. He'd been an altar boy as a child and felt the deep mystery of the Mass and the transformation of the bread and wine into the Christ. Ritual is what drew him to theatre.

"You could believe you were Hamlet's best friend when you played Horatio, right?" she said. That startled him. It was like she was hearing his thoughts.

"Yeah. When I was onstage, playing those scenes, I believed Hamlet was my best friend."

"And when he was dead at the end of the play, you felt truly heartbroken."

"I did."

"So this shouldn't be so hard for you. I believe in what the curandera tells us to do. You believe in me. So accept it and play this role straight on through until we have our baby. You usually just play a role for a few hours at a time for five weeks, maybe, but now I'm asking you to play this role until we have our baby. I believe you can do that, Dwayne. I believe in you. I want you to believe in me."

She had always believed in him, even when it was not convenient or fun. He knew that. He loved her so much. He truly wanted this for her. He wanted it for *them*.

Suddenly, he was weeping. What was this? Her words, her desire, her love touched him so deeply. He sobbed as she wrapped her arms around him.

"That's it, Dwayne," she said. "Now you know. Now you know."

He loved her so much. They hugged for the longest time until he stopped sobbing. Then they drank the teas. His tea did taste horrible, but also sort of intriguing. Or penetrating? He didn't know how to describe the sensation of drinking it, but he drank it down to the bottom and then took his wife by the hand and let her back into the bedroom.

As they made love, Angela felt that uncanny sensation again she'd felt in the curandera's storefront. Her consciousness zoomed in and in and in, down to the molecular level in which the swimmer came swimming and the egg greeted it with joy. She cried out in ecstasy.

My God, could they have done it on the very first try?

40

Sunday, June 24, 2005

The next day, still high from Dwayne's acceptance of the plan and their ecstatic love-making, Angela visited the Old Orchard Shopping Center with Bonnie. Since Bonnie and Chaz had divorced, she hadn't seen her old friend as much. They walked into Toms Price Furniture, which had just opened in the past year.

"Are we going to get a cocktail after this?" Bonnie said.

"I promise." She suddenly wondered if she should swear off alcohol for a while. The curandera hadn't said anything about that.

"May I help you?"

The young man in the Toms Price uniform looked them up and down a little too eagerly for Bonnie's taste. "You can back off a little, Cosmo," she said.

Angela chuckled.

His grin diminished substantially.

"We're here to look at your cribs and bassinets," Angela said. Bonnie cocked her head at Angela so abruptly, her vertebrae cracked loudly enough to be heard across the store. Angela hadn't told her what they were shopping for.

"Oh, I'm sorry. We don't carry cribs and bassinets. We do have youth beds and trundle beds."

"You don't have nursery furniture?" Angela said.

"I'm afraid not. I'm pretty sure you could find them at Nordstrom or Fields."

"Huh," Angela said. She turned on her heel and led Bonnie out of the building. "Marshall Fields and Nordstrom are so expensive. This Toms Price joint is supposed to be affordable."

"Let's go to Saks," Bonnie suggested, leading the way.

"Saks doesn't have furniture."

"I know, but I need a new dress." Bonnie clutched Angela's forearm. "Why are you looking for a crib? Are you pregnant? Why didn't you tell me?"

"I'm not pregnant. I have to do this…"

"You *have* to do this?" Bonnie stepped away as they were walking. "How is it you *have* to do this? You are aware that pregnancies last nine months. That allows plenty of shopping time."

Angela stopped. She couldn't explain. The curandera warned her that she must not discuss this process with anyone other than Dwayne. It had been four days since she'd met with the curandera, and her life already felt entirely different. Every moment, in some way or another, had become a prayer. There was no way to explain that to the hilariously sarcastic Bonnie.

If she had to talk with anyone in addition to Dwayne, she was allowed to talk with Ximena, who had been through it all. But no one else. Even with Ximena, she was not allowed to discuss specifics. This was a sacred process. Mockery offended the spirits, which is surely what most modern people would heap on her if she discussed it. Certainly, Bonnie would.

"Sorry. I don't *have* to. I want to."

Bonnie scoffed. "You do you, cookie. We went to your store first. Now let's go to one for me, and then we'll go to another one for you. Fair?"

"Sure," Angela said, though this made her crib search seem less like a sacred mission and more like a casual girl's shopping outing. Maybe Bonnie was the wrong person to ask along. Angela thought Bonnie could stand in for her maternal line. She didn't want to get her mother involved at this stage. She would drive Angela crazy. She could have asked Dwayne to go shopping, but the feminine line thing seemed important.

"Why do you want to have a baby, anyway?" Bonnie asked. "I mean, you spend all day with people's brats and then you'd have to come home to your own? Seems like a bit much."

"Teaching is not like having your own child. Don't you want children? Eventually?"

"Oh, God!" Bonnie said, her red hair flashing as a beam of sunset light caught it. "Chaz wanted children, but would he take time off to raise them? No way. His precious career. And, you know, did he have to go to Law School? Did he have to pass the bar? Not on your life. It takes nothing to become a PR man. And I should spend nine months like a freckled balloon? I didn't become the youngest woman partner at my firm to drop out and play pat-a-cake with a tiny clone of Chaz Ackersley."

"So, never?"

"I see kids caught in the middle in my divorces. If you can't stay married for twenty years—and I certainly didn't—should you really be subjecting children to your screwy life?"

"Wow." She and Dwayne had tough patches sometimes, but she didn't see them ever divorcing.

"For the love of God!" Bonnie exclaimed, pointing.

On the glass doorway of Saks Fifth Avenue was a large sign with CLOSED at the top. They thanked their faithful customers for the years of patronage, but Saks would no longer be doing business at Westfield Old Orchard Shopping Center.

"No more Saks?" Bonnie moaned. "And what is this Westfield bullshit? When did Old Orchard become Westfield? What is this world coming to?" She stood looking stunned for a moment, then collected herself. "You want to go get a cocktail?"

"Sure," Angela said. Apparently, today was not the day to buy a crib.

41

Tuesday, July 25, 2005

Dwayne plunged back into the second bedroom that had always been their shared office. Where was his messenger bag with his script and notes? He had to get out of the house and to his first rehearsal for *King Lear*. He couldn't be late for the first rehearsal! What a horrible precedent that would set! The table the two of them shared as a desk was pushed up against the wall. The back half was covered with photos of Angela's mother, grandmothers, great-grandmothers, and pictures and figurines representing her maternal line going back in time. The front half was set up as a changing table, as though a baby was about to arrive any day. There was a crib, a bassinet, a little dresser for the baby, pictures on the wall, and a mobile hanging above the crib. Everything a baby would need. It was his job to pour love into all these things to welcome a baby. That had become a major part of his life in the past weeks since Angela had started with the curandera.

But right now, he had to find his bag and get the hell out of here.

"Angela," he shouted. "Have you seen my bag?"

"Oh my God, why are you shouting?" she came out of the kitchen where she'd been sorting and storing a new batch of herbs she'd collected from the curandera. Another $700, but Dwayne was not supposed to fret over money. That would be counter-productive. "I need a calm atmosphere while I'm sorting the herbs."

"Of course. But I need to get out of here. Have you seen my bag?"

"Yes, I hung it up on the coat tree so you could find it easily on your way out the door."

"I wouldn't have trouble finding it if you didn't move it. And if we still had an office."

"Damn it, Dwayne. You have to love the nursery!"

"I do love the nursery. But right now, I'd love to be in the car on the way to my first rehearsal."

"Okay, but just wait!" She grabbed a sprig of herbs from the kitchen counter and lit them with the stove.

"Oh, for the love of God."

"Take this as it's offered, Dwayne, so you can be on your way with blessings." She breathed on the burning herb until the flame went out and smoke curled from it. Dwayne stood and turned impatiently while she anointed him with smoke before he burst out of the door and ran down the stairs toward the rusty Pinto parked out in front.

How had this become his life?

42

Slightly Later

The entire cast was laughing. Dwayne laughed, too, but it was hard to really enjoy it. They'd been going around the circle, everyone introducing themselves before Dwayne would give a little speech about what he intended for the show. Then they'd do a read-through of the script. When they got to Reg Camper, however, he followed his personal introduction with a story about the first time he'd directed *King Lear*, back at a storefront theatre way back at the beginning of his career—and then that reminded him of another story, and another, and then....

"Oh, but the worst," Camper said, all the actors leaning toward him with attention, "was *Who's Afraid of Virginia Woolf?* One of the cast decided we needed to do a drink-through. He hadn't discussed it with me. He snuck in bottles of booze. Gin for Martha. You know, whatever the characters were purportedly drinking. Poured the fake booze out of the prop bottles and replaced them with real booze when no one was watching. You know. It's the second run-through. I want the actors to feel the rhythm of the whole work, so I don't interrupt. I do notice the actors looking at their glasses at the first sips, but I don't think much about it." He smiled and looked around, a master storyteller enjoying the attention.

Dwayne looked at his watch.

"So we are getting toward the end of the act, and Honey stands up, a little wobbly on her feet. I'm thinking: *This is the most intensely she's played the drunkenness.*" The actors laughed again. "Our Honey was quite petite. If you know the script, there are all those lines about her being *slim-hipped*. And our actor was *quite* slim-hipped. She was slim-everything. So she stands up, unsteady on her feet. She's about to deliver a line, but suddenly she erupts vomit. A geyser of vomit. A volcano of vomit. Just burst from her mouth into the air like a fountain. And I think, oh, my God, she's so sick, until I smell it. This vomit is booze-soaked. The actor playing Nick looks so guilty. Drunk and guilty. He was the one who'd spiked the prop bottles. That was the end of run-through for that day."

Reg looked around, enjoying the attention of his rapt audience until he noticed Dwayne looking at his watch once again. He turned and looked at the clock on the wall behind him. "Oh dear," he said. "I was only supposed to introduce myself, but now I've gone and used up some of your rehearsal time."

"No, no," Dwayne said, battling against his sense of urgency. "This is a treat for us all."

"Oh, my God," Camper said. "That reminds me—just one more—I promise." And off he went into another story from Chicago theatre lore past. As soon as Dwayne heard what could possibly be a concluding note in Reg's story, he stood up, script in hand, looking absolutely ready to launch into his pre-read-thru speech, despite the fact that three more actors, seated past Reg Camper in the circle, had yet to introduce themselves.

"Okay." Howie Grange, the Goodman-supplied Equity stage manager, slid into the fraction of audio space between Reg's final word and the first word Dwayne could not get out of his mouth. "Take ten, everyone."

"Thank you, ten," everyone said, except for Dwayne, who said: "Take ten? What do you mean, take ten? We haven't done anything yet."

Howie tapped the face of this watch. "Take ten. It's time. We follow Equity rules at the Goodman." He got up and exited the rehearsal room as the actors started moving around.

"I do apologize," Camper said. "I suppose you had words to say and wanted to complete a read-through and start a discussion. And *Lear* is a long script. I don't suppose you'll be able to finish a read-through today now."

"It's such a pleasure for us all to be here," Dwayne said, trying very hard to feel it sincerely. "How often do we get the chance to hear these stories?"

"Once I get rolling," Camper said. "I do enjoy a story." He took a deep breath and leaned in toward Dwayne. "I did want to see your actors in action, but I am going to get out of your hair. You're going to love Howie Grange and Peter Burden. They are both at the top of their game." He clapped Dwayne on the shoulder and headed out of the rehearsal room.

That was a relief. But now he had just half his rehearsal time to get this show launched. He always felt the first rehearsal meant a lot to the process. He liked there to be a playful quality because that helped the actors to be wide-ranging in their experimentation. He liked that especially at the beginning when they were inventing the broad strokes of their characterizations. As the process continued, they would solidify what they were doing until, in the final run-throughs, they would become consistent and clear.

"Okay, we are back," Howie Grange announced ten minutes later as the actors settled back into their chairs around the big table. Howie wore his wiry grey hair in a no-nonsense crew cut. His seated posture was militarily erect. He wore a green polo shirt over a well-muscled torso and half-frame reading glasses down on his nose. When he looked out over the top of them, it appeared to be the look of judgment.

"Very good…" Dwayne said, hoping to move things along.

"Yes!" Peter Burden nearly shouted. "If I may…" He'd been seated next to Reg Camper. "…my little introduction." He smoothed down the lapels of his mauve velvet sport jacket with both hands.

Dwayne nodded reluctantly, but Peter was not looking at him or waiting for confirmation.

"This is my twelfth production here at the Goodman. Three in the Owen and nine on the Albert mainstage." He rocked his lean body in his chair like a proud hen settling on her eggs. "I think this is the first Goodman show for many of you?" he said, with a sniffy tone. "Except, of course, for Bobby here." He patted Bobby's arm, seated to his left, who'd also not yet introduced himself. "Bobby and I appeared in a show together."

"Bobby playing a thug," Coco interjected.

"Bobby has range, we all know," Peter said loftily. "For me, this is my sixteenth Bill Shakespeare production, one of which was here, six with Chicago Shakes, and the rest scattered around the city and the country. Three up in Stratford." He gave a little sniffy sound again. "I'll be playing Gloucester. One might have assumed I'd be playing Lear!" He gave Wallace a harsh look. "But maybe Dwayne didn't want a Black Lear." He took a short pause. "I'm sure my new colleague," he nodded at Wallace, "is absolutely ready." He gave a half-hearted, totally humorless smile and looked away.

Bobby sat looking at Peter amusedly. "Well, now," he said in his clear, deep voice. "Ain't you the sniffy bitch?"

Peter looked at him in shock and dismay. Bobby gave him an immediate hug around the shoulders. "Old castmates," he said. "We give each other the shit now and then." He laughed his low, deep chuckle. "Most of you know me. I founded and was the original artistic director of this company."

Dwayne sat up sharply, but Bobby plunged on before he could voice a correction.

"I'm delighted to be back. I'm delighted to be working again with my brother-in-arts, Dwayne Finnegan." He leaned toward Dwayne and started clapping, and the other actors followed into a round of applause for their director. "And to be working again with the incomparable Coco Nesbit, the only actor in the city of Chicago whose charisma may exceed my own." He gave a hearty self-depreciating laugh and led a round of applause for Coco, and winked at Melinda, whose applause was perhaps less enthusiastic than the rest.

"I'm playing Edmund, because, after all, a Black man has to play the most thuggish character in the play."

Dwayne sputtered a little. Bobby waved his hand at him. "Just tugging your chain, brother. We all know Edmund is the one both Goneril and Regan want to get into their bed…and who better fits that bill?" He laughed even more heartily. Orlando, who'd wanted to play Edmund, looked sulky. Bobby slapped Tom's thigh, who was seated to his left. "Tom Collins, ladies and gentlemen! Another of my long-time artistic partners." He led a round of applause again.

"I know Dwayne is dying to get started." Tom stood up and turned fully to Dwayne. "I just want to thank you for letting me play

Regan. Yes, in Shakespeare's day, all the women were played by men, but this is a new day. And this is my first role that was written as a female character. And I'm so excited to play her." His voice cracked a little with emotion, and he sat back down. Bobby put his arm around him and gave him a squeeze. Tom blew his nose.

"I guess I hadn't thought that through," Rocky said, his face settling into an intense collection of folds around his mouth and eyes. "How do I play Cornwall when you are playing Regan, *my wife?*" he said to Tom.

"Oh, pops," Coco said. "It's acting."

"No, no, no," Bobby said. "Your pops has a point. What does it mean that he is married to and I am seeking a liaison with a Regan who is played by a man?"

Tom waved a hand in the air. "Don't fret, boys. The actor has a dick, but the character has a pussy. You are married to or romancing the character, not the actor."

Rocky's eyebrows rose suddenly. "Huh! The actor has a *dick*, but the character has a *pussy!*" He gave a sudden laugh. "I guess that takes care of that!" He slapped hands with Bobby and grinned at Tom.

"Well, that was surprisingly easy," Dwayne said. "Okay then! Welcome, everyone!" Dwayne led a round of applause for them all. "All right, before we start the read-through…"

"I'd like to ask why we have such a long rehearsal process," Peter interrupted. "I've done twelve productions here at the Goodman, and I've never been involved in a show with so many weeks of rehearsal."

"That's what I thought," Wallace said. "But then I directed *Oedipus Rex* with a short rehearsal schedule, and it wasn't enough."

"It seems you are doing a lot of things you are ill-equipped to do," Peter sniffed.

"All right now," Dwayne warned.

"Peter, if you didn't want to be in a non-equity production," Howie Grange interrupted, "you shouldn't have accepted the role. Most of these people have day jobs. They can't do eight hours of rehearsal during the day and go home in the evening."

Of the two people Reg Camper had recommended to him, so far, Dwayne was liking the stage manager much more than the actor.

43

Wednesday, July 26, 2005

Dwayne pulled into his spot in the Government Center Self Park next to the Goodman Theatre, where Ingrid had procured the free parking pass. In his rearview mirror, he saw Reg Camper opening the door to his Escalade. The big man waved. He'd recognized Dwayne as he pulled in.

Dwayne yanked at the door handle on the Pinto. Nothing. He yanked again and put his shoulder into the door. It didn't budge.

Holy Magdalene and the rolling rock before Jesus' tomb.

He pulled the handle again and again, battering his shoulder into the door. He tried opening the passenger side door. It, too, was welded shut with the inexhaustible glue of oxidized steel.

Rust never sleeps.

Dwayne checked his rearview mirror. Reg Camper was still standing there, looking toward him with a bemused expression.

Oh, the humiliations of Saint Teresa.

He rolled down the window to climb out. His belt buckle got momentarily stuck on the top of the door as he tried to slide through. He folded his torso onto the roof of the car, pulled his legs out the window, and slid down to the parking lot pavement.

Reg Camper gave a slow clap. "If you are practicing for a guest spot on *Hawaii Five-O*, I think it needs a little work."

"You think?" Dwayne reached back through the window to grab the backpack with his script and notes. He attempted to pull the door open from the outside, but it was just as impervious to his efforts as it had been on the inside. How would he close the window?

"Did you finish the read-through last night?" Camper asked.

"Halfway through act three."

"Act three is a long one. Scene four with mad Lear on the heath and Poor Tom goes on forever. Are you cutting?"

"Some cutting. We're also replacing some scenes with music." Dwayne pulled his backpack onto his shoulder and stepped away from the car.

"Aren't you going to close your window?"

To close the window, he'd have to open the trunk, knock out the back seat, climb in, close the window, and climb back out of the trunk. Did he want to do all that in front of Tony-Award-winning Reg Camper? "Actually, I'm kind of *hoping* someone will steal it," Dwayne said.

"You might be disappointed," Camper said. "I set a briefcase on the hood of my Escalade, got into a chat with Nick Sanchez, and left my case on the car for six hours. When I came back, it was still there. Apparently, not many thieves circulate the Government Center Self Park."

"My hopes are dashed." Dwayne had scheduled a pre-rehearsal talk with his stage manager and Joan, but then Camper launched into a surprisingly long story about parking when the Goodman was still in the Art Institute. When Dwayne finally got to the rehearsal room, both Joan and Howie Grange gave him a look of disapproval.

"I ran into Reg Camper in the garage."

Howie Grange's eyebrows rose, and he nodded in recognition.

All the actors were chattering together. Bobby and Peter Burden were in a particularly spirited conversation, but keeping their voices low so as not to be overheard.

Dwayne clapped his hands twice and sat down next to Howie Grange. "All right, everyone. Let's pick up where we left off yesterday, starting with Act Three, Scene Four."

"Before we jump in," Bobby said. "I've got a question."

"Sure," Dwayne said.

"In the first scene, when Gloucester introduces me to Kent, Peter thinks I should find some way to tip my hand about my true nature. But I think Edmund's absolute evil comes in his ability to look innocent as he betrays his brother," he said, gesturing to Orlando, "and his father," gesturing to Peter, "and later the sisters," gesturing to Coco and Tom.

"I'd agree with you," Dwayne said.

"But look at the text!" Peter objected. "The same with Lear. Wallace gives us no foreshadow of his madness in the opening scene. When he disinherits Cordelia, Wallace sounds like a cranky old man. We should get an intimation of madness right off the bat."

"Nonsense!" Wallace huffed out a breath.

"All right…" Dwayne said.

"Look at the text!" Peter exclaimed. "Scene one. Kent says *majesty falls to folly…Check this hideous rashness*. Regan says: *he hath ever but slenderly known himself*."

"All right," Dwayne said. "The opening read-through is to explore the text, not to comment on one another's readings of the script."

Peter turned to Rocky. "Gouge out mine eyes now," he said, "that I not see this abomination."

Rocky chuckled deeply.

"You are calling my first read-through of the script an abomination?" Wallace complained.

"It could be better," Peter said.

"That's enough!" Dwayne insisted.

Bobby caught Wallace's eye, cocked his thumb at Peter, and shook his head dismissively. Wallace settled back in his chair.

"All right," Dwayne said. "If you have questions on the text as we go, feel free to stop the action. But please confine your questions to ones that impact your own performance. As an ensemble, we support one another's performances *in the roles in which we are cast*," he said pointedly, staring at Peter.

"We don't need to understand the full scope of the play, just our own parts?" Peter said, tossing his script on the table in front of him.

"Let's you and I talk privately at the end of the rehearsal," Dwayne said.

"Oooo, Peter's in trouble," Rocky mocked. Bobby let out a deep guffaw. Dwayne shook his head, amused despite his annoyance.

"Come on, let's read," Coco said. "We got an old king to drive to madness!"

"Evil-doers got evil to do," Bobby said.

44

Thursday, July 27, 2005

The next night, Bobby strode into the rehearsal space early. Joan and Ingrid sat at the table in the center, going over budget figures. Ingrid looked annoyed. Joan looked entirely neutral.

"The brain trust!" Bobby exclaimed. "I understand without you two, my company would have failed and folded."

"Your company ended when you spent the *Hamlet* money on a one-bedroom rental in Hollywood," Joan said flatly.

"Money," Bobby scoffed. "A company isn't money. It's people!" He opened his arms wide to the almost empty room. "You, me, Ingrid, Dwayne, Coco, Tom, Melinda, Peaches. We're all still here. The company continues. Nonstop. Indefatigable."

Joan scoffed.

"And now we're *here* in the friendly confines of the Goodman Theatre," he said. "It's a triumph."

Joan looked at Ingrid. "I must use the girls' room. Are we done?"

"Yes," Ingrid breathed. She laid her face on the table. Joan left the room.

"Trouble in paradise?" Bobby said.

Ingrid sat up and scratched her head vigorously with both hands. "Joan elected herself treasurer of the company, and now I can't move like I used to."

"As though anyone could slow down Ingrid Baardsen." Bobby gave a low chuckle. "That'll be the day."

"When it was your company—and Joan is right, this is not your company anymore—you trusted me to do my job. That's the way I like to work."

"That's how Ingrid Baardsen gets things *done*." He slid into a chair next to her. "So, how can they possibly stop you? You obliterate obstacles."

"I do, don't I?"

"Obliterate."

Ingrid leaned in toward Bobby and lowered her voice. "It's not just Joan. It's everyone. Dwayne. Reg Camper. Nick Sanchez."

"What's the blockade?"

Ingrid lowered her voice even lower. "I designed a set with mountains of antique furniture. The inheritance of betrayal…"

"Yes, you showed us the model."

"As Lear carries in his beloved Cordelia, dead in his arms at the end—as he himself dies of a broken heart—imagine that great stack of furniture bursts into flames!" she whispered.

"My god." Bobby leaned back. "That would be epic."

"But everyone says I can't do it. The fire marshals would never allow it because of the Iroquois Theater fire a hundred years ago."

Bobby blew a raspberry. "A hundred years ago. Like technology hasn't marched on."

"Exactly! Have you been to a rock concert recently? The flames shooting up? They do it in the arenas all the time!"

"You just have to prove it can be done," Bobby said.

"They don't even want to see."

Bobby leaned in until his nose touched her cheek. "Just do it," he whispered. "They'll become believers."

"That's what I thought. Don't show a concept. Show a reality."

Orlando walked into the room. Bobby and Ingrid leaned back away from each other. Bobby winked at her. Ingrid's face blossomed into a smile. She picked up her big canvas bag and exited the rehearsal room.

Orlando tossed his messenger bag on the table and began doing stretches. "What were you two whispering about?"

"Oh, nothing," Bobby said. "And how is Orlando?" He got up and began mirroring Orlando's stretches.

"Said the man who came to town and stole Orlando's role."

"You're not still mad I played Oedipus?"

Orlando snorted. "Ry and I saw Oedipus together. No. All' s forgotten there. We dodged the bullet when Wallace dumped us out of that mess. I'm talking about Edmund."

"Oh, now, not fair." Bobby continued mirroring his moves. "I asked Dwayne to cast me as Kent."

"But when Tom suggested Edmund, you jumped at it. The conniving object of the sisters' lust. You couldn't resist." He bent down and pressed his torso flat against his thighs.

Bobby attempted to mimic the move. He gave up. "Hey, I take what the director gives me. I'm no Peter Burden."

Orlando stopped moving abruptly. "How did you make the transition?"

"The what?"

"You went from doing little shows in Chicago to doing a movie with Sarah Michelle Geller. How did you manage that?"

Bobby chuckled a little and did a little circle walk. He stopped and pointed a finger at Orlando. "You don't want to know how *I* did that. You want to know how *Orlando Gunn* can do that."

"Yeah. Okay. Obviously."

Bobby moved quickly to him and put a hand on his right shoulder. "Don't waste this showcase. Important people will see you here. Yeah, Edgar has to pretend to be Poor Tom. Pathetic, insane, dirty Poor Tom. But *Orlando* must never lose his sexy, superstar self— if you are serious about making the transition. Yeah, be Poor Tom. But be Samuel L. Jackson as Poor Tom. Be Terrance Howard as Poor Tom. Be Laurence Fishburne as Poor Tom. You feel me?"

"Wow." Orlando backed off. "I'm not even sure how you'd do that. That's a lot to consider."

"Yeah." Bobby did a smooth dance move. "You *consider* that."

"Well, well, well." Wallace said, entering the room. "It's the *frères Gloucester.*"

"And so it is," Bobby replied. "The loving brothers. Of a loving father."

Wallace snorted. "Speaking of your loving father, Peter Burden…"

"Yes," Bobby said.

Wallace moved close to Bobby. "What did you think of his comment that I need to be foreshadowing Lear's madness right from the start?"

"What did you think?" Bobby said back.

Wallace shook his head and lowered his voice. He tapped a finger gently on Bobby's chest. "Look, I heard about your Hamlet. How good it was. I want *your* opinion. What did you think of what he said?"

"Bobby does give interesting advice," Orlando piped in.

Bobby breathed a deep sigh and rocked his head from one side to the other. "Okay," he said at last, as though forced into giving his opinion. "Always be the King." He looked at Wallace.

Wallace looked back.

"Always be the King?" Wallace said.

"*Always* be the King."

"Even when I'm mad, raving on the heath?"

"Always be the King."

"How does that make sense?"

"How does Kent's faith make sense? How does Gloucester's sacrifice make sense? How does Cordelia's undying love make sense? Because Lear always remains the King."

"My God." Wallace sat down. "I never thought about that."

"It can't just be pity," Bobby said. "Gloucester knows he's risking his life to support you. Cornwall gouges out his eyes for supporting you."

"Always be the King," Wallace mused.

"Absolutely."

"Interesting."

He sat down to mull it over as Dwayne and the other actors arrived.

45

Sunday, July 30, 2005

On Sunday, Dwayne began to see the problem. In the past week, he had the actors focused on table work. They read through the script, working on the meaning, intention, and emotion of the lines. He wanted them to fully comprehend what they were saying and why before getting on their feet. This was an essential process of discovery in any play, but even more so with the meanings hidden within Shakespeare's archaic language.

Yesterday, with Saturday's longer rehearsal, Dwayne got them onto their feet for the first time. Today, they were moving into Act Three, the middle act. The madness on the heath. Dwayne wasn't giving them specific blocking as yet. This was still exploration. He watched Wallace playing Lear's high rage:

"Blow, winds, and crack your cheeks!" he cried, throwing his arms up. *"Rage! blow! You cataracts and hurricanoes!"* he commanded. *"You sulphurous and thought-executing fires, singe my white head!"* He spun about in anger and rocked his fists in front of him. *"And thou, all-shaking thunder, strike flat the thick rotundity o' the world! Crack nature's moulds, all germens spill at once, that make ingrateful man!"*

What was off about this? Was he falling back on what he'd done as Titus Andronicus? Dwayne considered it. No, it wasn't like how he played the crusty old general.

"Let's stop for a second." Dwayne stepped out onto the rehearsal floor. "This is one of those huge moments," he said to Wallace alone.

"Yes," Wallace agreed. "One of those moments people remember forever—if I do it right."

"So what do you want in this moment?"

Wallace groaned. *What do you want in this moment?* was one of those questions Dwayne had been putting to his actors a lot in this first week. "I want to command the weather," he said.

"You're giving commands to the weather," Dwayne agreed. "But why? What do you want?"

"I want to be king. I want to restore my power. No?" He pushed both hands, fingers spread, back through his thick salt and pepper hair.

"You are the king, but you've found yourself stripped of power, stripped of followers, sent out into the storm with no shelter, betrayed by your daughters. You're now at the deepest recognition of your weakness."

"Yes. *Blow, winds, and crack your cheeks,* blah, blah, blah, *strike flat the thick rotundity o' the world!* Revenge! Right? I want revenge."

"Good thought. But let's go deeper," Dwayne said. "*You sulphurous and thought-executing fires, singe my white head!* Think of that."

"*Thought-executing fires,*" Wallace mused. "Right. When lightning crashes down near you, you cannot think a thing. *Oak-cleaving thunderbolts, singe my white head.* I'm seeking oblivion! A lightning bolt to the head."

"Yes! And not just personal oblivion. A king of your epoch identified with his realm. Your fertility guaranteed the fertility of the kingdom." Dwayne stopped for a moment. He felt something weirdly personal in that. He had a sudden memory of horrible tea in the back of his throat. *The king's fertility guaranteed the fertility of the kingdom?* Where did that come from? Joseph Campbell? *The Hero's Journey?* What did that mean about Dwayne leading these actors? Was he the king who was infertile? Angela said his swimmers were going sideways. Some had two tails. Some deformed. Did that mean he couldn't lead these people in realizing Shakespeare's greatest tragedy?

"Dwayne?" Wallace looked at him with concern, the deep wrinkles in his face arranged in a brow of sorrow.

"Right. Sorry. Lost in a thought there for a moment," Dwayne said. "Yes. Oblivion is right, I think. And then look at that last line. *Crack nature's moulds, all germens spill at once, that make ingrateful man!* Germens there in the sense of germ, like wheat germ: seed. He's commanding nature to crack the molds and destroy the seeds that make man. Oblivion to himself, as you say, but the end of humanity, as well."

"Wow, yes," Wallace said. "The most epic despair of all!"

"Yes," Dwayne said. "So what I saw from you in that scene was Lear focused on command. On wielding power…"

"Right, right, right," Wallace said. "But I am a man who always wielded power. And now I want oblivion because of how far I've fallen?"

"Try that." As Dwayne returned to his seat behind the director's table, he thought he noticed Bobby looking at Wallace and shaking his head.

Did Bobby really do that? Had Wallace nodded back?

Dwayne sat down. Weirdly, he noticed how his balls felt as he sat. Did they have a slight ache to them? Was he imagining it? Was he feeling the dysfunction that created malformed sperm? Would his seed always lack potency? Was he someone who lacked potency? Is that why, at thirty-one years old, he was still struggling to find his way into a lucrative adulthood? His old friends, Aleister and Chaz, had their ups and downs, but they excelled in their respective fields.

But why did his balls feel weird now? He'd never noticed the feeling of his balls against the chair so pronounced when sitting before now. Could he just go back to sitting without thinking about his balls again? Or was drinking a cup of that weird-ass curandera tea twice a day doing something to his testicles? And those burning herbs. The apartment always smelled like a grass-fire prairie these days. What was all that doing to him? Would his balls grow to twice their normal size? Would he walk bow-legged for the rest of his life? And Angela! Would she ever be the same? She was like a convert to a weird cult, praying to her ancestors. Dwayne did his best to do his part, but he couldn't help thinking sometimes that this was a big, weird trick being played on the two of them. If it didn't work, how crushed Angela would be! He dreaded the coming of that moment, and that made him try ever harder to believe it *would* work. If his ancestors could, in fact, hear his prayers, they would be impressed with his fervency.

Come on, Dwayne! You're in the Goodman Theatre, directing King Lear, *for fuck's sake! Focus!*

He liked what Wallace was doing somewhat better after their talk. He continued to watch, taking notes. But when Kent and the Fool took Lear to the shelter of the hovel on the heath, Orlando seemed somehow weird. By this point, Orlando's Edgar had disguised himself as the mad, homeless Poor Tom. Betrayed by his brother, Edgar had a price on his head, condemned to death if caught.

"Away! the foul fiend follows me! Through the sharp hawthorn blows the cold wind. Humh! go to thy cold bed, and warm thee," he said to Lear as they entered his hovel.

"Didst thou give all to thy two daughters?" Lear asked him. *"And art thou come to this?"*

"Who gives anything to poor Tom?" Was Orlando flexing his muscles as he spoke? *"Whom the foul fiend hath led through flame to ride on a bay trotting horse over four-inched bridges,"* He did a proud little gallop as he spoke. *"Bless thy five wits Tom's a-cold."*

Dwayne was tempted to stop the action, but he let it continue. He wasn't sure what to say. Every Edgar Dwayne had seen had played Poor Tom curled in on himself and covered in dirt so that no one would recognize him as the noble Edgar. But Orlando looked upright and physically strong. That was the problem, Dwayne realized. He wasn't disguising his physical self.

"What, have his daughters brought him to this pass?" Wallace replied. *"Didst thou give 'em all?"*

He liked how distracted Wallace looked. Wallace was starting to embrace Lear's madness.

At the break, Orlando strolled up to Dwayne. "What did you think? I'm trying something Bobby suggested. You know, to take me farther in my career."

"What's that?"

"He suggested I keep a kind of superstar presence. I want people to notice me, to make a impression. I want to break through to film as well as stage."

"Edgar is a great role for that," Dwayne said, "but not by maintaining a superstar presence. Edgar allows you to show incredible acting chops. You show the other characters Poor Tom, but you show the audience that you are seeing all the pain onstage. You see what's happening to Lear. What's happening to your father. You show the decisions you make. You play all that while also playing Poor Tom's madness, you'll impress every director or producer in the house."

"Wow," Orlando said. "Yeah, I hadn't been thinking that way. Thanks, Dwayne."

As he walked away, he gave a smirking salute to Bobby, but an annoyed Tom came and pulled Orlando away. Coco slid up to Bobby on the other side and bumped her hip against his as they stood. Bobby gave a slow smile. Coco gave him an arched eyebrow.

What was Bobby up to?

Jealousy and convoluted love affairs were beginning to complicate the relationships, Dwayne suspected. Would they get so intense that they'd undermine his work? Would everyone else's sexual potency unravel his power to lead?

46

Wednesday, August 2, 2005

The two actors of whom Dwayne felt most confident now stared at each other with doubt. He'd looked forward to seeing the pyrotechnics they'd bring to the stage. What was this?

"Back, Edmund, to my brother," Coco said to Bobby (or rather, Goneril said to Edmund). But that was the problem. Dwayne was not seeing Goneril and Edmund. He was seeing an oddly hesitant Coco talking to a mystified Bobby. *"Ere long you are like to hear a mistress's command,"* she said, giving Bobby a special ribbon. The last time she'd delivered this line, it was laden with desire. *"This kiss, if it durst speak, would stretch thy spirits up into the air."* She gave him a kiss so sexless it might have looked more appropriate from Judas to Christ than from lusty Goneril to crafty Edmund. She turned away without looking him in the eyes.

Saint Anthony of Padua, where are my lost performances?

"Yours in the ranks of death," Bobby said, looking mystified as to what had happened to all the fire in this scene. He exited.

Albany walked on stage, but Coco turned to face Dwayne. "Can we take a moment? I'd like to talk with you."

Stage manager Howie Grange looked to Dwayne. Dwayne nodded. "Take ten, everyone," Howie said.

"Fifteen," Dwayne corrected.

"Take fifteen, everyone," Howie said.

"Thank you, fifteen," everyone said.

Coco led Dwayne briskly to a dressing room down the hall and closed the door after them. "I think I need to see your friend, Aleister."

"Why?"

"He helped Melinda during *Titus Andronicus.* Then he brought my pops back to himself when he went full-blown into Uncle Bull."

"Yeah, but why would *you* need to see him?"

She sighed and sat down at the makeup table that stretched along the wall.

"I might have inherited Pops' mental illness."

Dwayne's mouth dropped open. He closed it, then cocked his head to the side. "Is it something that's inherited?"

"I don't know!" Coco said. "Do I look like a psychiatrist? That's why I need to talk with Aleister."

"Why do you think you're having the…dissociative identity thing?"

"Bobby," she whispered with extreme force. "I swore I'd never get into bed with that man again. I mean, not that he isn't fine. He's actually more fine than ever. I don't know if Sarah Michelle Geller strayed from Freddie Prinze, Jr., who also is fine, by the way, but I wouldn't have blamed her. Bobby's body is something to behold. And, frankly, he knows how to use it. But it's not like Bobby is the only man out there. It's not like if I wanted a man right now, I couldn't find one."

"No."

"So I would not be luring Bobby back to my crib if I wasn't dropping into some mental dissociative thing."

"Well…" Dwayne said doubtfully. "People fall back into relationships all the time. Some people even stay in abusive relationships for years. He's not abusive, is he?"

Coco cocked her head. "If anyone ever hit me, that'd be the end of them." She snorted, imagining the fate of such a person.

"So," Dwayne said. "No abuse. Just casual sex, right?"

"Yes!" Coco said. "But I was absolutely done with him in that way two years ago." She leaned in and lowered her voice to a barely audible whisper. "That's why I think it must be Goneril."

It took Dwayne a moment to figure out what she was saying.

"You think Goneril has become an alternate personality inside you?"

"What else explains it? I never would've hooked up with Bobby again. Ever! But Goneril lusts for Edmund. And then I started to feel jealous of Tom. Tom! Playing my sister, Regan. My rival for

Edmund's love. Can you imagine Bobby deciding to hook up with Tom?"

"Right." Bobby was about as heterosexual as a person could get.

"So, there. That proves it. Now I'm afraid to play her fully. I don't want to get swept into a dissociative personality disorder like Pops. You don't know what it's like growing up with a father who turns into Uncle Bull."

"I don't. But I do know actors who've felt overwhelmed by their roles without it ever turning into multiple personality disorder."

"Yeah, but how many of them had it run in their family?"

Dwayne didn't have an answer for that.

"So I need to see Aleister. Or else I'm going to have to drop out of the show."

"No, no, no!" Dwayne said. "Don't do that. Jesus. I'll get Aleister to talk with you." *Oh, please be available, Aleister!* "And in the meantime, can you get back to playing fully? The last time you and Bobby did that scene, it was electrifying. Let's get back on the horse!"

"I don't know, Dwayne." Coco sniffed and moved toward the door. "I need to take the rest of the night off." She took a deep breath and let it out. "In fact, please keep my things for me until tomorrow. I don't want to face anyone in the rehearsal room."

"Wait. Let's do a breathing exercise. Cleanse this feeling…"

She raised a hand for him to stop. She swept out the door without another word, down the stairs, out onto Dearborn Street, and into the night.

47

Friday, August 4, 2005

"I'm not taking charity," Coco announced as she swept into Aleister's consulting room in the office building at the corner of Lake and Wabash downtown. She set a picnic basket on the table next to the couch. She looked at him with a challenging expression, then looked out the window, down at the curve of the El tracks going around the corner far below. She turned back to him. "Whatever your rate, add thirty percent. I see you staying after hours for me. I know that's a favor to Dwayne. You get my money, my thanks, and my charcuterie." She flipped open the wicker picnic basket to reveal a demi-baguette, cheeses, crackers, prosciutto, sausages, olives, a split of champagne and a split of Bordeaux, as well as plates, glasses, and cutlery. "Some people call me a diva, but I consider other people's needs." She began spreading the foodstuffs on the coffee table in front of the couch. "You give up your happy hour to sit with me, it's the least I can do. However…" She handed him a corkscrew and gestured to the splits. "Part of your duty is to open."

Aleister chuckled. "How did I know a session with Coco Nesbit would be unlike any other?"

Coco leaned back and arched her left eyebrow. "How could it not?" She sat on the couch and gestured to the spread. "Please."

Aleister chuckled again and prepared himself a plate, then uncorked the Bordeaux. He poured himself and Coco a glass. He didn't actually think of this as a professional session. Even if it were, making the patient comfortable was always best, within reason. In any case, he didn't intend to charge her for the time. A conversation with this extraordinarily beautiful, eccentric woman was reward enough in itself.

"I don't know how much Dwayne told you…"

"He was going to tell me something, but I stopped him. He told me you wanted my help. Something was interfering with your work. I want to hear the details from you."

"Well, you were just a wizard with Pops when he dissociated into Uncle Bull."

Aleister remembered it well. He'd used basic hypnotism to help Rocky emerge from his alternate personality, the dangerous and violent Uncle Bull. "Is your father having trouble again?"

"Not him. Me!"

"In what way?"

Coco cocked her head at him. "How do you do that the way you do?"

"Do what?"

"You don't show surprise. You just welcome in whatever the next insane thing you might hear."

"I didn't hear anything insane. Yet." He spread a little cheese on a cracker and popped it into his mouth.

"You funny." She looked at him for a while. She changed her seating posture. She changed it again twice more. She sighed loudly.

"Okay! I think I inherited Pops' thing," she said at last.

"His dissociative identity disorder?"

"Yes. That."

"You've been suffering symptoms?"

"Just since we started on *King Lear*."

"Do you remember your episodes?"

"Oh, yeah."

"But it's an alternate personality?"

"That's right." She rolled up a slice of prosciutto and stuffed it in her mouth, then tore off a piece of baguette.

"Does this personality have a name?"

"Goneril."

"Isn't that the name of your role in *King Lear*?"

"Right. She's making me do things I would never do."

"Do you feel like yourself when you are doing these things?"

"Well…" She screwed up her face and looked at the ceiling, and then back at Aleister. "I kind of still feel like I'm myself. I mean, it's not like I'm doing things I've never done before. It's just I swore I'd never do those things again. There's no reason I *would* ever do those things again, except this Goneril personality is invading me. If I'm inheriting Pops' thing, it's like this might just be the beginning. I don't want it to advance to where I don't even know myself, and she's making my life an incredible mess. I mean, Pops has to stay on his meds, or he could go off the tracks. I don't want that for me."

"No," Aleister said. "What's she making you do?"

Coco got up, opened the door, and looked out into the reception room. No one else was there. She closed the door.

"Is everything I say in confidence? Like the Catholic priests? Or a lawyer?"

"Absolutely."

"You don't report *nothing* back to Dwayne?"

"Especially not Dwayne. But no. Nobody. Your privacy is sacred."

"Okay." She settled herself back on the couch and looked around a little. "This is a really nice office, by the way. I know furniture. This is nice furniture."

"Thanks." Aleister had upgraded the furniture after his book started bringing in startling amounts of money. He especially liked the vintage roll-top desk he'd put in. The carpenter had done a nice job of hiding the hole to pass through the wires for his computer.

"Did you select the artwork? They look like originals."

"I do like oils," Aleister said. Sometimes a patient needed to meander a bit. He never rushed anyone.

Coco looked down at her hands in her lap. She slapped her thighs abruptly and threw her hands in the air. "She's making me fuck Bobby. I swore I'd never do that again."

Aleister nodded.

She couldn't see any judgment on his face, one way or the other. "I would just never do that," she insisted. "I mean, I totally swore off that man long ago. Goneril is the only explanation."

"So, you're usually well-reasoned in your choice of sexual partners?"

"Well-reasoned?" She looked at him, amazed. "I don't know

about that. I was fucking your pal, Chaz, not that long ago. Sometimes I just see what I want and go out and get it."

"But Bobby is off-limits."

"I don't believe in *off-limits*, but I definitely decided no more Bobby. That episode was over and not to be repeated. When I decide that, that's it! I don't go back. Never have. Done is done. Period. Finito. Caput. I don't go back."

"But now you have."

"Yes. Well, you know Bobby. Bobby is a good-looking man. And when he's got his clothes off, he's twice, maybe three times, more good-looking. Most people look better with their clothes on. But Bobby. He's even better-looking now than back when he and I were, you know, first hooking up. And it's not just how he looks. And how that sculpted body feels. He's just way better…at…it. He made me come so hard, I was weeping. And he's going, *Yeah, yeah, yeah, little girl, let it all out.* And, oh my God, I came even harder. Multiple orgasms. I'm telling you. I've never had an experience like that. I couldn't walk. I couldn't talk. He tried to talk to me. He wanted to go for a drink. I was so…. Finally he just left."

Clearly Coco was aroused just telling the story. "So that was…" Coco stopped and stared into space.

"And you'd prefer to avoid that in the future," Aleister said.

"Well, it was kind of overwhelming. Still…" She considered it breathlessly for a moment, then shook her head hard. "But there's more to it than that. The *Goneril* in me is jealous of Tom, for the love of sweet baby Jesus. Goneril poisons Regan. Kills her out of jealousy. But why would *I* be jealous of Tom? Even if I wanted a real thing going with Bobby again, Bobby is never, ever going to fuck Tom. And why would I care, anyway? I don't care who else Bobby is fucking any more than he cares who else I might be fucking. And I never would've found out what it's like to fuck Bobby now if it hadn't been for Goneril. I would've steered clear."

"Right."

"You see, I take my acting serious. It's what I do. Having an offstage thing with Bobby messes with my onstage performance. I won't have that. Especially when I'm going on at the Goodman. That just messes with my whole philosophy of living!"

"I see."

"So, what do you think?" Coco leaned in toward him.

Aleister considered it for a moment. "First, I think there's very little chance that you've inherited dissociative identity disorder from your father. I've never seen any evidence in the literature of that disorder being inherited. It generally results from trauma. In those cases where a parent and child both suffer from it, trauma inflicted by the parent on the child is typically the cause of the child's disorder. Nor does it tend to arise in the subtle ways you are describing."

"I don't know if y'all was listening, but there was very little subtle about all that."

"Subtle in the development of the dissociative symptoms, I mean."

"Okay," she said, looking unsure what that meant.

"There are many anecdotal accounts of actors being influenced by the characters they portray, however. Might that seem the more likely source of your discomfort?"

"Well…" She mulled that over for a moment.

"Goneril wants Edmund, played by Bobby. You've noticed Bobby is more attractive than ever. Your recent experience with him was extraordinary."

"It certainly was."

"So even though you made this pact with yourself to swear off Bobby, there's nothing unusual about being attracted by him and backsliding. Just like someone who's trying to lose weight suddenly finds cheesecake irresistible."

"Huh! Then what do you think I can do about it?"

"There is a ceremony you can perform before and after rehearsals and performances that might help keep Goneril in her place."

"Really?"

"It's a combination of movement, breathing, meditation, and affirmations beforehand that allow you to access the character and then a similar set to shut her off at the end. It's like matched sessions of self-hypnosis."

"That sounds fantastic. Will you teach me?"

"Absolutely. But maybe you know it already. I learned it from Dwayne."

"Dwayne?" She stood up in outrage. "He didn't teach me that. Shit. Why was he holding out on me?"

48

Saturday, August 5, 2005

Dwayne was excited to get to the Saturday rehearsal. Saturday and Sunday, they had longer rehearsals. They could dig deeper. Get more done. It wasn't like the weeknights when most were showing up exhausted from their day jobs. And today they were working the final scene of the show. Dwayne couldn't wait.

But when he got to the spot out in front of his apartment where he'd left the company car, he did not see the ancient Pinto. Had he forgotten where he'd parked? He looked up and down Albion. No sign of the rusty heap anywhere.

St. Anthony of Padua, help me!

Dwayne cut under the CTA viaduct and turned up the next street. There, mid-block, the old Pinto stuck partially out into the street. There was no way Dwayne had left the car like that. The door was partly open. He had to tug hard to open it enough to get in. Once inside, shards of shattered metal littered the mat below his feet. He lifted his key to the ignition on the steering column, but the ignition switch was gone, and a gaping hole was left. Someone had broken it off the column, and a few wires hung out.

Someone had stolen the car! They stole it to drive one block from where he'd left it?

He looked again at the mess they'd made of the steering column, and then he noticed the white button of the manual choke beneath the dash. Of course! They'd stolen the car and couldn't get it to drive more than a block because they didn't know how to use a manual choke. They wouldn't even know the white button was a manual choke. And even if they did know, and somehow they knew how to use a manual choke, they wouldn't have known how to use this one, because it was installed backwards.

There were only two people in the continental United States who knew how to operate this car: He and Ingrid. It was theft-proof.

But now he was going to be late. It being a Saturday, the Red Line offered less frequent trains. He ran back under the viaduct, east on Albion to Sheridan, and down to the Loyola stop.

Waiting on the platform for a train was an agony.

He called Ingrid to let her know about the car. She thought it was hilarious and promised to swing by and fix it.

He arrived in the rehearsal room two minutes after the rehearsal was scheduled to begin, out of breath and sweaty. Fortunately, Joan had the actors up doing some warm-ups led by the young and admirably flexible Melinda. Melinda loved leading warm-ups, and the actors seemed generally happy about doing them with her, with the exception of Peter Burden, who went through the movements half-heartedly with a droopy look on his face.

"What happened?" Joan said to him quietly.

"It was the Pinto."

"You know how that car is. Plan accordingly."

"Somebody stole it."

She looked at him with something resembling surprise. "Why would anyone steal that heap?"

"Maybe for a demolition derby?"

Dwayne gathered his thoughts and cooled down as Melinda finished the warm-ups. He stepped into the center as the actors took their seats.

"Okay. Today, we are going to move into the final scene. We'll come back to choreograph the war scene and the Edgar/Edmund sword fight that precedes this with Ry's music and Tom's movement on…" He searched his mind. The stress had scrambled his memory.

"Wednesday," Joan prompted.

"Yes. Wednesday. Thanks, Joan," Dwayne said. "So, coming into Lear's entrance, we've got Kent and Albany in conversation center stage." He gestured to them, and they joined him in their positions in the center of the rehearsal space. "They've just sent Edgar to rescue Cordelia because the dying Edmund admitted he sent a captain to hang her. They are waiting here as Lear enters from upstage center, carrying Cordelia in his arms, followed by Edgar and the French Officer." Those four actors got into the places Dwayne designated. "Kent and Albany will split, backing off from this sorrowful sight, as Lear moves downstage center with Cordelia. Edgar will join Kent stage right and the French officer moves toward Albany stage left, and everyone will remain very still, putting all focus on Lear. Good?"

He looked around as the rest of the actors got quietly into place. Orlando whispered something to Wallace.

"No! Absolutely not!" Wallace said.

"I think it makes sense," Orlando insisted.

"No! No! No!" Wallace said.

"Is there a problem?" Dwayne said.

"Edgar wants to put Cordelia in my arms. He doesn't want me to pick her up."

"I'm talking about backstage," Orlando said. "Before we enter."

"Lear picks up his daughter and carries her on," Wallace said. "That's what I want to do."

"Seems reasonable," Dwayne said.

"It's not," Orlando said. "Wallace is playing a devastating scene. Is he going to remember safe lifting technique? We can't have our Lear throw his back out. I mean, Melinda is slim, but it's not like she weighs nothing." He turned to Melinda. "No offense intended."

"None taken." She turned to Dwayne. "I think Orlando's hand-off idea is good." She put a hand on Wallace's shoulder. "We can't have you hurt, Father. You do the heavy-lifting all through the show."

"It's kind of you to say so, but Lear lifts his daughter," Wallace insisted.

"He does," Dwayne agreed. "But then he dies. Whereas you have another performance the next day."

"Wait a minute," Orlando said. "We don't know that Lear lifts Cordelia. It's off stage. The officer and I discover you two. She and I have known each other since we were children. It's entirely possible that *I* would have lifted my friend Cordelia, and you held out your arms for her."

Wallace laughed grimly. "Okay. You win. Edgar can put Cordelia in my arms, but not because I'm a weak old man!"

"Absolutely not," Dwayne said. "Let's do it Orlando's way. Places, please, and let's try it."

Wallace put a hand on Orlando's shoulder so he'd wait until Wallace gathered his emotions. Then he nodded, and Orlando nodded back, and he lifted Melinda into his arms. Wallace carried her slowly toward center stage as the others parted to give him focus.

"*Howl, howl, howl! O, you are men of stone,*" Wallace declaimed. He did not sound entirely convincing to Dwayne. "*Had I your tongues and eyes, I'd use them so that heaven's vault should crack. I know when one is dead, and when one lives; she's dead as earth.*" He set her on the ground in front of him. "*Lend me a looking glass. If her breath will mist the stone, why then she lives.*" Lear took a mirror from the French officer and held it to her nose. Watching it, he began to shake his head and moan. Then he looked at the mirror as though he didn't know what it was.

"*O, my good master!*" Kent knelt down by Lear.

"*Prythee, away!*" Lear pushed Kent down. "*A plague upon you, murderers, traitors all! I might have saved her! Cordelia! Stay a little!*" He stood up and then knelt back down, as though he'd forgotten what the action was. He stopped and put his ear to her mouth. "*What is't thou say'st?*" He looked up at the others, frustrated. "*Her voice was ever soft, gentle, and low.*" He turned back and addressed her. "*I killed the slave that was hanging thee.*" His face turned suddenly savage, and he broke away from her. He stood up and waved his arms like a windmill, then stopped abruptly.

"*Tis true, my lords, he did,*" the French officer said.

"*Did I not?*" Lear shouted. "*I have seen the day, with my good biting falchion I would have made them skip.*" He mimed the waving of a sword and then stuck his hands in his pockets abruptly and pulled them back out. He looked back again at Kent with deep curiosity. "*Who are you? Mine eyes are not o' the best. Are you not Kent?*"

"*The same. Your servant, Kent.*"

"*And my poor fool is hanged! Why should a dog, a horse, a rat have life, and thou no breath at all? Thou'lt come no more. Never, never, never, never, never!*" He stopped. "*Do you see this?*" He looked suddenly shocked and pointed at her face. "*Look on her: look, her lips, look there,*" *look there!"* He put his hands to his heart and collapsed to the ground.

"*He faints!"* Edgar exclaimed. *"My lord!"*

"*Break, heart. I prythee break!"* Kent said.

"*Look up, my lord,"* Edgar said, seemingly seeing the soul of Lear rise.

"*Vex not his ghost,"* Kent insisted. *"O, let him pass! The wonder is, he hath endured so long. He but usurped his life."*

"*The weight of this sad time we must obey,"* Edgar said. *"The oldest hath borne most. We that are young shall never see so much, nor live so long."*

They held for a moment, then Dwayne said: "And lights down. Okay. Good."

"Oh, argh!" Wallace said, getting up from the floor.

"The first well-delivered line from him today," Peter Burden said from his seat.

Wallace approached Dwayne. "A word in private?"

Dwayne turned to Howie Grange. "Take ten, please."

"Take ten," Howie announced.

"Thank you, ten," everyone replied, looking at one another, surprised there was a break so early.

Dwayne led Wallace to the same dressing room he'd gone to with Coco earlier in the week.

"Sorry, sorry, sorry," Wallace said in his deep baritone. "I know you want to accomplish so much, especially on a Saturday. But I am so…." He stopped. He looked down at his feet. "I…" He shook his head vigorously. "I but usurp my life."

"That's nonsense," Dwayne said.

"I'm in a panic." He sat down abruptly and clutched at the seat of the chair between his legs.

"We are still finding our way in. This is *Lear*, for God's sake. You aren't going to get it immediately. We have time before we open."

"My whole career, I've been a failure. Maybe there's a reason for that. I had no business taking on Lear."

"I don't believe that."

"I can't focus my mind. There I am, with dead Cordelia in my arms, and I am seeing the actor, Melinda, and I'm thinking how I should have directed her differently as Antigone in *Oedipus*. I did a terrible job directing *Oedipus*."

Dwayne sighed. "You know what? You did do a terrible job directing *Oedipus*. You weren't prepared for it, and you approached it with an utter lack of humility."

Wallace looked shocked.

"I'm your director, not your cheerleader. I'm honest about your work. I owe you that. How else could you trust me? You are as ready to play Lear as you were not ready to direct *Oedipus*. I didn't have to give you the role of Lear. I could've had every veteran actor in the city of Chicago, equity and non-equity, begging me for the role. Directing *Lear* at the Goodman is the opportunity I have been waiting for. And I chose you. I chose our ensemble. And look what happened today. You had a young pup like Orlando looking out for your performance, making sure you didn't injure yourself lifting Melinda. He even found justification in the text for Edgar to lift Cordelia. They have your back. Literally. And what did Melinda say? *We can't have you hurt, Father. You do the heavy lifting all through the show.* That was one of the sweetest things I've ever heard. They love you, and they believe in you. They know you can do this."

Wallace's face suddenly crumpled up. "I love them, too," he said, beginning to weep. He threw his hands up. "*Now* I'm crying! Not when I'm carrying my dead daughter. *Now*!"

Dwayne laughed at him with affection. "You're fine. You'll have this."

"All right. God damn it. *Blow winds, and crack your cheeks! Rage! Blow, you cataracts and hurricanoes!* Let's get back in there."

"Now you're talking," Dwayne said. He watched the old man head back toward the rehearsal room.

Was he right about Wallace?

49

Later that Evening

At the end of rehearsal, Dwayne's costumer, Peaches, came bounding into the room. Eight pigtails bound tightly with mini-scrunchies erupted from her scalp in all directions. Each of them was dyed a different color, including black, ice blond, a variety of pastels, and midnight blue. She wore large sunglasses with rhinestones across the top. She wore pink yoga pants and a blue tutu, with an open orange satin blouse over a black ribbed turtleneck tee shirt. She threw her arms around his neck.

"Hello, Dwayne!" She gave him a big kiss on the side of the cheek and bounded off toward Melinda. "Hi, gorgeous," she said to her. She reached out more tentatively to take her hand.

"Hi," Melinda said cautiously.

Peaches backed off, her smile twisting. She giggled a little and bounded off to say hello to the other ensemble members. When she got to Bobby, she laid her hand on his chest and leaned in to whisper something in his ear. They both laughed, and she put her hands on his shoulders, and stood like that for a long moment, then bounded off again. She looked around the room uncertainly, and then slunk over to Melinda and left the rehearsal room with her.

Dwayne had seen Peaches in her manic phases before, but this one seemed extra energetic.

Everyone cleared out. Just Peter Burden, Dwayne, and Howie Grange remained. Peter cleared his throat. "A word?"

"Sure," Dwayne said. "I can lock up," he told Howie.

"Actually, I have to do that."

"Howie can hear this," Peter said. "After all, I'm the only one in this production who's worked with Howie before."

"Okay," Dwayne said.

"I think you see how this is going," Peter said. He leaned on the director's table that stood between himself and Dwayne and Howie, then straightened up again. "You've got an actor who has no business playing Lear on the Goodman stage. Or anywhere, frankly, in a city like Chicago."

Dwayne started to object, but Peter raised his hand. "Just let me say my piece, please, okay?"

"Okay," Dwayne said.

"I've been in two shows with Wallace. He played small roles—a supernumerary in one of them—and he wasn't particularly distinguished even in those. Look at what he's doing now. Why do *Lear* if you are not going to do it well? It makes no sense." Peter looked from Dwayne to Howie and back as if he were waiting for them to agree. "Would you prefer to stage another *Lear* with a mediocre White actor—something we've seen far too often—or stage a *Lear* with an exceptional Black actor, something we've seen far too little?" He looked at Dwayne and waited.

"Is that it?" Dwayne said.

"Absolutely not. Wallace has improved since I last worked with him. That was fifteen years ago. He could probably do a credible job with, say, the faithful Gloucester, or the virtuous Albany. Or even the cruel Cornwall. But Lear? He's never going to get there." He looked again for agreement.

"I disagree," Dwayne said.

"Give it another week," Peter said. "See if he's developing into a Lear of which you can be proud. In the meantime, talk with Reg Camper. I think he'll tell you I am capable of a Lear that will put your name on the map. You want to be known as a Chicago director whose time has come. You don't want to blow this chance. Nor do I."

"So you want me to swap roles between you and Wallace?"

"Yes! If he resents losing the title role and quits the production, you can find a new Gloucester. But don't wait too long. I would have preferred rehearsing it from the start, even though this is a much longer rehearsal process than…"

"Yes, you shared your thoughts on that," Dwayne said.

"Right. So if you could make this swap no later than August

sixteenth, I promise to put my whole heart and twenty-four hours a day into giving you the Lear you deserve. A Lear people will talk about for years."

"You are offering me nine days to dump Wallace."

"Give him Gloucester. It's a great role."

"I'm not going to do it, Peter."

"Don't decide tonight. We'll keep this under our hats. I know Howie is discreet."

Howie looked inscrutable.

"I'm not going to do it, Peter."

"That's how you feel *right now*," Peter said. "The residual pull of your ensemble. That's fine. See how you feel in a week. Talk to Reg. See if Wallace develops. Even if it's later than the sixteenth. I'll be learning both roles, so I'll be ready."

"I'm not going to do it, Peter."

Peter nodded reassuringly. "You don't have to decide right now."

50

Monday, August 7, 2005

"And look at this!" Peaches flipped over another large sheet of drawing paper to show her new drawings for the costumes. She waved her arms at it. "Ta da!"

Peaches was a great designer, but even with her best designs, she tended to present them in an apologetic way, as though she wished she could do better and maybe Dwayne would be better off with a different designer. Today was different. She was using huge sheets of drawing paper. She'd drawn her renderings with savage strokes. She was so confident it frightened him.

It wasn't that he didn't enjoy this version of Peaches. He truly did. And he loved her designs. It frightened him because the higher she flew, the deeper she crashed, and this crash might be horrible.

"I love them," he said. "I love them all. Let's go ahead with these."

"Hurray!" she shouted. She jumped around the room and gave him a hug.

"Peaches, listen," he said quietly.

"No, no, no, no, Dwayne. I know what you're going to say."

"You do?"

"You're worried about me. Melinda's worried about me. But there's something you don't realize." She took his shoulders and pushed him down gently into a chair. "I live for this," she said intently. "Most of my life, it's hard to be me. You know how I am. So nervous about everything. But when I'm *here*..."

"Here?"

"Don't be obtuse, Dwayne."

"*Here* as in manic."

"Don't use that word!" she shouted. She lowered her voice.

"Don't reduce me to a symptom. This is my *life*," she whispered. She knelt down beside him and put her lips to his ear. "I have to live this to the full when it comes so that I have something to look back on and to look forward to when I'm down and it's so so so so so so so so hard."

"Hey, babe, you guys done?" Bobby stood at the door, leaning against the doorjamb, looking like a model on the cover of *Ebony*.

"Oh, come on now," Dwayne said.

"What?" both Bobby and Peaches said.

"You sit," Dwayne said, steering Peaches into a chair by the shoulders like she had done to him.

He took Bobby out into the hallway and closed the door behind them. "You can't treat this ensemble like your private harem."

"I can't?" Bobby looked facetiously shocked, then gave a deep laugh.

"Bobby, come on. You can't be taking advantage of Peaches when she's like this."

Bobby rolled his eyes. "You know what she does, right?"

"Yes, I know."

"Well, would you rather she be out throwing herself at strange guys in bars, maybe meeting someone who beats her up or gives her a disease? Or would you rather she go home with an old friend who's going to give her what she wants, but who's also going to look out for her?"

Peaches stuck her head out of the doorway. "If you two are talking about little old me, I'd sure like to hear what you're saying."

"We're done," Bobby said. "Dwayne was just giving me notes. On the show. You know how evil Edmund is. He doesn't want me to go over the top."

"Right," Dwayne said. He narrowed his eyes at Bobby.

"Well," Peaches said coyly. "You could go over the top on *me*." She yelped and grabbed his hand and dragged him until they were both running down the hallway and around the corner, out of sight.

Dwayne shook his head. He gathered his things and headed down the hall to go home.

"Dwayne Finnegan on a Monday night!" Reg Camper said,

coming from the opposite direction. "Can you be rehearsing?"

"I just met with my costumer."

"Ah! It just so happens I have a decent bottle of scotch in my office, and it's a beautiful night on the Via Maggio. Might you care to join me?"

"I'd love to."

They took the elevator up to the fourth floor and retrieved the scotch from Camper's office, a couple glasses, and took them out to the balcony over North Dearborn Street. The warm August night enveloped them, and the lights of the huge Goodman marquee reflected on their faces.

Camper held up the bottle. "One of my board members makes occasional jaunts to Scotland to play golf. He often brings me back a bottle of extraordinary scotch. He says it's to enhance the excellence of my creative thinking." Camper laughed and poured out two healthy glasses. "I do enjoy the scotch, but I can't say I've ever had an exceptionally interesting thought because of it."

Dwayne lifted the glass to his nose. "Peaty. This makes me wish I'd had enough good scotch in my life to appreciate this."

"They say drinking steadily better scotches develops one's palate. On the other hand, why not start at the top?" He clicked glasses with Dwayne, and they sipped. Despite its pronounced smokiness, the scotch was exceptionally smooth. Dwayne nodded in appreciation.

"I hear your Lear is struggling," Camper said.

Ah, so that was the occasion of this invite. "I can't imagine where you heard that." Dwayne wagged his head back and forth.

"Our friend, Peter Burden, is being a pain in the ass?" Camper asked.

"He likes to share his opinions."

"He does," Camper agreed. "But as long as you and I are here enjoying the scotch, I'd be glad to talk, one director to another."

"My Lear has been having a few confidence issues," Dwayne admitted, "but I believe he'll find his way through."

"It's *Lear*," Camper said. "That's inevitable for any actor."

"How do you help an actor find the role?"

Camper thought that over. "I use stories," he said finally. "You know, we're in the business of telling stories. You're telling the story of *King Lear*. When I directed Brian Dennehy and Patricia Clarkson in *Long Day's Journey*, the actor playing Edmund struggled. I think he was overawed by Brian and Patricia, even though they are both exceptionally generous actors. I told so many stories of O'Neill's life. His early life. Brian did, as well. He's a great storyteller. Both of us love O'Neill. We've done so much of his work. Well, all those stories eventually cracked something open in the actor and freed him up. You know, Edmund is the character most closely based on O'Neill himself. We spent so much time telling stories; our stage manager was amazed we got the play up on the boards. But we broke open everything in that script."

"And that helped the actor find his way?"

"He did a brilliant job. Story-telling was an impulse from the beginning of my career. Then I read an interview with Mike Nichols, who, of course, was a great hero of mine. He also told stories to help his actors find their performances. If Mike Nichols was doing it, how could it possibly be wrong?"

"Right."

"The other thing is to make sure you've got the right cast. But you seem to be confident in your actors, even if Peter Burden thinks you're dead wrong." Camper gave him a long, hard look. Did Camper think Wallace was miscast? Dwayne broke his gaze and looked up at the Goodman marquee. This was the big time. Was he, in fact, sure of his Lear?

51

Wednesday, August 9, 2005

"Okay, everyone," Tom said. The actors watched him intently, holding their weapons. "A warning for those of you who were in *Romeo and Juliet*: this is going to be totally different. I don't want the fights to look like dance this time. This is the inevitability of tragedy. In this play, all choices lead to disaster. With every blow of a sword, we echo the thought: *Oh no!* Got it?"

The actors nodded. Tom got them on their feet and took them through the movements of the war in Act V. Shakespeare gives almost nothing in stage directions or dialogue for the battle between the British forces led by Lear's older daughters fighting Cordelia with the forces of France who want to rescue him. When the battle ended, Dwayne and Tom wanted the sensation of both sides having lost. Although the British warriors defeated the French invaders, they also defeated the defenders of their rightful king.

Once the actors had the movements down, Tom gave the nod to Ry and he led the band into the blues score he'd written to support the action. They played it up-tempo as the battle engaged and then brought it down to a dirge as the fight wore on. Everyone looked beaten. The music accentuated the feeling beautifully. Dwayne loved it.

From there, they jumped ahead to the sword fight between Edgar and Edmund, with the band playing furiously beneath the crashing of their swords until Edgar gave the fatal wound to his bastard brother.

"Let's take that again," Ry said. He turned to his drummer. "When you see that final stroke, break it down." The drummer nodded.

"Break it down?" Tom said.

"When the band is playing loud, the drummer hits a loud crack on his snare, and the band immediately drops the volume," Ry said. "In Chicago blues, that's called breaking it down."

"Ah! Good," Tom said. He turned to Bobby and Orlando. "Let's take the moves again. Stay in the rhythm, but don't dance it. And Bobby, make it look like Edmund might win this battle at the top and then start to be overpowered in the middle."

"Got it," Bobby said. "But maybe every other performance, I could win. How about that?"

"My name is Edgar, Earl of Gloucester," Orlando said in a Spanish accent, raising his sword. *"You killed my father. Prepare to die."*

The actors chuckled. "Thank you, Inigo Montoya," Tom said. "Let's take it again."

"This sword of mine shall give them instant way," Bobby (as Edmund) exclaimed. *"Trumpets, speak!"*

Ry stepped on a pedal that distorted his opening chords to sound like trumpets. The band wound into the blues score as Bobby and Orlando moved through the choreography of their fight. Then Edgar ran Edmund through with his sword. The drummer broke it down, and the music turned dirge-like. Finally repentant as he was dying, Edmund confessed he sent a captain to hang Cordelia and make it look like suicide. Edgar rushed to save her, but too late.

Ry's solo guitar faded as Edgar followed Lear carrying the dead Cordelia on stage.

"Howl, howl, howl! O, you are men of stone." Wallace declaimed mournfully over the low, dirgeful wail of Ry's guitar. *"Had I your tongues and eyes, I'd use them so that heaven's vault should crack."* It was like Wallace's voice and Ry's guitar were two instruments in the saddest blues ever. *"She's gone for ever! Dead as earth."*

It took Dwayne's breath away. Acting with the guitar had somehow boosted Wallace out of his confusion into true tragedy. He was a revelation all the way through to the moment he collapsed into death.

After the surviving characters delivered the final lines of the play, Wallace got up and staggered to where Dwayne and Tom were talking, pulling Ry along with him.

"Dwayne, Dwayne," he said in an intense whisper. "What if we add some of that guitar to the madness on the heath? Right at the height of my madness, a duet with Ry and me, lines and guitar, just like we did now. Not necessarily the same tune, but something. I loved that!"

Dwayne looked at Ry and lifted his chin.

"Yeah," Ry drawled. "We planned on just drums and lights to indicate the storm, but I know a riff that might work. I like playing under your voice." He put his hand on Wallace's shoulder and nodded. It was the friendliest thing Dwayne had ever seen from the ultra-cool Ry.

"Excellent!" Wallace said. "Can we try it today? Act Three, Scene Two?"

"We're ahead of schedule with the choreography," Tom said. "It's okay with me."

"Good," Dwayne said. "Let's try it."

They prepared the scene, and Ry's drummer rolled into the percussion he'd been using for the storm, with blasts of cymbals and cascading single-stroke and double-stroke rolls across the toms. He shattered the hi-hat cymbals together repeatedly with the foot pedal and fluttered the bass drum pedal, creating somersaults of the deepest thunder. He brought the full storm into the room sonically.

Ry pulled a long note over the top of the crashing, roaring percussion, and the bass player brought in a note and then a second note below him. A few more notes from the guitarists, and the drummer brought in a blues shuffle within the cacophony of the storm, and brought down the volume of his hammering. Ry nodded to Wallace.

"Blow, winds, and crack your cheeks!" Wallace cried, throwing his arms up. Ry pulled a long, wailing note on his guitar. *"Rage! blow! You cataracts and hurricanoes,"* The bass player walked up a trembling ladder of notes. *"Spout till you have drench'd our steeples, drown'd the cocks!"* he cried, blending harmonically with the notes Ry bent on his guitar. Ry crossed down from the musician's space to face off with Wallace center stage. He wailed another string of notes, and Wallace wailed back at him: *"You sulphurous and thought-executing fires, vaunt-couriers to oak-cleaving thunderbolts, singe my white head!"* He spun

about in desperation and rocked his fists at Ry. *"And thou, all-shaking thunder…"* Ry leaned back into a long shrieking note, the two of them looking like some version of Keith Richards and Eric Clapton trading fours. *"Strike flat the thick rotundity o' the world!"* Wallace fired back. *"Crack nature's moulds, all germens spill at once, that make ingrateful man!"*

"Wow! Fuck! Holy shit!" Peaches shouted from the doorway. "Oh my God, I showed up at the right moment! I can't believe… That was incredible!"

It was, in fact. Dwayne lost his worries about whether Wallace could attain a Lear to do them proud. He'd captured in this duet with Ry and the band, all the desperate, raging, suicidal angst of Lear's explosive rampage. It would need to be refined, and Ry would not face off with him on stage like that, but all the elements were there.

The sight of Peaches, however, was equally incredible. Dwayne had seen her in various stages of bipolar depression and ecstasy, but he'd never seen her as elevated as she looked now. Her garb of the day reflected her state. She wore a sparkly pink tutu over purple tights and sequinned ballet slippers. Above, she wore only a bikini top with embroidered daisies over her nipples. Rather than her typical slouch, she stood with shoulders back and chest out.

Wallace was so taken with what he and Ry and the band had just achieved, he was slapping Ry on the shoulder and shaking hands with the band. Most everyone else, however, was looking at Peaches, who then plunged forward onto the playing space.

"Wow! You were…wow!" she said to Wallace, shaking his hand vigorously.

"Thank you, Peaches," he said, suddenly noticing by her demeanor and garb.

"And you," she sidled up to Ry and brushed herself up against him like a cat. "That was super-sexy."

"Hey!" Melinda called from the seats. She got up and rushed to Peaches. "What the hell is up with you?" she shout-whispered.

Peaches backed off three steps. "Sorry, sorry, sorry!" she said. "I was just so knocked out by what I saw. I walked in the door, and they were…they were…doing *that*! Incredible. You saw it! Incredible."

"Okay," Dwayne called. "Let's take ten and regroup."

"Take ten," Howie Grange announced.

"Thank you, ten," everyone responded.

"I can tell you're…excited," Dwayne said quietly to Peaches, "but make sure to contain yourself when we start back into rehearsal. Okay?"

Peaches looked profoundly embarrassed. "I'm so sorry, Dwayne. I would never…. You know how much I respect you."

"I'll take care of her," Melinda insisted. She dragged Peaches off to a corner, where Peaches planted a big kiss on Melinda's lips, and Melinda shoved her down into a chair.

Never-ending thrills.

After the break, Dwayne got the rehearsal back on track. They continued refining the fight choreography and working with the band. Once in a while, he noticed Peaches vibrating in the seats, but she stayed quiet and off the stage. All in all, it was highly productive. At the end of the night, however, with the other actors walking out of the rehearsal room, Melinda and Coco discovered Peaches in the corner slipping her hand down toward Bobby's pants.

"The fuck?" Coco said to Bobby. She grabbed her bag and took off out of the room.

Bobby pushed Peaches' hand away and took off after her. "Hey, Coco! She's just taking that inseam measurement. There ain't nothing like me and you." And his voice faded out down the hallway.

Meanwhile, Melinda was staring at Peaches, who got up and fidgeted from foot to foot.

"What?" Peaches said. "What do you want to say?"

"I thought it was going to be different with you," Melinda said. "I know men can't keep it in their pants, but I thought you…" She shook her head. She took a shaky breath. "You said you *adored* me…"

"I do. I do. You know I do."

"But you're off latching onto Bobby and Ry and God-knows-who on the side?"

"My heart belongs to you."

"So what is this *fuck-me* outfit you're wearing?"

"It's for you!" Peaches cried. "Just for you."

Melinda waved a hand at her. "I just can't. This defeats the whole purpose of being with you." Melinda grabbed her things and walked out.

Peaches sat abruptly on the floor and began to weep.

Now what was Dwayne supposed to do? He sat down on the floor next to her.

This was going to be a long night.

52

Friday, August 11, 2005

"So she tried the bipolar medication," Dwayne said, lifting a forkful of linguine and clams to his lips. "I forget what it's called." He ate the pasta while Angela watched him from across the table. Usually, on a Friday night, they would order pizza and eat it in front of the TV with a rented DVD. But she had such energy tonight. She felt the spirits of her maternal ancestors around her. They loved the smell of pasta.

"She says the medication takes away her creativity," Dwayne continued. "She doesn't have the crushing depressions or the incredible manic phases, but she also loses all her will to design."

"Maybe she should think of some other career," Angela suggested.

"That's the problem. Nothing in her life seems interesting when she's on the drugs. She had a day job at a resale shop. She loves resale shops. On the drugs, she couldn't bring herself to show up, and she got fired. Now she has a day job at Vogue Fabrics, and she loves that. She doesn't want to lose it, and she doesn't want to stop designing. If the drugs make her life lose meaning, what's the point?"

"If she doesn't mind the chaos…"

"Well, she was heartbroken when Melinda dumped her. She really did adore her. But when the manic phase hits, she can't control herself. She goes man-crazy. The rest of the time, she doesn't date men at all."

"Could you excuse me?"

"Sure," Dwayne said. "By the way, this pasta is terrific."

"Thanks." She patted him on the shoulder and headed into the bathroom, closing the door behind her. Yes, it was coming again. She bent over the toilet and threw up, keeping it as quiet as she could.

Normally, she loved linguine with clams. So easy to make and so delicious. She sautéed plenty of garlic in olive oil and butter. She added the canned clams along with the juices in the can, some white wine, salt, pepper, oregano, and lots of fresh grated parmesan. Paired with some crunchy French bread heated in the oven and a green salad, it made a fantastic meal. It smelled really good, but after a few bites of pasta, all she could eat was the bread and the salad. And now it was all coming up.

Dwayne hadn't noticed anything. He was so taken up with *King Lear* and all his crazy people, there was hardly any room left in his brain.

This was the second day she'd experienced unexpected vomiting. Tomorrow she'd take a test and verify, but right now she felt pretty sure. Still, she was keeping quiet. She didn't want to set herself up for disappointment. That's what she told herself now, but if the test came out negative tomorrow, she'd still feel crushed. She knew that.

If it was positive, she'd be due at the end of the school year. Then she'd have the summer plus her maternity leave. Really, she'd like to take a full year off. Could they afford that? Maybe if Dwayne's career continued to take off.

She returned to the table. Dwayne looked from her face to the almost full plate in front of her.

"Are you okay?"

"I was just thinking the summer is almost over, and I have to go back to work soon."

"Yeah. That's too bad. But you look pale, too."

"I met Bonnie for lunch. We decided to get hot dogs. It's not settling well in my stomach. Should we watch the DVD?"

They carried their plates over to the TV. Once the movie started, just like magic, he didn't ask any more pointed questions for the rest of the night.

53

Saturday, August 12, 2005

Dwayne woke to the sound of his phone ringing. He grabbed it quickly so that it wouldn't wake Angela, but as he sat up, he saw she wasn't in the bed. "Hello?"

"Hey!"

It was the preternaturally loud voice of Ingrid on the phone. He swung his legs over and sat on the edge of the bed.

"I got your car down here, outside your apartment. I need to show you how it works and get out of here."

"What the hell time is it?"

"It's seven forty-five. It's late, Finnegan. I got places to go, people to see. Get your ass down here so I can show you how this works. Then you'll be able to drive to rehearsal."

"All right. Let me put some clothes on." He hung up the phone and headed to the bathroom. He really needed to pee, but the door was locked, and odd noises came from within.

"Are you all right?" he called through the door.

"Yeah. Give me a minute."

Did Angela's voice sound strangled?

He paced from foot to foot in the hallway.

Should he go pee in the kitchen sink? There was nothing wrong with that if he rinsed out the sink immediately. Maybe wash it with some dish soap. But if Angela came in while he was peeing, she'd be disgusted with him. He didn't want that.

He went back into the bedroom and laid out some clothes to wear, hopping from foot to foot.

The bathroom door popped open, and he dashed past Angela.

"Good morning to you, too," she said.

After the long blessed relief, he returned to the bedroom and pulled on his clothes. He heard the beeping of the Pinto out in front.

"Where are you going?"

"Ingrid is here. She fixed the car."

"That piece of junk." She flopped back on the bed.

Dwayne was about to dash out of the bedroom, but he noticed the oddness of Angela's complexion. Her cheeks were extraordinarily flushed, but the skin under her eyes, across her forehead, and in front of her ears was intensely pale. It made her look like a painted porcelain doll.

"Are you okay?"

"I'm fine. Go." She waved him away. "Just sleepy." She pulled the sheet up around her neck and rolled over.

He hesitated, heard the Pinto horn again, and headed out of the apartment.

How rude, to be sounding the horn at 7:45 on a Saturday morning!

In front of the building, Ingrid sat on the hood of the Pinto, twirling a set of keys on her index finger.

"About time, Finnegan!" she shouted merrily.

Was it possible? The Pinto looked even older and rustier than the last time he'd seen it.

"Get behind the wheel," she commanded. She climbed into the passenger seat as he got in. The doors actually opened all the way with minimal metal screech.

"Yes. You're welcome. I worked on the doors, too." Ingrid pointed to the steering column where the ignition key used to be. "See? I epoxied that over." Where the ignition had been, the column was now more or less smoothed over with a green substance. Dwayne tapped his fingernail on it. Rock hard. Ingrid handed him the key ring with a medium-sized key extended. "Your new ignition key. It goes in under here." She pointed to a silvery disk underneath the dash. Dwayne turned the key and heard the engine turn over.

"Don't forget the choke!"

Dwayne adjusted the manual choke, and the Pinto started right up.

"I tuned it up a little, too. Oh, and you've got a new way of using the turn signals." She pointed down to the hand brake handle between the front bucket seats. Now there were contact switches fastened on to each side with duct tape. Wires ran out of each of the switches under the floor mats. It looked like some kind of rocket launcher device.

"So you just lay your hand on this thing. You press the left one repeatedly to light up the left light and the right one to light up the right one." She pointed to the back window of the car. Red lights mounted with clear tape adorned the left and the right side of the window. As Dwayne pressed one or the other, the corresponding light flashed.

"Good lord," he said.

"Just be careful not to kick the wires out." She pointed to the wires that emerged from under the driver's side floor mat up the left wall of the car to the little fuse box.

"This gives new meaning to the word *customized*," Dwayne said.

"And no one will ever guess where the ignition switch is. If it was theft-proof before, it's twice as theft-proof now."

"That's for sure." He clicked the contact switches a few more times with his head turned to see the turn signal lights. "Thanks. I guess."

"Oh, come on! You love driving to rehearsal and parking free of charge downtown!"

"Except when it breaks down and I'm in a sweat because I'm going to be late."

"You shouldn't have any more trouble. Unless someone runs into you from behind and the damn thing bursts into flames!" She laughed heartily.

"I thought they fixed that," Dwayne said.

"Well, I imagine someone took it in for the retrofit," she said, patting the dash. "I mean, why wouldn't they?"

"But you don't know?"

"How would I possibly know?"

"Well, that's reassuring."

"Just watch your rearview, Finnegan! You don't want to go up in a ball of flames!"

"Thanks."

When he got back upstairs, Dwayne offered to make Angela breakfast, but she just wanted to sleep. He left an hour earlier than usual in case he got stranded by the car.

When he arrived in the rehearsal room, he was amazed to see Wallace and Chaz already there. They were watching a video on Chaz's laptop.

Wallace turned as he approached. "Hey, Dwayne, take a look. It's the 1953 Orson Welles *Lear*." He turned back to the screen.

"What are you two doing?"

"Wallace asked me for career advice PR-wise," Chaz told Dwayne. "How to get this production to raise his profile. So we're looking at some of the most high-profile Lears. I've got clips from Paul Scofield directed by Peter Brook, Patrick Magee, James Earl Jones…"

"And you've been looking at all these clips?" Dwayne didn't like this.

"Fascinating, Dwayne," Wallace said. "Such a range of approaches. I'm getting all kinds of ideas."

That's what he was afraid of. Not that Wallace would have new ideas, but that all these approaches might lead to confusion.

"And how does this relate to PR?" Dwayne asked.

"Well, it doesn't pertain to PR, per se," Chaz said. "But when you get an opportunity like this, the most important thing is to make sure the performance kicks ass."

"And you thought your input would be useful?" Dwayne stood with his arms crossed, his lips downturned at the corners. This felt very weird. Chaz was his boss at his PR firm, but Chaz also did PR for the Psychedelic Dream Theatre, where Dwayne was the client. So Chaz was in charge of him, and he was in charge of Chaz, and Chaz was one of his oldest friends.

"Well…" Chaz took two steps back from the computer. "I mean, it never hurts to take a look at the greats, right?"

Wallace snorted. "He tried showing me how to write a press release, but I was hopeless. Anyway, we talked to the Goodman PR people. They'll get the word out, so I think I'm okay there."

"So instead, you're offering acting coaching?"

Chaz gently closed his laptop. "I mean, not really…"

"Hey," Wallace protested. "Orson Welles was ludicrous, but we haven't seen James Earl Jones yet."

"That's probably enough for today," Chaz told him. "I need to talk with Dwayne for a minute."

Wallace frowned. "Well, okay." He headed off to the rehearsal room.

"I can tell you're not happy about the videos," Chaz admitted. "I won't do that again. But we have another problem."

"Oh?" Dwayne said.

"Hamilton Bottling Equipment fired us. They said we don't understand their market."

"I thought your theme for their equipment release was great. *However fast you run it, for this machine it's an easy cruising speed.*"

"They're still using that, but they didn't like anything else we gave them. I'm just not landing the new accounts we need."

"So what do we do?"

"Without Rocky and without Hamilton and without new accounts, I don't have enough to keep us both busy."

"Are you firing me?" Dwayne had hoped Chaz would put him on an account that had some human interest angle, like with Rocky's lawyers and their clients. Maybe one of his arts clients.

"I could explain the situation to Rocky and see if he'd take you back," Chaz suggested. "It wouldn't be PR, but they could probably find something for you."

"Oh God, no." Dwayne could imagine Brianna's face if he showed up again at Rockwell Nesbit III Personal Injuries Law. "No. I'll go back to the temp agencies. And bartending when my evenings open up. Sorry this didn't work out."

"I'm sorry, too. The last few weeks, I've been paying you, but I couldn't afford to pay myself. It's awkward when we've been friends so long."

"No, I understand. Rocky put us into this in the first place. Not your fault."

"Thanks, Dwayne." Chaz looked uncomfortable and then glanced at his watch. "I'd better get out of here." He grabbed his laptop and headed out the door.

Unfortunately, as the rehearsal progressed that afternoon, it became clear that Dwayne's income was not the only thing Chaz had taken away. The gains Wallace had made the previous nights were nowhere to be seen. Wallace was trying out movement and vocal inflections like Paul Scofield and Patrick Magee from watching those Lears with Chaz. It was so frustrating. When he was offstage, he saw Wallace huddling with Bobby, and Bobby giving him what looked like impassioned advice. Dwayne approached them, and Bobby skittered away.

It was so easy for an actor to give in to insecurity and lose his way, especially when playing the role of a lifetime.

Meanwhile, Peter Burden was giving Dwayne the eye and tapping his finger on his wristwatch.

One step forward, two steps back.

54

Wednesday, August 16, 2005

Dwayne watched Tom approach Bobby on stage. Had it been a mistake to allow Tom to play Regan? At first, Tom's Regan was intriguing. He played her in a hyper-feminine way that accentuated her shift to treachery. But it wasn't long before the hyper-femininity began to play as false. And then it got worse. Tom was floundering.

He and Tom had been in high school together. Tom had convinced him to enroll in Brad Cunningham's summer theatre workshop during their junior year, which changed his life. Tom contributed as much to their last two productions as Dwayne did. When Tom wanted to play Regan, he trusted Tom could do it. But now, it just wasn't working.

Tom had always been extravagantly fey. When Dwayne met him in high school, his clothing was a patchwork of decorations. He knotted scarves not only around his neck, but around his biceps, waist, and thighs. It took time before Dwayne felt comfortable with him. His sense of style modulated over the years, but his physical carriage always remained femme.

Dwayne was seeing that exaggeration in his Regan. He'd started out playing her as dangerously feminine, but now she seemed borderline silly. What had happened?

"Now, sweet lord, you know the goodness I intend upon you," he said, approaching Bobby and coyly laying a finger on the center of his chest. *"Tell me but truly. Do you not love my sister?"*

"In honoured love," Bobby replied. He took a half step away.

That was another problem. When Tom and Bobby were in a scene together, Dwayne was seeing Bobby instead of Edmund. Bobby was as extravagantly heterosexual as Tom was homosexual. Was this going to be a problem?

"But have you never found my brother's way to the forfended place?" Tom leaned back and laid one hand near his groin and another over his stomach.

"That thought abuses you," Bobby said, looking disgusted with Tom's suggestive gestures. Tom straightened up uncomfortably.

"I am doubtful that you have been conjunct and bosomed with her," Tom sniffed.

"No, by mine honour, madam." Bobby looked exactly like himself, denying a dalliance for which he was guilty.

"Be not familiar with her," Tom said, his voice rising to an outraged falsetto.

"Fear not," Bobby said.

Goneril and Albany stood ready to enter the scene.

Dwayne got up. "Let's stop there a minute." He took Tom aside. "How is this feeling to you?"

"I don't know," Tom said. "This is harder than I thought. For one thing, I'm so much taller than Bobby. It's making it hard for me to feel…feminine…with him. And I know so much about being feminine…" he rolled his eyes to lighten his tension.

"Right," Dwayne said. "The stylized femininity is not working now."

"I know, I know, I know," Tom whispered back to him. "I studied some of my trans friends who really pass, but I don't think I can do what they do, you know, and I watch Coco, and I watch Melinda. I'm not doing what I wanted to do as Regan. I'm sorry."

"Don't be sorry," Dwayne said. "You're going to find it."

Tom laid a hand on Dwayne's shoulder. "Thank you. I worried you'd lose faith."

"Not at all," Dwayne said. "So this femininity is not working, right?"

"I don't think so. Do you?"

"No. I agree. Listen. Let's try the opposite. No worries if it succeeds or fails. Try playing Regan like a man."

Tom cocked his head to the side, mystified. He lowered his voice and advanced the tilt of his pelvis. "Like a man?" he said with an exaggerated masculinity.

"Not a fake butch man," Dwayne said. "Play her more like…a neutral man, with a hint of Bobby."

Tom giggled. "A hint of Bobby? That's hilarious."

Bobby looked over at them. "What's that?" he said. Dwayne waved him off. The actors were accustomed to allowing one another privacy when Dwayne talked to them. Bobby drifted off to chat up Coco, who was waiting for her entrance as Goneril.

"These are powerful women, Regan and Goneril. Daughters of the King. They expect to be obeyed. They don't need to trade on their femininity. Try leaning toward something more powerful. You want Edmund as your lover. You want him to replace your dead husband. But your power comes from your inheritance. You *own* half the kingdom. You don't need to be shorter than him. He's your bitch. You aren't his. Still, you aren't sure of him, and you worry your sister has already laid a claim. After all, she is as powerful as you. But you are sure of yourself."

"Like Bobby is always sure of himself," Tom said.

"Yes, *that's* the part I meant," Dwayne said, wondering if that was a crazy suggestion. "Just a little taste of that."

"Okay!" Tom said. "Let's try it. Why the hell not?"

"Why the hell not?" Dwayne agreed. He clapped his friend gently on the arm. He turned to the rest of the actors. "Okay, everyone. We are taking Act Five, Scene One from the top again."

Tom approached Bobby again. *"Now, sweet lord, you know the goodness I intend upon you,"* Regan said in a deeper voice, not feminine or pleading. She stood tall and leaned back, judging Edmund. *"Tell me but truly, but speak the truth. Do you not love my sister?"* She glanced down her nose at Edmund, judging him.

"In honoured love," Edmund replied. He bowed to her.

Now this was working! Tom's Regan looked regal. His attempt at a neutral masculinity looked like a reserved femininity. And Bobby was reacting to her regal authority with a perfect subservience (laced, of course, with Edmund's ever-present deviousness).

"But have you never found my brother's way to the…" Regan gave a long and meaningful pause, her face entirely neutral, *"…forfended place?"*

Edmund looked away and then back at Regan. *"That thought abuses you,"* he muttered.

"I am doubtful that you have been conjunct and bosomed with her," Regan said haughtily. Dwayne loved it.

"No, by mine honour, madam," Edmund said hurriedly.

"I never shall endure her, dear my lord," Regan said, his voice rising in volume, but not in pitch. *"Be not familiar with her,"* she commanded.

"Fear not," Edmund said.

"Nice, nice, nice," Dwayne interrupted. He jumped up and approached Tom. "How did that feel?"

"How did it look?" Tom said.

"I believed it," Dwayne said. "You looked like a dangerous Regan, every bit capable of betraying your father and contending with your sister."

"Ha! Yes. It felt pretty good," Tom said.

Dwayne clapped him on the shoulder. "Excellent. Keep it! Let's continue!"

At the end of rehearsal, Peter Burden approached him. "I don't know if you noticed the date…"

"August sixteen. Yes, I have."

"And? Have you decided?" Peter looked at him, constraining his eagerness.

Dwayne had been worried about Wallace. Wallace had been doing so well, and then he'd lost his way again. When he was staying within his talent and his own ideas, he was excellent. Once he started looking at other performances and taking random advice, he lost it. Like Lear, giving away his authority to his daughters and still expecting to be the king, he was outsourcing the ideas that created the backbone of his character.

And what about himself as a leader? Dwayne's little kingdom was his ensemble. The best successes of his life came from leading this set of artists. Look what he'd done with Tom today. The trust of decades of friendship and artistic partnership could not be replaced.

He didn't have decades with Wallace, but he had led him out of mental traps and into a brilliant performance in *Titus Andronicus*.

When Wallace had been listening to him, he'd been making his way toward a credible Lear. Before others stuck their noses in.

Dwayne would do it again. He could lead these people. He *would* lead these people.

"I *have* decided, Peter," he said. "Wallace is my Lear. You are my Gloucester. And I look forward to us continuing together to make this the finest *King Lear* anyone has seen in the city of Chicago."

"Humph," Peter said.

55

Saturday, August 19, 2005

The phone rang at 6 a.m., waking Dwayne from a sound sleep. Angela glared at him, hair tousled and face pillow-wrinkled, as he answered the phone.

"Sorry to wake you, old man," a truly contrite-sounding Wallace said. "I had to make sure I caught you before you got on with your day."

"No danger there." Dwayne pulled himself up to a seated position.

"It's just." Wallace cleared his throat. "I need a little extra *Dwayne* time today."

"Okay," Dwayne said. "Before rehearsal?"

"An hour before, please," Wallace suggested. "In that little dressing room? I'd prefer to have a little *solo Dwayne* time, if you catch my meaning."

"Sure thing, Wallace. See you then."

But when he rolled over and closed his eyes, he could not fall back asleep. Wallace had had a steady march toward a good Lear through the first weeks of rehearsal. Then he'd had a break-through night capturing a truly fine Lear, collaborating with Ry's guitar. Then it went all to hell. His Lear since that night had been all over the place. *King Lear* depended on the quality of its Lear. Should he have given more consideration to Peter Burden?

He lay in bed for a half hour, resisting the urge to toss and turn. He didn't want to wake Angela.

So much depended on this play. The trajectory of Dwayne's successes had been based on his ensemble. It was his synergy with them that created such an interesting *Titus Andronicus* and *Romeo and Juliet*. And so he'd plunged forward with them in this assault on the heights of the Goodman Theatre.

He slipped quietly out of bed. He had no hope of getting back to sleep. He padded into the kitchen and looked in the refrigerator. Bread. Eggs. A pound of bacon. He could, at least, be a thoughtful husband. He put on the coffee and stripped bacon into the largest cast iron pan. Might as well cook the whole pound. Bacon reheated nicely enough. He turned the oven on at its lowest temperature to keep things warm until Angela woke up. He mixed up eggs with a dash of half-and-half and a shake of cinnamon and nutmeg, and put bread in to soak for French toast.

By the time he was halfway through his first cup of coffee and the bacon was cooked and staying warm in the oven, Angela tottered into the kitchen and poured herself a cup. She looked over the edge of the large mixing bowl at the bread soaking up the egg mixture.

"So you're finally acknowledging my nutritional needs."

"I know you love French toast."

"You are so clueless, Finnegan." She took a sip of her coffee. "Absolutely clueless." She waved her hand vaguely at the stove. "Go ahead, make my breakfast." She got a sudden startled look on her face, set down her coffee cup, and headed swiftly to the bathroom. His curiosity piqued, Dwayne followed. From inside the bathroom, he heard regurgitational sounds.

"Are you okay?"

"Just…wait," Angela said.

A few moments later, she came out, wiping her mouth.

"Well, I have room for breakfast now."

"Were you throwing up?" He followed her back to the kitchen.

"I've been throwing up," she said. "Not that you'd ever notice, *Mr. The-Goodman-Theatre-Is-The-Only-Thing-I-Can-Possibily-Think-About.*"

"You mean before today?"

"Good guess, Sherlock. Now, how about some French toast? Some of us are eating for two." She could not suppress the sneaky grin blossoming on her face.

"You mean? Oh, my God!" This was such an eruption of confusing emotions. Elation, fear, shock, love. It rushed through him in such a confounding combination that it took a moment to sort out anything like a proper response, and then, of course, he took his beautiful, sleepy, pregnant wife into his arms and kissed her.

"Well, this is a whole new world, isn't it?" he said, face to face, still holding her in his arms.

"I hope you weren't quoting *The Tempest* there," she said.

"No, no. That's: *Oh brave new world that has such people in it.*"

"Just shut up, Finnegan," she said, and kissed him back.

* * *

"I told myself: Wallace, don't be arrogant. This is *Lear*, for God's sake. Have some modesty." He paced back and forth across the little dressing room like a lion in a too-small cage. Dwayne sat in one of the chairs along the makeup table in front of the mirrors on the wall. "Be willing to hear advice," Wallace continued. "And I have. I'm trying everything I can think of, everything people suggest—you know, everything that isn't some hare-brained nonsense, because there's certainly plenty of that to go around—but everything from people who know what they are talking about. But the more I try, the more I think: Who the hell am I that I thought I was up to Lear? The greatest role in the English language?" Wallace stopped and glared at Dwayne.

"This is the perfect role at the perfect time for you," Dwayne said.

"Yeah, yeah, yeah, yeah," Wallace said, waving his hand dismissively. "I've heard you say that before." He groaned and sat down. "Bobby says I need to *play the King* always. Which, I guess, means always hold on to the majesty. But how can I do that when I've lost my mind, and I'm howling on the heath?"

"Bobby is a wonderful actor, but he's a crap director, believe me. Ignore everything from Bobby."

"He was talking about playing Lear so that it advances my career."

"The only way to play Lear so it advances your career is to play a great Lear. Anything else is nonsense and a murderous distraction."

Wallace cocked his head from one side to the other. "I guess I can't argue with that."

"I love Bobby, but he's no role model for you."

"Right, right, right." Wallace laughed and shook his head. "I guess that should have been self-evident. Okay, though," he plunged forward, "Chaz suggested I look at the great Lears that have been caught on film. And, I know, I know, what the hell does Chaz know? But after he showed me some clips, I got out all the DVDs from the library. They're so great." He stopped himself. "Well, not all. But I did catch a lot of admirable ideas."

"Yes…" Dwayne said. "About that…"

Wallace held up his hand, got up, and began pacing the room again. "I was standing in the hallway, pondering those ideas. Reg Camper walks up and says: *You look like you are deeply in it.* So I tell him what I'm pondering. He tells me: *It's always in the lines. Shakespeare tells you how to play it.* I say: How so? He says: *Look at the feather moment. Lear says: 'This feather stirs; she lives! If it be so, it is a chance which does redeem all sorrows that ever I have felt.' So he must be holding the feather beneath her nose to see if it stirs, desperate to see it stirring, to show she still breathes.*"

"Seeing what Shakespeare's lines tell you. That's good advice."

"But then I compared how two of the actors on the DVDs played that moment. The first held the feather to her nose, but the second just held it up in the air, nowhere near her nose, playing the madness nonstop."

"Every actor discovers his own approach. There's no one right way. Remember the first time you played lines against Ry's guitar? You struck right into the brilliance of the role."

Wallace considered that for a moment. He shrugged. "Peter Burden says a great Lear just delivers the lines."

"You went to Peter Burden for advice?" This was a startling thought.

"No, Peter came to me. He says it's not the actor's job to play the emotions. The emotions are in the lines. You deliver the lines, and the audience feels the emotion. If you are emoting, you deprive the audience of their experience."

"Have you seen him follow that advice as Gloucester?"

Wallace thought for a moment, then laughed outright. "Good lord, no. He screams like a little girl when Cornwall is gouging his eyes out. Then he's weeping and weeping with Poor Tom…"

"Please ignore Peter Burden. I don't believe he has your interests at heart."

"I did suspect…" Wallace leaned against the wall by the door and sighed. "So, do I ignore *everything everyone* is telling me? I feel like I've lost my way."

Dwayne got up and laid a hand on his actor's shoulder. "You aren't here to play the quintessential Lear. There is no such thing. You aren't here to play Lear according to me, or Reg Camper, or anyone else you can possibly imagine. You are here to play the *Wallace Proctor Lear*. That's why I trusted you in this role."

Wallace looked a little stunned. Then he shook his head. "But how do I do that, Dwayne?"

"You build on everything you've done and everything you've learned. In *Titus Andronicus*, you played the great Roman general who served his city and then was betrayed by the emperor whom he'd served. That betrayal drove him to rage and revenge. Now you are playing the great king who is betrayed by his daughters whom he put into power. That betrayal drives him into madness. Take what you did in *Titus* and build on it for Lear. You don't start from zero. You use your past roles and your life."

Dwayne enjoyed the look on his actor's face. Realization bloomed on his features like the sunrise igniting the landscape. Wallace sat abruptly in the chair by the makeup desk.

"I want to tell you a story," Dwayne said. "There was once an actor who was discouraged with his opportunities in the Chicago theatre. So he did a great thing. He wrote a one-man show for himself."

"Oh, Dwayne…" Wallace groaned, recognizing his own story.

"Listen! He created his own opportunity. He wrote a script that would demonstrate and feature his creativity to the great city in which he lived. He had a writing partner he trusted. His partner trusted him. They perfected the script. They pooled their money to produce the show. He would act. His partner would direct. But his partner lost faith. He panicked. He feared for his money, and his panic infected the enterprise and caused it to fail. His panic betrayed the promise of their partnership. That betrayal so devastated the actor that he fled from his dream for years. He fled like Lear flees from the betrayal of his daughters. He flees into his madness on the heath."

Wallace's face turned deathly pale. "Oh, my God." He got up from the chair and walked across the room. He stood looking away for the longest time. Finally, he turned back to Dwayne. "The way I felt. The way I retreated. The way he felt…"

"There's definite application," Dwayne said.

"So you mean, the *Wallace Proctor Lear*."

"Yes," Dwayne said.

"Take Titus and all my past roles, take my life, take the script…"

"Take it all and make the *Wallace Proctor Lear*."

"And ignore everyone else but Dwayne Finnegan," Wallace said.

Dwayne felt a rush of pleasure at his actor's newfound trust. "I will always be your honest partner."

Wallace took Dwayne in his arms and hugged him to his barrel chest.

When they began the rehearsal, Wallace looked so much more the master of his role. He was commanding as he demanded expressions of love from his daughters. He was confounding as he rejected his best-loved Cordelia. He was absolutely heartbreaking as he moved into the madness on the heath. But then, toward the end of rehearsal, he began looking confused. He had fallen somehow out of his Lear. What happened?

After the rehearsal, he begged Dwayne to get Aleister to talk with him. Aleister had done such great things for Melinda. Perhaps Aleister could help him.

Were all his actors going to insist on a session with Aleister?

He set it up for Monday.

56

Monday, August 21, 2005

"Wait a minute," Angela said. "That dish water is not even hot."

Dwayne lifted the colander from the soapy water. "It's warm. It's as warm as I always have it. And the rinse water is warmer."

Angela stuck her hand into it. "Are you kidding me? This rinse water is not going to kill any germs. If you don't disinfect the holes, bacteria can lurk in there, ready to leach into the next batch of pasta."

"Pasta goes through the colander with a load of boiling water," Dwayne said. "If there were germs on the colander, they'd be killed when the pasta got drained." This seemed reasonable to him. He wanted to finish the dishes so he could get together with Wallace and Aleister.

"Are you telling me I should be okay with you putting a germ-infected colander on the shelf with our clean dishes?" Her voice rose and then rose some more. Angela, pregnant with their first child, was unusually emotional these days.

"I'm sorry, I'm sorry." He turned on the hot water full until billows of steam rose from the sink. "I'll rinse it hot."

"Thank you," she said impatiently. "But I don't think you are taking this seriously. Why would you risk exposing me to unwashed toxins? This is the stage of pregnancy when women have the most miscarriages. Our child is hardly larger than a lima bean. A lima bean, Dwayne! Do you think a lima bean can fend off the bacteria you've got swimming in that sink? And what about me? Do you want to see me lying in a hospital bed where I might get exposed to a fatal staph infection? I mean, have you never, ever, for a moment of your life, actually loved me?"

"Um…" Dwayne said.

"Um. That's what you have to say! Um."

He looked at his watch.

"What?" she said. "Now you have somewhere else you need to be?"

"Actually…" Clearly, this was not a discussion he could cut short. This was Monday night, so there was no rehearsal. She'd been expecting he'd be home with her, and they could do some talking and planning. "Wallace wanted extra rehearsal time. He wants to meet with me and Aleister."

"Tonight?" Her eyes flared.

"Yes."

"Why can't Wallace learn his role on the millions of nights of rehearsals you've already got scheduled? Isn't he the one who thought he could direct *Oedipus Rex* in three weeks flat?"

"Yes, actually, but you saw how that turned out…"

"And Aleister? So this isn't really a rehearsal," she insisted.

"Well, not in the traditional sense."

"So why do they need you, Dwayne? Why can't Aleister tend to Wallace's neuroses on his own? Do I and our baby-on-the-way have no priority in your life?"

"Well, I prepared some new notes that I thought could help Wallace, too."

"Oh, great. Why don't you see if Wallace wants to carry your baby?"

"You know what? Let me call Aleister and Wallace to see if they can get along without me."

"And then what?" She pointed dead at his face. "Right. I see it. You think you *have* to be there. You think: *Oh God, this is my big Goodman Theatre chance, and Angela is going to run everything.*"

"No, no, I wasn't…"

"Saint whoever-the-fuck, patron saint of whatever-the-fuck, pray for me," she mocked.

"No, honestly."

"Just get out of here," she said. She huffed and pushed him to the entry and out the door. Thirty seconds later, she threw his messenger bag with his script and notes out the door after him.

He stood on the landing, considering whether to go back in.

"I can hear you breathing out there, Dwayne," she shouted through the door. "Just go to your fake rehearsal!"

He stood for one more minute.

St. Gengulphus of Burgundy, patron saint of difficult marriages, pray for me, he muttered.

He walked down the stairs.

Five minutes after Dwayne had driven away, the doorbell buzzed. She figured he must have walked out without something. Angela slammed open the door to discover Coco looking uncharacteristically abashed. "I know. You weren't expecting me."

"Dwayne isn't here. He's having some special session with Wallace," she said, still annoyed.

"I know. That's why I picked now to come. I wanted to talk with *you*." Coco cocked her head to the side and gave an uncertain smile.

"Oh." Angela stood up straighter. She wasn't expecting this. She'd never had a private, one-on-one conversation with Coco in all the years Dwayne and she had performed together. And Angela's opinion of her as a human being had taken a severe hit after Coco had participated in the demolition of Bonnie and Chaz's marriage.

"May I come in?"

"Well, I suppose so." She backed away from the door. Coco headed for the friendly conversation pit of the living room, where she'd attended any number of company meetings, but Angela went to the dining room and sat at the head of the table.

"Oh. Okay," Coco said. She got up and settled in on one of the side chairs at the table. She felt much more temporary in the upright wooden chair. She laid her hands flat on the tabletop. She looked up at the ceiling, then at Angela's face, and then down at the tabletop. "I understand that you probably dislike my…history. But I really wanted to talk to you, despite the fact that you probably got a low opinion of me."

"Why me?"

"You're not like any other woman I know. You're not from the theatre, but you are married to Dwayne, so you know our world. You're like a regular, normal person who knows things. The women I know are either performers or they don't understand the first thing about our life."

"So?"

"Well, that makes you unique." She looked at Angela with her eyebrows raised.

Angela clapped her hand on the tabletop. "Okay. I'm unique. But why are you here?"

Coco looked shocked. She'd never seen Angela this prickly.

"Right, right, right. Sorry. I'm a little nervous. I wanted some advice." She tilted her head far to the side. "Do y'all like being married?"

Angela opened her mouth, then closed it. She sat up straighter. "I thought you wanted advice. This sounds more like prying."

"Yeah. Sorry. It's not what I really want to know." She took a deep breath. "See, I've always been confident. I go for what I want. You know. I'm ambitious. And I know you'd understand that, because Dwayne is ambitious. I know you get that about us. And you are a woman. And you are married. And, to me, it looks like you got a great marriage. Both you're doing your things, and doing very *different* things. It looks like you got a lot of respect. And love. But me, I never let relationships get all that deep, because for performers, sometimes a serious relationship just holds you back. Or suddenly you're having kids, and bingo, there goes that career you wanted. Then life is all about the kids and keeping a roof over everyone's head and food on the table. I mean, that's not my problem because my pops gives me an allowance. I can do what I want. But still. I never thought about relationships as something I'd take to the next level. Once they impinge on my sense of well-being, sayonara, motherfucker. But now. I don't know. I started to think, have I fallen in love? And I needed to talk to somebody about that. Because I don't *want* to be in love. But if I am in love, I need to know. What do I do about it? I'm not equipped. But you—you're like a totally real person who isn't a performer but who understands performers. But more important, I think you understand love. You don't play at love on stage…"

"So what are you asking me?" Angela interjected impatiently.

"Could I possibly be in love with Bobby?" Coco looked horrified at the thought.

Angela laughed. Maybe this would be more entertaining than the walk by the lake she'd planned.

Coco shook her head. "Years ago, when Bobby and I hooked up for the first time, I remember Ingrid scoffed at me. She said everyone falls in love with Bobby at first, but they get over it. And actually, I *didn't* fall in love with him. It was all about the sex. But now it feels different. I even got Dwayne to set me up with Aleister because I thought maybe I had dissociative personality disorder like Pops, and my alternate personality was falling in love with Bobby. But Aleister said no, that wasn't it."

Angela held out her hands to frame the problem. "So you are worried you might be falling in love with Bobby. And you don't want to be. Is that right?"

"Yes." Coco sighed heavily. "In some ways, he's just the same as he's always been, hopping from woman to woman. But now there's more tenderness to him. His lovemaking is…deeper. He's also got so many of the attributes I admire in myself. I think about him all the time. What it's like to be in bed with him. But also what a life together might be like. We always been cheerleaders for each other. Could there be something more? What if he knew I was open to something more? Something bigger and deeper? Would that interest him?"

"You'll never know if you don't ask him."

"But what do *you* think? Do you think I'm really in love? And if so, is that a good idea? Or should I just get over it and get on with my life? Maybe love's a bad idea for a performer like me. You know, like, celebrity marriages seldom last."

Angela laughed again. "If you went to Aleister suspecting you were losing your mind, you might well be in love."

"Oh, shit," Coco said. "That's what *I* thought. But what should I do about it? Should I just get over it? I mean, you know Bobby. The chances of this working out seem vanishingly slim."

"You and I have never had a conversation this long, and I have to say, I love some of the phrases you use. *Vanishingly slim.* Ha!"

Coco shrugged. "I've been in a lot of plays."

"You'll never know what he's up for if you don't ask him."

"But what if I come offering love, and he refuses? Then what's it like when we work together? How am I going to be equal on stage with him if I'm the spurned woman?"

"You don't get real love without risk."

"*You don't get real love without risk.*" Coco's shoulders slumped. "So that's the wisdom?"

"I don't know if it's wisdom, but it's true. When you love, you open yourself up to hurt and pain, as well as joy. No one can hurt you like the one you love."

"I don't know if this is worth it."

"Sometimes it's the best. Sometimes it's the worst."

"I guess that sounds right." Coco shook her head in sorrow. Angela took pity on her.

"I was just going to take a walk by the lake," she said. "It's just two blocks away. Would you like to walk with me?"

Coco looked surprised and pleased. "Yeah. I would."

57

Meanwhile

Dwayne's stomach knotted as he turned west on Wacker Drive and saw the upper level was blocked off for construction. He took the ramp down to Lower Wacker on his way to Wallace and Aleister at the Goodman. Dwayne had had to beg his old friend to come in and talk with Wallace on this, the usual night off for the cast. Aleister would be coming straight from his Loop office after treating patients all day. Dwayne may have laid a bit of guilt on his old friend, and for that, he felt bad. On top of that, Angela was annoyed with him. But this was *King Lear*, for the love of God!

Dwayne never liked driving on Lower Wacker. He imagined Upper Wacker collapsing atop him and crushing him like a bug. He wasn't exactly sure how to get back to surface level. He took his first opportunity to turn left on Lower Michigan. As he rounded the corner, he heard a horrifying rending of metal as the car lurched left and dipped and slid out of control up the curb. An itinerant man screamed and leapt back as the Pinto careened up onto the sidewalk and crushed the man's shopping cart against the brick wall, flinging Dwayne against the constraint of his seat belt and banging his right ribs against the stick shift.

Longinus' lance, that hurt!

What the hell had happened? He'd turned the steering wheel, but instead of turning the corner, the car decided to slide sideways into the wall. The itinerant man began pounding on the trunk of his car and shouting. "What the hell's wrong with you? You could've killed me!" He continued to bang his fist.

Dwayne attempted to open the driver's door, but it was stuck again. He pulled on the handle and butted his shoulder into the door, an action that did not budge the door but caused intense, ringing pain to shoot through his right ribs.

Had he broken a rib on the gearshift?

Then a more horrifying thought occurred to him: He'd been in an accident. He didn't know if the past owners had taken this Pinto in for the recall. Was it about to burst into flames? Would he die a horrible, fiery death, leaving his child fatherless, Angela a widow, and his play without a director?

He pulled the handle and pounded his shoulder into the door again and again, despite the surges of pain in his lower right ribs.

Oh, the horror!

"You crushed my cart!" the man shouted.

"I can't open the door!" Dwayne shouted back.

The man took hold of the handle and opened the door without a problem. Dwayne climbed painfully out of the car, remembering to grab the messenger bag with his script.

"You crushed my cart," the man repeated.

Dwayne walked around the car and looked at the shopping cart flattened against the wall. Hundreds of aluminum cans had exploded out of it. "It looks pretty flattened," Dwayne admitted.

"That was a lot of work in there," the man said. "Thirty dollars, at least."

"How's that?"

"I was going to turn in that aluminum for forty dollars. My cart was full. That's my income."

"I'm sorry," Dwayne said.

"Sorry don't cut it. You owe me fifty dollars. I would have got fifty dollars for all those aluminum cans. And those shopping carts cost a hundred bucks. That's a hundred fifty bucks."

"That cart may have cost *somebody* a hundred bucks, but you can't tell me *you* paid a hundred bucks for it," Dwayne said.

The man looked down at the sidewalk and shook his head disgustedly. He looked back at Dwayne. "That's my livelihood."

Dwayne looked in his wallet. He had fifty-five dollars. He gave it to the man. "Here's fifty dollars for the cans and five more for the inconvenience of having to find a new cart."

The man looked at the money. "That's all you got?"

Dwayne displayed his empty wallet.

"Okay," the man said. "I guess that's fair enough." He gave back a five. "You saved me a long walk to Swerski Metal Recycling. That makes up for the cart."

"I love an honest man," Dwayne said as the fellow walked away.

He walked around to the front of the car. The right front wheel was collapsed flat under the car. It had broken off the axle when he turned the corner. Chunks and flecks of rusted metal littered the ground like confetti. Thank God the wheel hadn't collapsed somewhere in traffic. He could have been killed. Or killed someone else.

Meanwhile, waiting for Dwayne, Wallace had found Aleister in the Goodman lobby, and the two of them got Nick Sanchez to unlock the rehearsal room.

"So, what did you think I could do for you?" Aleister asked as they settled in.

"You were so helpful with Melinda, back in *Titus Andronicus*," Wallace said. "Maybe you could do with me what you did with her?"

Aleister sighed. "You understand that if I had a session with Melinda, anything we did would be confidential."

"Oh, yeah, absolutely." Wallace mulled that over. "What if you just did what you did with Melinda without telling me what it was?"

Aleister sighed. Why hadn't Dwayne shown up? Was this his plan, that Wallace and he have a private session? "Why don't you tell me what you want to achieve tonight?"

"I've never gone to a psychiatrist before," Wallace confessed. "Not that people haven't said I *should*." He laughed.

"But why did you ask Dwayne to bring me in?"

"I can't see clearly how to play King Lear because of all the suggestions I've gotten! The ideas fight with one another. It's maddening!" He got up and began pacing the room. "O, full of scorpions is my mind, dear friend. Canst thou not minister to a mind diseased? Pluck out from the memory a rooted suggestion? Raze out the written troubles of the brain?"

Were those lines from *Hamlet* or *Macbeth*? Aleister wondered. It didn't matter. "Did you have this problem when you played Titus?"

"Nobody gave me advice about Titus. Except my director. But everyone has opinions about *King Lear*." He continued pacing.

"I was impressed with your Titus. Why not ignore everyone but your director?"

Wallace stalked toward Aleister, his eyes wild. "That would be heaven!" he exclaimed. "But these other ideas have already attached themselves to me. It's like I'm covered in mental leeches, sucking away my powers of focus."

"Ah!" Aleister said. "Now we're getting somewhere. I think I can help you."

"You can?" Wallace looked at him in amazement.

"Yes. Is there somewhere you can comfortably lie down?"

"The Equity cot!" Wallace exclaimed. He led them to the nearby green room.

"Excellent." Aleister gestured to the cot, and Wallace lay down.

"Close your eyes and relax." Aleister selected some restful music on his phone. "Relax totally and bring your awareness inside until you can feel your blood moving through your body."

This was not like anything he had done with a client before, but he wasn't really practicing psychiatry here. He was inventing a guided meditation to help Wallace focus. He waited a long time as Wallace's breath slowed and deepened. Wallace finally said, "I feel it," in a dreamy voice.

"Very good," Aleister said quietly. "Now pay attention to my voice while staying relaxed and aware of the movement of your blood. Most people believe that the mind resides in the brain. In truth, the great network of nerves descending into the body through the spinal column and radiating out through all parts of the body—all of those nerve cells are a part of the physical mind. Now, move your awareness from the movement of the blood through your body to an awareness of this great network of nerves radiating down from your brain."

Aleister waited a long time, listening to the gentle music, until Wallace said: "I feel it."

"Good," Aleister said. "In various places along that vast network, you will find opinions and suggestions attached. Perhaps there is a suggestion that had a connection with the way you walk. You might find that suggestion clinging to nerves in your thighs. As you become aware of them, loosen their connection to you so that even if they don't go away totally, they can no longer exert an influence. You may find ones related to emotion around your heart. You might find ones related to thought patterns in your brain. There could be ones related to will in your spine. Become aware of them, one by one, and gently, by focusing on the nerve cells beneath, loosen their grasp."

Working with Dwayne's people had led him to do the strangest things. He was totally inventing all this on the fly. Was this completely ridiculous?

It wouldn't be if it worked.

Aleister watched Wallace. From time to time, his body moved subtly, or he made a gentle groan. Then he saw Dwayne's face looking through the window of the room. He held a finger to his lips and gently opened the door to let Dwayne silently in and gestured for him to sit in a chair. They sat there for some time.

"When you feel you have completed the voyage and loosened all the offending thoughts, you may return to us," Aleister said.

He held his finger to his lips again to keep Dwayne quiet.

They waited another ten minutes, and finally Wallace began to stir. He took a deep breath, opened his eyes, and sat up.

"Doctor, I believe you are a genius. Ha!" He turned to Dwayne. "Excellent. What do you think, old man?"

"I have no idea what you two were up to," Dwayne said.

"Are you free from the offending thoughts?" Aleister asked Wallace.

"I believe I am!"

"If they trouble you again, repeat that exercise. Now that you know how to do it, you can do it on your own."

"Excellent! Thank you, doctor!"

Aleister turned to Dwayne. "Do you have something to add?"

"I do, in fact. I worked this up this afternoon." Dwayne pulled out a printed sheet and showed it to Wallace.

"*Seven Steps to Tragic Death,*" Wallace read.

"Lear experiences seven emotional plateaus in the course of the action," Dwayne said. "Once you understand the levels and locations of these plateaus, you'll know how to play every scene."

"Really?" Wallace said. "That *is* intriguing."

"*Number One: Power and Fury.* You distribute your responsibilities to your daughters, but you still want to be king. When Cordelia displeases you, you disinherit her. When faithful Kent objects, you banish him. You split the kingdom between your two older daughters and travel to Goneril's castle with your hundred knights."

"Right," Wallace said. He turned to Aleister. "It's as though that idea attaches itself inside my brain."

"*Number Two,*" Dwayne continued. "*Defeat #1 50%* begins when Goneril insists you dismiss half your knights. You don't have the power you thought you'd reserved to yourself. You leave in fury, and you feel madness approaching."

"Yes. What am I if I'm not the King?" He turned to Aleister again. "This could be in my calves, those muscles, running out of Goneril's castle. Ha!" He stood up and flexed his knees.

"*Number Three: Defeat #2 100%* begins when you see Kent in stocks. Who would dare put the King's messenger in stocks? And then Regan refuses to take in *any* of your knights. You leave in fury again. Powerless."

"But now I have nowhere to go. I'm out into the storm without a roof over my head. I feel this in my thighs, digging deeper, pushing, heaving, pushing."

"Right," Dwayne agreed, though he wasn't exactly sure what he was agreeing to. "And that begins *Number Four: Inviting Oblivion.* Out on the heath, you invite the lightning to strike your aged head and wipe out all mankind. Madness begins."

"Oh, this is in the gut." He laid his hand on his abdomen. "I'll always be able to find that emotion right here."

"*Five* is *Embracing Madness.* You meet Poor Tom, who pretends madness to hide his identity."

"Yes, yes, yes," Wallace exclaimed. "The only possible cause of his madness would be how his daughters treated him. But I also call him a wise Athenian. A role model. Oh!" Wallace stopped and tilted his head up toward the ceiling. He took along breath in. "I feel this in the nerves behind my eyes." He grabbed Aleister and shook him. "This is amazing! You cleared the spaces around the nerves, and Dwayne is refilling them with incredible insight!"

Dwayne was tempted to ask what he was talking about, but decided to continue. "*Six* is *Worldly Defeat & Soulful Redemption*. Lear is transformed, in and out of madness, but when he regains himself, he can recognize Kent, Gloucester, and Cordelia. He feels love and appreciation for his true friends. He no longer identifies with his power. He tells Cordelia they can while away their lives in prison, happy as songbirds in a cage."

Wallace sat down and laid a hand over his heart. His mouth opened, and then closed, and then opened again. The wrinkles in his face deepened, and a tear rolled down his cheek. He covered his first hand with the other over his heart. He nodded at Dwayne, but did not speak.

"And finally, *Mortal Defeat and Death*. It begins as he carries in the dead Cordelia. There is nothing left for him in this world. His heart breaks, and he dies."

Now tears flowed freely down Wallace's cheeks. He clutched his hands tightly over his heart. Finally, he got up and hugged Dwayne and Aleister. "Thank you. Thank you. Thank you," he said.

58

Saturday, August 26, 2005

Rocky, playing Cornwall, stood over Peter Burden, playing Gloucester, tied to a chair. The rehearsal had been going nicely, and Dwayne was enjoying it deeply. Wallace had taken to sitting next to him when he was offstage rather than huddling in a corner with his script, getting ready for his next scene. He'd become so confident—and so good.

"Where hast thou sent the King?" Rocky/Cornwall demanded.

"To Dover," Gloucester replied.

"Wherefore to Dover, sir?" Regan demanded. She swirled the rehearsal skirt he wore as Regan aggressively as she moved in on Gloucester.

"Because I would not see thy cruel nails pluck out his poor old eyes; nor thy fierce sister in his anointed flesh stick boarish fangs." Gloucester cried as he struggled against the ropes that bound him. *"I shall see winged vengeance overtake such children."*

"See it shalt thou never," Rocky/Cornwall shouted. *"Fellows, hold the chair. Upon these eyes of thine I'll set my foot."* He approached with a spoon to dig out Gloucester's eyes. He stopped directly in front of him. But Rocky did not move any closer.

Suddenly, he turned. This was not part of the action. Did he look pale? He strode swiftly to Dwayne.

"I'm remembering," he whispered. "When I went to gouge out Gloucester's eyes, I remembered things I did as Bull. I've never remembered any of that before."

"Huh!" Wallace said, leaning in toward Dwayne's shoulder to overhear.

"Are you afraid you might slip back into *being* Uncle Bull?" Dwayne said. This was a horrifying thought. That was why he'd had the props department supply an aluminum mask to cover Peter Burden's face. He didn't want to risk a resurgent Uncle Bull actually gouging out one of Peter's eyes.

"I don't think I *slip*. I am either me or Bull—nothing in between. But I've never remembered anything of Bull until just now. As I was holding that spoon to gouge out Gloucester's eye, I suddenly remembered breaking Chaz's finger with a pair of pliers. I could *see* it!" He thought about it for a moment and then began to chuckle. He leaned yet closer. "You should have seen Chaz's face!" He laughed outright and then sobered up. "But that wasn't nice."

"Is there any risk you could drop into Bull and gouge out Peter's eye…"

"No, no, no," Rocky said. "It's just the exact opposite. I see that memory; I forget everything else. Cornwall's rage was gone. I'm just amazed, because I never remembered anything! People told me what Bull'd done, but otherwise, I had no idea."

"Interesting…" Wallace said.

"But I forgot my lines. I didn't know what we'd been doing. I've got this spoon in my hand, and there's Gloucester, so I remember what the scene is—but what was the last line spoken? I don't know."

"*Holy Dymphna, pray for us.*"

"What's that?" Rocky said.

"Look here, old man," Wallace said to Rocky. "Bull is a leech sucking on your life force, clinging to your nervous system."

"Well, now…" Dwayne knew where Wallace was going with this. Aleister had explained the exercise to him.

Wallace held a hand out to block Dwayne. "No, listen, this works. I had these thought-leeches in my calves, my thighs, my brain, and especially my heart. Dr. Aleister got rid of them."

Rocky took a step back. "What does that have to do with me?"

"Bull has been like a super-leech on your life! He sucked away your whole body, your consciousness, your time, everything. He's the definition of a parasite."

Rocky raised a finger. "Bull used to tell Yvette that she and I and Coco were all parasites on him. We were all living off *his* money."

"Gentlemen, can we get back to rehearsal?" Dwayne said.

"Rocky, why don't we discuss this…"

"Hang on," Rocky said. He turned back to Wallace. "So you think I'm remembering Bull now because he's clinging to my nerves?"

"Nerve matter, brain matter, it's all the same," Wallace said. "Your brain is the physical manifestation of your mind, and it's not just in your head. It's spread all over your body in your nerves. These parasite entities cling to it and suck your life energy. They keep you in confusion and weakness."

"You got all that from Aleister?" Dwayne said doubtfully.

"I did some follow-up research on the internet."

"And you know how to get Bull off me?" Rocky's eyebrows raised high.

"Absolutely. It worked for me. I did it on the Equity cot."

"And it worked?" Rocky narrowed his eyes.

"Have you seen the difference in my Lear?" Wallace said.

Everyone had noticed the difference in Wallace's Lear. That was the major topic of conversation all week. Rocky clapped his hands and pulled himself upright. "Okay, let's go."

"Wait a minute," Dwayne said. "You can do that after rehearsal."

"I can't perform until I get this parasite off me," Rocky said. "I'll be stuck every time I pick up the spoon." He pushed Wallace toward the door.

"No, no, wait!" Dwayne said.

"You can't put a price on your mental health," Rocky exclaimed, and the two of them disappeared down the hall.

Dwayne blew air through his lips. Aleister leading Wallace in whatever guided mind-game they'd done was one thing, but Wallace leading Rocky? Wallace's performance had taken a huge leap, that was for sure. But Rocky had an actual diagnosed mental disorder. Would Wallace make it worse? Had Dwayne been crazy to cast Rocky?

Clearly, he wasn't going to talk Rocky out of this exercise. He needed to make use of his rehearsal time any way he could and hope for the best.

"Okay, everyone, we are going to jump over and work on the Gloucester/Edgar scenes," he announced. "If you aren't in any of those, you are excused for the night."

59

Sunday, August 27, 2005

Ingrid wasn't sure how many designs she'd tried for building a fire rig, but not one of them had been good enough for the Goodman Theatre. The loft was full of the detritus of her abandoned attempts. She needed something beautiful, stunning, and absolutely safe. It needed to be something she could sneak into the building without anyone knowing. She usually preferred to beg forgiveness rather than ask permission. Well, she had asked permission this time and had been roundly denied. Never mind. Once everyone saw how amazing this would be, the naysayers would shut up. That's what Bobby said. Just wow them with the effect. They'd all be happy. And who knew more about wowing people than Bobby?

So the timing could not have been more amazing when she heard from Doug Slivesky, a guy who'd started in theatre lighting but now was making bigger bucks as a rock band roadie. He knew she was always hot for bargain equipment and called her. She headed immediately over to the outdoor bandshell in Douglass Park. Since she was living in the loft now, she'd removed her living paraphernalia from the van and had much more room for cargo.

She'd never spent much time in Douglass Park, and it took her twice around the weirdly shaped lagoons before she found her way to the band shell. A collection of roadies were drinking beer and getting things ready for that evening's performances. She found Doug, who introduced her to Haki.

"Your name is Hockey, like the sport?"

"Well, that's how it's pronounced," he said, pushing his waist-length braids behind him. "Doug said you might be interested in taking these propane tanks off my hands."

"Yeah," Ingrid said. "The fire rig, too."

"You should be able to get something for the copper. The hoses are probably a loss. The controller has a lot of brass fittings. If you take that all apart, there's probably some good scrap there." He looked terribly sad.

"How come you're scrapping it?" Ingrid asked. "Didn't it work?"

"Are you kidding me?" Haki said. "This thing was fantastic. Great billows of fire rolled right up out of it. The Rolling Stones didn't have a better fire rig. Except theirs was all electronic, and the light guys could run it from the booth. I had to set this baby up and run it by hand from backstage. It was all mechanical, which, really, when you think about it, makes it more reliable. I just fucked up on one little thing, and now the band says we have to junk it. Can't sell it. Can't give it away. They don't want the possibility of anyone getting injured and suing them. I invented it. I built it. But Hiss owns it. When we started using it, I got extra money to sell the rig to them, which seemed like a good idea at the time." He sighed deeply. "But now I got to do what they say."

"What was the fuck-up?" Ingrid asked.

"So dumb," Haki said. He showed her one of the two fire rigs. These were definitely DIY devices. Five brackets had been bolted on to each of two fifty-gallon metal drums, all the way around the circumference. U-bolts with set screws attached the copper tubes to the brackets, and each of the copper tubes was attached to flexible gas lines. The copper tubes had stainless steel nozzles sweat-soldered to the tips. Ingrid admired the design of the nozzles. This was what her designs had lacked.

"Looks nice," she said.

"It was nice. I angled the nozzles into the center so the jets of burning gas would come together into one big fireball and rise up. It was awesome. But look at this." He showed how one of the copper tubes was loose. "The mount cracked, and I just reset it with super glue. I should've rebuilt the mount. But instead, I guess the glue melted, and the tube got loose in last night's show and slipped sideways and burnt up Perry's wig."

"Jesus."

"Yeah. It's a good thing those guys are going bald; otherwise it would have been his head. But, man, he was pissed. He had to pull that burning wig off his head, and the whole audience saw his gleaming noggin. So, the band agreed. The rig has to be scrapped, not sold. No more fire rigs from Haki. They're talking to the Rolling Stones' guy. Like Hiss is going to be able to afford something like that," he scoffed.

"They won't let you fix it?"

"No way. Perry is the bass player, and bass players are really hard to replace. He wasn't really hurt. He looks like he has a little sunburn on one cheek. Those guys lack all logic. I mean, if you were going to start a *Kiss* cover band, would you call it *Hiss*? Ridiculous…"

Even though Haki had to junk his rig, he was still proud of his invention. It took very little prompting on Ingrid's part to get him to explain every bit of the workings.

They agreed on ten dollars each for the six propane tanks. Haki complained because four of them were full, but Ingrid insisted she'd get no more money for a full tank than an empty one. He gave her the fire rig and controller for free, since it would take so much labor to remove the valuable scrap from the parts going to the landfill. (She had to pretend she was just taking it for scrap.) Ingrid unbolted the brackets from the fifty-gallon barrels, rolled the barrels out to the curb where they looked like garbage cans, and left them there. She loaded everything else into her van to take it back to the loft.

She tried out the fire rig back in the loft, and it worked great. She began working up ideas on how she could disguise the hoses and tubes in her set design. She wouldn't fuck up like Haki and set anyone's wig on fire. Then she put some supplies in the big canvas bag she always carried and went to the Goodman to watch the end of the afternoon's rehearsal. She didn't really want to watch the rehearsal, but she had to test out the most essential part of her plan: the ability to work secretly on the Owen stage.

Near the end of the rehearsal, she slipped away and went down the stairs into the basement under the stage, making sure no one saw her. Everywhere she went, she passed framed posters and photos from past Goodman shows, but down in the basement under the Owen stage, it was just crates and storage and space under the trapdoors in the Owen stage floor. She found a place to hide and waited.

For someone with Ingrid's level of energy, waiting for the show on the Albert stage to end and everyone to leave the building was torture. The show ended at 10:30. She figured the cast and crew were probably out of the building by 11:30, but if a technical problem had come up, maybe techs would be there until 12:30. However, these were not idle hours for her. She worked and reworked and reimagined and redesigned how she would disguise and use the fire rig and controller on her set. One of the problems was that she would have to be in the basement running the controller while the fire was happening up on stage. How would she be able to watch it to make sure everything was working okay? She could set up some cameras and monitor them with her phone. She could use those security camera doorbells people had on their houses. She could probably get a couple of those fairly cheap. The fire wouldn't run very long. All the actors would have come to their final positions and be holding when the flames went up. So it should be safe.

Her brain was running on all eight cylinders.

She waited until 1:30 to come out of hiding, then she walked all through the Goodman building, entering each new area cautiously in case someone might be there. After forty minutes of searching, she felt assured the building was empty. The dry run was a success! When the day arrived, she'd be able to do her work undetected.

She took a nap on the Equity cot until 5:30 a.m. and then went back into hiding until 11 a.m. At that point, she came out of hiding and walked through the building toward the lobby. She even ran into the big man himself, Reg Camper, and exchanged a few pleasantries. No one suspected she'd been there all night. She walked out of the building, chuckling to herself, no one the wiser.

60

Tuesday, August 29, 2005

Wallace and Rocky were already in the rehearsal room when Dwayne arrived. They sat on the floor in some tortured version of the lotus position, both of them far from youth and flexibility. They sat with palms up, the backs of their hands resting on their knees.

What the devil?

"And one last deep cleansing breath," Wallace rumbled in his deep baritone.

Dwayne set his bag on the director's table and quietly watched. Wallace and Rocky seemed the unlikeliest of companions.

"Good," Wallace said. "Now we start from the nerve endings at the very top of our heads and follow them down all the way through the body. We loosen and let drop any unuseful thoughts and energies, any pernicious entities, any preconceptions or thought patterns, any invasive spirits that cling, and we let them go, cleansing our nerves."

"Ahhh…" Rocky moaned. Both of them kept their eyes closed, deep in a trance-like state. They sat for the longest time, breathing slowly, their bodies sometimes shifting and distant grimaces crossing their faces, as though they were vanquishing internal phantoms. After the longest time, they began making deeper, louder rumblings in their throats and stretched out their legs in front of them, shaking their feet. Wallace lost his balance and rolled onto his back, still shaking his legs and feet, stretched out prone. Their moans turned full-throated, and they vibrated their feet violently, giving one last shout together. Then they opened their eyes. Wallace sat up again. They looked at one another and laughed heartily, helping each other to their feet and sharing a vigorous embrace.

"Ha! Marvelous!" Wallace shouted.

Rocky clapped him on the shoulder. "You the man!" he

exclaimed.

Wallace pointed a finger at him. "Remember, review your four steps to tragic death. And I'll review mine."

"Four steps to tragic death?" Dwayne said.

Wallace turned as though startled. "Ah! The Master Director. Yes, we reviewed the arc of Cornwall's progression through the play. We found four distinct emotional steps before his servant kills him, like you found seven for me. Wait until you see Rockwell's performance today!"

Rocky nodded. "Wally really showed me some things," he agreed. Wallace turned sharply, surprised to hear his name shortened. Rocky moved off gently to one of the chairs at the back of the room and sat down with his script. Dwayne had never seen Rocky look so…what?…peaceful? He typically had an aggressiveness to his movements that fit with his portrayal of the fiery Duke Cornwall. What would he be like now?

"That thing Aleister taught me," Wallace whispered to Dwayne. "It's just magical! Rockwell loved it last night. He could feel Bull peeling away from the nerves along the middle of his spinal column. He thinks he'll be able to stop his meds."

"For the love of God!" Dwayne said. "I hope you didn't encourage that."

"No, no, of course not. He broke the finger of young Chaz with a pair of pliers." Wallace laughed heartily.

Why did he find *that* funny?

"But this exercise from Aleister, it's just genius," Wallace said.

"Right…" If he told Wallace that Aleister had just dreamed up the exercise on the spot, that might make Wallace tumble out of the gains he'd made. But he couldn't have Rocky think that this meditation could replace his drugs. "But he gave that exercise to you, for your specific needs," Dwayne whispered intensely. "Rocky's condition is entirely different."

"Pish posh," Wallace said. "I understand how incredibly powerful this therapeutic modality can be. And Rockwell absolutely felt it. He heard Uncle Bull squealing like a little pig when he was flushed from his system. Bull is *gone*!" Wallace laughed and nodded. "Great talk, old man. Got to prepare!" He clapped Dwayne on the shoulder and strode off to sit next to Rocky. He pulled out his script, and the two sat together, going over their scenes.

Saint Dympha, patron of the insane, pray for us!

As the other actors were arriving and going into their warm-ups, Dwayne stepped out into the hall to call Aleister.

"Maybe he did peel off Uncle Bull." Aleister said. "After years of affliction, Wallace found the cure."

"Be serious. We can't risk Rocky off his meds."

"No, no," Aleister agreed.

"Please, you've got to talk to him. But if you see Wallace, don't tell him that mumbo jumbo wasn't real."

"Hey, that was clinically effective mumbo jumbo."

"Please?"

"All right," Aleister said. "Since you said please twice. I'll tell Rocky since he performed the exorcism on his meds, he has to stay on his meds for it to be effective. The absence of his meds will alter the magnetic polarity of his nerves and attract Bull back again."

"Wow. Nice detail. Can you do it tonight?"

"Has anyone ever told you that you are a pain in the ass?"

"Nearly everyone. Please, oh please, Aleister?"

"All right. You don't have to grovel."

"I'm willing."

"I know you are."

* * *

Once all the actors had gathered, and it was time to start, Dwayne stood up. "Okay, everybody." He loved their collective look of expectation. They were all so talented. They'd worked so hard. "We'll soon be up on the set in the theatre. It's one week until previews. Two weeks until opening." Melinda looked both nervous and excited. Coco gave him a confident smirk. Wallace whispered something in Rocky's ear, causing him to chuckle. "As much as possible, we're going to be running the show without stops from now on. I want you to get the flow into your bodies. If you need to discuss something offstage, please take it into the hall, but be aware of your cues. We'll pick up whatever needs work at the end of the run. If something happens on stage, deal with it like you're in front of a live audience. If it's a total train wreck, I'll stop you, and we'll fix it. Otherwise, keep it going." Dwayne nodded to Howie Grange.

"Places for the top of the show," the stage manager called.

"Thank you, places!" all the actors called back, the enthusiasm clear in their voices.

Wallace began the show masterfully, playing Lear larger-than-life, jovial as he divided his kingdom and listened to his two older daughters exaggerate grandly about how they loved him solely and above all things.

Melinda approached him cautiously as Cordelia. *"Good my lord,"* she said reasonably, *"you have begot me, bred me, loved me. I return those duties back as are right fit, obey you, love you, and most honor you. Why have my sisters husbands if they say they love you all? Haply, when I shall wed, that lord whose hand must take my plight shall carry half my love with him, half my care and duty. Sure, I shall never marry like my sisters, to love my father all."*

Although Cordelia spoke lovingly, Lear looked confused. *"But goes thy heart with this?"*

"Ay, my good lord." She bowed to him.

He looked utterly baffled. Was this not the daughter he'd loved best? *"So young, and so untender?"*

"So young, my lord, and true."

An expression of profound pain crossed his face. *"Let it be so, thy truth then be thy dower."* He began the speech with profound regret, which swiftly transformed from regret into fury. *"For, by the sacred radiance of the sun, the mysteries of Hecate and the night, by all the operation of the orbs from whom we do exist, here I disclaim all my paternal care!"* And so he blasted irrevocably into the decision that would lead ultimately to his own destruction.

Dwayne took a deep breath. That was perhaps the most difficult moment in the play. Everything depended on Lear's rejection of Cordelia. If he was merely mad from the get-go, what sympathy could be felt for the old man? But here Wallace had given a moment in which we could see something inexplicable—but real—go on in his soul.

Masterful.

While Wallace had progressed step by step into a better and better Lear, Rocky had instantly changed to playing a totally different Cornwall. It was as though Denzel Washington's character in *Training Day* had been transported into *King Lear*. It startled Dwayne at first because it was so different, but as Dwayne continued to watch it, he had to admit, it worked. What gave him the greatest relief, however, was the scene in which Cornwall gouges out Gloucester's eyes. Rocky played it like the moment in which Alonso (Denzel) has Jake (Ethan Hawke) kill Roger (Scott Glenn). He played it with sardonic humor, coldly mocking Gloucester like Alonso mocked Roger as he died. This was not the dangerous fury of Uncle Bull. This was an actor in total control, making a conscious choice about the way he played the scene. He turned to see Aleister standing at the back of the rehearsal room, observing. He wasn't sure when his friend had arrived, but he was glad he'd seen that.

At the end of the night, Aleister went off with Rocky. Dwayne hoped that Rocky's issue would be resolved.

61

Wednesday, August 30, 2005

Ingrid had racked her brains about how she would sneak in the fire trick apparatus and the six propane tanks she needed to complete the run of the show. Two days before load-in, she realized she didn't need to sneak in all the tanks. She just needed one. After opening night, the fire trick wouldn't be a secret anymore. Everyone would have seen that she could provide actual flames safely. They'd love it! They'd congratulate her! Well, some of them might still be sulky about it, but so what? It'd be her triumph. She'd be able to bring in the other tanks in broad daylight. (And actually, she wasn't sure that the six tanks would be enough for the run of the show. She might have to get some refills. All totally doable).

On Wednesday morning, she met Peaches in the alley off Lake Street. A truck from the Goodman set construction shop in the Bridgeport neighborhood was already pulled up to the loading gate, bringing in set pieces for the show. She and Peaches carried in the first rack of costumes, working around the men and women carrying in the antique furniture and metal bracketing on which all that furniture would sit, rising up in the air on the stage of the Owen. As they turned in front of two men carrying a tall chifforobe, one of the men shouted, the chifforobe tipped, and the two men staggered, banging the top corner of the piece into the wall, gouging a nasty divot into the plaster.

"Hey, hey, hey," Nick Sanchez said, coming around from behind the two men. He put his hands on his hips in front of Ingrid. "I thought we agreed that you'd load in props and costumes on a different day than these guys."

"Well, you did suggest that," Ingrid countered. "But this was the best day for Peaches and me."

"Best day?" Peaches said. "I had to rearrange my whole schedule to make this day work."

Peaches did complain about loading in today, but congestion and confusion were exactly what Ingrid wanted. She wanted everyone to be too busy to notice what she was up to. However, now Nick Sanchez was looking right at her.

"We have just a few racks of costumes and some crates of props," Ingrid said. "We'll stay out of everyone's way."

"Please do," Sanchez insisted.

"It's a collaborative art form!" Ingrid said brightly.

Sanchez made a grumbling noise in his throat and walked off with his clipboard in hand.

After rolling in another rack of costumes, Ingrid looked around carefully to see that Sanchez was nowhere in sight. They rolled in a large trunk spray-painted on the sides with "PDT Props." Some of these crates did have props. This one had a propane tank and coils of gas hoses. Another had the gas control unit, copper tubes with stainless steel nozzles, and all the connectors. Peaches and she rolled in the one with the propane tanks, when suddenly Coco blocked their way.

"Okay, so here I am," she said flatly.

"Great!" Peaches said. "Could you hang in here for a minute?" She turned to Ingrid. "Since you wanted to load in today, I asked Coco to stop by and try on a costume. This one will need heavy alterations."

"We need to get this trunk put away," Ingrid said quietly.

"This will just take a minute," Peaches said. "Well, longer than a minute. But I don't want to keep Coco waiting." She smiled nervously.

"Nobody wants Coco to be kept waiting," Coco agreed.

"But…" Ingrid said.

"Right this way," Peaches said. Coco came first. After all, Ingrid had never brought Peaches to tears.

Ingrid sat on the trunk. She felt sweat begin to build up around the edges of her hairline. The whole point was to get the trunks with the fire equipment hidden away quickly. She didn't want to be sitting in the hallway where anyone might pass by. She didn't want questions about where she intended to store her props. She didn't want anyone to know how many trunks she was bringing in. But she also didn't want Peaches to be suspicious.

Then she heard Nick Sanchez's voice down the hall. Fuck it! She had to move. She rolled it over to the freight elevator and pressed the button. She heard it moving, but it was a large, slow elevator built to carry heavy loads.

Come on!

Nick Sanchez's voice was getting closer.

The doors opened, and she rolled in the trunk. She could hear the voices getting closer. She punched the button for the basement.

Close! Close, God damn it!

The doors slid closed just as the footsteps and voices were getting so close they'd be coming into view.

When the elevator opened, she rolled the trunk to the section under the stage and out of sight along the back. Then she ran up the stairs in case anyone who might question her was coming down to the basement.

When Coco and Peaches returned to the spot where they'd left her, Peaches looked around for the trunk, but she didn't ask about it. One of the wonderful things about Peaches was that she never questioned what other people were up to.

"Say, Ingrid, have you ever been married?" Coco asked.

"No." What was this about?

"You've known Bobby even longer than me. Do you think he'd ever get married?"

"Bobby?" Ingrid shrugged. "I'm guessing Bobby will have married three or four times before he's through."

"Huh." Coco thought that one over. "You prefer being single?"

"I don't think about it that much," she said hurriedly. She took Peaches by the elbow and began leading her back toward the truck. "Thanks. See you later. We've got to get back to work."

Coco looked startled by a new idea and began following them. "Oh, say, I can't believe I don't know this after all these years. Are you a lesbian?"

"See you later!" Ingrid hurried forward around the corner with Peaches.

"Was that question too personal?" Peaches said, looking back in the direction where they'd left Coco. "I mean, I'm such an introvert, but everybody knows all sorts of details about me."

"Why is that?" Ingrid kept moving.

"I blurt things. I get insecure, and then I blurt. And then I'm sorry."

"Huh," Ingrid said. "I guess when I talk, it's mostly about tech. Or my van. I like to talk about my van."

They got back to the truck and rolled a crate with weaponry and props into one of the empty dressing rooms. Sanchez was wandering around again among the tech workers, moving the metal superstructure onto the stage, so they continued with the final rack of costumes and crate of props. After that, they got the crate with the controller and nozzles into the basement. That was the last secret crate. And no one was the wiser. Not even Peaches suspected a thing.

Hurrah!

62

Thursday, September 7, 2005

Ingrid sighed. "Well, *that* still looks like shit. But your actors look fantastic." She sat watching the last moments of the first preview. She and Dwayne sat at the back of the second balcony, near the light booth, out of earshot of the audience. The audience was all on the main floor and the first balcony.

Dwayne nodded while finishing his notes for the actors.

"You worked miracles with Wallace. And Tom as Regan? I never thought that was going to work. I can't believe how good he was."

"Yeah," Dwayne said distractedly, still madly writing in his notebook. "He's good…"

"But that lighting effect for the fire?" She shook her head sadly. The Goodman lighting designer had tweaked it every night of tech, and it still never looked like actual flames licking up the mountains of antique furniture.

Dwayne looked up from his notebook. "Yeah, I don't like it, either. I tried to see it as a representation of Lear's mind—but Lear is dead. I tried to think of it as the spirits of Lear and Cordelia going off to the other world—but it just doesn't work. Let's cut it. The actors are giving us everything we need. Your set has made its statement. It all works without the fire."

"It does," Ingrid said. She had a weird little smile. "But I've still got one more idea. Just wait."

Dwayne sighed heavily. He hated when Ingrid would bring in some weird lighting device at the last minute and he'd have to fight her on it. He didn't want anything to throw off the actors. "We're already in previews," he said. "We open in a week. If you've got something new, let's see it tomorrow. After that, no more changes."

"The only real deadline is opening night."

"Seriously, Ingrid. Tomorrow."

She slapped her notebook closed and charged out of the Owen, calling behind her with a grin: "Don't you worry your pretty little head."

Most of all, he hated when she said that.

63

Monday, September 11, 2005

"Ooh, that's wet," Angela said. The sonographer nodded as she applied the transducer to Angela's stomach and began moving it around across her flesh. It was about the size of an electric shaver. Various squishy noises were coming from the device. Angela gave Dwayne a big, excited smile. This was her first ultrasound, and she was hoping for the best.

"Oh my," the sonographer said.

"What? What is it?" Angela said, panic in her voice.

"No, no," the sonographer said. "Nothing bad. Everything looks healthy. But look at this." She turned the screen so that Angela and Dwayne could see it more clearly.

"What?" It looked like a bunch of blobs to Dwayne.

"What are we looking at?" Angela said.

The sonographer moved the transducer until she had the image she wanted. Then she held it in place and used her other hand to point first at one dark blob on the screen and then at another. "See that? Twins."

Today being September 11, all morning on the radio at home and in the car, they'd been hearing remembrances of the attack on the Twin Towers four years ago. The word *Twins* hit Dwayne with an instant overtone of disaster. He looked at Angela.

Angela's mouth hung open. She closed it. "Twins?" She started to laugh. "Oh my God in heaven. The ancestors have outdone themselves. Twins!"

Every time he heard the word *twins*, in his mind's eye, Dwayne saw a huge commercial jet flying into the side of a tower and exploding.

"Look at my husband." Angela laughed to the sonographer.

"You're not going to faint, are you, Dwayne?"

"If you are feeling faint, put your face down between your knees," the sonographer said. "You look pale."

Dwayne did as he was told. He didn't feel faint, but he felt it was best to hide his face for a moment.

He was going to be the father of twins? How could that possibly have happened?

Well, he knew how it had happened. Sperm and egg and all. And, apparently, two daily doses of highly questionable herbal tea. He didn't know if an egg had split and they were going to have identical twins or if two eggs had fertilized and they would have fraternal twins. But how would he cope with being the father of twins? He could barely imagine taking care of one. How would he possibly take care of two?

Until this moment, he'd always been worried about his career and about their finances, and how they would afford a family, and whether he'd have to abandon his life as a theatre artist. But now, suddenly, in this moment of seeing the two tiny swirling masses on the screen that were going to grow like little parasites in his true love's belly into the size of actual babies and come out her vagina with all their needs and demands, now he wondered if he were up to the task as a human being. Could he be the father of twins? Could he raise them and take care of them, and foster their development into well-adjusted, happy, successful human beings?

It seemed highly unlikely.

If they were daughters, he might be no better than King Lear.

He'd never received any training in how to be a father. He'd been through grammar school, high school, and the university, and he'd never taken a single course in fatherhood.

Saints Cosmas and Damian, pray for me.

Maybe that should be their names if they were boys. Cosmas and Damian, patron saints of twins. Maybe that would bring blessings upon them.

"Hey, Dwayne," Angela said. "Are you coming back up for air?"

He sat back up.

"Well, you've got a little color again." She smiled at him.

"Twins!" she said brightly. "If we keep this up, I might catch up to my ma, after all." She laughed merrily.

Dwayne put his face back between his knees.

64

Thursday, September 14, 2005

Tuesday and Wednesday passed in some kind of dream. Now here he was at opening night, the night that would decide his future. In past productions, it had been mostly on him to get the critics to attend. His productions were a low priority for the press, so the critics tended to be spread out, attending over the first two weeks of the show. Once he'd had a critic attend the closing weekend. What was the point of that? But with Goodman's PR department behind him, all the critics were attending on opening night, which meant all the pressure was on this one performance of the show. It was still an hour before curtain, and, given his level of perspiration, Dwayne was wishing he'd brought an extra shirt.

Monday night with Angela had been one of the most extraordinary of their marriage. Angela decided she was the one who was driving home from the ultrasound, which was all to the good. Dwayne continued to be dumbfounded by the news. But then he pivoted into action and whimsy and did everything in doubles for the rest of the night. He made her cups of two different herbal teas (store-bought) when they got home. He made two entrees for dinner, including one of sausages. Angela had craved sausages since she got pregnant. Then he made love to her twice, once for each of their beloved little zygotes. All of this amused Angela to no end.

Angela had taken a personal day for her doctor visit on Monday. For the rest of the week, they'd hardly seen one another. She was back at work, and Dwayne was going in early every day to oversee every possible detail through the final days of previews. And now the night of opening had come.

Dwayne circulated among the technical people. One of the upsides of working at the Goodman, with their insistence on planning things out far in advance, was that everything ran more smoothly than the typical Psychedelic Dream production. Peaches was happy and excited, assisted by the Goodman costume people. The actors worked through their warm-ups. They were all checked in and moving around in various states of excitement and nerves. At forty-five minutes to curtain, Dwayne called for them to join him onstage.

Dwayne looked from face to face as they gathered in a circle onstage. All his actors were there, and Peaches and Joan joined them.

"It's my last night of duty as your director. From here on, it's Howie Grange that leads you. Opening night!" he exclaimed. They all cheered.

So many of these faces he loved. Tom, who'd been his friend since high school. How would his Regan be accepted tonight? Dwayne had cast an all-Black Gloucester family: Peter Burden as the patriarch, Orlando as good Edgar, Bobby as the evil Edmund, but his Lear family was an odd mismatch. Black Coco as Goneril, White male Tom as Regan, and pretty White ingénue Melinda as Cordelia. Would the critics crucify him for these choices?

But he loved these actors. They had shown so much soul, every one of them, in learning their roles, and acting as a united ensemble.

"I dreamed of directing a show on this stage," he told them. "Ever since I first walked in here, I have loved the possibilities of this space." He stopped and looked into each of their faces. "I am so, so happy to be here with all of you." They all smiled back at him. Only Peter Burden looked a little bored. "I had an idea what this *King Lear* could be, but you all have taken that and gone beyond into something much greater. Have fun tonight. Listen to each other. Live it like it's the first time. I'll see you on the other side."

They all cheered. It filled his heart with so much joy, tears came to his eyes, and he choked back a sob.

"Pull it in! Pull it in!" Tom cried, waving his arms so that they all pulled in together with their arms around one another. "To the greatest play in the English language on the premiere stage in the city of Chicago, the greatest theatre city in the world!" he yelled. "Huzzah!"

They all shouted after him: "Huzzah! Huzzah! Huzzah!"

"Break a thousand legs!" Dwayne shouted.

"Huzzah!" they all shouted, and there was much hugging and laughing. Then they all returned to their preparations, looking forward to curtain.

Dwayne circulated, checking to see where he could be of use, but everyone seemed fully prepared, which astounded him. But where was Ingrid? He'd seen her checking on things when he first arrived, but he hadn't seen her in the past half hour.

He went out to the lobby to greet the critics and hand out press kits with the Goodman PR assistant. After that, it was time to join Angela in their seats way at the back of the second balcony, just under the light booth. He liked to watch as much of the audience as he could on opening night to gauge their reactions and see how every scene played. He waved to Howie Grange in the booth as he took his seat next to Angela.

"How is it?" she asked him.

"Everything looks good." He leaned in towards her. "Should we tell anyone? Maybe in the after-party? That'd be fun."

"We aren't at twelve weeks yet. Let's wait. Tonight's all about your show. That's the way it should be."

"Okay," he said. "I'm just excited. Twins. I can't believe it."

"I thought you were going to faint on Monday."

"I thought so, too." He laughed. "But now I'm excited."

She smiled and hugged his arm to her. "Look at you. Proud papa. Goodman theatre director. Things are looking up."

He put his arm around her. "It sure does look that way." He gave her a warm kiss on the mouth as the house lights began to go down.

When Wallace entered for the first time, he entered arms out, like a beloved celebrity embracing his audience. He sucked every eye to him and owned the stage. He was a masterful Lear, living life from the highest heights to accentuate his fall that would follow. Dwayne enjoyed the show so much, he had to remind himself to watch the audience, and they seemed to be enjoying it, too.

Coco seduced with her speech of excessive love for Lear. Her Goneril was not to be trusted somehow, but Lear fell under the spell of her words. It was completely understandable. Tom's Regan ingratiated. She delivered her praise of Lear from an almost oily, servile angle, and Lear drank up the flattery.

He remained so puffed up by his older daughters' excesses that when Melinda's Cordelia expressed her dutiful and honest love for her father, admitting that when she married, half of her love would go to her husband, Lear became outraged. This was a moment on which Wallace could founder. Why would Lear disown the daughter he loved best? Why banish his most faithful knight, Kent, when he protested Lear's rashness? But the ego with which Wallace swept onto the stage, the pleasure with which he'd absorbed the excessive fawning from his older daughters, the mental confusion he showed when he began to divide up the kingdom made his shift credible.

The audience believed him. And that was the battle.

He held them all the way through the show, carried them as every bit of his power was stripped away, causing him to go mad, a madness only relieved when Cordelia came to rescue him. A madness that returned when she was killed. A madness that carried him right into death.

Dwayne saw tears glistening in audience eyes as Lear died. Every bit had been good. Even when an actor stumbled on a line, another actor picked them up, and although Dwayne saw it, he did not think the audience noticed anything amiss.

The last words fell to Orlando's Edgar: "*The weight of this sad time we must obey; Speak what we feel, not what we ought to say. The oldest hath borne most; we that are young shall never see so much, nor live so long.*"

Dwayne's heart felt so full. They'd all been so good. One sob escaped his throat in the emotion of so much goodness. He could feel the audience ready to surge into applause.

And then two great fountains of fire surged up on each side of the stage in front of the towers of antique furniture that made the background of Ingrid's set.

Dwayne suddenly remembered wondering where Ingrid was before the curtain.

The audience gasped. Some shouted their shock and surprise.

Then the shock turned to terror as some of the old, dry, antique furniture caught fire. This was not some technical effect. This was fire, out of control. The shouts of shock and surprise turned to screams of *FIRE!* Dwayne's beautiful audience turned suddenly to a mob in panic and surged toward the exits. Angela stood up beside him.

"Oh, my God! We've got to get out of here." The people all around them surged to the exits, screaming.

"Wait. Stay calm," Dwayne said. He got up and held her for a moment until they were alone in their aisle. The flames were dancing up the furniture, more of it catching fire. What the hell had Ingrid done? She had some kind of gas fire blowing up in front of the set, but why wasn't she turning off the gas? Surely she could see this was going wrong. Where the hell was she?

Then the fire curtain dropped, and he could no longer see the conflagration.

"Don't panic!" he shouted at the top of his lungs, trying to reach the audience below. "Walk slowly!"

But no one heard him. People jammed into the exits. Some were running, climbing, jumping over others who had fallen. Horror stirred up in Dwayne's chest.

"We've got to get out of here," Angela cried. "I've got the twins."

"Right," Dwayne said. "Follow me. I know a safe way." He led her over to the far side of the seating area and unhooked a chain with a *No Admittance* sign hanging off it. Behind was a set of stairs going up into the space above the theatre.

"This will get us out of here?" Angela sounded panicky. Going up into the smoke did not look like a good idea.

"Trust me," he said. He led her up the stairs and across a metal gangway over the top of the audience space, from which rows of lighting instruments hung. They crossed over the top of the theatre, smoke curling up around them. Dwayne handed Angela his handkerchief. "Breathe through this!" he said. He knew more people died of smoke inhalation than burns in fires. He held his breath until they got to the other side of the theatre and opened a door. Suddenly, they were in an upper hallway of the Goodman Theatre and out of the smoke. Dwayne took deep breath, and they both coughed a bit.

"How did the set catch on fire?" Angela said. "I thought you weren't allowed to use flames."

"We aren't. Apparently, Ingrid decided to put in a fire effect anyway and managed to set it up without anyone knowing."

"What a fucking idiot."

Far below, sounding very far away now that they were in this upper hallway, they could hear shrieks and crying, and then fire truck sirens screaming, getting louder and louder. Dwayne led Angela down the flights of stairs and out of the building. Then he dove back inside to see if there was anything he could do to help.

65

Friday, September 15, 2005

The next day at noon, Joan stood in front of the Goodman Theatre, as still as a statue. As Dwayne got closer, he realized she was standing with her eyes closed. Most unusual on a busy Loop street like Dearborn. A couple walked by, looking at her. They laughed and shook their heads.

"Joan," Dwayne greeted. She opened her eyes slowly.

"I'm gathering myself. I was not walking in there without you."

"No," Dwayne agreed.

"How is Angela?"

"She's okay. She's angry." Dwayne pushed the revolving door so Joan could enter before him. He followed through in the next revolving compartment. Joan stood inside, facing him.

"I was so worried about her in all that mess last night, in her condition. She didn't get caught up in the stampede, I hope?"

"I led her out through the lighting grid. We avoided the crush."

"I'm so glad."

Dwayne tilted his head to one side. "What do you mean, *her condition?*"

"The baby."

Dwayne looked around to see if anyone was in earshot. "What makes you think Angela is pregnant?" He knew no one could tell by looking at her. She wasn't showing yet.

"I can sense these things," Joan said. She started walking toward the Owen. "Do you want to know the sex?"

"Just… Just stop now," he whispered. "We haven't said anything to anyone. And don't you tell anyone that *you think* Angela is pregnant."

"I *think?* I'm pretty sure you just confirmed it. But don't worry. I can keep a secret." She pushed open the doors of the Owen and followed the entrance alley down to the back of the seats. Reginald Camper and Nick Sanchez stood on the stage, talking and looking at the *King Lear* set.

Last night, after Dwayne had gotten Angela out of the building, he went back to make sure his actors were safe. None of them had been hurt. Once the gas in the fire trick was turned off, the fire died almost immediately. Only two of the furniture pieces burned much. When the fire department arrived, which was quick, they hosed down the furniture with water in a way that seemed excessive. Dwayne got all his people safely out of the theatre. He had one glimpse of Ingrid, looking horrified at what had happened, and then he didn't see her again. Reg Camper cursed him out colorfully at a volume that made Dwayne's ears ring. On the way out of the building, he saw paramedics carrying people away on stretchers who'd been trampled in the panic. Some of them looked pretty bad.

This morning on the phone, Nick Sanchez told him the run of their show was cancelled and that Dwayne and his executive staff should come in immediately. He and Joan were here. Ingrid was not answering her phone.

Reg Camper turned to see them coming up the aisle.

"How could you possibly have thought this was okay?" he called.

"This was all Ingrid," Dwayne said, continuing to walk toward the stage and climb the stairs up onto it. "I told Ingrid we were cutting the lighting effect for fire. It wasn't needed. I had no idea she'd rigged up a real one."

"What about the doorbell monitors?" Sanchez said.

"Doorbell monitors?" Dwayne said.

"How did she get all that liquid gasoline in here?" he said.

"She used liquid gasoline?" Dwayne said.

"No," Sanchez said. "She used propane. I wanted to see if you knew about the doorbell monitors or the propane tanks. But at least you acted like you didn't."

Reg Camper shook his head. "You've directed too much Agatha Christie, Nick."

"Well." Sanchez shrugged. "Maybe."

"Come on." Camper led them down into the space below the stage and showed them the fire controller, propane tank, and hoses leading up through holes drilled in the stage floor below the stacks of furniture above. It was all cleverly disguised and fit into trunks that closed up to hide them completely. It included a baby monitor speaker. "She hid a monitor transmitter backstage. She could hear what was happening onstage, so she knew when to light it up. The doorbell monitors allowed her to see the action, but apparently not well enough to see that her set was on fire."

"Look over here," Sanchez said. He pointed to a sleeping bag on a yoga mat behind a row of stacked boxes. "Apparently she slept back here. She must have done her work at nights when no one was in the building."

"This is a high level of subterfuge," Camper said. "If she put that level of ingenuity into something useful, God knows what she could achieve."

"Well," Joan said. "This is a woman who lived in the back of a van through Chicago winters on very little income. She took a failing for-profit theatre company and turned it into an NFP with $150,000 in the bank."

"Yes, I'm sure she's a genius," Camper said dourly. "Let's call the MacArthur people."

"Where is she?" Sanchez said.

"She's gone," Joan said.

"Where?" Sanchez said.

"Gone, gone," Joan said. "She's gone. Not to be seen again."

"How do you know that?" Dwayne said.

"I went to the loft. All the things she'd brought in from her van were gone. The van was gone. All her personal stuff was gone. Her tools were gone. She's gone."

"We need to find her," Dwayne said.

"You'd better," Camper said. "I got calls from two of the lawyers on the Goodman Board already. Audience members from last night are planning to sue. They'll be coming after us, after you, and particularly after Ingrid."

"Ingrid isn't Ingrid," Joan said.

"What's that?" Camper said.

"I tried to track her down. Dwayne, Ingrid, and I are all on the company credit card. I tried to see if she'd used the card anywhere, and then dug a little deeper. The social security number she uses belongs to an Ingrid Baardsen of Saint Paul, Minnesota. I called her. Ms. Baardsen is ninety-one years old. She had no knowledge of our Ingrid. She had one child who died twenty years ago and no grandchildren. I got that much information, and then she decided I was trying to scam her and hung up on me."

"Ingrid isn't Ingrid?" Dwayne said. "But why would she have done that?"

"My guess is that she got in trouble in Minneapolis and decided to leave town under a new identity," Joan said. "Somehow she had this Ingrid Baardsen's personal information."

Camper shook his head. "Good lord."

"Anyway," Sanchez said. "Be ready to be sued. Get your things out of the building by Wednesday. After that, we junk it. And, obviously, don't come back here looking for work."

66

Saturday, September 16, 2005

"Do you know anyone in New York City, Kate?" Ingrid sat across from the old lady at the kitchen table. She'd restored her van with all her living gear in Kate's garage, safely hidden for the moment. No one had ever known about her time living in Kate's garage and doing repair jobs around the house for the old lady. No one knew about their connection, so that was good. But Ingrid liked the old lady. Even after she'd moved into the loft, she still stopped by occasionally to see Kate and pick up groceries for her and do the odd job.

"Oh, golly, no. No one in New York City. All our people were in Ohio, and then we made friends here. I've never even been to New York. When Bernie and I would vacation, we liked a road trip out west or down to Florida. One time we went to New Orleans, but that city was a bit much for us, to tell you the truth." She got up and refilled her and Ingrid's coffee cups and brought out a Heinemann's coffee cake from the refrigerator.

"I hear you." Ingrid took a deep breath. "I wasn't expecting this, but I'm going to be leaving Chicago."

"Oh, no!"

Her look of disappointment broke Ingrid's heart. Would anyone but Kate miss her like that?

"Yeah. I got offered a job in Los Angeles," she lied, "and it's just too good to pass up. I have to leave immediately."

"Oh, that's too bad." Kate stared into her coffee. "I mean, it's nice for you. A good job…" She cut a piece of coffee cake for Ingrid and one for herself. She let hers sit on the saucer.

"I feel pretty good that I got so many things on the house handled for you," Ingrid said. "The place is in pretty good shape. You shouldn't need a handyman for a while."

"I'm so grateful for that. I wish you'd let me pay you something."

Ingrid felt a flash of guilt. She wasn't doing anything that would take any money from Kate, just like she hadn't taken any from Ingrid Baardsen in Minneapolis. She was just kind of…sharing. "You've paid me more than you know," she said.

"I don't know what you mean by that. You've been so good to me, and all I've done for you is let you use my garage. It was just sitting empty."

"Well, now you can rent it out and make a few extra dollars. Also, you should call *Rent-an-Angel* to get someone to help you out like I've been doing. I used to work for them. They have a sliding scale rate. If you have less money, they charge you less money."

"If you think so. Why did you ask about New York?"

"I had another job offer there, but it wasn't as good. So I'm going to Los Angeles."

"So exciting! Job offers from all over."

Ingrid was glad Kate knew no one in New York. Kate wasn't likely to go there at this stage of her life, either. That would be Ingrid's next stop. She'd have to get used to being known as Kate Bennison. She'd make a side trip back to St. Paul to have new documents made. Better to use the same guy than to look for a new forger here. She needed to get out of town before anyone spotted her.

She remembered those people on stretchers in the lobby of the Goodman. The pain on their faces. They'd been trampled because of her. Those faces would haunt her for a long time.

Chicago would be dead for her now. No doubt lawsuits would be coming. It wouldn't take them long to discover her real name was not Ingrid Baardsen. She had no hope of graduating to the better-paid theatres. But she'd learned so much here. Minneapolis and Chicago were done. It was time to conquer the Big Apple. If she could make it there, she could make it anywhere. And this time, she wouldn't fuck it up so badly that she had to change her identity yet again.

"Well, I certainly will miss you," Kate said.

"I'm going to miss you more than you can imagine," Ingrid replied.

67

Meanwhile

By three o'clock on Saturday, Dwayne had still not gotten out of bed. Angela had gone in to see him three times. On the fourth visit, she threw a half-cup of cold water in his face.

"What the living fuck?!?" Dwayne said.

"It's time to get up, darling," she said sweetly. She raised a cup of coffee in her other hand to offer him.

"You threw water in my face."

"I always throw water on that pillow at three p.m.," she said. "Usually your face isn't in the way."

"You do not." He pulled his legs over the edge of the bed and sat up.

"Maybe not." She handed him the coffee. "Get up. Your life is not over."

"The life in which Nick Sanchez would never tell me *Don't come back here looking for work* seems to be over."

"Yeah, you mentioned that three times last night."

Dwayne followed Angela out to the dining room. Two fried eggs and two pieces of toast lay on a plate in his spot at the table.

"You made me breakfast?"

"A long time ago."

Dwayne picked up a piece of the toast. It was cold and stiff. Cold butter congealed yellow on the eggs. He sat down in front of it, dipped a corner of the toast into his coffee, and chewed it.

"Joan called. When she found out you wouldn't get out of bed, she said, Forget it, you'd be useless anyway, and hung up."

"She's probably figuring out how to get our stuff out of the Goodman." He stared ahead of him. "I just keep thinking…" He'd replayed it so many times in his mind. Lear, carrying the dead

Cordelia out in his arms, his sorrow and regret so intense he literally dies of grief. And then the solemn words from Albany, Kent, and Edgar, and the audience so caught in the tragedy, so silent in the Owen, so many people, absolutely rapt. It had been a heartbreaking triumph. Dwayne had been so proud. Tears rolled down his cheeks for what his people had achieved. So wonderful. And then the roar and the balls of fire billowing up both sides of the set, and the actors shocked out of that last, beautiful moment of the show—shocked and terrified—Wallace and Melinda jumping up out of their supposed deaths at the roar of flames on both sides of them, rushing to the front of the set and jumping into the front row of seats. What horror! What a travesty! Dwayne began to sob again, remembering it. Those flames betrayed everyone on stage, betrayed everyone in the audience, betrayed all of Dwayne's hopes for his future.

Don't come back here looking for work.

Who would hire him now? The man whose production had set fire to the Goodman. Horrifying. Ingrid had done it and disappeared without a trace.

She must've thought her flames would be so perfect, they would win everyone over. So arrogant. She couldn't possibly have done it just to ruin everything.

Could she?

But how could she have thought anyone would be won over when it went against the fire marshal? It made no sense. It was frustrating even to think about it.

"Ingrid giveth, and Ingrid taketh away," Angela said.

"What?"

"I was thinking about what a weird force of nature Ingrid was," Angela said. "The polar vortex shut down your production of *Titus Andronicus*, but she pulled something out of the rubble and created a theatre company from the remains. You were ready to walk away, but she convinced you to move forward with *Romeo and Juliet*, and that got you your big break with the Goodman. And then you direct an absolutely beautiful *King Lear*, and she sets it on fire and disappears. But you know what's constant through all of that?"

"What?"

"You directed three shows that, despite everything, were brilliant. Nobody can take that away from you."

She moved in and put her arms around him. He accepted the hug, even though he felt like it *had* all been taken away from him. Who would remember how good his *King Lear* had been? They would just remember the panic and the screams and everyone surging toward the doors, and people being trampled. Mostly old people. Two of them were still in the hospital.

"Are you hungry?" she said.

"A little."

"I'll make you something." She picked up the plate with the cold eggs and whisked them off into the garbage pail in the kitchen. She considered frying more eggs, but it was after three p.m., and it was pasta that soothed the soul. Generations of Guiseppelli wisdom said nothing soothed like pasta. Who was she to argue with the ancestors?

Dwayne sat down on the couch with his coffee. The door rang once, but he couldn't think of anyone he wanted to see, so he ignored it. After it rang three more times, Angela stuck her head into the room.

"Will you please get that?" she said, showing admirable patience.

Dwayne buzzed them in and was not overjoyed to see Joan and Chaz at his door.

"Good. You're out of bed," she said.

"Why are you here?" Dwayne slouched back to the love seat under the horseshoe of windows that curved around his living room.

"I'm pulling our fat out of the fire." She looked at Chaz. "That was your expression, wasn't it?"

"Yes," Chaz agreed. "An excellent and apt image."

Angela came out of the kitchen. "What's this? The rescue committee?"

"The salvage committee would be more like it," Chaz said.

Joan sat down on the edge of one of the couches. "The lawsuits will drive the Psychedelic Dream Theatre into bankruptcy. Before we get served any papers, I am paying all the actors and techs for the run of the show. We still had over a hundred thousand in the bank. I warned everyone to cash those checks before our funds are frozen.

Here's yours." She tossed an envelope onto the cable spool coffee table. "Second, there are firms in town that specialize in disaster PR, but Chaz knows us well, plus I believe he is fond of you." She pointed at Dwayne. "In fact, I thought you worked for him."

"He fired me."

"A lot of that going around," Joan said.

"I didn't fire him," Chaz protested. "I had to lay him off."

"Interesting distinction. Anyway, I've hired Chaz."

"And paid in advance," Chaz said brightly, patting a folded envelope in his shirt pocket.

"Why do we need PR?" Dwayne said.

"I'll get to that. Third," Joan said. "The upstairs mainstage at the C.R.A.P. is empty. I've paid Green for the next three weeks in advance. That's all I could get. Everyone is already paid for a five week run. We open *King Lear* at the Playhouse on Thursday."

"This Thursday?" Dwayne said. "Four days from now?"

"Yes," Joan said. "I've got a crew working right now moving all of our stuff to the C.R.A.P. The stuff that won't fit—like the furniture that went up really high at the Owen—we'll move to the loft. But my first priority is getting everything we can use over to the Playhouse."

"You decided this all on your own?" Dwayne said.

"Ingrid is gone. You were useless."

"It's not just up to you!" Dwayne complained.

"Yes, it is. I process emotion differently from you. You are not capable right now. So it's up to me. We'll have to find a new third board member, but we don't have to worry about that right now."

Chaz laughed and stopped suddenly when Dwayne looked at him.

"Also, you'll be playing Gloucester," Joan said. "As our only Equity actor, I had to pay Peter Burden the most, but he refuses to move venues."

"What about the understudy?" Dwayne said.

"His understudy refuses to move, too. As do most of the other understudies. They were more interested in having a Goodman credit than being in the show. But the rest of the cast are committed."

"This is just crazy," Dwayne said. "Who's going to come see a show that set the Goodman on fire?"

"That's the beauty of it!" Chaz jumped up and clapped his hands. "Everybody! And everybody is going to know about it. I just stopped by because I wanted to see your face when Joan popped all this. I'm already incredibly busy. Every newspaper, radio station, television station, blog, and smoke signal fire in the city wants the story of the little theatre company that set the Goodman Theatre on fire. It's the biggest news story I've ever pitched. It's incredible. And Ingrid having a stolen identity? It's the cherry on top. I'm trying to get an interview with the real Ingrid Baardsen in Minneapolis."

Dwayne's mouth hung open. "How does this make sense?"

"Are you kidding? This puts you on the map!" Chaz said. "Sure, we're never going to get any of those critics to come back and see the show, and no doubt they are going to crucify you for opening night. Your name will be absolute shit with them."

"Chaz?" Angela raised her eyebrows.

"Yeah, okay. But none of that's going to matter, because everyone else will be super curious about this show. It's a PR bonanza! Everyone will know about it. The curiosity-seekers will come in droves. We will absolutely sell out this three-week run—and then you'll have the word-of-mouth from the people who actually saw the show." Chaz's eyes suddenly lit up. "Say! Do you think you could set up a real fire trick for the end of the show at the Playhouse?"

"No!" Dwayne and Joan shouted simultaneously.

"Okay, I suppose not." Chaz held up his hand. "I know you've got a lot to digest, but we have to get to work. Get yourself ready, Dwayne. You're going to be giving a lot of interviews!" He rushed out of the apartment.

"Also," Joan said, "the lawyers will come after our personal money as board members. My accounting business is a Limited Liability Corporation, and I've shifted five hundred thousand of my savings into the LLC to protect it from the lawsuits."

"You have half a million dollars in savings?" Dwayne said.

"Some of my accounting clients have lucrative businesses, particularly in software. They prefer an accountant who processes emotions the way they do. They pay well for that."

"If you've got half a million dollars, why do you stage manage little shows like ours?"

"For fun."

Had he ever seen Joan looking like she was having fun?

"You are all endlessly interesting to observe," she said. "Would you like to discuss an LLC to protect your savings?"

"We don't exactly have savings," Angela said.

"We have debts," Dwayne agreed.

"Hmm." Joan cocked her head to the side, then continued without transition. "The stage at the Playhouse is smaller and differently shaped than the Owen, so I need you to come over and help me decide how to set things up. The frames that held the furniture up in the air are now cut to a size that will fit the lower ceiling height. We'll use less than half the furniture we had at the Owen. And then you'll probably want to schedule a run to get everyone used to the different space before we re-open on Thursday. Are you ready?"

Dwayne was still wearing pajamas. He clearly was not ready.

"I haven't even eaten yet."

"Eat," Joan said. "And meet me at the Playhouse. The crew is there now. We have work to do." She walked out of the apartment.

Angela started laughing.

"What?"

"These women in your life." She laughed some more. "Absolutely incredible."

68

Thursday, September 21, 2005

Thursday night. The first night of the new run at the Playhouse. Act Three, Scene Seven. Dwayne played Gloucester, replacing Peter Burden. He helped the king escape his ruthless daughters. Edmund betrayed him to Regan and Cornwall, and now he was bound to the chair before them.

"What mean your graces?" Dwayne pleaded. *"Good my friends, consider you are my guests. Do me no foul play."*

Regan hovered around him, threatening. Dwayne saw only Regan; Tom was so transformed. However, as Rocky approached him, he did not see Cornwall. He saw Uncle Bull.

"Come, sir, what letters had you from France?" Bull said.

"Be simple," Regan said, *"for we know the truth."*

"And what confederacy have you with the traitors?" Bull demanded.

Regan grabbed his beard. *"To whose hands have you sent the lunatic King? Speak!"* She pushed away his face, but despite her abuse, Dwayne's attention was still focused on Uncle Bull. Would he need to run off the stage for his own protection? He was bound to the chair, but the knots were not tight.

"I have a letter guessingly set down," Dwayne said, *"which came from one that's of a neutral heart."*

Bull took another step toward him. *"Cunning,"* he said.

"And false," Regan added.

"Where hast thou sent the King?" Bull thundered.

"To Dover," Dwayne replied.

"Wherefore to Dover, sir?" Regan slapped him across the face.

"Because I would not see thy cruel nails pluck out his poor old eyes; nor thy fierce sister stick boarish fangs in his anointed flesh," Dwayne cried. *"I shall see winged vengeance overtake such children."*

"See it shalt thou never," Bull said. *"Fellows, hold the chair,"* he commanded his servants. Dwayne's heart began to race twice as fast. Bull turned to the audience as he gestured to Dwayne. *"Upon these eyes of thine I'll set my foot."*

Should he run? Dwayne shook his head back and forth.

Saint Lucy, pray for me!

Should he run?

Bull closed in on Dwayne as the servants grabbed each of his arms. When he was fully in front of Dwayne, his back to the audience, suddenly he gave a little grin and winked just for Dwayne. This was Rocky, not Bull. Relief flooded through him. Good God! Would he go through this panic every performance?

The servants secretly raised the aluminum mask to cover his face. Dwayne groaned while Rocky mimed the gouging out of Gloucester's eye.

"Out vile jelly!" Cornwall threw a large green grape that had been dipped in strawberry jam onto the floor. He waited for the audience to see it, then stepped on it.

The rest of the night, Dwayne played his scenes with a bloodstained rag covering his eyes.

All the way through the show, the audience was fully with them. They got an enthusiastic round of applause at the intermission. The response was doubly gratifying because Chaz was videotaping sections of the show, actually stepping onto the stage to get close-ups of some of the speeches. (Because of this, today's tickets were free). Most of the actors kept in character admirably, although Bobby actually pushed Chaz away in one scene. (That did seem to be in character for his portrayal of the evil Edmund).

Dwayne wasn't sure if it was despite the trauma they'd suffered at the Owen or because of it, but the cast's performances seemed deeper than ever. That first night at the Playhouse was only half full, but at the end, after a stunned and mournful pause, the audience rose to its feet in a standing ovation.

In the dressing rooms after the show, the actors were exultant. Some were still shaking their heads, having been demoted from the glory of the Goodman to the penury of the Playhouse, but as actors, they were back. Pride in themselves mixed with the sorrow of their shared loss, and they embraced one another with a world-weary, deep affection for one another.

As Bobby left the men's dressing room, Coco waited for him in the hall.

"Nice performance, Edmund," she said. "I think everyone out there hated you extra hard tonight."

"Not as much as they hated you, my evil princess." He wrapped an arm around her waist.

"Maybe we need some loving to counteract all that hate," she suggested.

"I'm down with that." He leaned his forehead in toward hers, but she backed off.

"I am, too, Bobby." She pulled him back away from the doorway for privacy and lowered her voice. "But I wonder if this might be the time to explore whether we can be more than that to one another."

"Huh," he said. "Interesting." He leaned back against the wall. "You been with a few men. I been with a few women. But after these years, I got to admit, there's never been anyone on the level of Coco Nesbit. Maybe you think that about me?"

She leaned in and spoke softly, directly in his ear. "Why else would I suggest something more?" She put both her hands on his biceps.

He leaned over and spoke back into her ear. "All right then. Let's explore."

Dwayne came out of the dressing room. "Hey, some of us are heading over to John Barleycorn. You want to come?"

"Nah," they said in unison.

"We'll catch you next time," Coco said. Bobby winked, and they walked out arm-in-arm.

69

Monday, September 25, 2005

"I'm glad we're finishing the run, but I don't see a future for myself," Dwayne said to Joan. "Every critic in town wrote a damning account of our opening night. They didn't attack the actors, thank God, but they really had it in for me. Nobody is going to hire me."

"Maybe not right away," Joan said. "But ticket sales are already looking good. What would it mean if *King Lear* were a hit at the Playhouse despite terrible reviews and the disaster at Goodman?"

"I don't know."

"If it does well, we should find somewhere to extend the extension. That could do something for your reputation. Plus, Chaz is getting you interviews. You can set the record straight."

"Maybe."

"Let me show you something." She'd asked Dwayne to meet her at the loft Ingrid had been caretaking. She led him inside to the back and pointed up. Hanging from the fifteen-foot ceiling were a variety of lengths of recycled 1¼" pipe. Wrapped around some of them were lengths of lighting cable.

"She was already putting in a lighting grid?"

"And look at this." Joan led him to a closet and opened the door. Inside was a stack of lighting equipment in various states of repair, a lighting control panel, four propane tanks, three dimmer packs, ACX cables, and other lighting and sound equipment.

"She was building a theatre in here," Dwayne said.

"Once you eliminate rent, doing theatre would be super cheap if you pay people like we paid them for *Titus Andronicus*."

"I don't want to slide that far back."

"If we work fast, maybe we can bring *King Lear* here after the Playhouse. I got in touch with the owner of the building and told him what happened with Ingrid. I'm flying out to San Francisco to meet with him. If he likes me, he wants to keep the same deal with me that he had with Ingrid. We can do anything we want with the building, so long as we keep it in good condition until he sells it, which he thinks is ten years away. I'm going to see if he'll promise us six months' notice when he decides it's time to sell."

"Is that something you want to do? Make this into a theatre?"

Joan gave a little huff, then walked back toward the front office of the building. "We'll really miss Ingrid," she said.

"Ingrid set the Owen on fire."

"Well, not really," Joan said. "She scared everyone, and she singed some of our furniture, but the Owen did not suffer any fire damage. All the damage was from the fire department hosing everything down."

"Potato, potahto," Dwayne said.

"Why do people say that?"

Dwayne opened his mouth to answer. "Never mind," Joan said. "I'm saying we'll miss her technical acumen. She was capable of anything."

"Clearly," Dwayne said.

She looked at him with an expression Dwayne didn't understand. She shook her head. "Hiring someone to do what she would do for free will be expensive."

"Unless we find someone who shares the dream of creating their own theatre and offer them a piece of the action," Dwayne said.

"Start up a for-profit theatre?" Joan said. "You and me and an Ingrid replacement? Could we find such a person?"

"This is Chicago. People come here for just that crazy dream."

"Well, then." She frowned. "We have a long way to go to make this a theatre. Seats. Well, lots of things. And how do we raise money? We have all that furniture from the set. Ingrid set up connections with antique shops to resell that stuff. I found her list of downstate sources of furniture in the desk. Actually, that could be an ongoing source of income. If you want to buy and refinish furniture, I could set up an LLC. Solid Oak Enterprises, or something. There's some money to be made. It might be better than temp work. And if you have any savings, we could hide it from the lawsuits in that LLC."

"Wow." Dwayne laughed. "But do *you* want to do all this? You have a successful accounting business."

"I like the solidity of numbers," Joan said. "But I like the unpredictability of theatre, for my own entertainment. The question is: do you want to lead this? Because without Ingrid, your leadership needs to be much stronger."

70

Later that night

"Chaz is putting you on TV? Oh, la, la." Angela made a faux-impressed face as she brought a half pan of reheated lasagna to the table. She was acting light-hearted, but that was not the way she felt.

"The Wednesday morning show on WGN-TV," Dwayne said, leaning forward and cutting slices of the lasagna and putting them on their plates. "Chaz was right. Everybody wants the inside story of the troupe that set the Goodman on fire."

"When you were on Dean Richards' radio show, I was surprised how much you threw Ingrid under the bus. Aren't you worried about her suing for defamation?"

This wasn't what Angela actually wanted to know, but she wasn't sure how to phrase her real question.

"We talked to the Lawyers for the Arts. Since Ingrid is a fake identity, who are we defaming? Certainly not the octogenarian lady in Minnesota whose identity Ingrid stole. Ingrid, whatever her real name is, has no standing to sue. Besides, it's not defamation since I'm only telling the truth."

"Huh. And you're going on WBEZ?"

"Yes, and I've got interviews coming with the *Tribune*, *Sun-Times*, and Chaz is talking with the *Reader*. The publicity is working. People are buying tickets to *King Lear*." Dwayne smiled, but he had a hard time keeping the smile. "Fucking Ingrid," he breathed. He bowed his head and clenched his eyes closed.

"I know," Angela said. "This would've been your second week in the Owen. You would have had great reviews."

"I can't blame the critics—caught in that stampede. At least everyone is out of the hospital now."

Angela set down her fork. "Okay, you moved your show, you are doing all this, tickets are selling, but in the long run, what are *we* going to do?"

Dwayne had a piece of lasagna on his fork on its way to his mouth. He looked at it and set it back on his plate. He leaned back in his chair. "I think the door I wanted to open is now closed," he said.

"Permanently?"

"For years, at least. Joan thinks we could make the loft into a theatre space, but that means we go back to low-budget storefront theatre. We might be able to make a go of it and develop an audience. We have free rent. We might do excellent work there and make it into a really cool space. But would it ever bring in good money? Not likely."

"Tell me about this furniture business she proposed." Angela picked up her fork, but then set it down again. Neither one of them had much appetite at the moment.

"We've got all that antique furniture from the set. We're still using some. Ingrid set up connections with antique stores in the area. Joan and I plan to sell the excess stuff. Ingrid bought more than we needed, so there's some we never used. It looks like I could make money refinishing the rest and selling it, and maybe go downstate to get more. It could be an ongoing business."

"So you know how to refinish it, and Joan thinks there's money to be made?"

"She does."

"And she thinks you can make money with this theatre at the loft."

"She doesn't believe the theatre would bring in much, but she thinks if we could get a liquor license, the house could make money. We'd do some shows, and we'd rent the space to other companies. Maybe we do concerts. Ry has a great band, and he knows a lot of others. We had a number of ideas."

Angela sighed. "I wish Ingrid hadn't blown everything up and vanished. As screwed up as she turned out to be, she made things happen. With the three of you, I'd have no doubt about the loft idea."

"Well, hang on," Dwayne objected. "The success we've had was due to a lot more than Ingrid, Joan, and me. We've got some really talented actors in that ensemble. Plus, there are a lot of tech people in the city of Chicago. Maybe we can find another Ingrid. Someone less crazy but equally resourceful. After these past three shows, I know a lot more about how to make all this work." He sat up straighter in his chair.

"Well, well, well. Now I recognize you. I was beginning to think the fire had burned out in Dwayne Finnegan."

"Well, if it's not too late. This rent-free loft is an opportunity, but you are pregnant with twins. I thought I was on the verge of getting good-paying directing gigs. I'm not, but I still have to step up and make money for this family. Right?" Just saying it made his stomach begin to clench inside. This was his new reality.

"Yes, you do," Angela said. "But I'm only going to get three months of paid maternity leave. I don't want our twins to go to daycare when they're so tiny—and daycare for two would cost a fortune. So I don't want you in some office from nine to five. If you can make some money in a way that also lets you be a house daddy while I'm at work, I'm going to like that a lot better."

"Really?" Dwayne said. His stomach started to relax.

"Yeah," Angela said. "Did you think I'd want our kids being raised by strangers?" She shook her head and picked up her fork. "You know, I'd like to see this loft. Let's you and me and Joan go down there and look around and talk some ideas."

"Okay." Dwayne picked up his fork. His lasagna had gotten a little cold, but it looked more appetizing to him now.

"It occurs to me there must be actors and designers who have kids," Angela said. "That must make it hard for them to do theatre. What if you got together with some of them to do something cooperative?"

"Actually, that's a great idea. I do know people who've dropped out after having children. They might love to come back."

"Yeah," Angela said. "And come to think about it, what about audience members? Wouldn't the ones with young families come if the theatre had childcare? A place where they could leave the kids while they see the show—and maybe even have a drink afterwards?"

"Oh my God, Angela, you are some kind of crazy genius." He

took a deep, unsteady breath, and his eyes welled up with tears. He got out of his chair, pulled her to her feet, and embraced her. They shared the longest kiss. Then she leaned back away from him.

"So you think all that could work?"

"It could certainly all fit. That loft is huge. There's space for daycare, performance, a bar, a workshop, everything!"

"You just have to release your inner Ingrid."

"The notebook she left is a gold mine of sources of free and cheap stuff. I think this just might work. You really are a genius!" He gave her another huge hug.

"Okay, okay, you are lucky to have me," she agreed, breaking away and sitting down again. "But right now I need to have some of this lasagna. You know I'm eating for three."

The End

Find more information about Richard's events and upcoming work at www.richardengling.com and sign up for his newsletter.

About the Author

Richard Engling has spent a lifetime writing and performing, paying his bills as a teacher, truck driver, and copywriter, while performing as an actor, drummer in a jazz quartet, and working as the founding artistic director of Polarity Ensemble Theatre in Chicago. His writing career began in high school when his coffee shop theatre group needed material to perform, and they elected him to write it. Richard's books include *Body Mortgage*, *Visions of Anna*, and the Dwayne Finnegan novels, *Give My Regards to Nowhere* and *Romeo and Juliet Keep Their Eyes on the Prize*. His plays include *Ghost Watch* and *Anna in the Afterlife*.

Richard holds a Master of Arts in Creative Writing from Indiana University. He majored in Theatre as an undergraduate at Northern Illinois University. He lives in Evanston, Illinois, with his wife, Gail.

GIVE MY REGARDS TO NOWHERE

The First Dwayne Finnegan Novel
by Richard Engling

"ABSURD COMIC HI-JINX" —Chris Jones, *Chicago Tribune*

"As Carl Hiaasen does with his Florida-based satirical crime novels, Engling's gloriously silly narrative allows his readers to witness how the sausage gets made...Engling's satire on storefront theatre is thoroughly entertaining from start to finish."
–ChicagoOnStage

"a rollicking ride through the underbelly of the acting world"
–Midwest Book Review

"The chaotic shenanigans conceal a tightly constructed plot full of vivid dialogue that hones to comedy's fundamental principles: pleasure, surprise, folly, luck both good and bad, and a celebration of human ingenuity and resilience. *Give My Regards to Nowhere* reminds us that theater has always been sustained by dreamers who keep striving in the face of all the odds."
—Evanston RoundTable

Available wherever books and audiobooks are sold.
www.polarityensemblebooks.com

ROMEO AND JULIET KEEP THEIR EYES ON THE PRIZE

The Second Dwayne Finnegan Novel
by Richard Engling

"Fans of Evanston writer Richard Engling's 2023 comic novel about Chicago theater, *Give My Regards to Nowhere*, will be delighted to learn that he has written a follow-up. The rollicking sequel ... continues the adventures of Dwayne Finnegan, the sometimes brilliant, sometimes hapless, artistic director of the Psychedelic Dream Theater, as he struggles to mount a fresh production of theater's most famous romance. Naturally, comic obstacles abound."
–Evanston RoundTable

"A welcome return of the beleaguered yet indefatigable Dwayne Finnegan. Engling's years in Chicago's storefront theatre ensure that, no matter how complex life on and off the stage becomes, the events are always exquisitely believable. It's funny, yes, and engaging too, but also wise and moving."
– Liam Heneghan, author of *Beasts at Bedtime*

Available wherever books and audiobooks are sold.
www.polarityensemblebooks.com

VISIONS OF ANNA
by Richard Engling

"PASSIONATE, POIGNANT" —Elizabeth Cunningham

"Matthew Harken's urgent questions about his friend Anna's suicide and his own critical illness compel him to risk a perilous, spiritual quest. His heartrending, heart-opening journey through the interwoven worlds of memory, dream, and shamanic magic lead him not only to visions of Anna but to visions of grace. A passionate, poignant novel."
—Elizabeth Cunningham, author of *The Maeve Chronicles*.

"...a strong authorial voice, motivated characters, and a plot that propels the book... The novel's most transcendent moments occur in Matthew's flashbacks to the time he spent in Paris with Anna. Both young emerging writers subsisting on meager meals in less than modest living situations, Matthew and Anna immerse themselves in the Parisian literary scene. In recalling these memories, Matthew squires readers through a vision of The City of Light so charmed and romantic even he questions whether it truly was as magical as he believed it to be. Engling displays an enviable gift for dialogue and a painter's eye for clear detail."
—Jarrett Neal, *New City* (Chicago)

Available wherever books are sold.
www.polarityensemblebooks.com

BODY MORTGAGE

by Richard Engling

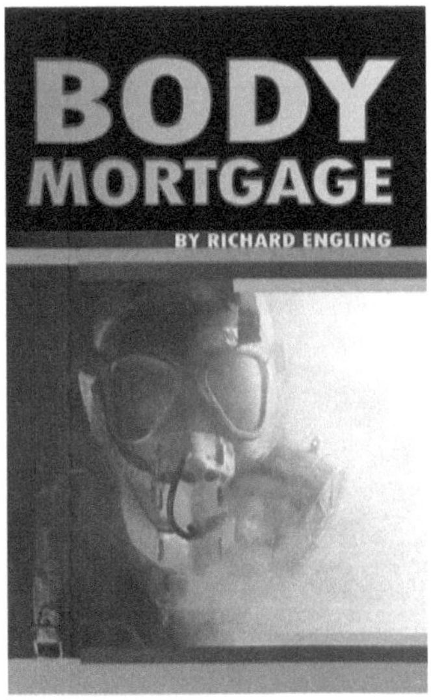

"Fast paced future thriller."
—SCIENCE FICTION AND FANTASY REVIEWS

"This is a neat SF detective story in the Mike Hammer / Philip Marlowe / Bladerunner mold...an engaging and well-constructed thriller, very enjoyable."
— BRUMM GROUP NEWS

A gritty thriller in a nightmare America where human parts are worth more than the whole.

The big market in Chicago used to be livestock. But now it's human body parts. People can mortgage their own bodies to organ transplant companies, but it's a gristly end when they can't pay up.

Gregory Blake is a private investigator in this savage city. His first mistake is to take on a client whose body is marked for foreclosure. His second is to investigate why the most powerful forces in town are in such a hurry to repossess. Blake thinks he knows all there is to know about the underworld. But never did he expect to be lost in the corporate corridors of perverse power—in the hell that future America has become...

Originally published by Penguin Books USA and Headline UK.

Available wherever books are sold.
www.polarityensemblebooks.com

www.ingramcontent.com/pod-product-compliance
Lightning Source LLC
Chambersburg PA
CBHW021030310726
48969CB00006B/1609